Dedicated to

Ann, my wife
Christel and Ann-Marie, my daughters

and

Basil Bastin and Donald Thomas,
who left this world much too early.

First edition November 2001

Published

in Belgium by Skylife.Frank Dassen
e-mail: dassen@flemishheights.freeserve.co.uk

in the U.K. with vital assistance of
John Fish B.Sc.
Publishers
of Tenby in Wales
e-mail: tenby.publishers@which.net

and

Straight Connections Pte. Ltd.
e-mail: jazzali@singnet.com.sg

Printed in Belgium
by Drukkerij Vuye bvba

ISBN 90-806812-1-0

Although based on the writer's personal experiences in Angola, all characters in this book are purely fictitious and any resemblance to real persons, living or dead, is purely coincidental.

Frank Dassen

FLY FREE

A story of flying and adventure, passion and intrigue
in war torn Angola

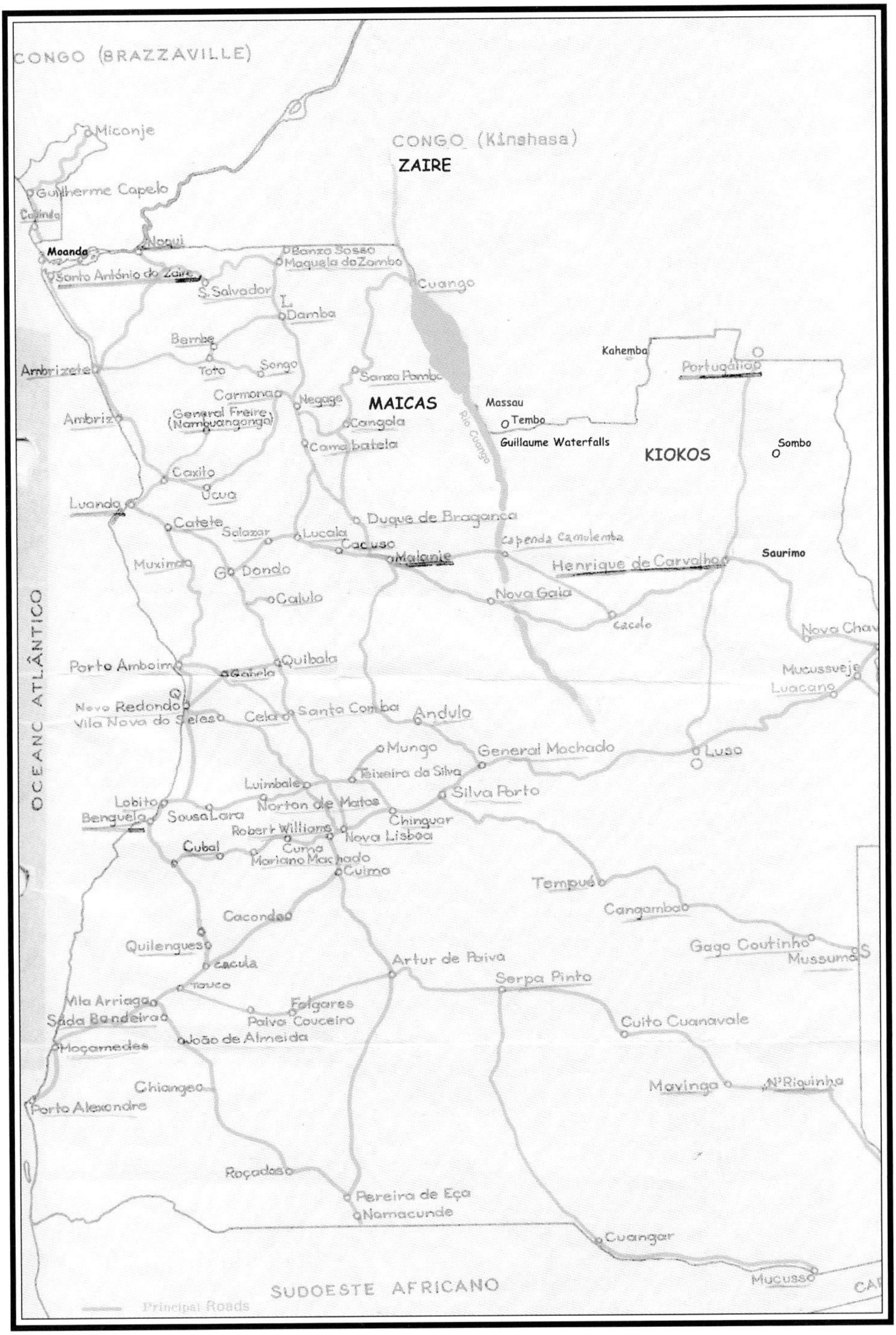
CONGO (BRAZZAVILLE)
CONGO (Kinshasa)
ZAIRE
Miconje
Guilherme Capelo
Cabinda
Noqui
Moanda
Santo António do Zaire
Banza Sosso
Maquela do Zombo
Cuango
S. Salvador
Damba
Bembe
Toto
Songo
Ambrizete
Sanza Pombo
Carmona
Negage
MAICAS
Massau
Tembo
Guillaume Waterfalls
Kahemba
Portugália
KIOKOS
Sombo
Ambriz
General Freire
(Nambuangongo)
Cangola
Camabatela
Rio Cuango
Caxito
Ucua
Luanda
Catete
Duque de Bragança
Salazar
Lucala
Cacuso
Malanje
Capenda Camulemba
Henrique de Carvalho
Saurimo
Muxima
Dondo
Calulo
Nova Gaia
Cacolo
Nova Chav
OCEANO ATLÂNTICO
Porto Amboim
Gabela
Quibala
Mucussueje
Luacano
Novo Redondo
Vila Nova do Seles
Cela
Santa Comba
Andulo
Mungo
General Machado
Luso
Teixeira da Silva
Luimbale
Silva Porto
Lobito
Norton de Matos
Benguela
Sousa Lara
Chinguar
Robert Williams
Nova Lisboa
Cubal
Cuma
Mariano Machado
Cuima
Tempué
Cangamba
Cacondo
Quilengues
Cacula
Gago Coutinho
Mussuma
Artur de Paiva
Serpa Pinto
Vila Arriaga
Sá da Bandeira
Folgares
Paiva Couceiro
Cuito Cuanavale
Moçamedes
João de Almeida
Chiangeo
Mavinga
N'Riquinha
Porto Alexandre
Roçadas
Pereira de Eça
Namacunde
Cuangar
Mucusso
SUDOESTE AFRICANO
Principal Roads

AUTHOR'S NOTE

Although "FLY FREE" is a work of fiction, a lot of the context is based on facts.

The company 'Skylift International' did not exist, but 'Young Cargo', a Belgian Air Charter Company did exist and operated humanitarian aid and cargo flights in Angola during the turbulent years of 1976 and 1977. I was Young's Chief Pilot at that time. My logbooks of those exciting years served as inspiration for the plot of this book.

The Angolan diamond mines were called 'Diamang'. They functioned much as described in 'Fly Free'. One of their aircraft was a Short Skyvan. It was not shot down, but was badly damaged by a SAM (surface-to-air missile).

The Cuban involvement in Angola is an historical fact, and so is the existence of the Organisation of Cuban Exiles and the Angolan political parties: the Popular Movement for the Liberation of Angola - MPLA, the National Union for the Total Independence of Angola - UNITA and the National Front for the Liberation of Angola - FNLA.

The names of the cities and provinces are the old Portuguese names prior to the 11th of November 1975, thereafter they are the new names of the post Independence era.

The lake in the vicinity of Massau does not exist. I situated it there, as it has a specific tole to play in the book.

The names and characters of political leaders, the lost treasure of diamonds and the daring escape out of the country are all products of my imagination. So is the tender love story. But the dangers of falling victim to the Secret Police and the hazards of flying in the always beautiful but often dangerous skies of Angola were exactly as depicted.

The Bristol Britannia was one of the most advanced military transport aeroplanes of the late 1960's. Young Cargo bought seven of them in 1975 from the Royal Air Force and converted them to freighters.

Finally, I would like to thank Ali Tasker, Heather Morgan, Bridget Little for the proofreading of the manuscript, and Richard Craig for his in-depth maritime expertise and advise. My gratitude also goes to Dirk Buytaert of the Aviation Society of Antwerp for the page layout and cover design. I am deeply indebted to them for their help, their patience and especially for their staunch support.

Frank Dassen
November 2001

PART ONE

LONDON 1995

Heathrow Airport, 3 March 1995

It was very cold for the time of the year with a sharp bite of winter in the air and showers of rain and wet snow drifting in near horizontal curtains across the airfield. Robert Stanfort, Chief-Pilot of Skylift International, stood at his office window on the second floor of the two-story cargo building. In front of him lay the wide rain-swept tarmac, its surface black and shiny like glass. A couple of old freighters stood in the far corner, their wings rocking in the gusty wind. His own aircraft, a Bristol Britannia, was safely parked inside the hangar.

As a new squall drifted over the field the windsock flapped wildly and a shower of sleet obscured the sky. The depressing spectacle made Rob shudder with disgust. Suddenly, the loud clattering noise of the telex shattered the silence. Rob swung around, his left hand reaching for the light-switch, his right hand tearing a slip of paper out of the receiver. He studied the text, then picked up the telephone and dialled the number of the operations room.

"Get over here, Ian," he said. "And bring Jock with you. Quickly."

Ian, just a fraction short of six feet tall but lean was a month away from his thirty-first birthday; a steadfast type with green eyes and going slightly bald. He was also Rob's Co-Captain, more or less engaged to Liz, a lecturer in modern history in Cambridge. As much as flying was important to Ian so was teaching to Liz and getting married was not one of their priorities.

Jock, the Flight-Engineer, was a stocky built Scot from Glenborrodale, in the north-west of Scotland. He was in his mid-forties, built like a tank and very rugged looking with pitch black hair, a full-grown moustache and a deeply tanned skin. Allowing his life to be ruled by the old nursery rhyme 'Needles and pins, when a man marries, his trouble begins' he was a fervent bachelor and a true sybarite who enjoyed first class food and drinks in the company of beautiful, unattached and very willing women.

Rob, as tall as Ian but strongly muscled and square-jawed with a wild mop of blonde hair and blue eyes full of self-assurance, had celebrated his thirty-first birthday three months earlier and was the only one in the team to have experienced married life. As a young Pilot Officer in the Air Force, finding a pretty girlfriend had been easy, the step to marriage even easier. As the months went by, he'd spent more and more time away from home, flying missions abroad or passing male-bonding hours with his friends in the Squadron's Mess. Apart from rather occasional sexual contacts, he and his wife had nothing in common any more, and they'd realized that the feeling they'd believed to be love was nothing but a barren infatuation. Soon thereafter their marriage had ended in a quick divorce. Since then, Rob had gone through a few shallow and short-lived relationships as none of his girlfriends had been able or willing to share his passion for flying and adventure.

Back in 1975, Ian and Rob were both pupils at the same boarding school, then student pilots with the R.A.F. Once graduated as Pilot Officers, they had both been transferred to Transport Command and had progressed from co-pilot to commanders on four-engined transport planes. In time, Rob had become C.O. of the Squadron and had appointed Jock as Chief Flight-Engineer in charge of training and checking of the squadron's engineers. Flying humanitarian aid flights and medevac missions in Africa and the Middle-East had created a strong bond between the three of them. When Rob's aunt unexpectedly had died, leaving him a house in Maidenhead and a very substantial amount of money, he had resigned and started his own airline with a surplus Bristol Britannia. Jock and Ian had been quick to come and work for him, not only for the better paid job, but also out of loyalty and for the joy of going through this new adventure together.

"Listen to this!" Rob exclaimed to Ian and Jock.

"To Skylift International. The Angolan Government is seeking a cargo company to operate relief flights between Luanda, Portugalia, Sao-Tome, Lobito, Benguela and Saurimo. Nature of the flights: food and medicines. Average number of flying hours per month: 120 hours. Payment 2,000 US dollars per flying hour. My commission 5%. Signed: Ernesto Veleiro."

Ian whistled softly between his teeth. "Two thousand dollars per hour and 120 flying hours per month. That's worth a fortune."

"That's correct," confirmed Rob. "If I subtract the actual running-costs of the business and the maintenance expenses of the Britannia, I could afford to give you both a hefty pay rise and still save up for a new aircraft."

The proposed contract was nothing but a miracle, Rob thought. Since the day he'd started his airline, flying cargo in Europe had become a cut-throat business where bigger and more affluent airlines were underbidding the smaller ones, leaving only the most dangerous, dirty or underpaid contracts up for grabs. Faced with that kind of competition, Rob had to keep his company solvent by making heavy financial injections, slowly but surely eroding his personal fortune. This contract in Angola could save everything! Suddenly he remembered that Angola was a war zone. His enthusiasm seeped away like water from a leaking drainpipe and his eagerness turned into doubt.

"Angola is not exactly a peaceful country," he announced. His voice heavily loaded with scepticism he added that since their independence from Portugal in 1975 the Government had been fighting a guerrilla war against the forces of the opposition UNITA. "Are you willing to take that risk, Ian," he finally asked. "... And what about you, Jock?"

Jock walked over to the window. Firing Rob a well-meaning look, he replied: "We know how precarious your financial situation is. You can't go on like this."

"I must admit that I would prefer somewhere more peaceful," added Ian, nodding his head in assent. "However, in order to survive, you need a contract. A regular contract that pays well. This deal is a unique opportunity. Go for it."

"What about Liz," insisted Rob. "Will she accept that you disappear for a couple of years in Africa?"

"Don't worry about that," answered Ian. "Just lately, she was talking about accepting an offer from Berkeley University in the States. She'll be all right." Half-jokingly, he added that it would be nice to live in the African sunshine without having to worry about making ends meet. Jock muttered something about not looking a gift horse in the mouth.

The doubt that had been flooding Rob's voice made place for determination. "In that case," he decided, "I accept, providing it's operationally feasible, of course."

"But what a coincidence, Rob," remarked Ian hesitantly, "... you were born in Angola, weren't you?"

"I was," replied Rob. "However, I don't remember much about it. Dad was a mining engineer with DIANGOL, the Angolan Diamond Mines. When I was two years old, my mother died of malaria. I stayed there until early 1975, when the fight for Independence became rather vicious and I was sent back to London to live with Dad's sister." Rob made an obscure gesture with his hand as if not sure how to express his thoughts. "I was barely eleven years old then," he said slowly, "... so it's rather vague, but yes, it would be interesting to return. I would be able to visit my mother's grave, and maybe uncover the secret about the mysterious disappearance of my father."

"He disappeared?" asked Ian. "What happened?"

"I don't really know," answered Rob. "When not managing the mines, my father was a very dedicated private pilot, and..."

"So that's where you got the flying bug," interrupted Jock.

"Most probably," acknowledged Rob, raising his shoulders. "To answer the question, Ian, I never found out what happened to Dad. One day, a few weeks after my return to the UK, he left on a flight and never came back. The wreck of his plane was never found. Once there, I'll try to find out, but ..." For a moment, Rob's eyes stared blindly into space, then he shook his head in a resolute manner. "... First things first. Let's find out what's going on in that country."

Without any further delay, he opened the International Jeppesen Manual, section Africa - a Pilot's Manual that covered all the airfields on the African continent. Flipping through the pages, his colour slowly turned an angry red.

"I don't believe it," he suddenly called out, slamming his hand down on the table, sending an ashtray and some papers flying. "The approach plates for the Angolan airfields haven't been updated since the start of the civil war! This book is nothing but junk."

"What did you expect," countered Ian. "With the war, they've got more important things on their mind than printing new maps and amending approach plates."

"Why don't you send Veleiro a message and tell him you're interested, but that you need updated charts and maps," suggested Jock.

"Good idea. Whilst I'm doing that, call the Foreign Office. Find out whether they have any up-to-date information about the situation in Angola. You, Ian, call the Daily Mail and the Telegraph. Ask them for the latest news from their war correspondents." As soon as Ian and Jock had left the office, Rob started to punch the keys on his telex.

"Bad news, Rob," said Ian half an hour later. "It seems that the Angolan Government is quite paranoid about having foreigners roaming freely around their country. The last time official journalists were in Luanda was during the trials of the Mercenaries, in July 1976. Since then, nothing. The only newsmen currently there are freelancers, following groups of UNITA in the interior. They report extensive fighting and guerrilla activities, but nothing about the condition of the airfields."

"Not much luck with the Foreign Office either," stated Jock. "The embassy in Luanda is manned by a small skeleton staff. They strongly advise all British subjects to stay away. In other words, if we go and get into trouble, don't expect the Embassy to get us out of there!"

Rob raised his eyebrows. "After all that, are you two still willing to go?"

Jock nodded. Ian smiled sadly. "How long can you go on running this company without that contract, Rob?"

"You must consider the fact," Jock declared, "that our jobs are linked to the survival of Skylift."

Rob raised his shoulders in a helpless way.

Veleiro's answer, when it came through, was short and very disappointing.

"There are no recently updated maps available," he wrote. "The international airport of Luanda is fully operational. If you need to know more about the airfields in the interior, you will have to come over and judge for yourself."

At that moment, the wind and storm chose to launch another powerful attack on the airfield. Raindrops streamed in long tears down the window, reflecting the lights around the tarmac and making them look like long wet smears of brightness. Rob's imagination instantly produced a vision of sunny beaches and waving palm trees. Like a rush of strong alcohol to his bloodstream, his mood changed, and the challenge of flying in the warm and maybe dangerous but very well paid skies of Angola became a temptation he could no longer resist.

A reckless smile brightened his face.

"Go and look for myself," he said very determinedly. "That's exactly what I'm going to do. I want that contract. We need it, but I'm not going to sign without knowing whether we can fulfill it."

"I'll find out which airlines are flying to Luanda," volunteered Ian. "Considering that Angola used to be one of their colonies, it's most probably the Portuguese National Airline, TAP."

"Fine with me," answered Rob. "Sort it out, will you, and book a seat on the first available flight." He put on his raincoat and strutted to the door. "Now, gentlemen, you'll have to excuse me," he said. "I have some packing to do."

Luanda, 8 March 1995

With a barely perceptible jerk, the red and white painted Boeing 747 of the Portuguese National Airline came to a halt in front of the airport terminal. Wondering whether the view outside matched the faint memories he had from his early youth, Rob pressed his face against the window. The airport layout and the control tower were vaguely familiar, but the large glass-fronted terminal and the tarmac looked strange.

The stewardess swung the cabin door open. Immediately, a gush of moist, warm air flooded the cabin with a strangely intriguing smell; a mixture of kerosene, hot tarmac and the sweet exciting scents of Africa. Rob took a deep breath and let his eyes feast on the deep sapphire-blue of the sky, the kind of blue that became visible in Europe only after a summer storm had washed all the dust and pollution out of the air. He snatched his bag out of the overhead rack, rushed down the stairs and well ahead of the other passengers, headed for the arrival hall.

Around him lay the vast and mainly empty expanse of the tarmac. In the left corner stood an old Fokker F27, its paint peeling in long streaks from its nose and wings. Dirty oil smears were running in stripes over the engine cowlings. A sleek and streamlined business jet was parked in front of the main entrance to the airport building. From the plane, a red carpet ran between two rows of potted palm trees to a door marked with large red letters 'VIP ONLY'. Comparing the shabby state of the F27 with the shiny jet, Rob reflected that it had to be the private transport of a high functionary, maybe even the President's. Shading his eyes against the glare of the sun, he looked up to the glass-topped control tower and noticed an impressive assortment of radar and radio antennas on the roof.

The old part of the terminal building gave an almost cheerful impression, with long red banners and brightly coloured pennants decorating its walls. As he was watching, a westerly breeze playfully swept the banners and pennants aside. The naked stonework underneath was soiled and pockmarked with decay, the contrast with the gaily coloured banners so shocking that it made the building look like an over-aged, but blatantly painted whore.

Chuckling at the analogy, Rob's eyes fastened on a row of heavily armed soldiers who were guarding the entrance to the VIP section. He saw their hostile faces, their fingers ready on the triggers of their AK47 Kalashnikovs. It reminded him that this country was fighting a bloody civil war and that neither arrogance nor audacity were much of a defence against bullets and rockets.

The arrival hall looked shabby with layers of dirt on the windows and the floor, which did nothing to decrease the general impression of neglect. Surprisingly enough, a set of noisy air-conditioners were working overtime. In contrast with the heat outside, the air was refreshing and cool. A full hour later, the suitcases of the Lisbon flight had still not arrived. Fuming, Rob asked a porter the reason for the delay. Instead of giving a reply, the man shrugged his shoulders and shuffled away.

The brightness of the day was turning to darkness when the luggage came tumbling down the luggage belt. Rob realized that all his haste to get out of the aircraft had been nothing but an exercise in futility. It occurred to him that he had a lot to learn about Angola, a country where time did not seem to matter and where everything seemed to happen at its own speed. Resigned to accept things the way they were, Rob walked over to the customs' clearance point.

The customs officer was a middle-aged man. A worn and none-too-clean blue shirt hung sloppily from his narrow shoulders. "Open your suitcase," he snarled aggressively. With obvious relish, he ran his hands through Rob's possessions. It soon became clear that Rob carried no contraband and his eagerness quickly changed into frustration.

"Whisky, gin?" he hissed, blowing the foul smell of old beer through his nicotine stained teeth. "Passaporte," he sneered finally. He punched a big red stamp in Rob's passport and waved him through, already looking with barely concealed expectation to the luggage of the next passenger.

At the door of the hall stood a tall and corpulent white man who was wiping his brow with a soggy looking handkerchief. His tropical suit stretched tightly over the rolls of fat on his belly. The view reminded Rob of a commercial for Michelin tyres. As soon as he saw Rob, the man came rushing over, a wide grin curling his lips.

"Senhor Stanfort," he yelled. The way he said Rob's name, it sounded like Stanfortey, with a long 'eee' at the end. "Senhor Stanfortey," he shouted again, grabbing Rob's hand and pumping it enthusiastically up and down. "I'm so glad to see you." Carried away by his own excitement, he put his arms around Rob's shoulders as if he were a long lost relative. Taken by surprise and afraid that Veleiro, in an outburst of Latin exhilaration, was going to embrace him, Rob hastily put his suitcase down and shook hands. "You must be Ernesto Veleiro," he mumbled.

Ernesto took Rob's suitcase in his left hand and pointed in the direction of the exit. "Let me show you the way." Quickly, he walked with a wobbling gait through the door and threw Rob's case on the back seat of a very battered old Volkswagen.

"It's getting late," he remarked casually. "You must be tired."

"Never mind that," responded Rob quickly. "My mind is full of questions. Maybe we can have a drink and..."

"It will have to wait," interrupted Veleiro. "Tonight, I have to take care of some other business. Tomorrow morning, we shall have breakfast together and we'll talk." Carefully navigating the Volkswagen between a myriad of potholes that littered the surface of the road, he added that after breakfast, they would go and see the Minister of Transport. "To get an idea of their requirements." Veleiro stopped talking for a moment and concentrated on his driving. As he changed to fourth gear, the old gearbox emitted a loud complaining sound. Smiling innocently, Ernesto shrugged his shoulders.

"I presume you want to start your inspection of the other airfields as soon as possible," he started.

Rob nodded affirmatively.

"I had thought so," confirmed Ernesto. "Tomorrow evening I have arranged a seat for you in the cockpit of DIANGOL's F27. They'll show you everything you want to see." Scanning the road in front of him, he hesitated briefly before completing his sentence.

"Remember to take an overnight bag with you. You'll be visiting the south part of the country, some airfields in the centre and finally Portugalia, in the north-east. The whole trip may take a day or two."

Surprised at the speed with which he was being launched into the operation, Rob pulled his attention away from the view outside and turned his head to face Ernesto.

"That old relic I saw at the airport, is that the F27 you are talking about," he shouted above the rattling noise of the old VW engine.

Ernesto nodded.

"Is it safe to fly in that aircraft?" Rob asked.

"Scared, are you?" jeered Ernesto, scornfully.

“No...” Rob yelled back, sounding as if he really wanted to say “Don’t be ridiculous.”

Briefly, he studied Ernesto’s face, trying to make up his mind whether he was serious or not.

For a while they drove on in silence. The atmosphere in the car became rather awkward, until Ernesto impulsively slammed his right hand on the dashboard.

“That F27 is the most modern civil transport aircraft they have available here, Captain Stanfortey,” he blurted out. A tone of well-played pique marked his voice. “The pilots of DIANGOL ...” His hand flew up from the dashboard and fluttered like a butterfly in front of Rob’s face. “They fly it everyday.” His dark eyes glowed with the intensity of his inner feelings. “Trust me, Captain,” he finally muttered. “I would not make you fly in a plane that is unsafe.”

Remembering the terms of the contract and the 5% commission he would receive for each flying hour, Rob realized that Ernesto had nothing to gain from his death.

“I bet you wouldn’t, Senhor Veleiro, because...” He chuckled when he considered the flippancy of what he was going to say, “... if I don’t come back, there is no contract.”

“I see we are beginning to understand each other,” Ernesto countered, raising one hand and pointing ahead through the windshield. “Here is your hotel.”

Very early the next morning, Rob was up and about. His head swimming with a thousand questions, he hurried to the restaurant where he chose a table by the window from where he had a good view of the Rua Vereador Castelbranco, a wide tree-lined avenue completely void of traffic.

“We don’t have a lot of traffic congestion here,” said Ernesto. He slipped into the seat at the other side of the table. “As you can see from the empty streets, communism has not brought prosperity to Angola.” He laughed sarcastically. “The few cars on the road are either official cars, or cars belonging to people like me.”

Ernesto lowered his voice slightly.

“The majority of the local population is so poor that they can’t afford the luxury of motorized transport.” Reaching across the table, he poured himself a cup of pitch black Robusta coffee, then refilled Rob’s cup.

“People here are short of almost everything that Europe has to offer,” he revealed, alternately smoking or taking a sip of his scalding hot coffee. “However, the country is not quite as poor as it looks. There is oil in the northern Province of Cabinda, and they have refineries in Luanda.” He drew his lungs full of smoke from his cigarette. “There are diamonds in the north-east, by the border with Katanga, but whatever they produce, whether it’s oil or diamonds, the Government is forced to export in exchange for hard currency.” Ernesto now sounded very irritated. Furtively, he threw a glance over his shoulder. “The true picture of the disaster lies in the interior of the country.” His voice was so low that Rob had to lean across the table to hear what he said. “The Government proclaims that there is peace, but we know better. Despite the elections of 1992 and the peace treaty of 1994, the belligerent forces continue their struggle. Even the presence of the newly arrived United Nations peacekeeping troops is not sufficient to stop the civil war which has been raging since 1975. What’s even worse, the Government troops are getting a beating. The roads are unsafe, the bridges over the rivers have been demolished and the railroads have been blown up or have fallen into disrepair. Only an aeroplane can get through.”

Rob asked himself whether he had the right to expose his men to this kind of danger. “Is that the reason why I’ve been offered the contract?” he inquired.

“No, not exactly.” Like a conspirator, Ernesto bent over the table and looked Rob straight in the eye. “A couple of years ago, DIANGOL bought two F27 aircraft.”

Ernesto lowered his voice even more. "Three weeks ago, one of them crashed in the vicinity of Luso. At least that was the official report. However, it is a well-known secret that the plane was shot down by UNITA. That F27 was doing the work that your Britannia will have to do..." A furtive smile slipped over his face. "If you accept the contract."

Rob faced him warily, again not sure whether he should go or stay. Despite the heat of the early morning sun, it suddenly felt as if a chill wind swept through the room. Hoping he knew what he was doing he forced himself to concentrate on Ernesto's words.

"They never found the wreckage of that F27," Ernesto said. "Therefore it is hard to say what *really* happened." The emphasis of his words lay on 'really', making it clear to Rob that whatever the Government said was not necessarily the truth.

"How can they fail to find the wreckage?" he asked. "Don't they have a Search and Rescue service here?"

Ernesto burst out laughing. "My oh my, Captain Stanfortey. You are quite a stranger to this part of the world, aren't you. Do you have any idea how large this country is? Even with ten SAR aircraft, they wouldn't be able to find a wreck in the tropical rain forests."

In a low voice, he told Rob the story of a Skyvan that had been lost in 1975. "That aircraft wasn't carrying a load of dried fish, but a king's ransom in diamonds," he uttered. "They used the most modern and sophisticated equipment, but found nothing and ..."

Rob's mind jumped back two decades, to the time he was told that his father had gone missing, presumed killed in a crash. "At that time, my father was working for DIANGOL," he interjected sharply. "He was declared dead a few days after his plane failed to reach its destination. Do you know who the pilot of that Skyvan was?"

"It was long before my time," replied Veleiro, "but as the rumours go, it seems that there were two pilots on board. The only traces they found of the aircraft were an engine and some metal cowlings which showed signs of damage caused by rocket fire." Veleiro sighed and raised his eyebrows. "That's all I know, Captain. I doubt that anybody alive can tell you more. Maybe, I could..." Interrupted by the arrival of the waiter, Ernesto didn't finish what he was saying. His mind in a turmoil, Rob decided to let the matter rest. If he accepted the contract, there would be time enough to find out the connection between the crashed Skyvan and his father's death; if there was a connection! He turned his attention to the menu.

"I'll have two boiled eggs and toast, please," he decided.

Ernesto roared with laughter. "You can forget that," he said, hiccuping with glee. "Whatever they put on that menu only exists in their fantasy."

The black waiter raised his eyebrows and walked away in a very dignified manner. Outside, a flock of large seabirds swooped low by the window. Their cries sounded faint but sharp through the thick glass.

"The waiters will do that again at lunch time," Ernesto said a little later, still enjoying Rob's embarrassment. "Don't even bother to read the menu. The only food they have available is dried fish and rice, and tomorrow it will be rice and dried fish. There is nothing else any more."

Busy weighing the risks of the operation, Rob rivetted his attention on the slice of dry bread and the watery jam the waiter had placed in front of him. Ernesto made a mocking gesture to his frugal breakfast.

"This is what they serve as food in an international hotel," he said sarcastically. "It makes you wonder what ordinary people out there have to eat. I'm not surprised that many of them find it difficult to believe that Communism will bring them happiness."

As a reply, Rob managed a thin smile. As soon as he finished his breakfast, they left the hotel.

"I'll introduce you to the people you will be working with in the future," Ernesto said. "First, we'll see the Minister of Transport, then the Manager of the Civil Aviation Department. He'll inspect your flying license and the Certificate of Airworthiness of your aeroplane."

Afterwards, Rob met some of the Board Members of DIANGOL. They gave him a general idea of the nature of the flights, mainly transporting food, medicines and petrol from the coastal airfields to cities in the interior. Lunch, as predicted, consisted only of dried fish and rice. At 2 o'clock they visited the DCA - the Directorate of Civil Air Transport - who would be organizing the cargoes and provide trucks, workers and kerosene for the Britannia. By the time they were finished, the sun was sinking to the horizon. In less than one hour, Rob was scheduled to take off on board the F27 to start his inspection tour in the interior. After a dull day running from one office to another, in spite of the shabby condition of the Fokker, it was something he was looking forward to.

Ernesto drove him to the hotel where he picked up his overnight bag and his flight kit, then they hurried back to the airfield. At half past seven, Rob walked across to the F27. A thin layer of fog started to drift over the tarmac. Above his head shone a myriad of stars, and the colour of the sky was a deep bluish black. Far away to the east, the narrow crescent of the moon was lying on its back marking the beginning of a new lunar month.

In the cockpit of the F27, Rob introduced himself to Captain Sobreiro, Chief-Pilot of DIANGOL.

"Welcome on board, Rob," said Sobreiro, his teeth looking very white in the dim light of the instruments. "Just call me Sobreiro. Everyone else does." With an abrupt movement of his hand, Sobreiro signalled the load master to close the door and slipped his headset over his ears. With his eyes partly closed, he listened to the ATIS - the Airport Traffic Information Service - and adjusted his flight instruments. As Rob was struggling with the unfamiliar seat belts of the co-pilot's seat, Sobreiro started the engines and put the flaps to the take-off position. As soon as the wheels came clear of the ground, Sobreiro lowered the left wing and swung the F27 in a sharp turn to the left. Rolling out in a southerly direction, he made a few corrections to the aileron and rudder trim, then switched the autopilot on and turned his attention to Rob.

"I'm afraid I don't know anything about your Britannia, Rob. You'll have to judge for yourself what your plane is or isn't capable of doing."

Reaching under his seat, he produced an old aeronautical map that showed the main features of the land and the contour of the hills and mountains in varying shades of green and brown. He folded it open and put it on Rob's lap.

"That's where we're going tonight." Using his finger to trace a line on the map, he showed Rob a track that roughly followed the coast from Luanda to Benguela, a city that lay 210 nautical miles to the south. Ten thousand feet below the left wing, Rob saw a white stretch of beach, the breaking waves glowing phosphorously in the light of the moon. Inland, as far as he could see, not one light was visible. "I always fly a few miles out over the ocean," Sobreiro emphasized. "Never over the coast!" He waited a moment, then, reading the question in Rob's eyes, he explained that the coastal plains were full of UNITA groups. "I wouldn't like to be at the receiving end of one of their rockets."

Rob remembered what Ernesto had told him that morning, about the other F27, which had been shot down. "I heard about that - um - accident in Luso," he replied, his voice sounding as if an ice cube had suddenly got stuck in his throat. "What about navigation? Don't you use radio beacons?"

Sobreiro started to laugh. "What beacons?" He asked contemptuously. "They haven't been working for ages, man. They are either destroyed by the fighting or broken down because of the lack of spare parts." He shook his head. "No, the only method of finding your way around in Angola is by the good old method of dead-reckoning, using aeronautical maps supplemented by road maps."

As if it was an echo, the question Rob had asked himself earlier exploded again in his brain. "Is it justified to take this risk?" Deep in thought, he took a sip of coffee from a paper cup the load master had pushed in his hand.

As he saw Rob's confusion, Sobreiro lifted his hand and gave him a resounding whack on his thigh. "I want you to come and work here, Rob. Honestly, we need you." All the humour gone from his voice, Sobreiro's expression became very serious. "However, Rob, you must know that since Independence, this is a whole new world with a set of completely new rules. If you want to survive, you'll have to learn them all very rapidly."

His brain loaded with indecision and doubt, Rob felt as if there was not enough air in the cockpit for him to breathe. Even the whistling noise of the engines and the hiss of air that caressed the windshield grew to a bewildering concert. His lips betrayed his confusion by twitching nervously. Again he questioned the sense of taking the risk. To hide his feelings, he turned his attention back to the map.

Twenty minutes later, slightly to the left of the plane, a small cluster of lights broke through the monotony of the night.

"Benguela," Sobreiro said. He pulled the throttles back and trimmed the F27 for a slow descent.

Ahead of them, the light of the moon cut a long and widening yellow strip through the rolling waves. Sobreiro steered a course that brought them in low over the water of the bay. Rob studied Sobreiro's way of closing with the field, his approach path safe over the emptiness of the sea. A line of lights appeared out of the dark. As they came closer, Rob saw the line split in the double row of runway lighting. A few feet from the ground, Sobreiro pulled the stick back and greased the plane on to the concrete surface of the landing strip. After the engines were shut down, the load master opened the side door in the fuselage and the unloading of the cargo began. Happy to be able to stretch their legs, Rob and Sobreiro walked the full length of the runway.

"That's what's left of a bombardment by the South Africans," said Sobreiro, pointing to the left.

Rob saw a cluster of large circular holes, each one of them repaired with a rough layer of light coloured cement.

"It happened back in 1975," Sobreiro expanded. "Since then, not much has been done to mend the damage. Look there." Rob followed the direction of his finger and saw the control tower, the glass still missing in the windows. He waved to the controller who waved back, shouting something unintelligible. "The control tower is still in a mess," Sobreiro said. "But the airfield is perfectly usable, and that's the main thing."

Sunk in a kind of private reverie, Rob followed Sobreiro into the big hangar. In earlier days, the hangar had been used as a maintenance base for aircraft. Now it had been transformed into a warehouse that was packed to the rafters with huge piles of jute bags; by the smell of it, they were all filled with dried fish. The stench, mixed with the moist and stagnant heat of the day, made the atmosphere inside almost intolerable. Rob pulled a handkerchief in front of his nose and mouth and followed Sobreiro into the depths of the hangar.

"Look over there, that might interest you more than piles of dried fish," shouted Sobreiro. At first, Rob saw nothing but an object covered in dirt and filth, its outlines hidden behind a curtain of flying dust. As he came closer, the shapes materialized into the elegant and tapered wings of a motor-glider. All of a sudden the stench and heat were forgotten. "My God," he exclaimed. "A Motor Falcon!" Gently, he wiped the dust away from the nose of the plane. The proud name 'Albatross de Benguela' appeared from under layers of grime. Behind the first Falcon, he noticed a second one, apparently in the same perfect condition. "These planes are equipped with a small Limbach engine," he said excitedly, reaching over to open the cockpit. "They can take off without any assistance and cover a distance of 400 miles at a speed of 70 knots."

"I know," replied Sobreiro. "As a member of the flying club, I used to fly them quite often. Since Independence, private flying has been banned. The club doesn't exist any more but each time I land here I pay the Falcons a visit ... for old time's sake."

Gazing at the instruments, Rob's lips folded in a sad grin. "What a shame to leave these beautiful planes here to rot," he whispered sadly. "They are worth a lot of money in Europe. Do you think I could buy them?"

"I can't help you there, Rob," replied Sobreiro. He turned away to walk back to the exit. "You'll have to talk to the Military if you want them. They're in control now."

"I might just do that," said Rob. He used his handkerchief to wipe the dust from his hands. "However, I must get my priorities right. First the inspection of the airfields and the decision as to whether I will or won't accept this job, then we'll see."

After the stuffy air in the hangar, the evening breeze smelled sweet and cool. They managed to get a lift in one of the trucks that belonged to the fishmonger. The city was dark, the streets were deserted and the houses looked like rows of tombstones. The driver of the truck dropped them in front of a small hotel, with the promise to pick them up at 7 o'clock.

The next morning, Sobreiro paid for their rooms in kind, two bars of soap and half a carton of cigarettes.

"The only 'real' currency nowadays, Rob," he whispered.

In spite of the early hour, they were met at the entrance to the airport by a group of hollow-eyed begging children. They were clad in rags. Rob's heart missed a beat when he noticed the distress on their young faces.

"The innocent casualties of this rotten war," Sobreiro said sadly. "And there is nothing I can do to help. It's heartbreaking, isn't it?"

Rob noticed a young girl with only one leg, who was supporting herself on crutches, and a very young boy who had a dirty bandage around his eyes.

"Victims of land mines or stray bullets," Sobreiro explained. "The war touches everybody, whether they are pro-Government or pro-UNITA, be they adults or children!"

At 8 o'clock, they took off. Every so often, when flying low over the land, Sobreiro pointed to the blackened remains of a destroyed and looted village, or the gap in a railway line where once a bridge had spanned the river. After climbing above 12,000 feet, a slight haze covered the scars of the land and they flew on in silence. That day they inspected the airfields of Luso and Huambo. Apart from an evident lack in ground equipment, Rob could find no apparent problems. Early in the evening, just when dusk turned to dark, they touched down in Portugalia.

"Now you'll discover how nice life in Angola can be," said Sobreiro triumphantly as he brought the car to a standstill in front of the old colonial villa where they were going to spend the night. "Because the diamond mines are one of the highest revenue earners, they enjoy a special status. Here, they don't live like radical communists. Quite the contrary, I'd say."

Rob felt strangely affected by the appearance of the old villa that looked very much like the house he had shared with his parents and their housekeeper. To confirm his intuition, he pointed towards the end of the lane.

"Tell me, Sobreiro," he asked hesitatingly. "The church is just around that corner, isn't it? And opposite the church is the police station?"

"That's amazing," exclaimed Sobreiro. He sounded genuinely puzzled. "How do you know that? Have you been here before?"

Rob smiled at Sobreiro's surprised tone.

"I have," he acknowledged. "Some thirty years ago. I was baptized in that little church and my mother is buried here, but I'll tell you all about that later. First a bath and some food, then we can talk."

A black house boy opened the door. Another boy brought them a bottle of ice cold Casal Garcia. Rob took a sip of his drink and was pleasantly surprized as he felt the caress of the slightly sparkling wine in the back of his mouth.

"If anything, I'm a little envious that I can't be based here with you," Sobreiro commented, throwing a meaningful look at Rob. "If you accept the job, that is..."

The next half an hour, Rob spent in the luxury of a large antique bath tub, another tall glass of Casal Garcia in his hand. As the hot water soaked the dust of the last two days out of his pores, his muscles began to relax but his head continued to be filled with confusing thoughts. At one moment, he was thinking about the soldiers at the airfield in Luanda, their Kalashnikovs and the unfriendly look on their faces. Next, he heard the echo of Ernesto's words: "The F27 was shot down, Rob, but the Government doesn't want to admit it." Sobreiro's voice reverberated in his ears. "I always fly a few miles away from the coast to avoid the rockets." Then, the view of destroyed villages appeared before his eyes, and the children he had seen that morning in Benguela. Wounded and mutilated children, who were hungry and wore rags instead of clothes.

The more Rob thought about it the more difficult it became to make up his mind. His ideas went from doubt to anguish. In a quick gulp, he drained his glass and filled it again from the bottle he had taken with him to the bathroom. "What shall I do?" he asked himself. On the one hand, there was the suspicion that he was being pushed by events into something that was foolhardy and very dangerous, something he didn't want to happen. On the other hand, because of the shaky financial situation of his company, he didn't have very much choice. Unless he wanted to flirt with bankruptcy.

Gradually, the alcohol of the fruity wine began to drive the spectre of catastrophe away. With each sip he took, the world began to look more and more as if he was wearing rose-tinted glasses and wallowing in the luxury of the hot bath, his mind came to rest. Finally, he thought about Sobreiro, who had been flying in Angola all his life and who had never been shot at!

"We'll have to follow Sobreiro's example," he mumbled. "As soon as we arrive here, we'll have to learn the rules, fast." He suddenly realized that he had thought in terms of 'as soon as' and not 'if' as if subconsciously his mind had already decided to give it a go, and he started to smile. Later, when he went down the stairs and sought his way to the dining room, heavy raindrops started to fall. The soft tones of Beethoven's "Moonlight Sonata" were accompanied by the patting noise of rain on the corrugated roof. In the dining room, the walls were shining with the light of a wood fire. The table was covered with a white linen cloth. As Rob saw the culinary miracle that the Zefa the cook had prepared, the spell of life in Africa suddenly invaded him.

The meal started with a plate of small river lobsters, freshly boiled and served with a delicious green salad and mayonnaise.

"The rivers here are full of freshwater lobsters," explained Sobreiro. A devious expression appeared in his eyes when he added that Zefa could also make the entree with thin slices of snake or crocodile meat. "I can assure you, Rob, you'd swear you were eating scallops."

"I'm not very sure whether I'd like that," shuddered Rob, a quiver of disgust running down his spine. "Change the subject, please."

The lobsters were followed by a mouth-watering moambe, a typical African dish made from bread-root, chicken and fresh vegetables.

As soon as the table was cleared, Sobreiro leaned back in his chair and pulled a packet of cigarettes out of his shirt pocket.

"Now, tell me how it happened that you were baptized here in the church, and how your mother came to be buried in the cemetery," he said.

Rob revealed that his father had been working for DIANGOL as a mining-manager, responsible for the exploitation of the diamond-rich soil. "My parents came here in the early sixties. I was born in December 1963 and my mother passed away in 1965. I stayed here until the spring of 1975, when my father sent me back to Europe to be away from a country that was on the brink of a civil war. Back in Europe, I didn't remember much about this place, but coming here has brought it all back. It feels almost as if I never left."

"I see," replied Sobreiro. "And your father, is he back in the UK now?"

"No, he never left Angola," Rob clarified. "When he was not busy managing the mines, he spent his time flying around the countryside in his own aeroplane. Quite often, I used to fly with him." For a moment, Rob fell silent, a faraway expression in his eyes. "Shortly after I left, my father disappeared. They never found a trace of his aeroplane and they never recovered his body." He helped himself to more wine.

"Yesterday morning, I was talking with Ernesto Veleiro. He mentioned a Skyvan once owned by DIANGOL that had been shot down in the same period that my father went missing. That made me wonder, Sobreiro. It's too much of a coincidence that two planes disappear at the same time, leaving no traces of either of them. Could it be that DIANGOL's plane and the plane my father was flying, were one and the same?"

"In '75, I was in my early teens," said Sobreiro. "My family was not working for the mines, therefore my memory about what happened then is blank, but I'll have a look in the archives. However, in my opinion, it's doubtful. A Skyvan is a rather complex piece of equipment. Hardly the plane a private pilot would be flying..." He shook a cigarette out of the packet and lit up.

"Maybe at a later stage, I could have a talk with the 'older' workers of DIANGOL," said Rob. "They might remember my father, maybe recall what happened then..."

"If there are still some of those old-timers around," replied Sobreiro. "Working in the mines is exhausting. It's very rare to find a miner who is older than 45 years of age, but we'll try. Who knows..." Sobreiro blew a plume of smoke to the ceiling and softly rapped his knuckles against the tabletop. "Something else, Rob. Yesterday, we were talking about the problem with the rebels. Now that is something I can explain." He revealed that he was Portuguese, born in Angola, and that he had visited Portugal only twice in his life. "As such, Rob, I feel more Angolan than Portuguese and I understand the dark forces which are tearing this country apart."

He sucked on his cigarette and continued to talk in a low voice. "This war between the Government and the guerrillas is nothing but a tribal war, Rob." Sobreiro's voice suddenly had a hard edge to it. "Do you know who is responsible for it?"

Rob looked at him thoughtfully.

Sobreiro beat himself theatrically on his chest. "We are responsible for it," he exclaimed. "We... The whites, who for centuries have colonized Africa; the British and the French, the Belgians and the Portuguese. For hundreds of years, we have plundered and stolen. We have exhausted the richness of the soil and have hunted for ivory and valuable animal skins. All that in the name of religion and civilization." Unable to control his agitation, he stood up and stamped around the room. He topped up his glass, pushed the bottle of wine across the table and sat down again. "Have another drink," he said. His voice sounded hoarse with a mixture of rage and sadness.

Rob did, then moved his chair a little farther away from the table and stretched his legs.

"The biggest blunder of all is that our ancestors drew the borders with complete disregard for the ethnic boundaries," said Sobreiro excitedly. "Whole tribes and families were split apart. Ethnic groups who previously had lived in the security of their own borders were suddenly forced to live together, people who were very different from each other, divided as they were by centuries of tribal laws and ancient customs." Sobreiro took a sip of his glass. "We, the whites," he went on. "We didn't care that we were splitting families apart. We didn't care that a few blacks were killed in one or other tribal dispute. That was not important. All that mattered was the possession of the land and the profits to be gained from it." Laughing harshly, he jumped up and walked over to the fire. For a while, he stood there, watching the play of the flames.

His mind slightly clouded from the wine, Rob raised his voice. "Why should that be a reason to make war now, Sobreiro?"

"That's the sixty-four-thousand dollar question, Rob. Let me try to explain. Angola is made up of more than twenty different ethnic groups. The main ones being..." Sobreiro raised one of his fingers. "First, the Bakongos. They live in the northwest corner of Angola and are related to the Bakongos of Zaire." He raised another finger. "Second, we have the Kimbundus. They are relatives of the tribes in Katanga. Their territory stretches from Luanda to Saurimo. A third group, the Ovimbundus, live in the south of the country by the border with Namibia." Instead of raising more fingers, Sobreiro lit up another cigarette, then continued: "There are also the Mbundus, the Nganguelas, the Nyanekas and the Humbas. Last but not least, there are the mulattos. They are of mixed blood, the result of centuries of inbreeding between white and black. They live mostly in the cities and don't really belong to any of the tribes."

At that moment, the door opened and Zefa entered the room, carrying a tray with coffee and cognac. Sobreiro stopped talking and waited until the coffee was poured. After Zefa was gone, he took a sip of his brandy, smacked his lips, and carried on with his speech. "When the Portuguese came to this part of the world, they claimed the country for the crown, drew the borders rather arbitrarily and forced all the different tribes to live together in one new big country. They called it Angola." Sobreiro's body, illuminated by the light of the flames, threw a strangely deformed shadow on the wall. "With the Portuguese Army as peace keeper in the country, all went well for centuries, the tribes living together in some kind of enforced harmony, until recently, when the fight for freedom flared up. In no time, the struggle to get rid of the Portuguese became also a war between the main tribes, as each one of them wanted to gain control of the country." Sobreiro revealed to Rob that Nevo, the President, was a Kimbundu and a communist.

"As a result, most of the Kimbundus are members of the MPLA and communists, Rob. On the other hand, Joshua Matindi is an Ovimbundu, and he is the leader of UNITA."

Rob nodded. "Now I begin to see why it is a tribal war," he said. "Kimbundus against Ovimbundus..." Walking over to the large veranda door, he looked out into the dark of the night. It was still raining. Every once in a while, the low scudding clouds became visible when a flash of sheet-lightning brightened the horizon. Whilst admiring the play of nature, Rob's mind was filled with the troubles, dangers and miseries of this enormous country.

"UNITA is getting more and more powerful," remarked Sobreiro from behind his back. "Matindi is slowly strangling the governmental forces."

Slightly dazed and confounded by all the knowledge, Rob returned to the table. The light of the wood-fire was much fainter now, hiding the corners of the room in dark shadows.

Sobreiro stretched his arms above his head. "The situation is so tragic, Rob," he said. "Whether they are with the Government Forces or with Joshua Matindi, the soldiers don't really want to fight. They want peace, they want to go home and live with their families, but the irony of everything is that the country is bankrupt. The big industries are almost completely shut down and agriculture doesn't exist any more. Therefore, the only thing a man can do to make enough money to feed his family, is to join one of the armies and fight, and it goes on and on... In the mean time, thousands and thousands of people are suffering, children are dying from hunger, a stray bullet, or from stepping on a mine."

They sat still for a while, listening to the rain and the heavy echoes of thunder rolling through the night.

"Poor Angola," sighed Sobreiro finally. "When is it finally going to end? All those deaths, all those tears."

The rain still fell down in torrents when they went up to their rooms. Before he closed his eyes, Rob concluded that his decision to come and work here was the right thing to do.

"It will not only solve my financial problems," he said to himself, "... it will also bring help and relief to the people of Angola. However small this help will be." He switched off the light, turned over, and went to sleep.

The next morning the rain had stopped. It was still damp with veils of mist hanging between the trees. In the garden of the villa, the air was heavy with a strong smell of moisture. The beauty of the morning was lost on Rob. He wanted to fly as soon as possible back to Luanda, to telephone Ian and Jock and inform them about his decision. Then one more meeting with the Minister of Transport to sign the contract, and back to London to get the operation started.

After breakfast, he went to the cemetery in search for his mother's grave. The church was closed, but the gate to the well-kept churchyard was open and he found the grave in the old part of the cemetery under the canopy of a full grown hibiscus tree. Rob went down on one knee and said a prayer.

Half an hour later they were airborne. As the propellers of the Fokker F27 whined down in front of the terminal building in Luanda, it was almost 3 p.m. in the afternoon. Rob removed his headset, looped it over the hook on the side panel and looked out of the window.

"Isn't that strange?" he said sharply. "Ernesto is bound to make a lot of money on this contract, and yet, he doesn't even bother to come and pick me up."

Sobreiro heard the amazement in Rob's voice and shrugged his shoulders.

"He probably didn't get our message," he said. "You know how it is nowadays, most of the time the long range radios don't work."

"Yes, I know, Sobreiro, and when they work, nobody is listening!" Smiling, Rob slapped Sobreiro on his back. "See," he said. "I'm already beginning to know the African system."

Together, they walked over the deserted tarmac, admiring the clouds on the western horizon which were coloured in red and yellow by the light of the sun.

Pointing to a fat thundercloud, Sobreiro began to sing. "Here comes the rain again." He pulled the door of his car open and threw his flight kit on the back seat. "Come on, Rob, I'll drive you to the Tropico. I'm sure Ernesto will be there."

"Not that I need him to sign the contract," replied Rob, "but he is my agent, and I have to play the game by the rules."

They drove on in an amicable but complete silence. Rob sat staring out of the window, his mind full of plans and blind to what was happening around him. In the Rua Vereador Castelbranco, Sobreiro stopped the car in front of the hotel. Rob recognized the big neon sign that lit up the facade. As if wakening from a deep trance, he forced his eyes open.

"Jee," he mumbled, fumbling around in his bag to find the key of his room. "That was quick, Sobreiro, thanks." He didn't bother to stop at the reception counter to check for messages, but ran straight to the lifts. The metal grille of the ancient elevator closed noisily behind his back. For a couple of seconds he stood there in the dark, furiously punching the buttons until it dawned on him: "No electricity, damn it."

Swearing, he almost fell in his haste to get out of the useless cage. His feet clattering on the bare stone steps, he ran the stairs two by two until he reached the seventh floor. Once in his room, with sweat running down his face, he dialled Ernesto's number, mentally counting the ringing tones of the phone. At twenty he gave up. After a second of hesitation, he called the number of the operator. "Any messages for Captain Stanfort?" he asked. "Stanfort!" he repeated, "STANFORT, room 744." There were no messages and Rob slammed the receiver back on the hook.

"What the hell is Ernesto up to?" he shouted, frustrated and very much on edge now. Rob's nose caught his own scent, a sour mixture of sweat, dirty clothes and dust. Shrugging his shoulders, he decided to have a shower. He quickly stripped off his filthy clothes, threw them in a corner of the room and walked over to the wardrobe to select a fresh set.

As he opened the door of his wardrobe, he saw that the cupboard was empty and his heart skipped a few beats. Very confused, he looked again. There was no denying it. His old leather suitcase and all his spare clothes were gone. A feeling of dread started to rise somewhere in the region of his stomach.

"What the hell is going on?" he yelled. Forcing himself to ignore the emotions of fright and worry, he tried to convince himself that there must be a perfectly logical answer to the question.

"Of course," he mumbled. "During my absence the management must have given my room to another guest. My luggage must have been put in storage." He hastily slipped back into his three-day old clothes and ran down the stairs. Forcing his voice to sound artificially jovial he asked Juan, the receptionist, what they had done with his luggage. Juan looked at him, something like fear showing in his eyes.

"Captain Stanfort, I ..." he muttered.

At that moment, the electricity came back on and with a screech Tjaikovsky's '1812' started somewhere halfway through the overture on the hotel's audio system. Trying to read Juan's expression, Rob kept his eyes locked on his face. "Come on, Juan," he prodded.

Covertly looking over his shoulder to the other side of the counter where two Army officers were trying to chat up the girl on duty at the cashier's desk, Juan shook his head. Rapidly approaching boiling point, Rob clenched his fists together.

"Don't play games with me, Juan. Tell me straight, what's the matter?"

In the bright lights of the reception counter, Juan's black colour turned a dirty grey, his eyes revealing an emotion of naked fear.

As he saw that, Rob suddenly remembered Sobreiro's words: "This is Angola, Rob, where life is cheap." His uneasiness shifted into second gear and became a flood of worry. "Juan," he stammered finally. "Tell me, have the police been here? Have they been looking for me?"

"Not the police," Juan whispered, one hand nervously tapping the mahogany wood of the desk. "The Secret Police, SECPOL. They have arrested Senhor Veleiro."

Rob's heart lurched. SECPOL's reputation in modern day Angola was reminiscent of the GESTAPO's in occupied Europe during the Second World War. There he was, lost in Luanda without anybody to turn to. Or was there? He hurried back to his room, double locked the door and dialled Sobreiro's number. "Listen," he said when Sobreiro picked up the phone. "Veleiro has been arrested and my room has been raided. All my clothes are gone, and I'm afraid I'm on the wanted list of SECPOL."

"If I were you," stated Sobreiro, "I'd contact the British Embassy, to get legal assistance."

"You must be joking," shouted Rob. "Since the outbreak of the war, most of the staff have been called back to the UK. Besides, we have been warned in London to stay away from here. Nobody from the embassy is going to help me."

"In that case, get a seat on the first available plane and get out of the country!"

"What?" Rob's voice was edged with disbelief, "... but I haven't done anything wrong," he stuttered. He began to shout defiantly. "Understand me, Sobreiro, if I run away I'll never find out what this is all about, and I'll lose the opportunity to discover what happened to my father! What's more, I'll lose this contract, and I need it if I want my company to survive."

For a moment the telephone remained mute, the silence in the room so profound that Rob could hear his own heartbeat. "Did you hear me, Sobreiro?" he shouted again.

"Yes, I heard you. Shut up for a moment and let me think."

Rob tried to imagine Sobreiro, sitting in the comfort of his home. All his instincts told him to get out and save his skin, but his feelings of outrage and pride forced him to reject that solution. He jumped with alarm when in the room next door to his, somebody flushed the toilet and the pipes of the plumbing produced a loud groaning noise. "I've done nothing wrong," he muttered again. "It's not fair."

Suddenly, Sobreiro's started to talk. "If you are so keen on clearing your reputation, I'll try to arrange an appointment for you with the Minister of Internal Affairs. As C.O. of the police and SECPOL, he should know what's going on."

Rob mulled the idea over in his mind.

"Remember," Sobreiro said with emphasis. "It's a knife that can cut both ways. Once in their hands..." He did not finish, the risks too obvious for Rob to be ignored.

Again, Rob felt the empty feeling of being completely on his own, like a swimmer in the middle of the ocean with no land in sight, waiting for his strength to give in and the water to drag him down.

"I accept," he replied hoarsely, too proud to give up. "And screw the consequences, but I must admit that I'm scared out of my wits. I don't want to spend the night on my own here. Imagine if those thugs from SECPOL come back to pick me up, I'll never have the chance to explain myself." He hesitated. "Have you got room to put me up, Sobreiro?"

"I don't sleep with men ..." said Sobreiro in an attempt to release the tension, "... but I can offer you my sofa. Will that do?"

"Try to keep me away."

"I'll be down in ten minutes."

Rob put the phone down. Afraid of his own shadow, he walked over to the wall, switched the light off and cautiously drew the curtains aside. Where the street lights had been vandalized, some patches in the street were darker than the rest.

As forecasted by Sobreiro, it had started to rain again, a light drizzle that formed wet yellow circles in the feeble light of the street lamps. Rob tried to see through the cavernous darkness under the trees. Once his troubled mind thought he detected the hazy shadows of two people who stood there, watching the entrance of the hotel. He waited patiently. After a while it became clear. The shadows were only what they seemed to be. Shadows!

With fear bitter as bile in his throat, he tried to convince himself that everything would be all right. "Certainly don't surrender to paranoia," he reminded himself.

By his watch, almost fifteen minutes had gone by since he put the phone down. He grabbed his flight kit and very carefully crept down the service stairs at the back of the hotel. Instead of using the main exit, he turned right and walked down the corridor that gave access to the kitchen. Ignoring the sign that said 'PERSONNEL ONLY', he pushed the door open. He also ignored the guilty look in the eyes of the cook, who tried to hide two bags behind his body. They were filled to the brim with the leftovers of the evening meal. "To be sold on the black market," Rob figured.

He hurried towards the back door, his feet crushing a couple of cockroaches which crawled by the dozen over the slippery floor. Outside, he found himself in a rain-swept courtyard, one wall lined with smelly dustbins. Two hungry cats scattered as he came near. In their hurry, they knocked over one of the bins which clattered loudly over the cobblestones. Scared of being discovered, Rob froze and hid against the wall. No one bothered to investigate the source of the noise and Rob slipped into the narrow passage that ran alongside the wall of the hotel towards the Rua Vereador Castelbranco.

At the end, Rob looked around the corner. No one stirred. The street was empty. The rain hit him fresh in the face, cooling his flushed skin. Sighing, he forced himself to relax a little, but every minute that passed felt like an hour. The constant rain plastered his hair to his scalp and drenched his shirt and trousers. In his anxious mood, he hardly noticed it and kept looking at his watch.

"Come on, Sobreiro," he muttered. "Pull your finger out! What the hell is keeping you?"

As time crept by, his imagination began to run wild. "Could it be that Sobreiro, in order to put himself in a better position with the new rulers, had gone to inform the police?"

In a surge of hysteria, Rob imagined he could hear the sound of sirens. Fearing that any moment a Black Maria with a squad of SECPOL would come screaming around the corner, he felt the urge to turn and run. Then he remembered the friendship that had been forged between the two of them during the last three days. Ashamed of himself, he shrugged the thoughts of distrust away. Finally the old blue car pulled up in front of the hotel. Rob made a dash for it and let himself drop heavily down on to the front seat. Immediately, Sobreiro pulled away from the curb.

"I started to see ghosts everywhere," Rob admitted guiltily. "You know, Sobreiro, for a moment I even thought that you were going to show up with the police."

Obviously shocked by his words, Sobreiro swung his face around.

Rob knew that he had made a terrible mistake.

"I'm not one of those vultures!" Sobreiro spat out, his eyes flashing with anger. Totally ignoring Rob, he drove on in silence.

Rob tried desperately to find the right words to explain the depths of his despair. After a full five minutes of time had elapsed, Sobreiro gave a deep sigh and punched Rob on his shoulder. "I guess I can understand you," he remarked quietly.

Rob knew he was forgiven.

The rubber strips of the wipers, worn out after a life under the tropical sun, drew thick, wet smears over the windscreen. It made the road look like the surface of a lake, the car like a boat navigating through a thick wet fog.

"I know what this atmosphere of oppression can do," said Sobreiro. "I've seen it happen time and time again, but you can trust me. I'm on your side, Rob. The only reason I arrived late was that I had to make a couple of calls to arrange an appointment for you at the Ministry."

They drove on in a trusting and warm silence. It was Rob who spoke first, giving voice to his worries. "I hope I'll be able to clear my name," he said. "After all, I've got nothing to hide. You can confirm that. You were with me most of the time."

Sobreiro threw him a sideways glance. "They don't want me to go there with you, Rob. The Minister insisted that you come on your own, and he is a strange fellow. Some people call him a fair man, others tell me he is merciless." He steered the Volkswagen around an exceptionally large pothole, then his voice turned harsh again. "It even seems that, if the deal is worth it, he is not unwilling to accept a bribe, but in your case, I wouldn't try it, Rob. It would be like walking a tightrope without a safety net. You could fall down and break your neck!"

Rob looked out through the side window, his breath misting the glass. "Jesus Christ, Sobreiro," he asked. "What am I going to do?"

"I personally know that the Minister is a man who will make use of people for as long as they can serve his purpose," Sobreiro replied. "Once that is finished, he drops them dead. Now, let's face it, Rob. You and your company have a very definite purpose. They need a transport aircraft here. They need it badly, and you are the only one who can deliver. If you remain a free man, of course. Therefore I think you stand a very good chance."

Sobreiro's words gave Rob something to hold on to, a little hope, but nothing to justify the feeling of optimism that suddenly rose in his heart.

Luanda, 12 March 1995

The Ministry of Internal Affairs was located in an old building on the corner of the Rua do Carmo and the Avenida Vidal. Formerly known as the Portuguese Office of Colonial Affairs, the large edifice had lost a lot of its former grandeur. The facade was dirty and grey and the walls were covered in a layer of dirty-white bird droppings. A pair of guards, dressed in the uniform of Angolan troopers, scrutinized Rob as he climbed the two flights of steps. Mustering all his courage and firmly suppressing a feeling of dread, he entered the building.

"I would like to see the Minister," he said cautiously to the receptionist.

The employee, a mulatto, made a pretence of concentrating on a piece of paper that lay in front of him on his desk. "The Minister doesn't receive visitors, go away," he mumbled.

"I have an appointment," insisted Rob. "Here is my card."

The receptionist threw a peremptory glance at Rob's card. "Ha, Captain Stanfort."

"So they are expecting me," Rob thought. Too late to turn back now. The mulatto wasted no further time and showed him to the lift. Accompanied by a grinding noise, the old elevator started to ascend. At the third floor, it stopped with a jerk. In front of Rob lay a long corridor, the far end in semi-darkness. The walls and the floor smelt stale and old. At the end, the mulatto knocked respectfully on the door of a large corner room. Almost immediately a green light above the door lit up. The mulatto pulled the door open and ushered Rob inside.

Rob found himself in a large, beautiful room, each wall at least 25 feet long, the ceiling decorated with delicate old frescos. Two large bay windows in the western wall offered a splendid view over the bay of Luanda and the Fort of San Miguel. Beyond the harbour lay a lagoon. From where he stood, Rob saw flocks of birds darting low over the soft green water, and further west he caught a glimpse of the deep blue of the South Atlantic. In the corner between the northern and the western wall stood a heavy and beautifully carved teak desk, its position so strategically chosen that the person behind the desk would never have to face the harsh light of the tropical sun.

The Minister, Sebasto Calio, was a big man, strongly built with powerful shoulders. His face, once good-looking, was now heavily marked with signs of ruin, left by years of guerrilla fighting and heavy drinking. Layers of fat hid his thick neck and his skin looked baggy and grey. Not bothering to shake hands, he motioned Rob to sit down. With his other hand, he waved the receptionist out of the office.

"Well, Captain Stanfort," he said in a deep melodious voice. "It seems that the person who was supposed to act as intermediary between our Government and your company has gone missing."

Rob nodded. Paler than ever, he tried to show a confidence that he did not really feel. "That's right, your Excellency," he replied, forcing himself to remain calm. "It's a mystery to me."

As if searching his soul, the Minister's eyes made a study of Rob's face.

"I would be very grateful if you could throw some light on this matter," Rob risked to say.

"WHAT?" Calio's black eyes became mocking, narrow slits. "Grateful you say. That's rather old-fashioned. But yes, I guess people like you would be grateful."

Rob seemed unable to sit still. To force himself to relax, he kept his eyes fixed on a point on the wall somewhere above the Minister's shoulder.

"Listen, Captain," Calio declared. "I hope we can solve this problem amicably. We need people like you to help us with our transport problem, but I have to be sure that we can trust you. Therefore, tell me, how long have you been working together with this..." With carefully studied nonchalance, he browsed for a while through the pages of a thick red file. "... This Veleiro?"

"As a matter of fact ..." Rob's voice sounded ridiculously high. "I have not *yet* been working with Senhor Veleiro. The reason why I came to Angola was to evaluate the possibilities of a co-operation with your Government. Just recently, I had a meeting about that with the Minister of Transport. He can confirm my good intentions." Feeling like a little mouse in the paws of a big black cat, Rob pulled a stack of telex messages out of his briefcase and handed them over to the minister, making a desperate effort to give a calm and unworried impression, but suddenly jumping when the telephone started to ring.

Noticing Rob's strange reaction, Sebasto Calio raised an eyebrow and reached for the telephone.

"Not NOW," he shouted angrily, "I said I didn't want to be disturbed."

Thoughtfully, he placed the receiver back on the cradle. "You seem to be rather nervous, Captain Stanfort," he said cautiously. "Are you sure you're telling me the truth?"

Rob knew that if he did not act confidently, he was damned. "Quite sure," he replied. "It's all there in the telexes."

"In that case, may I ask you to wait outside for a while. I have to call my Superintendent at SECPOL and make some inquiries."

The Minister made a dismissing motion with his hand and started to dial a number. Rob walked on stiff legs to the exit and gently closed the door behind him.

"Hello, Lopes," articulated Calio in the telephone. "Sebasto Calio here. Listen, I get the impression that Stanfort has nothing to do with Veleiro's clandestine activities. He is worried shitless, but honest, and certainly brave." He listened briefly to the reply from the other side. Suddenly, his right hand made a wildly fluttering motion. With plain disapproval in his voice, he interrupted the conversation.

"*What did you say*," he yelled. Listening attentively, he pressed the telephone closer to his ear.

"Well, I'm sorry that Veleiro died before he could give you the names of his conspirators," he said assertively. "Anyway, what *did* you find out before Veleiro dropped dead?"

Shifting the telephone to his left hand, he scribbled a few notes on a writing pad. "Buying diamonds on the black market and smuggling them out of the country with the help of an officer in the Customs Department. All right, Lopes, hold on."

Calio tossed the phone down and walked over to the window. For a while he stood there, looking at the view but seeing nothing. He suddenly made up his mind and hurried back to his desk.

"Listen Lopes, what Veleiro has been able to say is proof enough that Stanfort is innocent. Officially, I don't want to know anything about your messy business. I'll make up a story, and tell Stanfort that I couldn't find out what really happened. You, from your side, let the matter rest and get rid of the body."

Lopes seemed to say something funny, because Calio suddenly smiled.

"I'm sure you did," he said, grinning, "... but, Lopes, tell your bullies to use a velvet glove in the future. Dead prisoners can't give information."

About to put the phone down, Calio remembered something. "Just to be on the safe side. If Stanfort and his men come and work here, I want you to keep track of their actions. You never know with foreigners what they're up to."

"Don't worry," replied Lopes. "I've got a couple of men inside DIANGOL. They'll tell me everything I need to know."

Calio hung up and pushed the button of his intercom. "Tell Stanfort to come in," he ordered.

"I haven't been able to find out a lot, Rob!"

Rob immediately noted the difference in Calio's voice. The hard edge had disappeared, and the use of his first name, was that an indication that his reputation had been cleared? Or was the Minister just playing a game with him?

"What I found out is, that Veleiro was engaged in smuggling diamonds out of the country," explained Calio, "... and that could only be the tip of the iceberg. Veleiro is now in a high-security prison, for further interrogation."

Rob didn't know what to reply. With each word the Minister said, his hope was surging, but he didn't dare to take his luck for granted.

"Forget about Veleiro," Calio droned on. "I already have. What I know for sure is that you have nothing to do with the crimes he committed. That's the most important point, isn't it?"

Suddenly, the weight seemed to be lifted from Rob's shoulders and his future looked much brighter.

"Your luggage will be returned to you," commented Calio. "And you can go ahead with your plans. If you still want to have the contract, of course."

For a moment Rob got the impression that it had been a set up, then he remembered Sobreiro's words - "I'm not one of those vultures, Rob." - and he knew it had not been a trick.

Terminating the interview, the Minister stood up. "I won't keep you any longer," he said, shaking his hand. "I'm sure you still have a lot of work to do, but believe me," His voice sounded almost like begging. "The sooner you can start, the better. We need you urgently."

Rob let himself out. He ran down the stairs, perfectly aware that the whole affair was a can of worms. How else could it be explained that the Minister, although suspecting that smuggling diamonds was only the tip of the iceberg, deemed it necessary to tell Rob that he had already forgotten about Veleiro's existence. Surely, as the Minister of Internal Affairs, it was his responsibility to find out the full extent of Veleiro's crimes.

"Or had Veleiro already been executed?" Rob asked himself.

As he stepped out in the sunshine, a shudder of relief ran down his spine. Promising himself to stick to the job and steer clear of Sebasto Calio and his clique, he walked over to Sobreiro's car.

"Thanks to you, I got the contract," he shouted, pulling the door open. He briefly explained what had happened. "... But I'll have to watch my back, and I'll have to tell my crew to do the same."

Sobreiro nodded pensively. "I agree," he said. "In the mean time, shall we get some work done and drive over to the Ministry of Transport. To sign the contract?"

Later that night, a pretty stewardess on board of the Portuguese Airlines' Boeing 747 showed Rob to his seat in the first class compartment, courtesy of the Ministry of Transport. As she brought him a vodka & orange, she was immediately attracted by his deeply sun-tanned face and his blue eyes.

His stomach pleasantly aglow with the effect of the vodka, Rob let himself sink in the luxurious upholstery of his armchair. Slowly, the cobwebs of worry, fear and stress began to disappear and a smile drifted over his lips.

The stewardess saw it and read it as an invitation. Casually, she sat down on the armrest of the opposite aisle seat and started a light-hearted conversation, allowing her skirt to show a little more of her slender legs than usual.

Rob felt the warm sensuality of the girl. "She is virtually throwing herself at me," he pondered, toying with the idea of chatting her up. After all, he was the only passenger in the first class compartment and the coach section was two thirds empty. It was not likely that they would be disturbed!

One of the good effects of a strong vodka was that it made Rob's anxieties and tensions fade away. As a side effect, it increased his level of fatigue and killed his feelings of sexual desire. Even his mind became too exhausted to stay aroused. Rob decided to give it a miss. Instead, he thought about the contract he had in his pocket, the key to wealth and a lot of adventures.

Gradually, his thoughts drifted to what Sobreiro had told him that night in Portugalia, about the real causes of the civil war and the tale about the Skyvan that had been shot down with a treasure of diamonds on board. And about his father...

"I wonder what it was really like, in 1975," he pondered. His eyes fell closed, a half-full glass of vodka still clutched in his hand.

PART TWO

ANGOLA 1975

Above Northern Angola, 29 October 1975

A small aeroplane suddenly emerged from slanting sheets of rain. The noise of its engines rose sharply above loud cracks of thunder. It was late afternoon in the middle of the rainy season. Huge storm clouds raised their heads far above the earth, their anvil-shaped crests ablaze with gold, red and yellow from the light of the dying sun. Lower down in the semi-darkness above the roof of the forest the clouds disgorged a torrent of rain that forced its way through a canopy of leaves, soaking the soil and transforming the rivers into wild flash-floods.

A furious gust of turbulence rocked the wings of the Short Skyvan. A savage attack of fist-sized hailstones hit the windscreen. The view from the cockpit became a greyish blur.

To maintain visual contact with the ground, the pilot, Joey Oviero, pushed the stick forward and slipped into the cleft of a narrow valley. A bolt of lightning split the darkness apart, outlining the shape of the rocks and the tops of the trees. The booming sound of thunder almost lacerated his eardrums. A second later, as if somebody had cut the power, the strobe-like flash of lightning vanished and Oviero found himself back in a dull grey, wet, and very dangerous twilight.

Through the rain-swept windscreen, his eyes found a break between two shoulders of rock. Beyond, the rainfall was less intense and the visibility improved drastically. Wishing he had never left the airfield of Saurimo, Oviero flipped the Skyvan on its side and headed for the gap.

Situated a few miles to the west of the city of Enrique de Carvalho, Saurimo was an old Air Force base, built by the Americans in 1953 as a bulwark against the rising threat of communism in Africa. All went well until 1964, when the Angolan drive for independence from Portugal was born and three political parties emerged, one financed by Moscow, the other two by capitalist countries. Instantaneously, the three parties became rivals, fighting each other as much as they fought the Portuguese. To avoid getting involved in an internal Angolan conflict, the Americans pulled out and the base at Saurimo became an empty shell. Since then, the calm tranquility of the place was only occasionally disrupted by the noise of aircraft engines when DIANGOL's Skyvan came in on one of its cargo or passenger shuttle services from Portugalia, its home base in the north of the province.

DIANGOL, short for 'Diamantes de Angola', was one of the largest producers of diamonds in the world. Even after years of guerrilla war and reduced production, the balance sheet still showed a turnover of over 80,000,000 US dollars.

Another violent gust of turbulence shook the aeroplane. The shock contracted Oviero's belly muscles. He looked out through the rain-splattered windshield, tears of frustration and effort flooding his eyes. With an irritated gesture, he swept them away. To check his position, he glanced quickly at the map that sat in a holder by his left elbow.

A sudden premonition of danger made him look up. The huge trunk of a baobab tree loomed out of the misty background, its top hidden in the clouds.

"Jesus..." he yelled, desperately jerking the stick towards his stomach. With a sickening pitch the Skyvan lurched through the thin branches at the crown of the tree, the broken pieces of wood beating a frenzied rattle against the aluminium skin of the fuselage. Suddenly the tree was gone, but so was the earth. Cautiously handling the stick with his left hand, Oviero let the nose of the plane sink, feeling more than knowing that the ground was coming up to meet him. Finally, the nebulous grey gave way to the wet landscape and he allowed himself to relax... until another cloudburst hit the plane and forced him once more to change course.

His fight with the elements lasted a further forty minutes, then the intensity of the storm started to decrease. Looking down at his watch, Oviero was astonished to see that sunset was only thirty minutes away. A few lighter patches appeared in the closed ranks of clouds, letting the sunlight fall on a ridge of low foothills.

According to the map, the highest hills peaked at 2,500 feet above sea level. For a moment, he was undecided whether he should go up or down. Going up would put him in the clouds, forcing him to navigate by dead-reckoning. On the other hand, going down would give him the luxury of better visibility, enabling to hold on to the contour of the land, which would make it easy to find his way. However, flying at low altitude in rising darkness and surrounded by hills was one of his biggest nightmares, the risk of flying into the side of a hill too much of a gamble! Now that the turbulence was mostly gone, Oviero preferred the safety of altitude. He pulled back on the stick and urged the altimeter to creep up to 3,000 feet.

For almost twenty minutes, he flew blind, navigating purely on instruments and praying that his dead-reckoning was accurate enough to get him to his destination. At last, the clouds broke open. Almost immediately, Oviero recognized the characteristic bend of the Luachimo River; a bend shaped like a striking cobra, its head pointing in the direction of the runway, with at its far end DIANGOL's single hangar. With a quick movement of his right hand, he pulled the throttles back. Next, he pushed the flaps to 30 degrees. As he turned the Skyvan on to its final approach, the lustrous colours of a giant rainbow arched across the grassland beyond the airfield. The ground came rapidly near. A few feet above the runway, Oviero gave a short burst of engine-power to ease the descent. Slowing down in level flight, he gradually brought the nose up, refusing to let the wheels touch the ground until finally, with the screeching sounds of rubber touching concrete, the Skyvan came home.

Oviero parked the plane by the old hangar and switched off the engines. With the gyroscopic instruments spinning down, he let his head drop back against the headrest of his seat. Fighting the storm had left him bone-weary. His legs felt like rubber and the muscles of his hands and shoulders were aching as if he had been working for hours with a sledgehammer.

Reaching over to the left, he opened his side window and breathed in deeply. Outside, it sounded unnaturally quiet, the silence only broken by the chirping of crickets and the soothing whisper of a soft evening wind. Strangely enough, deep inside, he felt an odd conflict of feelings. Happiness at being alive mixed with a sensation of loss, as if a major part of him was still up there amongst the clouds.

Inside the hangar, Anthony Stanfort heard the arrival of the Skyvan. He wiped his hands on an oily rag and threw the door of the hangar open. Carefully threading his way between large puddles of water, he walked up to the aircraft. Stanfort, the Mining Manager of DIANGOL, was a thin wiry man in his middle forties. He was also a fanatic private pilot who spent all his free time at the airfield, either working on his de Havilland Chipmunk, or taking it up for a training flight.

"Hello, Gringo," he called, his strong voice echoing in the calm of the evening. "Do you enjoy flying in this kind of weather?"

"Sure do, Bwana," answered Oviero jokingly. He made his way to the exit of the plane. "Can I help it if I'm a bit crazy?"

"A bit?" Stanfort queried. He made a sweeping motion with his arms. "Even the birds were staying on the ground today."

"Yes," replied Oviero. "I noticed that, but I had to come home. A three day's absence, flying supplies for the mine between Luso and Saurimo, eating rubbish and sleeping rough in a sleeping bag on the floor of my plane is about all I could stand."

"Now you mention it, you are smelling a little ripe!" Stanfort added teasingly.

Bantering happily, they entered the hangar. The floor was partly covered with a huge pile of junk. Against the left wall lay a collection of rusty pistons that had been removed from an old engine. The remains of a vintage truck stood forgotten in the far corner. An enormous workbench, covered with a collection of tools, took up all the space to the rear of the building. In the middle of the hangar, as beautiful as a rose in a field of nettles, stood a shiny Chipmunk, Anthony Stanfort's prized possession.

The plane was an ex-trainer of the South African Air Force, bought by Stanfort during one of his trips to Johannesburg. Oviero had taught him the art of flying aerobatics, spinning and turning the Chipmunk in graceful loops through the warm African skies.

Oviero and Stanfort began to prepare the Chipmunk for the air show they had organized for the next weekend, a friendly competition to determine who deserved the title of 'Aerobatic Champion of Portugalia'. However, the topic of their discussion was not the flying contest but the increasing instability caused by the guerrillas in the formerly peaceful province.

"A lot of things have happened during the last few days, Joey," Stanfort said. "The worst of all was an attack on Sombo."

Sombo was a small mining camp 100 miles to the south of Portugalia. Stanfort quickly related how a group of guerrilla fighters had blown up the bridge over the Chiumbe River and destroyed the only radio link the camp possessed.

"It was the manager's safe they were after," he explained. "There was less money than expected, and in a surge of blind rage they slaughtered the manager and gang raped his wife." Stanfort swallowed hard.

"How do you know all that?" Oviero asked.

"When we didn't receive any radio messages from Sombo, we got worried and sent out an armed rescue team. By then, the attack was already two days old. For all the rescuers accomplished, they might as well have spared themselves the trouble. The only thing they found were the corpses of the manager and his wife and the fire-blackened ruins of the mining installations."

Visualizing the horrible sight, Oviero's eyes focused on a point in the distance.

"What happened to the workers?" he asked.

"They were lucky. They managed to run off into the bush when the attack started," Stanfort replied. He shot a troubled glance at Oviero.

"I'm very worried about the situation, Joey. Here in Portugalia we are protected by our own security forces, but who knows what these guerrillas are up to?" He took a rag out of the Chipmunk's cockpit and unscrewed the oil cap on the engine.

"I know what you mean," called Oviero. "If it can happen in Sombo, it could also happen here."

"Another reason why I'm glad that Rob is in the UK," stated Stanford. "Of course, I miss him like mad, but at least he is safe!" He sighed wistfully and added, "If only Manuela would go back to Europe..."

Manuela Rodrigues, Stanfort's girlfriend, was secretary to the Chairman of DIANGOL. They had met two years earlier in Luanda during a management meeting. By then a widower for almost ten years, Stanfort had asked her out, and gradually their friendship had become a loving and caring relationship.

"Why doesn't she leave?" asked Oviero.

"Because of me, and because of her father. It's a no-win situation. I'm unable to leave because of my work in the mines. Manuela's father won't leave because of his coffee plantations."

Concentrating on filling the fuel tank from a jerrycan that he kept balanced on the leading edge of the wing Oviero let his mind wander to the yield from the mines for the last three months - 30,000 carats of uncut diamonds, a fortune worth more than 12,000,000 dollars.

"I hope the rebels will never find out what you're concealing in your safe," he shouted.

Stanfort shrugged his shoulders. A cunning smile crinkled his lips. "Even if they manage to open my safe, they'll be very disappointed," he laughed. "The bags in my safe contain nothing but cheap industrial stones. The real expensive diamonds are safely hidden somewhere else."

"Crafty bastard," replied Oviero, showing his teeth in a wide grin. "Remind me never to play poker with you. Compared with you, Machiavelli is just a novice." He jumped down from the wing and completed the inspection of the plane. Satisfied that the job was well done, he closed the engine cowlings over the Gipsy Major engine. "The Chipmunk is ready to fly," he said. "Time to go home now. I'm dying for a cool glass of wine."

"Excellent idea," replied Stanfort. "Isn't it fortunate that I happen to have a fresh bottle of Casal Garcia in my fridge."

Early next Saturday afternoon, a few hundred spectators were lined up either side of the runway - a cosmopolitan mixture of off-duty mine workers, Portuguese engineers and a slightly self-conscious delegation of the mulatto community, mostly employees from the mine's administrative offices. For the auspicious occasion of a free air show, the miners had brought their entire families. Boosted by the festive atmosphere, they rapidly became exuberant and carefree. Some of them began to clap their hands moving to the rhythm of music from a portable radio and others raised their voices in a happy song.

Oviero stood staring at the crowd, a surprised but bemused look in his eyes.

A platoon of heavily armed security men, all facing the dark line of the forest that bordered the runway, reminded him of the fact that the country was not at peace and that right at that moment danger might be lurking in the dark shadows beneath the trees. Sighing, he looked up in the sky and briefly studied the drift of the clouds. He then climbed on to the wing of the Chipmunk and secured the safety straps in the empty rear cockpit. Loose straps had the tendency of getting tangled up in the flight controls, and that could spell disaster. Finally convinced that all was in order, he watched Stanfort climb into the front cockpit. He gave him a hand to buckle his belts, then tapped him on the shoulder.

"Have a good time, buddy," he said. "Show them what you can do."

Stanfort pushed the starter button. The motor caught with a deep throated roar and the propeller dissolved in a circle of silver.

As the Chipmunk was a tail-dragger, its long nose stood high above the ground, hiding Stanfort's view of the taxi way. To see where he was going, he stuck his head out of the cockpit and taxied out in a zigzag course, alternatively looking to the left and the right. It was hot in the small cockpit, the sun burning mercilessly down on his head. Upon reaching the runway, he set the parking brakes and advanced the throttle to 1,700 rpm. He then checked the ignition by switching the two magnetos, one by one, from *ON* to *OFF*, then back to *ON*. Satisfied that his engine was performing faultlessly, a sudden knot of tension rose in his stomach. He knew the feeling, anxiety mixed with a kind of stage fright that would disappear as soon as he was up in the air. Stanfort wiped the sweat from his forehead, threw a last look at the engine instruments and, with a deft movement of his left hand, pushed the throttle forward.

Almost immediately the tail came up. The small plane accelerated rapidly and the trees by the runway became a greenish blur. As soon as the airspeed indicated 65 knots, Stanfort pulled the stick back. The Chipmunk leapt from the ground.

At a height of 3,000 feet, he threw the plane into a graceful series of loops and rolls, the figures following each other so precisely that they all seemed to be part of one continuous aerial ballet. For his finale, Stanfort circled higher and higher until, at a height of 5,000 feet, he cut the engine. Simultaneously, with a brusque jerk, he pulled the stick into his stomach and kicked the left rudder forward. The Chipmunk flicked over on to its back and came tumbling down to earth in a vertical spin, the wings twirling around like a falling leaf.

A horrified shout rose from the crowd.

"Something has gone wrong," yelled somebody. "The plane is out of control."

At less than 1,000 feet from the ground, Stanfort pushed the stick forward and stopped the spin with a touch of the right rudder. He straightened the plane out, lowered the flaps, and let the wheels, after a gentle sideslip, kiss the ground.

The crowd, very relieved, clapped their hands.

With an almost regal wave of his hand, Stanfort acknowledged the applause. He knew he was good, but with anticipation he looked forward to Oviero's show. After all, Joey was the 'pro', his instructor and ex-fighter pilot of the Portuguese Air Force.

Oviero walked out in front of the spectators and placed a white handkerchief in the middle of the runway.

"Stanfort's show was excellent," he shouted loudly. "I'll try to do better."

He explained that for the conclusion of his show he would fly inverted over the runway with the tip of the tail barely ten inches above the concrete. "I'll pull up when passing this spot," he concluded, pointing to the white piece of cloth.

A cry of disbelief greeted his words.

It was immediately evident that Oviero's mastery was indisputable. Barely airborne, he flicked the Chipmunk on to its side and climbed up to a height of a thousand feet above the ground. He started his show with a loop, followed by a flick roll. The perfect execution of the manoeuvre made it look as if the monoplane hung still in the air, only suspended by magic.

Mesmerized by the spectacle, the spectators held their breath.

Finally, Oviero pushed the throttle fully open and climbed to 2,000 feet, aiming the long nose of the Chipmunk to the beginning of the runway. As soon as his airspeed reached 140 knots, he rolled the plane on to its back.

The tension became unbearable. Some of the spectators nudged each other and pointed to the plane.

"That's the low pass he was talking about," they whispered excitedly.

Accelerating rapidly, Oviero hung upside-down in his safety-straps, the fabric cutting through the thin cotton of his shirt. As the runway came rapidly nearer, an intoxicating gush of adrenaline rushed through his veins. He suddenly felt invincible. Shouting with joy and lust for life, he fearlessly pushed the plane down, focusing his attention to the line that marked the middle of the runway. With a slight touch of rudder and stick, he stabilized his attitude, the tail of the Chipmunk barely clearing the ground. At this height and speed, Oviero had the impression that the runway was just a grey smear. Seconds later, the white dot of the handkerchief streaked by.

With a sigh of relief, Oviero threw the throttle open and pushed the stick forward.

The spectators burst into spontaneous applause. They shouted and yelled. Some even cried from the stress of their emotions.

Suddenly, the engine of the Chipmunk backfired violently. The crowd fell silent. In unison, they turned and looked in the direction where the Chipmunk was hanging in the air, struggling for height, a thick cloud of black smoke belching out of its exhaust.

The motor backfired again. This time a long red flame shot out from under the engine cowling and the disc of the propeller became visible like the spokes of a slow turning wheel.

Oviero's instincts for survival immediately took over. He quickly completed the roll, simultaneously looking for a place to land. Unfortunately, his speed was too slow and his height too low... The plane was caught, as pilots called it, in the corner of death, no height... no speed...

With the sickening sound of a cardboard box being crushed, the Chipmunk plummeted down amidst the high grass at the end of the runway. The silence that followed lasted only for ten seconds, then the air filled with cries of horror.

"Oh, God," prayed Stanfort. "Don't let him die...." He started to run. "Please Lord, don't let the plane burn..."

The Chipmunk was lying on its side, the left wing buried under the broken fuselage. The motor had been torn out of its bracket by the force of the impact and lay smoking between two brick-coloured termite hills.

Oviero hung head down in his straps, his torso half out of the cockpit and blood pouring from a deep gash in his forehead.

"He's still alive!" Stanfort shouted, feeling his pulse. "But for how long?"

A few hours later, Oviero opened his eyes. He was lying in a small white room in the mine's infirmary. Suffering from a pounding headache, he immediately closed his eyes again.

Stanfort, who had kept a faithful vigil during the time his friend was unconscious, walked over from the window and sat down on the chair by the bed.

"Well, Joey," he said, relief echoing in his voice. "You scared the shit out of me. It must be true though that drunks and reckless fools have a special guardian angel."

"Sorry," whispered Oviero, carefully opening his eyes again. "I think I've damaged your Chipmunk."

"That must be the understatement of the century," complained Stanfort. "My plane is a write off. You're lucky. You only bruised three ribs, cut your forehead and fractured one of your legs." He pushed himself out of the chair and walked over to the door.

"Relax," he said, looking back over his shoulder. "And rest well. Try to get out of here as soon as possible."

Oviero felt his eyes grow heavy. Before he drifted off, he heard Stanfort say mockingly: "Since you crashed, I guess I'm the winner of today's competition!"

Luanda, 4 November 1975
Rua Henrique Couceiro, Headquarters of DIANGOL

Manuela Rodrigues, secretary to Rolando Saldanha, General Manager and Chairman of the Board of Directors, was 29 years old and a strikingly beautiful woman. Her dark eyes reflected the sadness she felt deep in her soul.

"Only ten more days", she thought. "Then Angola will become independent from Portugal and the old colony, with all its deeply rooted conventions and customs, will cease to exist."

Comrade Alfonsino Nevo, leader of the MPLA, short for Popular Movement for the Liberation of Angola, would become the new President and Angola would be nothing more than a satellite of Moscow.

Rolando Saldanha stood up from his chair and let his eyes scan through the meeting room. Slowly, he took in the collection of antique paintings and wall tapestries. His eyes came to rest on a row of pictures, each one depicting one of his illustrious predecessors. As the next meeting of the board would be presided over by the Chairman of the Revolutionary Council, whose members had already been appointed by Comrade Nevo, it came to Saldanha that his picture would never be added to the collection. His lips twisted in a grimace of self-mockery and he banged his gavel on a wooden block.

"Gentlemen... Friends!" The room fell silent. "In a little more than a week from now, our DIANGOL will be nationalized and the new communist leaders will run the company in their own enlightened ways, I'm sure."

His words were greeted with contemptuous sniggering. In a plea for silence, Saldanha raised his hands. "Let me introduce Senhor Emilio Silva," he continued, pointing to a narrow faced, very well-dressed gentleman who was sitting at his right side. "He is a special envoy of the Portuguese Minister of Foreign Affairs."

Saldanha, his face very pale now, raised his shoulders in a helpless gesture. "I'm afraid that the Minister has made a decision which affects us all. Losing control of DIANGOL is bad enough, but what the Minister has decided, is completely beyond my comprehension. Therefore, I'll leave it to Senhor Silva to tell you the news." After these grave words, Saldanha sat down, his teeth locked on the stem of his old, well-smoked pipe.

Emilio Silva stood up and pulled a few sheets of paper out of his briefcase. Smoothing the wrinkles in the documents, he quickly scanned the text. He found what he had been looking for and briefly traced the words with his finger, then he put the papers on the table, clasped his hands behind his back and coughed to clear his throat. "The transfer of ownership of DIANGOL is a fact," he said. His voice sounded impatient as if he was eager to say what he had on his mind and get it over with. "Nothing can change that, and DIANGOL will cease to be Portuguese property."

Silva turned his head slowly, making eye-contact with each one of the assembled Board Members. "My mission is related to the diamonds, which are still in Portugalia awaiting transportation. More precisely, Gentlemen, thirty thousand carats of diamonds."

The silence in the room became heavy and uncomfortable. Nobody, except Rolando Saldanha, had the slightest inkling of what was to come.

"The Minister in Lisbon," continued Silva. "With the support of the whole Government, has decided to give the new rulers of Angola proof of Portuguese goodwill. Therefore, once the official Declaration of Independence is signed, we'll hand over this treasure as a token of our full support to the new Government."

The news fell like a thunderclap out of a clear blue sky. It was received with shouts of indignation and anger.

"What ..." yelled Julio de Armano. He jumped up, his face flushed with suppressed anger. "Give the diamonds to a bunch of murderers and terrorists. They don't deserve it. We should give the money to the families of faithful Portuguese who died as victims of their terror campaigns..." To emphasize his words, he thumped the table with both his fists. "Nothing but murderers!" he shouted. "Murderers!"

"Yes," roared Fillip de Virgo. "I go along with that. What's more, I'm convinced that the proceeds of the diamonds, instead of going to the poor people of Angola, will disappear into the vault of one or other private bank in Switzerland."

The other members of the Board also started to voice their protests.

"Gentlemen, Gentlemen," interrupted Senhor Silva. He raised his hands in a gesture of surrender. "I don't have to spell it out to you that I agree with your objections. I even sympathize with your indignation..." His soothing words had the calming effect he had been aiming for and he managed to regain the full attention of the Board.

"But," he continued. "There are much more important matters at stake than hurt pride and rightful indignation! With this gesture, our Government hopes to gain the confidence of Nevo and his ministers. That will allow us to obtain a foothold as advisors." Silva paused briefly to allow his words to sink in. "As such, we would, in a certain way, decrease the negative influence Moscow would have in the running of Angola."

Juan de Carvalho, a descendant of an old colonial family, took some time to absorb the implications of Silva's words. His great-great-great-grandfather had been one of the first Portuguese to settle in the colony. Until last year, he had been earmarked to follow in the steps of Rolando Saldanha as the next General Manager of DIANGOL. Smiling ironically, he eventually asked: "What could possibly be the influence of the Portuguese Government in Angola? Why would Nevo and his associates listen to anything that comes from Portugal?"

Silva's intelligent eyes swept from Carvalho to the others. The grin on his face showed that he had been expecting this question. "It's a simple matter of confidence, Senhor Carvalho. Nevo has been trained in Moscow. He is, by definition, a true-blooded communist. However, he is a smart communist! He has seen what the Soviets have done in other countries in Africa. The Soviets have always worked along the same lines: first win the confidence of the new leaders, then grab hold of the country's assets."

Carvalho had to admit that Silva was right.

"I agree, the Soviets have given millions of roubles in military aid," Silva pointed out. "Nevo knows that they intend to demand a very high price for that. Given the slightest chance, the Soviets will overfish the territorial waters, overcrop the land and drain the national resources. In short, they will bleed Angola dry. Nevo knows all that," repeated Silva. "He doesn't want this kind of economic rape of his country. Therefore, he is more than willing to keep an open door to the West as a safety net."

He could read in the eyes of the board members that his words were beginning to make sense. "So that's the reason why it is important for Portugal to keep a foothold in Angola," he continued. "Otherwise the danger of slowly surrendering the whole of Africa to the communists becomes too great. I don't have to tell you the consequences for the rest of the free world if one day all the African countries were to unite under the 'Hammer and Sickle' and give the Soviets full control of all the treasures of African soil. It would be like a knife at the throat of freedom."

Silva's words touched a raw nerve. Indeed, it would be a very dangerous situation for the free world if most of the world's supply of uranium, copper and cobalt became the property of the Eastern Bloc countries.

"I don't want to preach doom and gloom," Silva concluded in a softer tone, "but it's maybe here in Angola, with your help, that we can put the first obstacles in front of the communist advance in Africa. So believe me gentlemen, the 30.000 carats of diamonds will be well spent."

"Why not just tell Nevo to go to hell and help Matindi and his UNITA movement," argued Carvalho. "They have no sympathy for the communists. Rather the contrary I should say. I'm sure they would use the revenue of those diamonds to make their opponents bleed to death."

His voice very frank now, Silva countered: "And risk an open war with the Soviet Union?"

They all knew what Silva was getting at. When the Independence of Angola had been discussed, it should have been a purely Portuguese-Angolan affair. However, with the stakes at hand, it had developed into an international intrigue, with Moscow and Cuba openly pushing Nevo and his MPLA in the seat of power, and the Western World supporting UNITA and FNLA. The outcome had been predictable. As usual the West had been too weak to stand up against the Soviets and the very irony of the situation was that, with the complicity of the Socialist Government in Portugal and the reluctant but tacit approval of the U.S.A, the MPLA had officially been recognized as the new ruling party in Angola.

"Changing that agreement is a game that cannot be played without causing a serious conflict between East and West," stressed Silva. "The Soviets will never allow the MPLA to become the scapegoat of an international intrigue. Anyway, the decision about the stones has been taken in Portugal, so it's useless to have an argument about it. The real reason why I came here to talk to you was not to explain why Lisbon had taken this step, but to ask for your help in bringing the stones to Luanda before Independence Day." He let his eyes circle the room.

"Does any one have a suggestion?"

Everybody's head turned towards Filipe de Vigo, the man responsible for the security of the installations of DIANGOL in general and for the transport of the diamonds in particular.

De Vigo stood up and draped his jacket over the back of his chair. The air conditioning was, as it happened so often these days, unserviceable. With a look of intensity in his eyes, he faced Senhor Silva. "At present, I don't see a safe way to transport the diamonds to Luanda. Let me explain." He walked over to a large blackboard that stood on an easel in the corner of the room. Quickly drawing the outline of the borders, he specified the difficulties involved with the transport of the stones.

"The total distance from Portugalia to Luanda is about 900 miles. The road goes through Camaxile, in the Province of Lunda, to Malange and then via Salazar to Luanda." With a piece of coloured chalk he drew a rough sketch. "The main reason why the diamonds are still in Portugalia is that UNITA and FNLA are in total control of that part of the country. They are well equipped with plastic explosives, and they use them with complete abandon." Vigo's words painted a grim picture of the damage and terror that was caused by the war.

"You must realize that the FNLA and UNITA receive a lot of assistance from Zaire, Senhor Silva. Their training camps are in Katanga, just over the border from Portugalia. To make matters even more complicated, some of our employees are members of the FNLA." Vigo shook his head in a helpless gesture. "As soon as we make plans to transport the stones, the rebels will be told, and they will ambush the convoy." Looking at Silva, Vigo took a packet of cigarettes out of his shirt pocket.

He lit up and blew a cloud of smoke to the ceiling. "I strongly advise you to forget about transporting the stones by road, Senhor Silva."

"Maybe it's not necessary to go all the way by road to Luanda," suggested Saldanha. "Looking at the map, I think it would be possible to bring the diamonds by truck to Luso and then by train along the Benguela railroad to the west coast."

"No, that's also excluded," replied de Vigo. "Luso and the surrounding area are a stronghold of UNITA. A train wouldn't stand a chance. Forget it."

"Then I suggest to transport the stones by air," Carvalho said. "After all, we still have the Skyvan. It hasn't quite the range to get to Luanda without making a refuelling stop, I agree, but that problem can be solved by installing an extra fuel tank."

Manuela Rodrigues cleared her throat. Her eyes bright with anxiety, she mentioned haltingly that there was a problem.

"I think you all know that Anthony Stanfort and I are..." She hesitated for a short moment. "Well let's say that we are very good friends. Yesterday evening I managed to get through to Portugalia by means of the HF radio. The connection was permanently distorted by static interference, but strong enough to get the latest news, and..." Manuela's eyes fastened on Carvalho's face, "... your suggestion of using the Skyvan is not feasible." She explained that Oviero, during the aerobatic show, had pushed his luck too far and had crashed.

"His life is not at risk," she stressed. "He has suffered a broken leg and some bruised ribs, but he can't fly!"

"Stanfort is also a qualified pilot, isn't he," asked Carvalho. "Surely he must be able to operate the Skyvan."

"No, I'm afraid he can't," answered Manuela. "Anthony is only qualified on single engine aircraft. The Skyvan is much too complicated for him. Unless you are willing to wait until Oviero is fully recovered, I'm afraid you'll have to find a different way."

Rolando Saldanha, clever as an old fox, came up with another proposition. "The decision to hand over the diamonds to the new rulers," he proclaimed, "was made by our Government in Lisbon. Because of that, it's only just that they should pull their own chestnuts out of the fire. Let the Army do the work. They still have a few units of the Portuguese Armoured Forces in Luanda. One of them is a tank unit, I believe. They are equipped with half-track vehicles and heavy tanks! What's more, they are well trained in anti-guerrilla activities. Let them go to Portugalia. It will relieve us of the responsibility."

Senhor Silva had to admit the validity of the proposition. It was the only way, and the safest.

"I thank you all for your assistance," he said. "I will take it upon myself to organize the mission with the military commander." As an afterthought he added: "I'm convinced that the transport of the stones won't be a problem. Surely, our tanks are more than a match for a bunch of guerrillas."

Army Barracks Luanda, 4 November 1975

"This mission is of the utmost importance," Silva said to the C.I.C. of the Recce Units.

Colonel Mendoza picked up his telephone and instructed his aide-de-camp to send for Comandante Oliviero Carvo.

"Carvo is my most experienced platoon leader, Senhor Silva. If anyone can get through to Portugalia and back, it's him. However, there is something you should know. The guerrillas were responsible for the death of his wife and son. He will not like this kind of assignment."

Mendoza was right.

As soon as Oliviero learned what Senhor Silva wanted him to do, his face twisted with horror. "It goes beyond my comprehension that our Government in Lisbon is wasting a fortune on a bunch of murderers, who are glorifying in slaughtering innocent women and children," he shouted. "It's an act of treason, committed by cowardly politicians, hiding in Lisbon, whilst we are fighting and suffering." Oliviero breathed deeply to calm himself. "For those reasons, Senhor Silva, I cannot accept this mission!"

Silva went red in the face and, hardly able to speak, threatened to throw Oliviero in jail. "For refusing a direct order," he shouted. "As we are in war with the guerrillas, I might even have you shot!"

With no way out, Oliviero was forced to concede and grudgingly made his plans. Depending on the terrain, weather and guerrilla activity, he figured that the round trip would take between seven to ten days. At 6 p.m, he briefed his men. They spent the next five hours refuelling and arming the vehicles of the platoon. They also loaded a fuel truck with high octane fuel and a trailer with spare parts and ammunition required for the 1,800 mile voyage. Shortly after midnight, they left the barracks.

Moving in a standard Recce-order, the platoon was headed by the Jeep and the half-track of the Recce section. The commander of that section was Sergeant-Major Jaqui, a veteran of ten years of guerrilla warfare. Stockily built and very tanned by permanent exposure to the tropical sun, he was also Oliviero's Second-in-Command. Corporal Bernardo was in command of the half-track, an armoured vehicle vaguely resembling a truck, the rear axle equipped with two sets of caterpillar tracks instead of wheels. With Bernardo were eight infantry soldiers, each one of them a specialist in Recce manoeuvres. Next in line came Oliviero's tank, a Walker Bulldog. Its main weapon was a 76 millimetre canon. On top of the turret, capable of firing 600 bullets per minute, stood a heavy .50 calibre antiaircraft gun. Behind Oliviero's tank followed the fuel truck and trailer, the most important element in the platoon, as it contained their fuel and oil reserves and spare ammunition. At the end of the column came the half-track of the mortar section commanded by Sergeant Diego, and a second Jeep.

It was now six-thirty in the morning. The early morning silence was shattered by the rattling and clanking noises of the armoured vehicles. Behind the column, the western skyline was still very dark. Far ahead, the first brightness of dawn began to mark the horizon. As the Recce platoon progressed eastward, the sun crept around the curve of the earth, colouring the flat base of an early Cumulus in scarlet and pink. Gradually, the heat of the sun burned the thin layer of morning fog away. The countryside became visible, the green, flat land of the plain dappled with brown, the roadside coated in reddish dust. Like ghosts, the buildings on the outskirts of Catete, a city 60 miles to the east of Luanda, appeared out of the haze.

Oliviero was standing upright in the turret of the tank, his eyes staring blindly in the distance.

His mouth contorted in sudden agony as he remembered that evil day, when a group of guerrillas had launched a bombing attack on the Banco National in Luanda, and he had found, amongst the bodies of the victims, the torn remains of his wife Gabriela and their son Dominico.

Oliviero had never discovered who was responsible for the attack, whether it was a group of the MPLA, the FNLA or UNITA, but from then on he hated them all, whether they were pro-communist or pro-capitalist. Sometimes, when his blood boiled hot with hatred, he had to restrain himself forcefully from firing his machine gun point blank in the middle of a protesting crowd, whichever political doctrine they proclaimed.

"Animals!" he spat, "nothing but a bunch of animals!" His only hope was that the padre, who had conducted the funeral service at the cemetery in Luanda, had told him the truth.

"Believe me," Padre Bruno had said." Don't give in to hatred. After you die, you will be reunited with your loved ones."

Oliviero fervently hoped that it was true. That once his time was up, he really would be reunited with his son and wife in the immensity of the hereafter. Only then would he be happy again.

Once past the city of Catete, the slow-moving column progressed through a stretch of relatively flat plains and low sandy hills. As they advanced further to the east, the sandy hills gradually receded behind them. Instead came the dense foliage of the tropical forest.

In his Jeep at the head of the platoon, Sergeant-Major Jaqui sucked the damp smelling air into his lungs.

All around him, the forest was alive with the noise of hundreds of birds. The sunlight dappled in patches through the dense foliage and created patterns of light and shadow.

The beauty did not touch Jaqui. His senses crying out with alarm, he stooped a little lower behind the small protective shield of his .30 machine gun.

Half a mile behind Jaqui, Oliviero was studying the terrain through his binoculars. Ahead of him, the road disappeared into a wooded valley that lay like a giant bowl between rows of curving foothills. The lower slopes of the hills were covered with a dense thicket of bushy undergrowth and flat topped acacia trees, the higher slopes and the crests were a wilderness of tangled rocks and boulders.

Oliviero clenched his teeth. Each bush and each rock could be the potential hiding place for a guerrilla armed with a Molotov cocktail, he thought. Or, worse still, a Rocket Propelled Grenade RPG, a weapon so powerful that it could pierce the heavy armour of the Walker Bulldog.

The biggest threat of all lay in the numerous wrecks of old cars and trucks which over the years had broken down and littered the sides of the road.

A favourite trick of the guerrillas was to cram an innocent looking wreck full of TNT and wait patiently for an unsuspecting prey to come close, then plunge the detonator down and blow the target and its occupants to kingdom-come.

Oliviero's worry for the safety of his platoon became fanatical. A couple of miles back, in the open field, he had been able to see for miles over the surrounding land. Now, his view to the left and right was restricted to a mere fifty yards. In front of him, the visibility was even worse, the road and the forest partially hidden behind bulging clouds of reddish dust. Anything could be hidden in there. Oliviero decided to play it safe. He hit the transmit-button on his radio.

"Platoon halt..." he ordered. "All sections to take cover by the side of the road in a defensive position, and One-six to report to the command tank."

Call sign 'One-six' was the code name of Sergeant-Major Jaqui.

Using the cover of the ditch by the side of the road, Jaqui quickly ran back to the tank. Oliviero jumped down and spread his map on the ground, his right index finger tapping the chart.

"Jaqui," Oliviero confided hoarsely. "I don't trust this terrain. There is too much forest and not enough visibility." He hesitated for a moment, scratching his chin. "We'll have to slow down and make it a true 'Recce Jump and Reconnoitre' advance."

Jaqui knew what that meant. He would have to take his Jeep and the first half-track and race ahead of the rest of the platoon. After a fast run of a few hundred yards, they would put the vehicles in hiding and search the forest on foot. Only when certain that it was safe to go on, he would give Oliviero the 'all clear' signal. Whilst the rest of the platoon then moved up to a new defensive position, Jaqui and his men would make another quick dash, followed by another recce on foot, and so on, and so on...

As if he had read Jaqui's mind, Oliviero said: "I know it's a tiresome exercise, Jaqui. However, if we want to stay alive and reach the safety of the open plains behind the forest belt, it's essential."

Jaqui nodded, his eyes hovering over the map, his mind already busy evaluating the most dangerous spots.

Oliviero wiped his forehead with a sodden handkerchief. He slipped it back into the pocket of his tank-suit and pointed to a spot on the map where the road made a sharp curve to the left before disappearing between the slopes of the hills. "Instruct your men to infiltrate the forest there," he said firmly. "That's a good place to start." Jaqui, a survivor of a thousand 'jump and recce' infiltrations, nodded his approval.

With a thoughtful expression in his eyes, Oliviero added: "Do it as fast as you can, but don't take any chances. If in doubt, call me on the radio and we'll use the canon of the tank to blow the enemy to the devil." To put more emphasis on his next words, Oliviero put one of his hands on Jaqui's shoulders. "I don't want to lose any of you!"

"Si, Comandante," replied Jaqui, slightly embarrassed by the unexpected sentiment in Oliviero's words. "Don't worry, I've done this kind of work for years. I'm not going to allow the scum to make a fool out of me."

A sombre velvet veil drifted over Jaqui's eyes and a painful tone marked his voice. "In the past I've seen too many dead and I've lost too many friends," he whispered emphatically. "Believe me, Comandante. The only corpses I want to see are the corpses of dead guerrillas." To mark his disgust with the endless horrors of war, he turned around and spat on the ground. "We'll get the pigs," he said, his voice very convincing now. "Don't worry, we'll get them."

Jaqui saluted, turned around and walked back to the head of the column. After a short rest to allow his men to swallow a piece of bread and a mouthful of water, he gave the order to resume the advance.

Followed by Bernardo's half-track, Jaqui's driver raced forward until they reached the first bend of the road. Even before the Jeep came to a full stop, Jaqui jumped out and motioned the half-track into a defensive position.

"Get out, men," whispered Corporal Bernardo. "Let's go and do our job, and remember to remain silent." Without waiting for a reply, he leapt out of his half-track. Accompanied by four of his men, he made his way through the dense bush. Out of the corner of his eye, he saw Jaqui disappear into the thicket on the opposite side of the road, the other four infantrymen running fast to catch up with him.

It was stifling hot under the thick foliage. Bernardo felt as if his lungs were suddenly filled with cotton wool. Immediately his shirt stuck like a wet rag to his shoulders. Swarms of mosquitoes came buzzing around his head. Behind him he heard the faint noise of clothes scraping against branches and the dry sound of breaking twigs, occasionally the mumbled curse when a battle dress got stuck in the thorns of a bush or the occasional slap of a hand on naked flesh when a soldier slapped a mosquito away from his sweaty skin.

"Sshh!" he whispered harshly. "You sound like a herd of elephants."

Very much aware of giant spiders and poisonous snakes which dwelled in these forests, Bernardo carefully moved forward in a wide arc, aiming for a point that lay well behind the curve in the road. Alert to any abnormal sound or motion, he slowly swept the barrel of his rifle from left to right. His eyes never wavered in their search for danger.

Suddenly he was startled by a flock of wild birds taking flight, the noise of their flapping wings the signal for a large animal to flee the safety of its lair. In its panic, it galloped through the branches of the undergrowth. One of the soldiers behind Bernardo jumped with fright and fired a volley of shots in the direction of the running animal.

"Stop that you fool!" shouted Bernardo, more scared than angry.

Slowly he crept on. Judging that he was well beyond the bend in the road and having found no sign of danger, he cut through the undergrowth and rejoined the road. Emerging from the bush, he blinked his eyes against the brightness of the sky which looked unnaturally blue compared with the greenish hue under the trees. There was no sign of Jaqui yet.

Bernardo told his men to take cover in the ditch. For himself, he picked a well-protected spot under a wild hibiscus tree. He sat down, comfortably stretching his legs. Desperate for a smoke, he reached for his pocket. About to light up, a thoughtful expression slipped over his face. The hand holding his Zippo lighter froze in mid-air. The smell of tobacco carried a long way, even in the most dense parts of a forest. If there were guerrillas in the area, they would soon pick up the smell. Smoking a cigarette could then very well be the last thing he did in this world. Bernardo decided to wait until they were safe.

Ten minutes later, without as much as a rustling noise, Jaqui appeared from behind the bushes facing the place where Bernardo was hiding. He lifted his right hand, his thumb raised in the agreed signal that no traps had been found and that all was clear.

Bernardo replied by giving the same sign and quickly ran across the road to report his findings.

"What about the shots I heard," inquired Jaqui.

"A soldier wetting his pants when he heard a fleeing animal," informed Bernardo.

"Stupid kids," said Jaqui mockingly. After rejoining the vehicles, he reported to Oliviero that it was safe to move on.

Like this, it went on for hours, a quick rush followed by a recce on foot, followed by the next quick rush. With always that hollow feeling of doubt and worry a permanent companion. By the time they came out of the forest, the sun was almost down below the horizon. According to the map, Oliviero saw that the worst was over. Between this position and the city of Malanje lay nothing but flat fields dotted with the trunks of a few isolated baobab trees.

As he looked up, he saw, barely five miles ahead, the lights of the city beckoning through the falling dusk. All his senses urged him to go on and reach the safety of the city before it was completely dark. Knowing his opponents very well, something stopped Oliviero in his tracks. The guerrillas were masters at setting booby traps when it was most unexpected, when safety was in sight and vigilance was at its lowest.

However, here in the open, where guerrillas could not hide close to the edges of the roads, the only danger Oliviero could think of was a land mine. A mine could easily rip a Jeep apart. Destroying a tank was far more difficult. Oliviero's Walker Bulldog was the strongest vehicle in the platoon, its armour almost five inches thick and capable of speeds of well over 40 miles per hour.

If at that speed the tank hit a mine, the worst that could happen was a broken track, the damage easy to repair as they carried sufficient spares in the trailer.

Besides, Oliviero considered, the area around the city was well controlled by local security forces. It was highly doubtful that this road would be mined. He turned to Jaqui. "This time, I'll lead the way! Give me half a mile lead, then follow with the rest of the platoon."

Without waiting any longer, Oliviero pushed his interphone switch down. "What are you waiting for, Jose," he shouted to his driver. "Let's go man, and keep your foot on the throttle until we reach the walls of the city."

5 November 1975

The military barracks in Malanje were situated on the Avenida Diego Pinto. It was five-thirty in the morning. The vehicles belonging to Oliviero's platoon were parked alongside the long wall that marked the southern boundary of the parade ground. The windscreens were opaque from the early morning dew. Here and there, the feeble light of a torch threw a cone of brightness. The noise made by one of the drivers whilst checking the engine of his Jeep sounded muffled through the darkness. From the black solid shape of the tank came the metallic clang of empty jerrycans. Gradually, the morning became bright enough to light up the courtyard. First the gentle purring of the Jeep engines broke the silence. Soon it was followed by the heavier grumbling of the two half-tracks. One by one, the soldiers took their places in the vehicles, using the last minutes before departure to make a final and thorough check of their weaponry.

Oliviero stepped out of the building. The smell of coffee still strong on his breath, his eyes darted from vehicle to vehicle, appraising the state of alertness of his men and the condition of their equipment.

Jaqui saluted stiffly. "We are ready, Comandante. All vehicles checked and serviceable."

A sudden gust of wind blew a cold caress over Oliviero's skin. Some dead leaves whirled in a crazy dance in the corner between two walls.

"The men seem very much on edge today," Jaqui added. "I've never known them to be so nervous."

Oliviero noticed the strong aura of anxiety. "It will disappear as soon as we hit the road," he replied. As the words left his mouth, a shiver of forewarning ran over his back. To hide his feelings, he forced a smile and pushed Jaqui in the direction of his Jeep. "Time to move out," he said.

Jaqui walked away in silence.

With feigned confidence in his voice, Oliviero called after him: "You'll see, today will be like yesterday, Jaqui. Believe me, we'll do just fine."

He jumped on the track of his tank and pulled himself over the side into the turret. As Jose noticed Oliviero's presence, he tossed the butt of his cigarette away and squeezed the two levers of the starter coils together. The heavy grinding noise of a cold engine whined through the hull of the tank. The cylinders slowly rotated through their starting cycle.

Jose counted the revolutions: "One, two, three..." At twelve, he gave a couple of clicks on the fuel injector and flicked the magnetos on. With a deep roar, the 400 horsepower engine burst into life.

Oliviero slipped a lightweight tank helmet with built-in speakers over his head and fixed the elastic connection of the microphone around his throat. "How do you read me, Jose?" he asked through the interphone.

"Read you five by five, Comandante."

"And you, Sergio?"

"Loud and clear," replied the gunner.

To relax the mood with light hearted conversation, Oliviero added: "It's damn cold this morning, isn't it?"

"Yes, it is, Comandante," answered Sergio. "However, in a short while, it might be getting very hot."

Oliviero knew that Sergio was not referring to the rise of the sun and the resulting increase in temperature, but to the dangers on the road between Malanje and Saurimo, their next stopping place.

In his mind, Oliviero pictured the road they had to follow.

The first one hundred miles were relatively safe. After that came the high plateau, during the dry season, a drought stricken wilderness of foothills and flatlands, flecked with high boulders and thorny bushes, and a few isolated and mostly abandoned villages. Now, during the rainy season, the high plateau was transformed into a vast area of marshlands and malaria infested swamps, making the risks of travelling this road a hundred times higher. At this time of the year, safety was not only threatened by booby-traps or guerrilla attacks, but by additional dangers, such as landslides, flooded rivers or collapsed bridges.

No wonder the men were so reluctant to move on!

As soon as the red-hot circle of the sun appeared above the horizon, Oliviero pushed the transmit-button on his radio down.

"One-six, this is Six, move out."

Jaqui's driver, Carlo, had been waiting for the signal. With a sudden release of pent up tensions, he let out the clutch and rammed the accelerator down.

The Jeep shot forward, spraying two plumes of gravel and dust from its rear wheels. A scraggy dog, excited by the screeching of spinning wheels, appeared barking from behind a tree and chased the vehicle. "Hey," yelled Jaqui, holding on with two hands to the edge of his seat. "Slow down, Carlo! We're not in a race to Saurimo, you know."

Carlo bared his teeth in a wolf's grin and eased up on the throttle until the Jeep ambled along at a sedate 30 mph. With the moist morning air whistling over the lowered windshield, the speed of the car made the air feel colder than it really was. Jaqui pulled up the collar of his battle dress.

"I'ld give a fortune this morning for a warm, cosy place in one of the half-tracks," said Carlo, shivering.

"Well, I wouldn't," replied Jaqui. "I know what an RPG grenade can do to a half-track." He told Carlo what he had seen during a battle in Benguela, when the platoon had been attacked by a group of UNITA fighters. "It was just before you joined us, Carlo. One of the infantry half-tracks suffered a direct hit. The grenade went through one inch of armour plating as if it was made of butter and faster than you can count to three, the metal shell was glowing."

Jaqui's description of the events was so vivid that Carlo felt as if he had seen it.

"The temperature inside that half-track must have been more than a 1,000 degrees," continued Jaqui. "In an instant, it was transformed into a charnel-house full of burning clothes and a soup of wrinkling skin, boiling flesh and blackened bones."

Carlo, swallowing his horror, did not reply.

"Now you know why I prefer to ride in a Jeep," concluded Jaqui."I couldn't stand to be locked up alive in one of those metal coffins."

Gradually, the heat of the sun began to replace the chill of the morning. Oliviero adjusted the small ventilator in the turret and let a stream of lukewarm air cool his forehead. Finally, when he could stand the heat in the tank no more, he swung the hatch open and stood straight up in the turret, his torso exposed from the hips up. Knowing very well that each boulder or bush could be the hiding place of an armed guerrilla, his hands closed around the grips of the .50 calibre machine gun.

In sharp contrast with the danger it presented, Oliviero noticed that the surrounding land was extremely beautiful. After the rank odours inside the tank - a mixture of rubber, petrol fumes and gun oil - the air smelled sweet with the scent of wild flowers. Once in a while Oliviero could hear the raucous noise of a powerful engine as the Jeep of the Recce section or the half-track raced up against the slope of a hill to reconnoitre the road ahead. When reaching the edge of the high plateau, Oliviero looked down at his watch. It was 11 a.m. According to the plan, they were barely thirty minutes behind schedule. The road ahead was completely empty. During the last hour or so, Oliviero had not seen a single vehicle, not even an old dilapidated farm truck.

This worried him! The complete absence of traffic was like the menacing silence before a storm, when all the birds went into hiding.

At 11.30 a.m, they approached Xandel, a small village on the southern border of the Milando Park. In its heyday, Xandel had been a rich and famous place, well known by the tourists for its shops filled with beautifully crafted crocodile shoes, handbags and other local artefacts. Nowadays, the place lay empty, abandoned by the tradesmen who had lost their livelihood as the tourists stayed away. Only the empty ruins of stone houses remained, the streets littered with broken glass, ripped-out doors and broken furniture.

"Stop here for a moment, Carlo," ordered Jaqui. The village had been built on the slopes of a row of low foothills. From where he sat, he could follow the meandering track of the steeply descending road, until it disappeared behind the first houses of the village. Alongside the road and to the left of it lay the Loeie river. Normally a placid river, the heavy rains of the last few weeks had swollen it into a raging torrent which had burst its banks and inundated the lowlands. The emptiness of the flooded plains was only broken by a splattering of tiny islands and reed covered mud flats.

Jaqui lifted a pair of binoculars to his eyes and studied the land at the other end of the village. There was a stone bridge, he noticed. The distance between the last houses of the village and the bridge was not more than fifty yards. On the other side of the bridge, the road became much narrower. It was in fact nothing but a widened dirt track that ran over some kind of a ridge.

Jaqui turned his attention back to the village. "Switch the engine off, Carlo," he commanded. He slipped out of his seat and crept forward until he reached the first dwellings. The only sounds he heard were the flapping of a door in the wind and the cries of a couple of hawks who were circling the thermals.

His sharply tuned instincts warned him that something was not as it should be, as if he could smell the scent of danger that hung like a heavy cloak between the skeletal remains of the houses. Knowing that the only way to find out for sure, was to go and reconnoitre on foot, Jaqui returned to his Jeep and reached for his radio. "Six this is One-six. This place stinks. I'm going to dismount the infantry and search the village."

Jaqui quickly briefed Corporal Bernardo and his men about what to do and what to look for.

As he spoke, he noticed a twitch in the corner of the eye of one soldier and the nervous fiddling of fingers by some of the others, the normal signs at the start of another dangerous infiltration.

"Everything you can find is important," Jaqui stressed. "Such as leftovers of food, scraps of paper or cigarette stubs."

Their senses on full alert and covering each other back to back, they made their way through the village, looking for anything that appeared abnormal. Upon reaching the last house before the bridge, they had found not one single trace of human occupation. It was evident that the village was empty. Also the bridge to the east of the village proved to be free of booby-traps.

"The village has been empty for a long time judging by the absence of ashes in the fireplaces," said Corporal Bernardo, a wide grin on his face. "This place must have been abandoned long before the start of the rainy season."

Reluctantly, Jaqui had to admit that Bernardo was right. There was nothing to substantiate his feeling that something was wrong. Nothing to suggest that the advance of the platoon should be delayed any longer. Jaqui grabbed his microphone and called Oliviero.

"The village is clear," he reported. He could not help himself from adding: "But I don't know why or what, Comandante, I smell a rat."

Oliviero knew Jaqui. He had learnt to trust his instincts over the years they had been together. If Jaqui said that he smelled a rat, it could very well mean that there really was something wrong with the place. Oliviero considered ordering another search, but that would mean another delay, and after Xandel, they still had four more hours to go.

Divided between Jaqui's doubts and his own eagerness to reach the safety of the camp in Saurimo, Oliviero surrendered to impatience. "Jaqui, if you with your experience can't find real signs of a trap," he said. "Then I'm sure the place is safe." His voice turned slightly abrupt. "Let's move on. No more wasting time."

That decision would haunt him for the rest of his life!

Jaqui kept his eyes fastened on the microphone, hoping that Oliviero would change his mind. Not that he questioned Oliviero's decision. Always concerned with the safety of his men, Jaqui knew that Oliviero would never send anybody deliberately to his grave. This time however, Jaqui could not silence his blasted inner voice. "Was it a sign that the danger he sensed was not just imagination," he asked himself.

A sudden gust of wind whistled through the empty shells of the houses and sent a bush of dry weeds tumbling over the road. The desolate view increased Jaqui's feeling of dread. Looking up into the sky, he noticed that even the circling hawks had disappeared. Resignedly, he told Carlo to move on.

As soon as Jaqui moved forward, Oliviero instructed Jose to put the tank into a more advanced position, somewhere between the last houses of the village and the bridge. Jose shifted the engine into forward gear and drove quickly through the village. Just ten yards behind the last house, he found a small hollow by the side of the road, its depth just enough to put the tank in a turret down position. Less than a minute later, only the upper rim of the turret and the barrel of the MI.50 remained visible.

In the mean time, Jaqui's Jeep, closely followed by the half-track of the infantry section, was approaching the bridge. As he could discover nothing out of the ordinary, Jaqui allowed his nerves to relax. This time, he admitted to himself, Oliviero had been right. His own omen of danger had been nothing but a delusion. Blissfully unaware of what had been bothering Jaqui, Carlo kept his eyes on the road, skilfully guiding his Jeep between deep mud-filled holes and slivers of broken glass. Just before starting to cross the bridge, Jaqui radioed Corporal Bernardo and ordered him to stop.

"I'll cross the bridge first," he said, "... and check the first few five hundred yards of the road. Cover me with your machine-gun. As soon as I am on the other side, it's your turn to make the crossing."

Bernardo acknowledged the message with a short: "Roger, understood and out."

As if he was leading a cavalry charge, Jaqui waved his hand forward. "Go ahead, Carlo," he shouted. "Let's see how fast you can get across."

Carlo smiled and put his foot down. At the other end, he swung the Jeep on to the dirt road. Some twenty yards down the track, in a flash, Jaqui saw the reflection of sunlight on something that glittered, something that spanned the whole width of the road. "You've been a fool, Jaqui," cried his conscience. "A fool for ignoring your own intuition. You knew that something was wrong. Only, the danger was not in the village or on the bridge. It's here on the dirt road beyond the bridge."

Abruptly, the small hairs on his arms stood straight up, a nervous shiver ran over his back and he felt the uncontrollable urge to urinate. "A tripwire!" he yelled, simultaneously throwing his upper body sideways, his torso hanging far out over the empty road. "Guidado!" he yelled again to warn Carlo. "Watch out, a tripwire!"

For Carlo the warning came too late. Before he realized what Jaqui was saying, the tripwire slipped under his chin and cut like a garrotte deep into his throat. With blood gushing out of the cut, his windpipe crushed by the impact and already choking from the lack of air, Carlo threw up his hands in a futile attempt to claw the wire out of his flesh.

Out of control and driven by its own momentum, the Jeep slipped sideways over the shallow slope of the road. Its tyres lost their grip on the muddy surface. Carlo's smothered cry of agony was abruptly cut off when the steel wire sliced through his larynx.

Struggling desperately to get out of the car, Jaqui's foot got caught behind the swivel mounting of the .30 machine gun. Before he managed the pull himself free, the Jeep rolled over. Jaqui saw the world tumble round, the earth and the mud appearing where the sky ought to be. As it fell upside down in the foul smelling waters of the flooded plains, the Jeep made a big splash and partially submerged under the surface.

From his observation point on top of the turret, transfixed and horrified at the same time, Oliviero saw what happened. Stunned by the suddenness of the atrocity, a deep feeling of guilt shot through his brain.

"Oh, Jaqui," he mumbled, his voice low with shame. "I should have listened to you. Now it's too late."

Sweat running into his eyes, Oliviero asked himself whether the tripwire was the prelude of something much more sinister. The idea that the rest of his men could be in mortal danger propelled him into action. No matter how much he cared for Jaqui and Carlo, it was the safety of the rest of his platoon that mattered now. Feelings of remorse and sorrow would have to wait until later. With a rapid gesture, he pushed the switch on his transmitter down.

"Six to all units. Suspect an enemy attack. All vehicles to take cover." At the same time, he pulled himself upright in the turret and observed the layout of the terrain. The only vehicle between him and the partly submerged Jeep was the half-track of Bernardo's infantry section. Halfway across the bridge, it was in a very vulnerable position. Again, Oliviero keyed his radio. "Bernardo. Pull back immediately."

Throwing a quick glance over his shoulder, Oliviero noticed that the road behind him was empty. He hoped that the fuel truck and the rest of his platoon were safely hidden behind the houses of the village. Looking back at Bernardo's half-track, he observed that it had cleared the bridge and was reversing slowly. "Come-on, Bernardo," he yelled, involuntary starting to punch the rim of the turret. "Get moving!" His words were barely cold when he saw a blinding flash of flame on the armour of the half-track. A fraction of a second later the loud whooshing sound of an explosion hit his eardrums. "By God," he shouted. "Bernardo's half-track has been hit!"

"That's your fault," added his inner voice. "You should have listened to Jaqui. Now it's too late." A new wave of guilt tore at his guts.

Inside the infantry half-track, it was a living hell. "Get out of here, all of you," shouted Bernardo. He threw himself forward and tried to force the rear door open. As he struggled with the handle, splinters of shrapnel burst through the inside of the vehicle, cutting through the driver's body. Other red-hot splinters ripped the engine compartment open and tore the fuel tanks apart. With a hollow noise, the volatile gases caught fire. Instantly, the half-track became a blazing furnace. All of a sudden, what was left of it exploded in a loud rolling 'BOOMBOOBOOM', sending hardly recognizable figures of men like discarded pieces of cardboard through the air.

Thirty yards away from the explosion, the Walker Bulldog was hit by pieces of steel and fragments of armour plating.

Ducking low to avoid being hit, Oliviero slipped down in his narrow seat inside the turret and slammed the hatch closed. The only light inside the tank were a few flashes of sunlight that fell in through a set of viewing slits. As soon as Oliviero got used to the semi-darkness, he grabbed his microphone.

"From Six to all units. Battle reports!"

Waiting for a reply and eager to know what was going on, Oliviero pushed his face against the rubber padding of the viewing port at his battle station. At first, he could see nothing but a patch of the flooded plains.

"Traverse the turret to the right, Sergio, quick. I want to see what's happening to the half-track."

By his left knee, he felt Sergio move, then he heard the whining noise of electric motors. Gradually, as the turret turned more and more to the right, Oliviero got a glimpse of the road, his view at times obscured by patches of dark, sticky smoke that drifted by like a bank of black fog. Slowly the infantry half-track swung into sight. Immediately, Oliviero realized that there was nothing left but a burning hulk, the flames occasionally flaring high when they found something new to consume.

"They are all dead," his inner voice said again. "Your fault."

Utterly shocked, Oliviero wished he could turn the clock back to start the day all over again. Shaking his head in a helpless gesture, he looked down at his watch. "Five minutes since Jaqui crossed the bridge. Five minutes and eleven men dead."

Suddenly, he remembered his request for battle reports, and realized that he hadn't received a reply from any of his units. "Are we the only survivors? Has the rest of the platoon been wiped out too?" Quickly, he keyed his transmitter. "Six to all units. Repeat! Urgent request for battle reports."

For a while he heard nothing but the faint hissing of static in his headset. The reply, when it came, was loud and strong.

"Six, from Two-six."

Two-six was the call sign of Sergeant Diego, the leader of the mortar section. His half-track, Oliviero knew, was at the tail of the platoon.

"Go ahead, Two-six."

Diego confirmed what Oliviero had prayed for, that the fuel truck was safely hidden amongst the ruined houses of the village, that Diego with his half-track and the second Jeep had taken a defensive position on the eastern side of the village from where they had an unrestricted view of the surrounding land.

"Thank God," Oliviero whispered. His mind reeled when he thought about what would become of them if the guerrillas had managed to destroy the fuel truck. They would be stuck in this Godforsaken place forever.

"I know where the guerrillas are hiding," Diego reported. "That rocket propelled grenade RPG came from a small island in the flooded terrain to the north of the village. Their exact map coordinates are..." To study the lines on his map, Diego went silent for a moment. "The coordinates are N4/E6," he said finally. N4/E6 referred to the grid on the small scale military maps they used in the Recce units.

Rapidly, Oliviero located the intersection of the grid lines on his own map. "Roger, Two-six," he replied. "Set up your mortar and home-in on the enemy target. We'll engage them from here with our gun, and keep on firing until I tell you to stop."

At the same time, he punched Sergio on his shoulder. "Now we know where they are, Sergio," he shouted excitedly. "Go ahead, blast the bastards with a few rounds of High Explosive shells."

Sergio rotated the gun control handle to the left. Eager to get a good view of the target, Oliviero pressed his eyes against one of the viewing slits. Another cloud of smothering black smoke drifted by, hiding the target from view. Oliviero smelled the stink of burning oil and rubber. His ears picked up the noises of battle, the BOOMS of mortar bombs alternating with the high whistling screams of RPG grenades.

Suddenly, an RPG exploded on the edge of the hollow where the tank was hidden. Splinters and pieces of shrapnel rattled like hailstones against the armour plating of the turret. Oliviero wished he could crawl into a tiny little hole, somewhere far away from these infernal noises, somewhere where he would be safe. Another sharp explosion made him cringe. The stench of cordite filled the tank. The foam rubber coating of his battle station reeked of sweat and oil, but also of fear; fear which rapidly became anger.

A new kind of courage was born in him. Very determinedly, he called Jose and Sergio on the interphone. "Listen, Sergio," he said. "You too Jose. We are going to move up the bank under cover of the smoke from the burning half-track. While Sergeant Diego is distracting the enemy with his mortar, we'll find the target and blow it to hell." Oliviero paused a moment to let his words sink in, then he shouted: "Go, Go, Go!"

Jose, sweating like a pig from the heat in the tank, shifted the tank into forward gear. With a clumsy movement, the massive weight of the tank started to move forward. Inside the tank, the tension rose, all three of them expecting at any moment the impact of an RPG, the searing heat followed by final oblivion.

As they burst through the blinding smoke screen, Oliviero noticed two tiny islets, barely two hundred yards away from the road and slightly to their right. They were nothing more than two heaps of mud, covered with reeds and long strands of stringy grass, their level barely rising a few feet above the surface of the water. A long burst of tracers sprouted from the largest of the two.

"I've got them," yelled Sergio, already swinging the long barrel of the canon into a firing position. "I've got the bastards."

Oliviero's feelings of guilt finally found release in action. Jumping up, he threw the hatch of his battle station open. A volley of bullets whistled by like a swarm of angry bees.

Oliviero did not care.

His blood boiling in his veins, he locked his fingers around the trigger of the .50 and sprayed the island with a long volley of large calibre bullets.

Sergio delicately adjusted the position of the gun until the barrel was pointing exactly at the centre of the enemy stronghold. "Cannon ready," he announced. "Firing now!" Eager to revenge his dead comrades, Sergio slammed the trigger down. The loud coughing sound of the gun hit his ears. Suddenly deaf to the world, he saw the impact of the shell, dead on target. His excitement at seeing the impact of the heavy grenade was almost erotic.

At the place of the impact an immense spout of water rose high into the air, the water mixed with mud, the remains of three guerrilla fighters, their weapons and all their equipment. A few concentric rings ran in widening circles over the muddy water. The echo of the explosion rumbled away like long thunderclaps between the gently rolling foothills.

The silence that followed was unnatural, the kind of silence that can only exist in a place where men have been fighting each other and where people have died brutal deaths.

Now that the carnage was over, they took the time to recover the bodies of Jaqui and Carlo from underneath the Jeep and bury them. All that remained of the men inside the burnt shell of the half-track, were ashes.

After paying their respects, Oliviero gave the order to start up the engines. Badly shaken but very alert, they moved on. Four hours later, undisturbed by any further attacks, they reached the camp at Saurimo.

6 November 1975

The next day, by noon, what was left of the platoon was parked in a camouflaged position half a mile west of the bridge over the Chikapa river.

The fuel truck and Oliviero's tank had found a cool spot under the thick foliage of a small copse of hibiscus trees. Sergeant Diego's Jeep and the remaining half-track stood closer by the bridge, concealed from the road by an outcrop of sand coloured rocks.

"What a wild place," remarked Oliviero to Sergio.

Sitting on top of the turret, with one of his legs dangling down the side, he swept his binoculars from left to right to scrutinize the landscape. The bridge was a complicated structure made of massive steel pylons, girders and crossbeams, designed to support the weight of heavy trucks and mining equipment. Four hundred feet beneath the level of the bridge, the wildly tumbling waters of the river were forcing their way between two high walls of rocks.

Sergio used the short pause in the advance of the platoon to take a break from the stale air inside the tank. His back comfortably supported by the base of the gun, he sat on the warm metal of the hull. The air around him was fresh with the perfume of wild flowers, and his eyes followed the flight of two falcons searching for prey. Worried about the state of his vehicle, like a mother about the health of her child, Jose spent his time making a quick inspection of the tank.

"Once we are over that bridge," Sergio remarked. "The worst is over. Only 60 more miles, a little more than an hour, and we'll be in Portugalia."

Oliviero did not agree with him. The disaster of the previous day still fresh in his mind, he was determined not to make the same mistake twice. "Never again will I allow myself to be ruled by impatience," he had sworn, and this bridge looked much too dangerous to be crossed without being thoroughly examined.

His mind made up, he leaned down in the turret and grabbed his microphone to call Sergeant Diego, his new Second-in-Command, to rejoin the tank.

During a long and sleepless night, filled with sorrow for the loss of Jaqui and his men but pragmatic enough to know they had to move on, Oliviero had been straining his mind to find the right man to replace Jaqui.

Bernardo would have been the most obvious choice, but Bernardo was dead. Jose or Sergio were both very experienced in Recce manoeuvres. However, Oliviero could spare neither of them, as Jose had to drive the tank, and Sergio was the only qualified gunner in the platoon. Finally, when the grey light of dawn broke through the curtains, he had decided to give the job to Diego. A reluctant decision, as Diego, a mortar man, had no experience in Recce operations like Jaqui. On top of that, Oliviero wondered whether Diego had that special gift, that delicate but so crucial difference in character that determined whether he was merely a good follower of orders or a true leader of men.

Through his binoculars, Oliviero saw the Jeep with Diego on board surge up the road. It pulled up behind the tank, dust swirling around its wheels. Diego jumped out, barely able to conceal his nervousness and uncertainty about what it was that Oliviero wanted him for.

Oliviero flipped the butt of his cigarette away between two boulders. He bent down and gave Diego a hand to help him climb up on to the turret. "Come and sit here next to me," he said. "Let's have a talk about what has to be done."

Oliviero noticed that Diego was looking rather tense. To help him relax, he offered him a cigarette. He lit himself another one. After blowing a cloud of smoke in the air, he pointed to the bridge.

"That's a Bailey Bridge," He looked at Diego searchingly. "Are you familiar with that kind of construction?"

Diego slowly shook his head and shrugged his shoulders.

"Only from a distance, Comandante. Only as a target for my mortar."

"I thought so, Sergeant. Therefore, I'll tell you exactly what to look for."

Very patiently, Oliviero explained to Diego that he had to spread out his men and make them walk in double file across the bridge. "Look for recent tyre tracks or footprints," he explained. "Check each nook and cranny that could be a potential hiding place for a booby-trap or a mine. In brief, look for anything suspicious. Take your time. When you reach the other side, put your men in a defensive circle amongst the rocks."

Oliviero's calm voice had the desired affect.

Now that he had been given exact instructions, the uncertain look in Diego's eyes became brighter and a flicker of a smile crinkled the corners of his mouth. "Understood, Comandante," he vocalized. "You can count on me." He jumped down from the tank and ran back to his Jeep, yelling to his driver to start up the engine.

"I want to go with him, Comandante," Sergio exclaimed impulsively. "I'm sure that I'm a better Recce than him." The way he said '*him*' made it clear that he had not much confidence in Diego's capabilities. "I know how to check a bridge. I've done it many times before I became a gunner."

"No, you can't go with him, Sergio," Oliviero replied. "I need you here in the tank."

Sergio sucked a great cloud of cigarette smoke into his lungs. "One extra pair of eyes could make all the difference, Comandante." A barely concealed tone of contempt slipped into Sergio's voice as he added: "Diego is *only* a mortar gunner."

Anger suddenly flared up in Oliviero's eyes.

"I know better than you that Diego is not a very experienced Recce, Sergio, but he will do as I tell him, and so will you!"

On the way back to where his section was lying under cover, Diego's thoughts were a mixture of apprehension and elation. Elation because of his promotion to Recce leader; apprehension because he feared that the men were very reluctant to accept him as a worthy successor to Jaqui. As leader of the mortar section, his men had never doubted his word. As far as mortars were concerned, they knew he was one of the best. Now however, as Recce leader and Second-in-Command, it somehow felt as if he had to start from scratch again to prove himself.

As he reached his half-track, Diego quickly gathered the men together. Kneeling down, he drew the outline of the bridge in the sand and told them what they were going to do. "One row of soldiers will search the left side of the bridge, another row the right side. I will search the centreline. Use your bayonets to probe between the planks to check for concealed detonators or tripwires.

"If," he stressed the word if, "you find something strange, anything at all, don't touch it. Just call me."

The men grunted. Now that action came near, the heat felt oppressive. From the distance came the rumbling sound of thunder. Diego shaded his eyes with his hands and looked up into the sky. A dark patch of angry clouds was sailing in from the west.

"Let's be quick about it, men," Diego said, his voice hard and flat. "I don't want be caught out by rain. That would wash all traces of tyres or footprints away."

They advanced slowly towards the bridge. The first four hundred yards of the road were easy, with a lot of cover from rocks and flowering bushes. Closer by the entrance to the bridge, all this disappeared. The roar of the tumbling waters became very loud, drowning out all other noises. Diego's mouth went dry. He put on a brave face, concealing his anxiety behind a mask of bravado.

The bridge was about twelve feet wide, its surface of wide wooden planking covered with a layer of dust. From that, Diego concluded that no traffic, neither on wheels or by foot, had crossed the bridge since the last fall of rain. That was at least half a day ago. "It proves nothing," he decided. A trap could have been laid days, even weeks before.

Diego gave a series of swift orders. Obediently, the soldiers spread out and moved from pylon to pylon, one soldier checking for booby-traps, the other one covering him with his rifle.

As they ventured further and further out onto the bridge, the tension increased. Suddenly Diego jumped when a soldier behind him accidentally kicked a pebble down from the bridge, the loud Ping-Pong noise of the stone as it fell down between the metal girders straining his already frantic nerves almost to breaking point.

"You imbecile," he whispered between clenched teeth.

In the open air halfway across the bridge, the already oppressive heat became even hotter. Overhead, brewing storm clouds drifted in front of the sun and swept the blue of the sky away. Diego realized it was only a matter of seconds before the storm would break loose.

"Let's work a little faster, men," he instructed.

The clouds suddenly burst open. It became almost dark. The escarpment on both sides of the river disappeared behind sheets of rain. Diego felt the water run down his body, its freshness cooling his skin.

About thirty yards before the end of the bridge, Diego suddenly heard one of the soldiers shout something. "Look. Sergeant, look there." He twisted his head around and caught the puzzled gleam in the soldier's eye. His finger was pointing towards the edge of a manhole, its metal frame protruding slightly above the surface of the bridge. Rain flowing down his face, Diego prodded the soldier. "Go on," he said. "Take the others with you and continue searching the surface of the bridge." He nudged his chin in the direction of the manhole. "I'll go and have a good look down there." And if there is a booby-trap, he thought excitedly, I'll find it. It's exactly what I need to establish myself as a competent Recce leader.

Going down on one knee, he slipped the point of his bayonet under the rim of the manhole. It lifted without any resistance. Diego placed it on the road beside him. Inside the hole was a set of rungs. Diego put his feet on the footholds and descended the ladder slowly and carefully. It was dark on the narrow metal walkway, dark but relatively dry, a relief from the lashing rainstorm outside. Once his eyes got used to the darkness, Diego saw that the walkway ran underneath the full length of the bridge. The metal structure was a maze of vertical pylons, each one connected to the other by thick crossbeams and steel girders, the whole construction fixed together with big round-headed rivets.

At the place where crossbeams and girders were joined, Diego noticed concentrations of bird nests. The planking of the walkway was covered with a thick layer of bird droppings.

"A maze like that could hide a thousand traps," he considered, taking a step forward. The sudden movement started a panic amongst the birds who lived under the bridge. Screeching loudly, they fled. Diego slowly inched forward.

Above his head, the rain tapped monotonously on the planking of the road. At places, through gaps between the planks, water came flooding down, washing slime and bird shit from the girders.

Squeezing his eyes half closed against the filth that fell in clots on his head and shoulders, Diego didn't notice a particularly large patch of slimy muck on the walkway. He slipped. With a bang he came down on his side and slipped halfway over the edge, his stomach and legs hanging out over the void, with the raging river hundreds of feet below him.

"Oh, hell!" he screamed.

In a panic he threw out his arms and grabbed the edge of the narrow walkway. With a gigantic effort, he pulled himself up until he could reach one of the metal crossbeams. Seconds later he managed to drag his legs to safety over the planking. His muscles were aching, his breath came puffing through his wide open mouth. Apart from bleeding hands, where the rough and splintered planks had cut his skin, and some aching ribs, he was unhurt.

"Jesus, look at the mess I'm in," he hissed. His uniform was covered with a mess of dirty grey and green streaks. "And phew, what a smell... Disgusting."

As soon as his heartbeat came back to normal, Diego stood up and worked himself forward, walking a little slower this time, a little more carefully. Suddenly, he saw it. Three fat sticks of dynamite, connected with detonating cord, the whole bunch attached with dark brown tape to one of the beams under the main section, the detonator cord disappearing somewhere in the dark of the structure above. On the next beam, Diego discovered another set of three sticks of dynamite. He climbed up the girders and cut the detonating cords loose. The two packs of explosives, he threw in the river. Once it was done, a warm glow of success flooded over him. "That will show them," he said. "Now the men will see that I know my job. Now they will accept me."

His head swelling with pride, Diego did not ask himself why those sticks of dynamite had been so easy to find. Why, if there were so many good hiding places in the semi-darkness under the bridge, they had not been better concealed.

In his haste to get out of there and enjoy his victory, Diego failed to notice the real trap, a large bird's nest, solidly wedged in a corner between two heavy cross beams, the deep and comfortable hollow of feathers the safe hiding place for thirty pounds of high explosive. He also failed to see the pressure-sensitive detonator that lay on a crossbeam beneath the planking of the centre section, where the bridge reached its greatest span across the river.

At the end of the walkway, Diego crawled out of the manhole. He hurried back to his Jeep and reported to Oliviero what he had found. "Two charges of dynamite," he shouted in the microphone. "I have disarmed them. The bridge is safe now."

"Well done, Sergeant Diego," replied Oliviero. "Go on and cross the bridge with your Jeep. Once the Jeep is safe on the other side, take the half-track over. After that, I'll send the fuel truck."

The metal structure of the bridge barely moved under the weight of the Jeep.

The half-track was a much heavier vehicle. Its weight made the middle of the bridge sag by almost half an inch. Half an inch was not enough to reach the plunger of the detonator. With two vehicles safely across the bridge, Oliviero relaxed.

He waved the fuel truck forward.

The planks of the deck groaned under the ponderous weight of the truck and its trailer. The girders bowed under the colossal stress. The open space between the cross beam and the detonator closed rapidly. Oliviero swung his binoculars in front of his eyes.

What saved the truck was the fuel the platoon had burned during the previous days and hours. It made its weight just light enough to pass over the danger point without fully depressing the head of the plunger. Unhurt, the truck reached the other side of the bridge.

Oliviero suddenly realized he had forgotten to breathe. With a deep sigh, he let the air stream out of his lungs. "Our turn, men," he said to Jose and Sergio. "Tonight, the beer in Portugalia will be on me." Jose smiled and pushed the accelerator down. The wide caterpillar tracks of the tank moved slowly forward.

As if nature wanted to witness what was going on, the rain abruptly stopped. Oliviero looked up and let the sun caress his face. The Walker Bulldog moved across the bridge. At the middle of the bridge, the cross beam could not hold the tremendous weight of the tank. With a sharp thrust, the plunger of the detonator went all the way down.

The silence of the afternoon was ripped apart by a monstrous explosion. The ground at the threshold of the bridge shook. The supporting pylons of the structure folded like sticks of firewood. The sides of the gorge caved in. A cloud of dust, rocks and boulders thundered down to the level of the river. Propelled by the gigantic might of the explosives, the Walker Bulldog rose slowly into the air. A stream of unused shells, a couple of maps, and a signal gun fell out of the gaping hole that had been torn in its flat bottom.

Inside the tank, Jose sat dead behind his controls, his spine crushed by the force of the explosion. Sergio lay dead under the breech of his gun, his torso smashed to a pulp by a load of heavy high explosive HE shells. Oliviero was pinned down by the weight of the radio rack. Cut by sharp edges of metal, the main artery of his left leg was pumping bright red blood.

"Jesus," he prayed. "Help me..."

At the apex of its climb, the tank seemed to hang still for a moment, then it flipped over and fell through the gaping hole where the bridge had been. Halfway down the narrowing gorge, the barrel of the gun found a gap between two giant rocks. For a moment it looked as if the Walker Bulldog was suspended against the side of the gorge like a big brown beetle. The weight of the tank was too immense for the strength of the turret. With a loud screeching sound of tortured metal, the lower part of the tank tore itself free from the main body. Holding the corpses of Jose and Sergio, it crashed down into the river and disappeared under tons of foaming water.

Trapped in the upper part of the turret, Oliviero was dazed with shock, but still conscious. With each beat of his heart, a spurt of blood gushed out of his wounds. As if his brain was slowly shrinking, he began to feel strangely dizzy. He tried to focus his eyes. It appeared as if he was looking through a long and black tunnel that became rapidly narrower and darker.

Oliviero realized that he was dying, but looking upon death as a welcome friend, he was not afraid.

Once dead, he would not be plagued by feelings of hatred and guilt any more. There would be no more nightmares of killings and blood and tears. "And I won't be lonely any longer!" he mumbled. The last conscious thing he did, was pray.

"Oh God, let it be true what the Padre told me, and allow me to be reunited with my darling Gabriela and my son Dominico..."

Two hours later, the remnants of the platoon reached Portugalia. Sergeant Diego called Luanda and reported the disaster. Rightfully, Senhor Silva considered it too dangerous to transport the diamonds back to Luanda on board a convoy that consisted only of one Jeep, one half-track, a fuel truck and a group of very demoralized soldiers.

"We don't have any other choice but to leave the diamonds where they are," were his parting words. "Let the new Angolan Government make their own arrangements for their recovery." The diamonds stayed in Portugalia. Five days later,

11 November 1975, Angola became an Independent Republic.
Luanda, 11 November 1975

Independence Day in Angola should have been a day of joy! Instead, it became a day of shame, the day the guerrilla fighting which had been going on for more than ten years exploded into a full-blown Civil War.

Independence from Portugal, and the recognition of President Nevo's MPLA party as the legal Government in Angola, was the result of a political intrigue between East and West. Yet, nobody in the whole world had bothered to ask the people of Angola whether they wanted to live as communists under the leadership of the MPLA.

Only a part of the population accepted Alfonsino Nevo as their rightful leader. The others wanted to live as they had been living for centuries, with their tribal councils and their own customs. They welcomed Joshua Matindi, the charismatic leader of UNITA, as their guide to a new future. Consequently, on the 11th of November 1975, not only one but two new Republics were born.

President Nevo and his MPLA movement took their seat in Luanda. They opted for a one-party Government with a Marxist regime, and called their Republic the "People's Communist Republic of Angola."

In Novo Lisboa, the second largest city in Angola and former colonial capital, Joshua Matindi and a coalition Government of UNITA and FNLA heralded the birth of the "Democratic Republic of Angola". They guaranteed parliamentary freedom and pluralism, and a totally democratic voting system.

The Soviets reacted immediately by sending shiploads full of tanks and planes to Luanda. The Cubans came next. Fifteen thousand soldiers to help their MPLA "comrades" in the struggle against UNITA and capitalism. UNITA received aid from America and South Africa. Mercenaries from all over the world joined Joshua Matindi's Army, and heavy fighting broke out.

A mass exodus of people began.

On 14 November 1975, the airport in Luanda looked like a disaster area, with military equipment blocking the tarmac and obstructing the taxi ways. Inside the building, conditions were worse. The air conditioning was down, the air was hot and humid and smelled of sweaty bodies. The people in the hall were divided into two groups. The first group consisted of expatriates: a mixed bunch of men, women and children; embassy personnel, employees of foreign companies, businessmen, doctors, nurses and teachers. They were fleeing because of the increased threat to their safety as a result of the Civil War. The second and larger group were Portuguese colonialists. They were leaving because ownership of properties and the possibility of making a living no longer existed. Both groups were treated equally with hatred and suspicion.

Manuela and her father Alvaro, a man in his mid-sixties, belonged to the second group. As the light eastern winds pushed a whiff of air through the open windows, Alvaro took a deep breath. "How much longer are they going to make us wait, Manuela?" he muttered. "They'll never give us an exit visa. Let's go home."

Manuela shook her head. "Stop being defeatist, Papa. It's only a matter of time, you'll see."

Alvaro let his thoughts drift to the luxury he had known in the past and compared it with the misery he experienced now. For six generations, his family had been in Angola, controlling coffee plantations, processing plants and a shipping company.

When the troubles had started ten years ago, other families had sold up and left the country. Convinced that the West would never allow Angola to fall prey to the communists, Alvaro had stayed on and, to defend his birthright, had become a supporting member of UNITA. It was only after Independence, when the new MPLA Government seized his coffee plantations, that he realized how misplaced his confidence in the West had been.

Alvaro sighed deeply. "If I had sold up years ago, we would still be rich, Manuela. Now I don't have two escudos to rub together."

"Helping UNITA in their fight against communism was right, Papa. I agree, we've been let down, but we can't turn the clock back."

Playfully, Manuela tapped her father on his shoulder. "What's that nonsense about not having two escudos to rub together. You still have money in the bank in Lisbon, haven't you. Not a fortune, but sufficient for a comfortable retirement."

Alvaro frowned. "What about Stanfort, Manuela. Don't you want to stay here with him, instead of coming with me to Portugal?"

"I would, but he isn't staying for long. Just a matter of finalizing the hand-over of the mines to the new management. Once that's done, he'll join us in Lisbon, and he is very adamant that I leave now, with you."

"He's right, you know," confirmed Alvaro. "It's safer for you to be out of here. Remember what happened in the Belgian Congo when they were given Independence in the early sixties. The white population was hunted like wild animals. Men and children were shot; women gang raped and murdered."

"It won't be like that in Angola," asserted Manuela. "MPLA and UNITA have been fighting for a long time, and there have been very few cases of attacks against Portuguese women."

"You're right, but I agree with Stanfort. You'll be safer in Lisbon!"

Alvaro's eyes became heavy with the heat and, hypnotized by the constant sound of babbling voices, he fell asleep. When he woke up, it was late in the afternoon. Finally, their name was called.

"You can go," the emigration official said, pointing to Manuela. A malicious smile on his face, he put a big red EXIT stamp in her passport. "But you," he snarled to Alvaro. "As far as I can see, you haven't paid your income taxes. Before I can consider your request, Comrade Rodrigues, you'll have to settle your debts."

A rebellious glare showed in Alvaro's eyes. "The value of my properties, which were confiscated by your Government, should be more than adequate to cover the amount of my taxes," he exclaimed.

Shrugging his shoulders, the emigration official spat on the ground, the spittle barely missing Alvaro's shoes. "Go away, man," he said. "You are too stupid to understand what I mean."

It suddenly dawned on Alvaro that the pretext of income taxes was nothing but a scam. Even if he did find a way to pay, he would never be given an exit visa. From now on he would have to live with the idea of spending the rest of his life in Angola, prisoner of a Government who considered the refusal of an exit visa adequate punishment for his capitalist status and his aid to UNITA.

The official made a gesture of dismissal. "As for you," he said to Manuela. "You can still go. Leave the old fool here." His lecherous eyes swept over her legs and breasts. "There's so much more for you in the world than this..."

Exhaling sharply with disgust, Manuela threw her passport back on to his desk. "Cancel my exit visa," she said proudly. "I won't leave without my father. If he has to stay, so will I, and if there is a way out for both of us, I'll find it."

Smiling spitefully, the official pulled a blue pencil out of his shirt pocket and invalidated her visa.

For a short moment, Manuela allowed her mind to turn to bitterness, then she threw up her head in an act of defiance. Taking her father by the elbow, she guided him to the exit of the hall.

One week later, Manuela received a summons to report to the office of SECPOL in the Rua do Esquadrao. She was met by a small man. He looked haughty and devious, but gave the impression of being very intelligent. His eyes were tiny and lay close together on either side of his wide flat nose. They reminded her of the eyes of a viper and a shiver of apprehension ran down her spine. With a curt gesture of his hand, the man motioned her to sit down. "I'm Lopes Pereira," he said. "Inspector of SECPOL."

Manuela's apprehension turned into cold despair. Having heard the name before, she knew he was one of the most powerful men in the country, master over life and death of all who had the misfortune of falling into his hands. She felt the urge to run away and hide.

"We both know that your father has severe problems," Lopes said conversationally. He stood up and walked around the desk.

Suddenly, his breath smelling sour and specks of saliva spraying her skin, he shouted: "He is an idiot, Manuela. His membership with UNITA could mean the death sentence. As a matter of fact, he should have been arrested already."

Manuela's eyes filled with tears. "But, Senhor Lopes," she cried. "He is an old man, a broken man. Hardly somebody who could be a threat to the safety of the country."

Lopes got hold of a jug and poured himself a glass of water.

"I'm prepared to do anything to save my father from being arrested," Manuela continued.

Lopes crinkled his lips in a vicious smile. As she saw that, Manuela stressed: "Anything, I'll do anything you want to obtain my father's freedom."

Lopes smile turned into pure loathing. "First, don't call me 'Senhor', he sneered derisively. "Since Independence, we address each other as 'Comrade'! Second, I'm not interested in your white flesh. However, there is something else you can do to save your father. Pull yourself together and listen." He placed his seat in a more comfortable position and put his right leg across the corner of his desk. "I'm a loyal communist, Manuela, a trustee of our President, Comrade Nevo. He has expressed worry about the safety of the diamonds in Portugalia. As you know, they belong to the Government now!" Lopes took the time to light up a cigarette. "Not that I distrust the new members of the Council," he said slyly. "But 30,000 carats of diamonds can be a hell of a temptation. That's where you come in, Manuela. I want you to become my eyes and ears at DIANGOL. I want you to come and tell me anything you hear about plans to transport the stones. I want copies of letters and reports and ..." With a rapid movement of his hand, he pushed a tape recorder with built-in microphone across the desk. "I want you to tape all conversations and discussions during the meetings of the new Revolutionary Council."

A blank stare marked Manuela's eyes as she realized that Lopes wanted her to spy on her own colleagues. She felt numb with horror. "Don't ask me to betray my colleagues, Comrade Lopes."

"It's either that, Manuela, or the cellars of the Old Fort for your father. So make up your mind and do it fast."

Manuela realized that she would not be allowed to leave the office before Lopes had his answer.

Sensing her despair, Lopes decided to tempt her with a carrot on a stick. "Remember," he said quietly, his voice again soft and gentle. "I have my powers straight from the President. If you handle your job well, and if I'm satisfied with the result, I'll personally talk to the President and ask him to pardon your father. With that pardon, getting an exit visa won't be too much of a problem."

A surge of hope flooded Manuela's heart.

"However, in case you do not wish to co-operate..."

Barely daring to breathe, Manuela waited for the rest of his words.

"Then your father will be arrested tonight, and I'll put you in a brothel for the Cubans. I'm sure they would know what to do with you!"

Manuela knew that she was trapped. Whether she wanted to or not, she would have to accept. Not collaborating with Lopes would result in her father's death, and she would end up as a whore in a Cuban brothel, a fate almost worse than death.

On the other hand, working for Lopes could mean freedom for her father. If he kept his promise!

Left with no choice and holding on to Lopes' pledge like a drowning person to a piece of driftwood, Manuela agreed to become an agent for SECPOL. Deeply confused and ashamed, but feeling a slight glimmer of hope for the future, she turned away from the loathsome man and left his office.

Government House, Luanda, 17 November 1975

President Nevo walked over to the large bay window of his office and stared briefly at the beautifully landscaped but neglected garden. Suddenly remembering something, he hurried back to his desk. After searching briefly, he picked up one of the letters and let his eyes scan the rows and rows of figures that covered the document. The part he was looking for was somewhere in the middle. He read it attentively, then let the letter flutter down on to the cluttered surface of his desk. As if mesmerized, he smashed his fists together. "Problems everywhere," he moaned. His face wrinkled in a deep frown. "Nothing but problems."

Turning on his heels, he looked at his faithful friend and confidant, Roberto Cabral. "Roberto," Nevo began. "You know that I trust you like my own brother. That's why I appointed you as President and Chairman of DIANGOL. There is too much at stake to leave it in less reliable hands."

Knowing that Nevo was just leading up to something else, Roberto sat back in his chair and folded his hands together. The President stepped around his ornamental desk, let himself heavily down in his armchair and pointed meaningfully to the assortment of documents that littered his desk. With a harsh tone that defied all contradiction, he groaned. "Debts and negative balance sheets, that's all I have... The Russians want money, the Cubans want money, I have to find ways to pay my own soldiers, and I have to buy arms and ammunition." He lifted his hands helplessly. "Not that I don't have the resources to pay, Roberto. On paper, at least, I've got 30,000 carats of diamonds, worth twelve million dollars. But where are those blasted diamonds, Roberto? Where are they...?" His fist came down like a crack of thunder on the document that lay in front of him. "According to this report they are still in Portugalia." With a smirk on his lips, he added mockingly: "Because the stupid Portuguese managed to get themselves killed by guerrilla fighters!" His voice became soft and almost pleading. "I desperately need this twelve million dollars, Roberto. I want you to find a solution for the transport of the diamonds."

Roberto raised his eyebrows and shrugged his shoulders. "Alfonsino, the area between Malanje and Portugalia is swarming with UNITA fighters. The roads are unsafe. Most of the railway bridges have been blown up. No train or truck can get through!"

Very agitated by Roberto's words, Nevo jumped up from his chair and flapped his arms like a bird. "I don't want to hear any of that non-constructive drivel," he shouted. "You have first-class people to help you. There is General Pia for instance. As Commander in Chief of the MPLA Army, he can ask for assistance from the Cubans. They have heavy tanks and armoured vehicles."

"You know very well that Pia was not exactly my first choice as Commander of our Army," remarked Roberto. "If I remember well, it was the Cubans who suggested his name." With a glint of distrust in his eyes, he added shrewdly: "Sometimes I wonder whose side Pia is really on."

His words put a twinge of doubt about Pia's loyalty in Nevo's heart. Searching his memory, he recalled the day when Pia had been nominated as Commander in Chief of the Army. Roberto was right. It was the Cubans who had suggested Pia's name. "Because he is fluent in Portuguese and Spanish. That will make it easy to coordinate between your Army and ours."

Cabral's sharp brain suddenly detected another problem with Nevo's suggestion. "There is another reason why we cannot afford to ask the Cubans for help," he commented. "If that bunch of 'Che-Guevaras' get their hands on the stones, they'll ship them to Cuba, and we won't get a single diamond. Believe me."

That was also true, Nevo contemplated. The Cubans would not hesitate to keep the diamonds as compensation for their military assistance.

Instead of being grateful for Cabral's advice, Nevo became angry. One of his faults was that he couldn't stand being corrected by anyone, not even Roberto. And now, Roberto had not only dared to prove him wrong once but twice in the space of a few minutes.

Nevo felt one of his blind and vicious rages building up. His eyes started to bulge, his eyeballs almost popping out of their sockets. With a desperate effort to keep his self-control, he locked his jaws together and swallowed hard, but all his efforts were in vain. With a voice that echoed from the crystal beads of the giant chandelier, he yelled: "I don't give a damn what you do or how you do it, but you'll have to find a solution, Roberto." To add strength to his words, he battered the dark mahogany surface of his desk with his fist. "Do whatever you have to do, but I need that money *now*. Not the day after tomorrow, not tomorrow, but now..." Clenching his fists so tight that the knuckles shone white through his dark skin, Nevo took a deep breath. "Don't sit there like an imbecile," he finally spat out. "There is nothing you can do by sitting on your bloody arse. Get out of here, go to your own office and organize something with the help of your assistants. *Immediately!*"

Still ranting and raving, Nevo turned his back on Cabral and stormed out of the room, slamming the door closed behind him.

"Si, Comrade Presidente," muttered Cabral. Still shaken from being at the receiving end of Nevo's anger, he phoned his secretary at DIANGOL and instructed her to arrange a meeting of the full Council. He then slipped his old leather bag under his arm and, with what was left of his dignity, strode out of the office.

It was a relief to find himself back in the fresh air outside the Government building. The day was pleasantly warm with only one or two storms building up to the west, far away over the ocean. Burdened by the problem of how to retrieve the diamonds, Cabral instructed his driver to take him directly to DIANGOL's headoffice. As they drove through the streets of Luanda, his feeling of frustration and resentment slowly started to dissipate. Nevo's sudden irrational behaviour was not exactly a new experience for him. He had seen it happen many times before, but this was the first time that he had been on the receiving end of it, and he had to admit that it was quite an experience. In spite of himself he started to smile. "Tomorrow, he'll have forgotten all about it," he whispered. "After all, we have known each other for so long." However, it remained a fact that the retrieval of the diamonds was vital if he wanted to remain Nevo's main adviser and confidant. To force fate to become his ally, Cabral superstitiously crossed his fingers.

During the short drive to DIANGOL, although preoccupied with the problem at hand, Cabral noticed with a certain feeling of regret, the drastic changes Independence had brought to the city. In the sixties, Luanda had been described as the most beautiful and cosmopolitan city in Africa.

The years of fighting had claimed a heavy toll. The once magnificent Avenidos were now a jungle of dry shrubs and dead trees, the surface of the roads a labyrinth of potholes. Here and there, piles of rubbish and stones marked the places where luxurious houses had been destroyed by gunfire. Electricity in the city was available for only a few short hours a day, water an even more infrequent luxury, its quality so bad that it was barely drinkable. To make matters even worse, there was a shortage of food and medical care, and unemployment was rampant.

His driver swung the car into Rua Castelbranco. The wide boulevard was lined with two rows of Royal Palm trees; mostly dead. Their long, pointed leaves littered the pavements. A red-painted Soviet tank, a monument to glorify the success of the revolution, stood prominently at the place where for centuries the statue of the Portuguese explorer Salvador Benevides had graced the corner of the boulevard. Carefully, Cabral's driver negotiated the car around a hole in the surface of the road where a looter had removed the inspection cover of the underground drainage system. A little further down the street, the road was blocked by a huge crowd. In front of the crowd stood a big harbour tractor, its towing-hook connected to a set of steel cables which hung like strings of spaghetti around the head and torso of the statue of Diego Cao, discoverer of Angola and founder of Luanda.

"That's another statue they are going to pull down," the driver remarked cautiously.

As he looked out of the window, it struck Cabral that, to an outsider, it must give the impression that the MPLA was only able to implement the new system by eradicating all traces of the past. It was a sobering idea, an idea that made him wonder about the rightness of it all.

With a nostalgic knot in his stomach, he thought back to the time when he had been fighting in the bush. It had seemed so much simpler then.

His driver turned around in his seat, an excited expression on his face. "They're ready to start, Comrade," he said, eager to please. "It won't be easy..."

The tractor driver pulled the cables taut and he let go of the clutch. The tractor's tyres clawed a spray of red laterite out of the ground. The statue slowly tipped a couple of inches forward.

"I bet he won't be able to pull *that* thing over," Roberto's driver said excitedly.

"I think he will... Look," Cabral replied, pointing ahead. "The driver is no fool. He is going to rock the statue forwards and backwards and use its own momentum to topple it."

He was right. The driver, high on the seat of the tractor, suddenly let go of the accelerator. Driven by its own inertia, the statue whipped up and went slightly over its apex. As it moved forwards again, the driver threw the full power of his engine against the tautly stretched cables. Belching a cloud of black smoke, the tractor reared up on its wheels.

Accelerating rapidly, the statue went over its centre of gravity. The enormous head, thirty-five feet above the ground, swept through a wide arc. One hand of the old explorer pointed high up in the air, as if complaining about this undignified behaviour.

As the colossus hit the ground, it smashed with the loud ringing noise of breaking bronze. A roar of approval went up from the crowd. This was the moment they had been waiting for. Armed with sledgehammers and pickaxes, they attacked the fallen statue and hacked it to pieces.

"The money they'll get from that scrap will be spent on food." Cabral's driver remarked.

Straight away, Cabral remembered Mao Tse Tung's claim that there was something constructive in all destruction. "Mao was right," he mumbled, a taste of bitterness in the back of his throat. "Tonight, because of this senseless demolition, some families will actually go to bed with full stomachs."

Fifteen minutes later, they reached the headoffice of DIANGOL. Roberto Cabral ran up the steps two at a time and rushed through the corridor that led to the large meeting room. In an attempt to catch his breath, he walked slowly to his chair at the head of the table and threw a quick glance around the room. He noticed General Mario Pia, Commander in Chief of the MPLA Armed Forces. As usual, Pia was wearing a very elegant dress uniform, his chest garnished with shiny decorations.

There was doctore Armande Aliba. Only interested in running his group of geologists to find new fields of exploitation, he kept himself totally absent from any involvement in politics.

Vigo and Armani were also there. After the Declaration of Independence, as a gesture of goodwill, they had accepted to stay on temporarily, as advisers to the new members of the Council. Still, the fact that they had kept their Portuguese nationality made them in the eyes of certain members of the Council, untrustworthy. And there was his secretary Manuela, who, after the disaster with her father's exit visa, had considered herself very fortunate to be reinstated as Roberto Cabral's private secretary with DIANGOL.

Cabral pulled his armchair back and sat down. With a vague motion of his hands he invited the other members to be seated. Before starting to speak, he waited until the scraping noises of chairs had calmed down. "I'm sorry that I had to call you out at such short notice," he commenced.

Seated at the other end of the table, Manuela took a notebook and a pen out of her handbag. Very unobtrusively, she turned her bag around and pointed the hidden microphone of the recorder in the direction of the assembled Members of the Council.

"Comrades," Roberto said reflectively. "I've just received a terrible reprimand from our dear President. When I say a reprimand, I put it very mildly..."

Knowing the reputation of the President, they all smiled politely.

"That's why I had to call this emergency meeting." Briefly, Cabral explained what was expected of them. "Sending one of our own military patrols is totally out of the question. The roads are too dangerous. Has any one got another suggestion?"

General Pia was the first to raise his hand. "I completely agree with you, Comrade Cabral."

Pia's words did not come as a surprise. Mainly concerned with the advancement of his own career, Pia generally agreed with people in power. Hiding his contempt for the man, Cabral made a show of concentrating on Pia's words.

"I strongly advise against sending any military patrol to Portugalia." Pia explained. "Intelligence reports show that Joshua Matindi has made a very big effort to reinforce his guerrilla forces in the eastern part of the country. Consequently, we haven't got a cat in hell's chance of getting through."

The other members of the Council nodded their agreement.

"The only way it could be done in my opinion is by sending a MiG17 fighter plane."

"You must be joking, General," exclaimed Armani. "The landing strip in Portugalia is far too short for a jet."

Roberto Cabral smashed the head of his gavel against the wooden block on the table. In unison, the Board Members turned to him. "We have to find a solution without any help from outsiders. By outsiders I mean Russians, Cubans, East-Germans, whoever. I don't want to give them the satisfaction of discovering that we can't look after our own interests."

A big thundercloud drifted by. A sudden downpour of rain erupted. The accompanying gusts of wind created a surge of air in the room, sucking the white lace curtains out of the window. Instantly the room felt colder, the air fresh but somewhat damp.

Grateful for the cooler air, Cabral continued. "It's bad enough that we have to rely on Russians and Cubans to fight our battles against UNITA. No gentlemen, for this mission, we cannot rely upon anybody."

"Comrade Cabral," argued General Pia pompously. "We don't possess one single plane that is capable of flying to Portugalia. If we can't use a MiG17, the only other solution would be to use one of the big Soviet helicopters and..."

"I said no foreign involvement," interrupted Cabral. "And that includes helicopters."

Vigo's eyes suddenly lit up. "There *is* one aeroplane in Angola that is capable of flying this mission," he remarked. "A plane that doesn't belong to the Cubans, nor to the Russians." He fell silent for a moment, then thinking out loud, he added: "The mechanics will have to install an additional fuel tank, but that is not too big a problem."

"Where would you find that plane, Vigo?" asked Cabral.

"In Portugalia, Comrade Cabral. The problem is the pilot. He is grounded with a broken leg," replied Vigo.

Manuela's heart missed a beat. "You plan to use the Skyvan," she exclaimed from the other end of the table. "Who is going to be the pilot? Oviero can't do it, his leg is still in a cast..." Her voice trailed off when she realized whom Vigo had in mind, and a red hot flush coloured her cheeks.

Surprised at her startled reaction, Vigo remembered that she was Stanfort's girlfriend. "That's right, Manuela," he said gently. "I was indeed thinking about the Skyvan." He turned his attention back to Cabral. "As to the pilot... You know Stanfort, Comrade Cabral. He is not only our Mining Manager, but he is also a very good pilot. I myself can bear witness to that as I have had the pleasure of flying with him on many occasions. What's more, gentlemen, Oviero is an excellent instructor."

Nobody but Manuela seemed to realize what he was leading up to. Vigo decided not to test their patience any longer.

"Gentlemen, I'm not a pilot, but I know that there is very little difference between the basic controls of the Chipmunk and those of the Skyvan. Therefore, I believe that Oviero is capable of teaching Robert Stanfort how to fly the Skyvan." A look of excitement appeared in Vigo's eyes as he explained that the whole beauty of the arrangement was that Stanfort didn't need to be on his own in the plane. "Although incapable of pushing the rudders because of his broken leg, Oviero can still assist the pilot by sitting in the co-pilot's seat. He can read the check-lists and operate the more complicated aircraft systems. As such, Stanfort would merely have to handle the flight controls."

Vigo's proposition was so simple that nobody could find fault with it. Except Pia. "What did you mention earlier, about the requirement for an additional fuel tank," he asked.

Vigo shrugged his shoulders. "The total capacity of fuel in the tanks of the Skyvan is not sufficient to fly non-stop from Portugalia to Luanda, Comrade General. Therefore, the mechanics will have to provide an auxiliary fuel supply. That's only a matter of a couple of fuel barrels and a wobble pump," Vigo added laughingly. "Even I could rig a system like that."

"That's excellent, Vigo," commented Cabral. "Let's set it in motion."

Walking behind Roberto Cabral, they all headed for the radio room. Manuela stayed behind. Feeling as if the ground was trembling beneath her feet, she gathered her papers together and stopped the tape recorder. Up to now, she had done what Lopes had asked her to do. At first, very much plagued by feelings of remorse and guilt, she had reminded herself over and over again that spying for SECPOL was her father's only chance of survival, and she had been able to repress her feelings. After all, Cabral, Vigo, Pia, Armani and Aliba, were just business acquaintances, strangers really. Now however, because of Vigo's plan, Stanfort would get involved, and Stanfort was definitely not a stranger!

Torn apart by her loyalties and not knowing what to do any more, Manuela started to cry.

"Please God," she whimpered in between her tears. "Help me. Don't put me in the position of having to choose between my father's freedom and my lover's safety."

The radio room at DIANGOL was situated on the top floor of the building. Vigo quickly consulted the chart with the recommended High Frequencies for that time of the day and switched the transceiver on. "Dundo, Dundo, this is Luanda on 5658, do you read?"

Dundo was the name of the camp in the vicinity of Portugalia where the administrative offices of the mines were located. Vigo waited impatiently for Dundo to reply. Apart from static and crackling sounds, he heard nothing in his headset. Irritated by the weird propagation patterns of long-range radio waves, he switched over to another frequency. "Dundo, Dundo, from Luanda, transmitting on 8865. Come in please." He twisted the squelch button a fraction to the right.

"Yes, Luanda, this is Dundo, go ahead with your message." The voice of the operator in Dundo sounded slightly distorted with the static interference of a tropical thunderstorm somewhere far away over Central Africa.

Vigo squeezed the microphone between his strong fingers. "Let me speak to Comrade Stanfort," he said. "Quickly!" To calm his nerves, he lit up a thin black cigar and sucked the smoke hungrily into his lungs.

Ten minutes later, Stanfort's voice burst through the loudspeaker. "Hello, Luanda, Stanfort here, what's going on?"

Vigo explained his plan.

Excited by the idea, Stanfort hardly waited until Vigo was finished. He rushed out of the door, jumped over the low railing that separated the balcony from the road, and hurried over to Oviero's villa.

Lying comfortably in a deck chair on the terrace, Oviero was reading a novel. Barely able to speak with exhilaration, Stanfort told him what Vigo had suggested.

"Hmmm, I don't know," replied Oviero. He lifted a glass of Casal Garcia to his lips and took a sip. "Transporting a fortune in diamonds for the President is not exactly the same as flying mining supplies to Saurimo."

"Not that different, just another kind of cargo," countered Stanfort, and willing his friend to accept the challenge, he emphasized, "I'm sure we can do it."

"I'm not so sure," replied Oviero teasingly.

"Come on, Joey, I'm begging you. Together we can do it. We have been in tighter corners before."

Bored after the long period of inactivity and sorely tempted to get some action, Oviero stood up and hobbled to the end of the terrace. Slowly he turned around and, grinning with anticipation, he nodded his head. "OK, let's do it."

Before Stanfort had time to run off, he warned him that it would take a day or maybe two to teach him the basics of the Skyvan. "The flight controls are slightly different from the controls of the Chipmunk," he said. "Also, the Skyvan is much faster, with two engines, and there are a lot of emergency procedures to be studied."

"With you as instructor," Stanfort said confidently. "I'm sure I'll manage."

"Yeah, I think you will," admitted Oviero, already savouring the idea of flying again. A big smile broke over his ruggedly handsome face. "Go ahead and call Vigo. Tell him we'll start your flight training tomorrow."

Stanfort was off in a flash.

"Tell him," Oviero shouted after him, "... that if all goes well, we'll be ready by the 19th or the 20th for the ferry flight."

Later that evening, Manuela walked furtively down the pavement of the Rua do Esquadrao. When reaching number 15, she rang the bell. Almost immediately the little spy hole in the door was opened. Manuela recognized the bloodshot eye of

Luis Cordi, one of Lopes' aides. "It's me, Manuela," she whispered. "Is Lopes in?"

Luis opened the door and pointed to an oblong of yellow light at the end of the corridor. Manuela entered the office.

Behind the desk, hidden behind a pile of files and illuminated by the glare of a strong desk light, sat Lopes. He swung his hand in the direction of a chair. Manuela shook her head, indicating that she preferred to remain standing.

Without speaking, Lopes grabbed the small cassette out of her hand and slipped it at once in the slot of his tape player. Leaning back in his chair and studying Manuela through the narrow slits between his heavy eyelids, he concentrated on the recording. Feeling as if Lopes was undressing her with his eyes, she shivered with loathing. She forced herself to show no fear, no feelings at all.

"Well done, Manuela," Lopes whispered between his teeth when the tape reached its end. "I see that I have succeeded in making a secret agent out of you."

Confronted once more with the truth that she was nothing but a vile traitor, her heart started beating like a drum and her lips began to tremble.

A vicious smile twisted Lopes' lips when he saw the distress on her face. "Come now," he sneered. "Once in a while we all have to do things which are not so nice or honourable, but the reward you stand to receive makes it worthwhile, doesn't it?"

Two tears ran down Manuela's cheeks. To soothe her feeling of guilt, she suddenly felt the need to hear again Lopes' promise. "I'm only doing it because you vowed to let my father go free," she cried. "Please guarantee me that you'll keep your word."

Lopes laughed scornfully. "We'll see about that when the diamonds are here, Manuela! Then, and only then, will I consider letting your father go free. In the mean time he should be happy to be alive."

He turned his black eyes towards Manuela, as if he wanted to pierce her brain. "Being alive is more than can be said of some of his cronies who were executed this morning in the cellars of the Old Fort." He raised his hand and pointed to the door. "Now get out of here."

Very confused and realizing that a promise from Lopes was as hollow and worthless as an empty bottle to a dying man in the desert, Manuela ran out into the darkness of the street. As she ran, the hollow clack-clack-clack of her shoes on the cobbles sounded like the spiteful laugh of Lopes, following her, haunting her...

Portugalia, 18 November 1975

Anthony Stanfort woke up as the early morning light filtered through the curtains of his room. Enjoying the bliss of being alive, he yawned and stretched his arms above his head. The delicious aroma of freshly brewed coffee, bacon and eggs came drifting up from the kitchen. Cookie is early as well, he thought. He suddenly remembered what was going to happen that day. "The Skyvan ... The training!"

Suddenly itching to get started, he jumped out of bed and walked out on to the balcony. The garden was still moist from the nightly rains and smelled fresh and cool. Dozens of blue, yellow and red coloured birds were soaring like darts between hibiscus and bougainvillaea trees, singing and chirping like the instruments of an early morning concert. High in the pale blue sky, a few small Cumulus clouds drifted by on a light westerly breeze.

"Excellent day for flying," Stanfort decided.

He quickly showered and dressed. Hurriedly, he devoured the breakfast his cook had prepared, then he ran out of the door, jumped into his car and raced to the other side of the compound.

Oviero, in the same impatient mood as himself, was already waiting for him on the veranda of his villa.

"Nice day, Anthony."

With a cheerful expression on his face, Oviero unlocked the rear door of the Mercedes and slipped sideways on to the back seat, dragging 'his damned plastered leg' behind him.

At the airfield, whilst Oviero struggled to get out of the car, Stanfort threw his weight against the rusty hinges of the side entrance to the hangar. Screeching and squeaking, the door swung open. The only light in the hangar came from dozens of fingers of dust-speckled sunlight that fell through holes in the walls and the ceiling. For a moment, blinded by the contrast between the brightness of the day outside and the murky shadows inside, Stanfort stood still. "You wait until I have the main doors open, Joey," he yelled. "No use coming in here yet." Chuckling with glee he added: "With your famous clumsiness, you'll only manage to break your other leg as well." He walked over to the sliding doors and threw the switch that controlled the electric motors. Haltingly, the large doors started to slide over the rusty tracks.

As soon as they were fully open, Oviero, strangely attracted by what he was going to find, hobbled over to the corner where the broken remains of the Chipmunk had been stored. "The Skyvan can wait a while," he said hoarsely. "Since the accident, I haven't been here. I have to see this first." Prodding the cockpit seat with the rubber tip of his crutch, he exclaimed: "It's a real miracle that I'm still alive, but I'm afraid your plane is never going to fly again, Anthony."

Stanfort shrugged his shoulders. "Don't worry, man. I knew that already. Especially now that Angola is struggling for its very existence, I can't see how, where and when I'd be able to get the spare parts."

"Still, I am very sorry, Anthony. Maybe one day, I'll be able to make up for it."

"Forget it, Joey. Just teach me how to fly this big bastard." Stanfort climbed on board the Skyvan, his arms full of flight handbooks and reference manuals.

Much slower and very cautiously, Oviero squeezed himself sideways into the co-pilot's seat and manoeuvred his broken leg into the open space beside the rudder pedals where it would not be an obstruction to the flight controls. Once comfortably seated, he stretched out his arms. It was a perfect fit. Even with his chair all the way back, he could still reach the starter buttons of the engines, throttles and the prop-controllers. Satisfied, he grabbed hold of the Aircraft Flight Handbook and let his finger run over the index. "Here we are, Anthony," he announced. "Normal and Abnormal Flight Procedures. If we manage to get this done today, we can be proud of ourselves. Here take a look at this," he said. He pushed a copy of the check-list into Stanfort's hand. "During the night I've spent a lot of time thinking. I'm convinced that splitting up the tasks of flying the plane between the two of us is the best thing we can do."

Stanfort listened attentively.

"I can't teach you all you have to know in just one or two days," Oviero explained. "This plane is much too complex in comparison with the Chipmunk."

Knowing that Joey was right, Stanfort nodded.

"Therefore we'll do it as follows. I'll handle the starting of the engines and the power settings for take off, cruise, descent and landing. The Skyvan has a fixed landing gear, so we don't need to worry about that. You, Anthony, will only handle the stick, flaps and rudder."

"That already sounds complicated enough," answered Stanfort. Feeling slightly lost when he looked at the big array of instruments and handles that covered the control panels in front of him, he moaned. "Even the stick looks different to the joystick of the Chipmunk. It looks more like an oval steering-wheel."

"That's no problem," chuckled Oviero. "It's much easier to work with a wheel than with a stick, look..." He rolled the control wheel to the left and pointed his index finger to the left wingtip. "Look, left aileron up, and right aileron down."

"And when I invert the movement," completed Stanfort, rolling the control wheel over to the right. "The right aileron goes up and the left one down."

"That's it," confirmed Oviero. "You've got it."

They spent the whole morning reading chapters in the Flight Handbook. Stanfort let his hands run over the different handles and flight controls, repeating the vital actions over and over until they became routine. What he lacked in experience, he made up for in pure determination.

"What's the speed for the take-off?" questioned Oviero.

"70 knots," replied Stanfort, "... and the cruise speed is 130 knots."

"What is the landing speed?"

Before Oviero had finished asking the question Stanfort cut in: "80 knots, with the flaps in the full down position."

"What are the vital actions in case of fire warning on the left engine?"

"Close the left throttle," said Stanfort. "Shut down the engine and push the right rudder to compensate for the asymmetric thrust." He hesitated a second. "Finally push the button on the left fire extinguisher to kill the fire."

"Is that all?" prodded Oviero.

"I guess so," said Stanfort falteringly. "No wait, I also have to adjust the rudder trim against the asymmetric thrust and continue the flight on one engine. Maximum flight altitude 7,000 feet, depending on the weight of the plane."

"Good," admired Oviero, grinning widely. "Perfect, I really believe that we'll make it."

In the afternoon, after a quick lunch, they continued the cockpit training. Finally satisfied with Stanfort's work, Oviero gestured to a couple of mechanics to push the Skyvan out in front of the hangar. The beautiful blue sky of the morning had disappeared. Instead, a line of thunderclouds had begun to darken the horizon to the west of the field. The eastern skyline had already vanished behind a bank of low stratus clouds. Oviero briefly studied the movement of the clouds. "Hmmm," he said, pointing to the west. "The way the wind is blowing, it will take at least two hours before that storm will drift over the field. Time enough for you to get the feel of the plane and make a couple of circuits and 'touch and go' landings."

He had little doubt in his mind that one or two circuits would reveal immediately whether Stanfort was capable of doing the job.

Oviero's simple words suddenly brought it home to Stanfort that the moment of actually flying the Skyvan had arrived. Instantly his hands felt moist. Accompanied by one of the ground mechanics, he made a walk-around inspection of the Skyvan to make sure that all rudders and ailerons were moving freely. No oil leaks, no damage to the flaps and no dents in the propellers.

While Stanfort slid back into his seat and adjusted the height of his chair, Oviero opened his side window. He looked carefully around to make sure that nobody was standing in the vicinity of the propellers and pushed the starter button. With a soft whining noise, the left propeller began to turn, first slowly, then faster and faster until the noise turned into a high whistle and the blades of the prop became an invisible blur. As the white needles on the counters stabilized at 1,200 revolutions per minute, Oviero flipped the generator switch on. He repeated the procedure for the second engine. Outwardly completely relaxed and whistling to himself, his eyes remained fixed on the engine instruments to catch any malfunction or excessive temperature. "Look," he said finally, sweeping his index finger over a row of instruments. "After starting the engines, Anthony, you have to check the oil pressure, vacuum pressure, fuel pressure and the generator amperage, understood?"

Lost in the complexity of the procedures and slightly numb with the amount of information he had to absorb, Stanfort nodded automatically. Noticing the stress that marked the face of his friend, Oviero gave him a friendly tap on the shoulder. "From now on it's easier," he promised. "Go on, taxi out and let's have some fun."

Stanfort released the brakes and allowed the Skyvan to roll slowly forward. Even the simple manoeuvre of taxiing the plane took some adjusting to. He was used to the Chipmunk, a tail-dragger. To steer the Chipmunk on the ground he only had to push either the left or the right wheel brake. Simple enough. The Skyvan however was equipped with a tricycle landing gear. The direction had to be controlled by means of a wheel - similar to the steering-wheel of a car - that was built into the side wall of the cockpit. After an initial spell of overcontrolling with exaggerated steering inputs and lurching drunkenly from left to right across the runway, Stanfort got the hang of it. "It feels almost like driving my old Mercedes," he shouted above the whistling noise of the engines. He lined the Skyvan up on the exact centre of the runway. Suddenly, he felt again that strange and hollow feeling in his stomach. Admitting to Oviero that he was feeling jittery was not on. He was much too proud for that. Hoping that Joey would not notice the slight tremor that distorted his voice, he announced: "I think I'm going to like this plane."

The reply came high above the whistling noise of the engines, "All set, Anthony. Are you ready to go?"

His fingers wound tight around the black plastic of the steering-wheel, Stanfort confirmed: "Yes, I'm ready."

Slowly, Oviero nudged the throttles forward. "Remember," he stressed once more. "When I call out 'V1', you have to pull the stick gently backwards until the nose of the plane reaches an attitude of 10 degrees above the horizon. Not more, otherwise the plane might stall, and we don't want *that* to happen at low altitude, do we?"

In reply, Stanfort shook his head and released the brakes. The Skyvan shot forward, the acceleration so fast that Stanfort had the impression he was trying to run behind a racing car, quite unable to catch up with it.

"Keep it straight!" yelled Oviero. To emphasize his words, he hammered the coaming of the dashboard with his hands. Stanfort kicked the rudder pedals and stabilized the plane on the faint white line that marked the centre of the runway. Too soon as far as he was concerned, he heard Oviero shout: "V1".

Immediately, Stanfort pulled the stick back. The nose shot up, much too high. "Ease the stick a little bit forward," shouted Oviero. The rumbling noises of the tyres against the tarmac fell away, instead came the sound of the air stream around the windshield. Suddenly Stanfort jumped, startled by a savage howl from Oviero.

"Lower that nose! Do you really want to stall the plane."

At two thousand feet above the ground, sweat running down his spine, Stanfort wound the trim a couple of turns forward to maintain the same height. Oviero went through the ritual of pulling the engine controls to the cruise power settings. Stanfort adjusted the trim.

"Make a few turns to the left and the right to get the feeling of the plane," Oviero instructed.

A little more relaxed now, Stanfort rolled the ailerons and banked the plane to the left, almost immediately reversing the turn. "It's a little slower in response than the Chipmunk, but I like it," he shouted cheerfully as he felt his confidence return. Deep below he saw the U-turn of the Luachimo River, the water tainted a muddy brown and red. To the south stretched the red scar of the open mining area, where bulldozers were scraping the surface of the earth to expose the diamond layers. A little further to the left lay the factory buildings where the diamond-rich soil was washed and sieved to extract the valuable stones from tons and tons of worthless rubble.

"Hey, Anthony..."

Stanfort suddenly realized that Joey had been calling him several times. "Sorry," he said apologetically. "I was a little distracted. The view from up here is so beautiful."

"That's not good enough, man," scolded Oviero. "You have to concentrate on your job." The twinkle in his eyes made a mockery of his anger. "I wouldn't like to hit the landscape because you are floating away on a cloud." Grinning, Oviero pulled the throttle levers back. "Time to show me how you land this plane."

Stanfort banked the Skyvan into a shallow turn to the left. Fighting with the controls to hold the plane in the extended centreline of the runway, he pointed the nose to the beginning of the landing strip. Oviero noticed the tight line of Stanfort's jaw. To relax him, he started to talk him through the landing procedure. "Good Anthony, you're doing fine. Keep the nose a little higher and roll in a little more trim to release the back pressure on the stick."

All went well until they were a few feet above the ground. Stanfort saw the ground coming near, but used to the smaller size of the Chipmunk which sat much closer to the ground, he still felt comfortably high when the landing gear hit the surface with a teeth-shattering jolt. Oviero was ready for it. He rammed the throttles forward, shouting: "Overshoot, pull the stick back and go around!"

The second landing was more controlled, the third acceptable. With the fourth landing, Stanfort managed to grease the tyres smoothly against the rough concrete of the runway. Oviero opened the throttles again. "Jesus, Anthony, that was beautiful," he said admiringly.

A blustery updraft battered the wings of the Skyvan. Looking out of the cockpit, Oviero noticed that the line of thunderclouds, which earlier on had been hanging far to the west, had moved closer towards the airfield. They still managed to make a couple more circuits, alternatively reducing the power on the left or right engine to simulate an engine failure. As if a tap had suddenly been turned on, the skies broke open, beating a wild torrent of rain against the windshield. The sun hid her face behind angry clouds. Here and there, a bolt of lightning drew a crooked shaft of light through the sky. Immediately, the visibility fell to less than one mile.

Stanfort, sensing the urgency of getting the plane on the ground, kept a sharp eye on the threshold of the runway and pulled the Skyvan into a steep descending turn to the left. Just before touchdown, the first gusts of the tropical storm grabbed hold of the plane and violently rocked the wings. In spite of that, Stanfort managed to plant the wheels firmly in a positive landing on the ground. Without bothering to use the brakes, he let the plane roll to the end of the runway and swung it into the safety of the hangar. "That was bloody fantastic!" he yelled wildly, his voice high with excitement and knowing that he had done rather well. "I loved every second of it. Especially that last bit."

"I'm delighted with your performance," declared Oviero. "Considering you're a novice on heavy aeroplanes, I honestly think you're doing a fine job. In fact, I feel that your performance is good enough to program the flight to Luanda for tomorrow."

Stanfort felt himself glow with pride. "... But I still have a lot to learn about handling the plane on one engine," he muttered modestly.

"True," Oviero replied. "However, if that happens, you won't have to deal with it on your own. I'll be with you all the way. If something unanticipated comes up, I'll tell you what to do!" He laughed carelessly. "Not that I expect something to go wrong, Anthony."

The rain persisted doggedly throughout the rest of the afternoon and evening. Stanfort and Oviero sat together on the balcony of the villa under the refreshing breeze provided by three wooden ceiling fans, the airflow helping to keep the mosquitoes away. As the centre of a squall line drifted to the east, the long echo of a thunderclap rolled away through the valley. On the low table in front of Oviero lay Michelin Map 155 of Central Africa, opened at the pages showing the land between Portugalia and Luanda.

"There are two different routes we can follow," he specified. "The southern track over Angolan territory, via Saurimo, then west over Malanje to Luanda. As the crow flies, a total distance of 700 nautical miles." He scratched his chin, a pensive look in his eyes. "That distance is too great for a direct flight. To get the range, we shall have to top up the fuel tanks during the flight, and that means loading a couple of fuel barrels in the cargo hold, a wobble pump and a set of rubber hoses."

To have some time to consider the second possibility, Oviero poured himself another glass of wine. After taking a sip, he returned his attention to the map and drew with his pencil a second track, a line that ran almost due west from Portugalia to Luanda. "That's the second possibility," he revealed, a conspiratorial tone in his voice. "That distance is only 480 nautical miles, well within the range of the Skyvan." A sudden boyish smile curled the corners of his mouth. "The first part of that route runs over Angolan territory. The second part follows the border between Angola and Zaire. Then, a slight problem arises!"

His face clearly outlined by the light of the anti-mosquito candles, he tapped the map with the point of his pencil. "There, we have to cross a small enclave of Zairean airspace, in the extreme south of that country."

"But, Joey, we can't fly that route. Zaire doesn't have diplomatic relations with the communist Government in Angola," Stanfort cut in. "They'll never give us the permission to overfly their territory."

"Who said anything about permission?" Oviero argued. "That part of Zaire is an empty quarter, nothing but bush and swamps. Hardly anybody lives there."

To emphasize his words, he banged his fist against the table top. "We have to take that second route, Anthony. I know, the Council in Luanda expects us to take extra fuel to fly the longer distance, but installing two barrels of kerosene and a set of old-fashioned wobble pumps is totally unrealistic. Who's going to handle the wobble pumps anyway?" Oviero didn't wait for Stanfort to reply. "You?" he asked rhetorically. "You are supposed to fly the plane... Me? I can hardly move around on a piece of level ground, let alone in an aircraft that's jumping and shaking in thermal currents. Believe me, Anthony, compared with the nuisance of installing an additional fuel system and having to operate it, flying without permission over an empty stretch of Zaire is a very small risk to take."

"What about the Zaire Border Guards?" Stanfort threw in. "Don't we risk being shot at?"

"You forget something," replied Oviero arrogantly. "I was trained by the Air Force as a fighter pilot. Before I joined DIANGOL, I was based in Huambo, flying F-104s. One of the things I remember distinctly from briefings during that time is that the Zaire Border guards don't possess Radar. Consequently, they won't even know that we are violating their airspace."

A sudden outburst of static discharge flickered like a giant Saint-Elmo fire between the clouds, throwing blue and white coloured flashes on the bushes in the garden. Oviero slammed his hand on Stanfort's back. "You're right, amigo," he said, smiling. "We should not be flying over Zaire. Therefore, to avoid detection, we must maintain a height of at least thirteen thousand feet above the ground."

Stanfort knew that it was useless to argue with Joey when he was in one of his exuberant and overconfident moods. Instead of making any remark, he stared blankly into the night and sipped his drink.

The heavy thunderstorm slowly drifted away. The intense activity of lightning and thunder gradually died out. The torrential rains gave way for a monotonous lazy drizzle. The only sounds to be heard were the loud croaking noises of bullfrogs by the river, the dripping of water from the overhanging roof of the balcony and the soft creaking sound of the wooden ceiling fans.

"That route over Zaire," Oviero remarked, "is actually a very easy route to fly. Look." Again, he drew his pencil over the track on the map and made the original line much bolder.

"From Portugalia we fly to Kahemba. Kahemba is just over the border with Zaire, so by that time we should be at 13,000 feet. From there, we'll fly straight across the high-plateau to the Rio Cuango and the Guillaume Waterfalls." He turned around to face Stanfort. "Have you ever seen those Falls?"

Stanfort shook his head.

"Well, you'll see them tomorrow. They are not as big or as spectacular as the Victoria Falls, but they are quite a sight."

Won over by Oviero's obvious determination and enthusiasm, Stanfort smiled. "I'm sure they'll make an excellent reference point for our navigation."

"The best thing of all," concluded Oviero, "is that the flight time to Luanda will be only three hours and forty minutes. And remember, Anthony, in Luanda, Manuela will be waiting for you."

Stanfort could hardly remember the last time he and Manuela had been together. Instantly butterflies started to flutter in his stomach. He reached for the bottle and poured the wine that remained into their glasses.

"Let's drink to that," he said, handing a full glass to Joey. "To the success of the flight."

"I'll drink to that as well," said Oviero. Under his breath, he added: "May God help us!"

19 November 1975

Shortly after dawn, Stanfort was out at the airfield to prepare the Skyvan for the flight to Luanda. Leaving the refuelling to the ground-mechanics, he took a neatly folded navigation chart and placed it in the pocket beneath the left side window. The flight plan, with the different headings for the legs of the trip and the timings, he put in his transparent plastic knee-board.

From the cargo hold behind him came the joyful voices of the cargo handlers who were busy stowing a heavy crate, marked with bold black letters:

MOTORPARTS
DIANGOL
DUNDO

"Make sure you tie that crate down," Stanfort yelled over his shoulder. "I don't want that weight flying through the cabin in the event we hit turbulence."

As soon as the mechanics reported that the fueltanks were full, Stanfort made a careful inspection of the aircraft. Happy with the result, he jumped in his car and rushed back to Portugalia to pick up Oviero. At 8 o'clock they were sitting in the cockpit. Anthony Stanfort stowed his pilot's case by his seat and plugged in his headset.

Oviero looked back to the big crate that stood prominently in the middle of the cargofloor. "What the hell is that?" he queried, raising his eyebrows.

"Oh that," laughed Stanfort. "That belongs to the power-generating plant. It's one of the diesel engines they use to run the big generators, and it's due for overhaul. I thought, since we are going to Luanda, we may as well take it with us and do something useful for DIANGOL. Because these diamonds here..." As he said this, Stanfort gave a meaningful tap on the leather flight case he had placed next to his chair. "These diamonds are destined for Angola's dear President. DIANGOL won't get a penny."

Unhurriedly, they went through the starting procedure and took off. Fifteen minutes later they reached an altitude of 13,000 feet. The sky was pure azure and void of all clouds. Without any apparent effort, the Garrett turbines maintained a comfortable speed of 130 knots. They flew over the valleys of the Chikapa, the Luele and the Luxito rivers. The banks of the rivers and the slopes of the hills were clearly visible in the early sunlight, the waters still hidden under a milky shroud of fog.

"All those rivers flow almost exactly north-south," remarked Stanfort. "Navigating here is so easy that I don't need a compass. As long as I cross all the rivers at the same angle, I must arrive in Kahemba. Even a child could do that."

Slightly drowsy from the monotonous droning of the engines, Oviero didn't bother to give a reply, but clapped his hands in a mocking gesture.

Exactly on time, they passed over the small town of Kahemba. Seen from 13,000 feet, it appeared to be a motley collection of huts, each one of them surrounded by a wall of mud to enclose the cattle. Stanford gently swung the Skyvan to the left, until the needle of the gyrocompass indicated 258 degrees. "Next leg, one hour and five minutes," he said, punching the button on his chronometer and looking down to find his first reference point, the intersection of the road to Mutombo and the northern arm of the Rio Cuango.

From this height, although the plane moved at a speed of 130 knots, he had the impression that they were hanging still in the air and that it was the earth that was slowly rotating beneath them.

Watching the rising column of smoke from a bush-fire, Stanfort concluded that the winds were stronger than expected and their direction slightly more from the south west. Consequently, he turned the nose of the Skyvan slightly to the left to compensate for the additional drift.

To check their track, Oviero turned the dial on his Aristo computer to verify the computations. "Well done, Anthony," he admitted. "I see I can leave my entire existence safely in your hands. Just keep the plane straight and level and with the right side up." He sighed contentedly and wriggled himself into a more comfortable position in his seat.

A thin layer of ground haze came with the rising heat of the sun. Stanfort concentrated on the few landmarks he could still see. Initially, the road that ran from Kahemba to the west was a well-maintained road, clearly visible from the air. Gradually, this road became narrower, until finally it petered out into a slim trail that curved aimlessly through the marshy grassland.

To the left of the Skyvan, the big white canopy of a bulging Cumulus cloud rose rapidly in the air. Three large birds, African Eagles, circled effortlessly with widespread wings in the thermals. Stanfort felt a little twinge of jealousy. To be able to fly like that, on your own wings and without an engine. Admiring the smooth and easy movements of the birds, Stanfort thoughts went back to his time in the Flying Club, when he used to fly gliders as a hobby.

Oviero's angry voice shook him out of his daydream. "Watch your height, Anthony. You're screwing up!"

Stanfort quickly made a quick scan of the instruments. Instead of 13,000 feet, the needle of the altimeter indicated 14,000 feet! Lost in his reverie, he hadn't noticed that he had allowed the Skyvan to follow the climb of the eagles. Rather self-consciously, he rolled the trim wheel a fraction of a degree forward to let the Skyvan sink gently back to its normal cruising altitude.

As the Skyvan progressed to the west, the growing heat of the day pushed more and more clouds in the air and the weather became heavier. Turning to the left to avoid a build-up, then again deviating to the right to avoid a large thunderstorm, Stanfort managed to maintain his original track. Minute after long minute went by. At last, he saw the cloud of moisture that marked the place where the waters of the Rio Cuango made their plunge over the Guillaume Falls into the lower basin that led to the Zaire river.

"Hey, Joey," he announced. "I think I can see the location of the waterfall."

Oviero leaned forward in his seat and studied the clouds. Next he looked at the surrounding landscape. "Yes," he replied finally. "I recognize this area. The Falls are another two or three miles ahead. It's a pity though that the cloud cover is so intense, otherwise you'd see an awesome sight."

"Correct me if I'm wrong, Joey, but according to the map, we are now out of Zaire. In that case, can't we descend to a lower altitude and make a couple of turns over the Falls? Who knows when I will get another chance like this?"

"You're right, Anthony. Why the hell not." Throwing all caution to the wind, Oviero pulled the throttles back and allowed the Skyvan to sink steeply to a lower altitude. "Just aim at the centre of the spray-cloud," he told Stanfort. "We can get the most sensational view from there."

By now the sun stood high in the sky. Its light transformed the river into a stream of molten gold. The spray which hung over the Guillaume Falls looked like a painting of a thousand rainbows. As they entered the cloud, fingers of moisture ran over the windshield.

Stanfort descended slowly, maintaining speed and heading. At six thousand feet, the Skyvan broke through the base of the cloud. Beneath them lay the magnificent spectacle of the Falls. On their left, on the high plateau, the wide and muddy waters of the river ran slow and calm. On their right, where the bed of the river flowed through a very narrow gorge, the waters became a savage torrent. Compensating in height and speed for the lack of width, they cascaded over the steep walls of the escarpment and dropped for more than five hundred feet before reaching the bottom of the valley. Stanfort swung the Skyvan around in a succession of steep turns. Forgetting the time, they admired the view and enjoyed the spectacle. Behind the waterfalls lay a dense rain forest.

Oviero leaned over, intensively studying something he saw between the giant trees.

"What's that there?" he yelled, pointing. "There between the trees on the Angolan side of the Falls, by the side of that jungle road."

"I don't see a thing," answered Stanfort. "It's most probably the reflection of the sun in a bend of the river."

"Hell, no! It isn't," contested Oviero. "I'm sure that for a moment I saw the silhouette of a military scout car. I don't trust it, Anthony! So close to the border with Zaire, it could very well be a group of guerrillas who have just crossed the border." Suddenly sure they were in danger, he threw the throttles forward. "Quick," he yelled. "Let's get out of here."

His instinct as a former fighter pilot did not betray him. They were in peril, but his urge to get away came too late! Just as Stanfort swung the Skyvan in a steep turn to the right, Oviero saw a burst of smoke. Something rose out of the dense foliage of the trees, the trail climbing steeply towards the Skyvan. "Shit," he shouted, swearing at his own stupidity. "The bastards have fired a Stinger rocket."

A second burst of smoke rose up from the forest. "Another Stinger!" Oviero yelled. Violently, he pushed the stick forward and dived the Skyvan in the opposite direction. The first Stinger passed far to the left and lost contact. The second Stinger locked on to the exhaust of the right engine. It hit the leading edge of the wing where the engine was attached to the main spar.

The rocket exploded with a deafening bang.

The blast ripped the engine out of its bracket and threw the heavy mass of metal into space. Pieces of aluminium and shrapnel tore holes in the fuel tanks. A flood of kerosene gushed out of the perforated tanks, forming a widening trail of mist that hung like a grey vortex in the sky. A few pieces of metal found their way to the cockpit and shattered the right windscreen in a shower of fragmented perspex.

"God, Oh God," whimpered Stanfort as the Skyvan flipped over in a spiralling dive. Using all his brute strength on the elevator and the rudder, Stanfort was able to bring the nose up. "Joey, help me, please," he screamed. "Tell me what I have to do." Reaching over, he shook Oviero violently by his left shoulder.

Oviero would never reply.

A sharp point of shrapnel had torn through his brain, exiting his skull through the socket of his left eye and covering the instrument panel with a slimy layer of blood. Stanfort's frantic movements made Joey's body roll over to the left. His empty eye socket stared Stanfort blindly in the face. "Oh, my God," he shouted, suppressing a sudden urge to vomit. "Shit, Joey! What do I do now, and how can I do it without your help?"

In shock and unable to absorb the violent death of his friend, Stanfort yelled and cursed. A constant stream of sweat dripped from his forehead, the back of his shirt stuck against the leather of the seat. His left leg, under the strain of preventing the plane from falling down in a spiral, quivered like an arrow. Almost subconsciously, he was aware that he had lost one of the engines, and he tried desperately to remember the vital actions in case of engine failure, but his mind seemed to be blank.

An uncontrollable wave of panic enveloped him. Stanfort wanted to jump out of the plane, even without a parachute. Just to be away from the horror of it all.

Slowly, he started to realize that he had to get a grip on himself. Then and only then would he be able to control the plane and prevent a crash. His instinct for self-preservation took over. "Come on, man," he said loudly. "Remember the drill. You know what to do, you did it several times yesterday."

Suddenly, it hit him. "Adjust the trim to release the pressure on the rudder."

He turned the little knob of the rudder trim a couple of turns to the left. It worked. The pressure was decreasing. He turned the knob a little more, until the terrible forces on the pedal disappeared.

Next, he became aware of the roaring noise of the air that came howling through the gaping hole in the windshield.

"That must create an enormous resistance," he mumbled, pushing the throttles forward. He let his eyes fall on the instruments. "Speed 90 knots. All right. Height 4,000 feet. Not bad, but I have to remain on the north side of the ridge. Fuel..." That again brought a wild surge of panic, the needles indicating an empty tank on the right, the left side barely containing one quarter of a tank. Not nearly enough to reach halfway to Luanda! "God damn it," Stanfort screamed. "That rocket must have made a sieve of the wingtanks." In a reflex, his left hand reached for the radio transmitter.

"Luanda, Luanda," he shouted in the microphone. "Mayday, Mayday. Badly damaged by rocket fire in the vicinity of the Guillaume Falls. Need assistance urgently."

He released the transmit-switch, hoping for a reply. Not even the sound of static filled his headset. It was only after his third attempt to reach Luanda that he noticed an enormous hole in the radio panel, with a large piece of shrapnel sticking out of it. No wonder he got no response.

Now that he had the plane under control, Stanfort didn't want to give up, but to land in this area was impossible. Below him, there was nothing but the green canopy of the rain forest and the tree-lined banks of the Rio Cuango. The shores of the lake were excluded, as they were to close to the place were the guerrillas were hiding, and in Tembo, the nearest village, there was no airfield.

Stanfort racked his brain for an alternative. Where in God's name was he going to find a place to land this wreck of a plane?

Desperate to find a wide and long sand bank, Stanfort switched his attention to the bottom of the Guillaume Falls, where the raging waters again became a river. His hope was futile. In the rainy season, the Rio Cuango ran at least fifteen feet higher than during the rest of the year. Instead of discovering sandy banks, Stanfort saw nothing but a truculent muddy flow bordered by a dense growth of man-high reeds and mangroves.

Ditching the plane in the river was not a very good idea either. The mangroves were the habitat of the reputable Cuango Crocodiles, whose tanned skins were very much in demand by leather workers in Luanda.

"Crocodiles!"

Wasn't there something Oviero had told him once about a landing strip here in the area, just to the north of the Guillaume Falls. A place that, years ago, had been used by DC3s who brought parties of hunters to the swamps of the Rio Cuango.

He recalled Oviero mentioning that the landing strip lay not only immediately next to the river, but also conveniently close to a small village where the hunters hired trackers to help them stalk the crocodiles. "If a DC3 could land there, a Skyvan should have no problem at all. What was the name of that place again?" Looking around in the cockpit to locate his map, Stanfort searched between the two seats, by the trim wheel. The map wasn't there.

Reluctantly, he looked over to Oviero's side of the cockpit. The map wasn't there either. Worrying that it had been sucked out through the broken windshield, Stanfort anxiously searched the rest of the cockpit. His heart lifted as he suddenly recalled that, when approaching the Guillaume falls, he had stowed his navigation equipment in the side pocket under the left window.

He retrieved the chart. To prevent it from blowing away on the hurricane-like wind that howled through the cockpit, he stuck it under the plastic cover of his knee board and traced the route he had been following since leaving Kahemba. Finding the Rio Cuango was easy. Following the course of the river, his fingers moved slowly upwards. Barely 30 miles to the north lay a tiny village. "Massau," he read, spelling the name with his lips. "Yes, that was the name Joey had mentioned."

However, in the vicinity of Massau, there was no sign of a landing strip.

Desperately, Stanfort moved his eyes further north on the map. For hundreds of miles, he found only virgin marshlands and unbroken forests. Disappointment rising bitterly in his throat, he checked the date on the map. "August 1965..."

Due to the guerrilla problems, the damn chart had not been updated for more than ten years. In all that time, twenty bush strips could have been built! With a rush of confidence and nowhere else to go, Stanfort decided to believe what Oviero had told him. If there was a strip, it had to be in Massau. Carefully avoiding the position where they had been shot at, he made a wide turn to the north and started to follow the eastern shore of the river. His eyes aching from the harsh glare of the sun in the water, he tried to match each bend with a position on the map. Now and again, he lost sight of the river when the shores came close together between two towering escarpments of grey-brown rock.

Stanfort was not too worried about that. He remembered Joey mentioning that the position of the landing strip was close to a place where the Rio Cuango threw its waters between two narrow shoulders of rocks. After that followed a succession of rapids, then the river widened out and became a big lake that looked like a giant tadpole, its head pointing to the south and its tapering tail curving away to the north-west. It was just not possible to miss a lake that was six hundred feet wide and several miles long.

At the reduced airspeed of 90 knots, it took a little over twenty-five minutes to reach the vicinity of Massau. Far away to the left, Stanfort could see a tiny village, like a circular smudge of brown in the green of the forest. However, there was no sign of a lake. Nor was there a landing strip. A quick glance at the fuel indicator made his heart race faster. Barely forty minutes of fuel left, maybe slightly less!

Stanfort considered the possibility that the village he saw was not Massau, but another village, so tiny that it was not even marked on the map. He decided to track for ten minutes further northbound. As the time wore on and the lake remained out of view, doubt began to eat away at his self-confidence. Finally, he had to admit that according to his watch, he was too far to the north of Massau and that in spite of all his careful exploring, he had missed the lake. Resolutely, he turned the plane around in a wide and flat turn and retraced his track, flying southbound along the western shore. This time, to make sure he didn't lose sight of the river, he descended to a lower altitude.

Alarmed by the noise of the engine, a flock of flamingos launched themselves in a hasty rush before rising majestically into the air, the pink colour of their wings in sharp contrast with the muddy water of the river. To avoid colliding with the swarm of birds, Stanfort remained at an altitude of 1,000 feet. Rounding another curve, the shores of the river drew apart and Stanfort found himself in front of a vast expanse of water. To his right lay the tiny village he had seen before. Looking to the left, he discovered that the eastern bank of the lake was a near vertical wall of rocks, which rose more than five hundred feet above the surface of the water. Stanfort immediately realized that on his first northbound course, the rock wall had acted as a screen, preventing him from spotting the lake. He turned the Skyvan to the right and searched the western bank for any signs of a runway.

The shore of the lake was merely a couple of feet wide, the sand concealed by thickets of reeds. Behind the shore, the land was flat and dotted with acacia trees, thorny bushes and grass. Through it, clearly outlined, ran a long line that was much too straight to be made by nature. "Yes," Stanfort yelled at the top of his voice. "That's it!"

As he came closer, he saw that it was a landing strip, a length of laterite coloured earth, at least 5,000 feet long and 100 feet wide. To Stanfort, who had been expecting to find nothing but a sandy trail more or less clear of bushes and rocks, it looked as big as the main runway in Luanda.

Turning a few low circuits around the field, he made a careful study of the strip and the surroundings. The strip looked good. His elation at having found the strip changed suddenly into a spasm of panic.

"Will I be able to land this wreck on my own without Joey's assistance?" Stanfort asked himself. Reluctant to leave the relative safety of altitude for the dangers of the approach, Stanfort flew another circle, and another, telling himself that he had to make sure that there were no obstacles on the runway or holes in the surface. Deep in his guts however, he knew that all that circling around was nothing but a delaying tactic, inspired by fear. Hastily checking the fuel indicator, he observed that the needle was hovering close to the zero mark.

"Come on man, you can do it," he muttered. "You must do it! Postponing any longer is foolish, unless you prefer to run out of fuel."

He looked around for the check-list, but the check-list was gone. It lay somewhere in the forest at the foot of the Guillaume Falls, together with the right engine and the broken perspex of the windscreen. Racking his brain, Stanfort tried to remember the vital actions Oviero had forced him to memorize, but the roaring sound of the air streaming through the shattered windscreen and his lack of confidence made it impossible to concentrate.

Looking for help, he instinctively glanced over to the right. Oviero couldn't help, but merely the fact of seeing him gave Stanfort some strength. It was as if he heard Joey shout: "Get a grip on yourself, Anthony. You don't need a check-list to fly this plane. Look for the basics."

To find a clue as to what to do, Stanfort started to scan all the instruments in the cockpit. The good engine, he didn't have to bother about. The propeller control was already in flight-fine pitch and the wheels were down, because the Skyvan had a fixed landing gear.

Suddenly he knew. "The flaps!"

He needed the flaps to reduce the airspeed for the landing. Locking his eyes on the indicator, Stanfort reached over and pushed the spoon-shaped handle of the flap control down. The needle on the indicator obstinately remained at zero. Stanfort tapped the instrument with his index finger. The needle didn't move.

Throwing a glance over his shoulder to verify the position of the wing flaps, he noticed that they were still fully retracted. "Damn it," he cursed. "The bloody system must have been shot to pieces."

Having no flaps was nothing less than a disaster. He would have to approach at a much higher speed than normal. That would make the landing far more risky.

"Christ," he whimpered. "How is this going to end?"

His hands lay slippery with sweat on the stick. Again, Stanfort felt that ghastly sensation of cramp in his bowels. The fuel instrument told him that the tank was empty. "The bloody engine must be running on fumes," he swore. Whether he wanted to bring the plane down or not, he had to do it now. Tightly gripping the stick, he swung the crippled Skyvan in the direction of the landing strip. In his urge to make the turn, he overcontrolled the rudder. The nose of the Skyvan yawed wildly over the horizon. Frantically, Stanfort groped for the knob of the rudder trim and adjusted the setting.

By now so single-mindedly involved in holding the plane stable, he failed to reduce the power at the start of the descent. With the nose pointing down towards the ground, the airspeed began to build up rapidly to 90 knots, then 100 knots.

As he came lower, Stanfort got the impression that the landing strip was covered with water, reflecting the sunlight as if it was a giant mirror, a phenomenon caused by the heat of the sun warming up the ground and making the thin layer of air above it vibrate in rising heat waves.

Cursing, he squeezed his eyes half closed against the glare and concentrated on keeping the nose of the Skyvan exactly on the beginning of the strip.

Unnoticed, the needle on the airspeed indicator rose to 120 knots. The Skyvan was now merely three hundred feet above the ground. Fighting with the rudders and the stick to keep the plane in the extended centreline of the runway, Stanfort forgot all about speed and engine power and trim settings. The noise of the wind flowing in through the window rose to a high pitched wail. It finally dawned on Stanfort that something was wrong.

"That noise," he thought, "where is that coming from?" He sneaked a look inside the cockpit and let his eyes sweep the flight instruments. As he noticed the airspeed he twitched fiercely. Immediately, he realized that he had fallen into the same trap as some student pilots, too much concentration on what was happening outside and not enough attention to the instruments inside.

It flashed through his mind that with a speed of 120 knots, he would never be able to put the Skyvan on the ground. His breathing became fast and difficult. Swearing loudly at his own foolishness, Stanfort jerked the throttle to idle and kicked the rudders neutral. Simultaneously his right hand rolled the rudder trim to zero. Finally, in a desperate effort to reduce the speed, he pulled the control wheel back.

"Where is that damned runway now," he cried.

The threshold lay directly beneath the nose of the plane. Afraid of overshooting the runway and not willing to go around to try another approach, he gave a wild shove on the control wheel and forced the nose down. Instead of settling down in a landing attitude, the Skyvan, its airspeed still well above 110 knots, kept floating on a cushion of air a few feet above the ground.

Stanfort saw the end of the runway come swiftly near. Terrified of running out of runway and landing into the lake, he desperately rammed the stick forward. The nose wheel hit the ground with a colossal bump. The shock caused the plane to jump steeply into the air. Stanfort remembered what had happened the day before, during his first landing with Joey, when he had made a similar bump.

"Overshoot!" he yelled. "Make an overshoot!" He threw the throttle of the left engine forward. The nose of the Skyvan flicked viciously to the right. It was only then that Stanfort recalled that he had to use the left rudder to correct the effect of asymmetric thrust.

His action came too late. Propelled by the left engine that was howling under its full power setting, the plane rolled over with a startling suddenness. Its forward speed carried the plane far out over the river. The badly damaged main spar of the right wing could not sustain the forces of inverted flight. The wing broke off. Spinning around its top axle, the Skyvan dropped into the river with a tremendous splash. Under the terrible force of the crash, Stanford's seat belts broke and he was thrown forward, crushing his skull against the lower edge of the instrument panel.

The force of the crash also caused the big cargo door in the rear of the aircraft to break open. The Skyvan floated away on the current until it hit a row of submerged rocks. Eventually, the weight of the water that filled the cargo hold became too heavy for the little buoyancy that remained in the fuel tanks and the Skyvan disappeared under the surface of the lake, taking the mutilated bodies of Oviero and Stanfort down with it to the gloomy depths.

Fifty feet down, the wreck settled sideways on to the bottom, the broken part of the right wing squashed beneath the bulk of the fuselage. A long silvery stream of air bubbles rose swiftly to the surface. As the light but steady current took hold of the left wing, the fuselage swung around until the nose of the plane pointed upstream towards the springs of the Rio Cuango. The river water flowed in through the broken windshield and out again through the gaping hole of the open cargo door, taking all that lay loose in the aircraft with it.

Stanfort's flight case, which had been standing by the left side of his seat, tumbled upside down. One by one, the bags of diamonds slipped out of the case. A couple of bags got stuck behind the metal supports of Oviero's seat. Other bags were slowly pushed out of the fuselage and dropped down to the muddy bottom of the river. Some of the bags contained a little more air than the others. They rose to the surface and drifted away. During the next two days, spills of kerosene and oil continued to float to the surface. After a few more days, the spills stopped and the final traces of the crash disappeared.

The Rio Cuango, hiding the terrible secret of the sunken Skyvan beneath its brown-red waters, continued its journey to the basin of the Zaire river.

Luanda, 19 November 1975

In Luanda, they had received a HF radio call from Dundo with the message that the Skyvan had left at ten past 8 a.m.

At first, when the plane did not arrive at the Expected Time of Arrival (ETA), nobody was overly worried. After all, this was Angola in the first days of its rather volatile Independence, where the distances from one side of the country to the other were enormous and communication between cities almost non-existent.

As the hours passed by without any sign or news of the flight, the atmosphere in the board room of DIANGOL became heavy with apprehension.

Vigo was the first to voice his opinion. "They must have landed somewhere to avoid a line of thunderstorms."

"I thought they had long range HF radio on board," countered Roberto Cabral. "In case of a diversion, I'm sure they would have called us."

"No, Comrade," replied Vigo. "Heavy thunderstorms are full of lightning. Radio waves can't pass through that electric barrier."

"Maybe their radio broke down," suggested Manuela. Unable to stop thinking about the risks involved in the flight, she felt something like terror clutching her heart. "Or they had another, more serious problem," she cried fiercely. "Maybe they had to make an emergency landing in the bush. Maybe they are hurt."

General Pia, who generally judged other people's integrity by his own standards, shrugged his shoulders. "They may have taken the opportunity to escape with the diamonds to Zaire or to Uganda."

Manuela looked up. "What was that?" The corners of her mouth started to twitch with anger. "Stanfort and Oviero are risking their lives for those diamonds and you dare to insinuate a thing like that. It's disgraceful!"

The other members of the Council buried Pia's offensive comment under an avalanche of protests. Trying to defuse the emotions and resentments that were building up, Roberto Cabral raised his voice.

"Stanfort and Oviero are entirely trustworthy, General. It's quite unnecessary to make an insulting remark like that."

As the day turned into night and there was still no news of the Skyvan, they had to admit that something had gone disastrously wrong. Roberto Cabral steeled himself to express their thoughts. "I think we have to accept that there has been an accident."

Manuela started to cry quietly.

"We shall have to swallow our pride..." continued Roberto Cabral, "... and ask the Cubans to organize a Search and Rescue mission.

To show their full support, the Cubans immediately assigned two Mi13 SAR helicopters from their base in Luanda. Equipped with the most up-to-date search equipment, they were capable of finding the slightest trace of metal beneath the green umbrella of the forest.

When told by Roberto Cabral that the Skyvan carrying the diamonds was missing, President Nevo exploded with rage.

"It's your bloody stupid fault, Roberto," he roared.

"All hope is not lost," ventured Cabral timidly. "I managed to get two Cuban SAR helicopters to comb the jungle."

"You're a disgusting fart, Roberto," bellowed Nevo. "A few days ago, you claimed that all Cubans were thieving 'Che Guevaras', and now you go down on your knees to beg for their assistance. Haven't you got any self-respect?"

In a new fit of anger, Nevo swiped all papers and pens from his desk. "Get out of here, imbecile," he yelled, "... and get the search started."

As Roberto Cabral hurried out of the office, Nevo's final threat sounded loud from the four walls. "I hope for your sake that the Cubans will find the diamonds. Otherwise, your future as President of the Council is over! I may even have you shot!"

19 November 1975

Colonel Guario, a qualified helicopter pilot, was delegated by the Cubans to DIANGOL as SAR coordinator. Very confidently he informed the Council Members that they would start the search early next morning. "Let me assure you," he stressed, "... if they are down there somewhere, we shall find them."

Unaware of the fact that Oviero had taken a short-cut by flying a more direct route from Portugalia to Luanda, Colonel Guario instructed his pilots to take off at first light and search the supposed flight path of the Skyvan - a flight path that lay far to the south of the real route Stanfort and Oviero had flown.

The two Mi13s took off from Portugalia at 6.30 a.m. on the 20th of November. Climbing to an altitude of 5,000 feet, they flew parallel courses at a lateral distance of five nautical miles, and began to search a strip of land, 20 nautical miles wide, on either side of the assumed flight path of the Skyvan. Soon after passing Saurimo, the forest yielded the wreck of an old DC3, a plane that had gone missing many years before. On the 23rd November, in the forest close to Malanje, one of the Mi13s found the rusting remains of a crop-dusting aeroplane, the bleached skeleton of the pilot still strapped to his seat.

Over the next six days, the two Mi13s tracked and retraced the presumed flight path of the Skyvan three more times. No more traces of downed aeroplanes were found and faith in finding Stanfort and Oviero alive and well, began to fade.

"I'm afraid that after all this time, I can't believe they are still alive," Colonel Guario said, wiping his brow as if to brush his worries away. "To cover all possibilities, we'll give it two more days to search a more northern track between Portugalia and Luanda. After that I'm afraid we'll have to admit that..." He did not finish what he was saying. Everyone in the room knew exactly what was on his mind.

In the early morning of the 28th November, they were waiting as usual in the radio room at DIANGOL. The room smelled of stale cigarette smoke mixed with the aroma of freshly brewed coffee. It was the last full day of searching for the lost pilots. By tonight, unless a miracle happened, hope would have to give way to sorrow. Apart from a couple of hours of snatched rest, nobody had really slept during the last few days. Vigo could feel the fatigue deep in his bones. Deep dark shadows lay under his eyes. To clear his brain, he lit up another cigarette and glanced at his watch.

It was almost 9 o'clock. Outside, a miserable drizzle hid the sky from view. The shrill sound of the telephone abruptly broke the silence in the room. Involuntarily, Manuela gave a cry of alarm. She picked up the phone, closed her eyes and listened intently. "It's for you," she said, handing the phone to Colonel Guario. "Somebody from Heliflight HQ."

Hardly daring to hope, she walked over to the window and leaned against the sill. The light that fell through the window enveloped her in a hazy box of greyish light and her face, colourless and frozen, looked like a statue carved out of ivory.

Guario launched a series of quick questions. He patiently listened to the answers, his lips gradually drawing together in a thin line and his eyes roving over the people in the room. After what seemed an hour, he put the receiver down. "The C.O. of Heliflight ..." he clarified, absentmindedly pointing to the telephone. "One of his Mi13s has reached Tembo, a small village by the foot of the Guillaume Waterfalls. It seems that, when flying over the forest, their onboard equipment detected traces of metal."

Manuela felt her heart go suddenly cold with intuition.

Colonel Guario added: "The helicopter could not land in the forest. To find out more, they landed in Tembo, on the village square. They've left now with a search party to have a closer look at the suspected wreckage!" Guario's voice became very wary now. "There's more," he articulated. "When talking to some of the villagers, the crew discovered that about one week ago, a small blue and white painted aeroplane flew very low over the Falls."

"A blue and white aeroplane," shouted Vigo, hardly able to control his agitation. "There are not many aircraft like that in Angola. It must have been the Skyvan."

"What the hell was the plane doing there anyway?" Roberto Cabral asked. His eyes fluttered to the map as if it would give him the answer. "Tembo is far to the north of where they should have been."

"Unless Oviero had taken a direct route," mumbled Vigo. "I know, with his kind of overconfidence, it's just the kind of thing he would do to cut the distance by a couple of hundred miles."

"It's possible," admitted Cabral. "Let's call Dundo on the HF and confirm with the mechanics that extra fuel tanks were fitted in the Skyvan."

Five minutes later, they had the confirmation that no extra tanks had been installed. The possibility that the Skyvan was the blue and white plane seen by the villagers near the Guillaume Falls, became a certainty.

"That's not all," added Colonel Guario. "The crew also reported that according to the villagers, the plane was hit by a fire arrow!" He raised his left hand in a gesture of sympathetic compassion. "I'm afraid that with fire arrow, they actually mean anti-aircraft rocket," he clarified.

Almost oblivious of what was happening around her, Manuela had to grip the sill of the window with both hands to prevent herself from falling.

At 8 p.m. in the evening, they were still waiting for news from Tembo. By now, more than ten hours had elapsed since the helicopter crew had started their search. It didn't seem possible that so much time had passed and so little had happened. Hardly a word had been spoken in the room. None of them had eaten anything. They had been chain-smoking and sipping coffee, silently watching the round black mouth of the loudspeaker, willing it to come to life. Outside it was dark again.

As if nature didn't care about the tragedy that had happened, the sky was speckled with a thousand brilliant stars. The darkness in the room was broken only by the soft yellow glow of the bulbs in the radio transceiver. Suddenly, the loudspeaker burst to life. Although expected, they all flinched. Colonel Guario bent forward and reached for the transmit-button. Before he could answer the call, the voice came again, more impatient now.

"Luanda, this is unit 15 of Heliflight, do you read?"

This time, Colonel Guario was ready for it and he pushed the transmit-button down. "Go ahead 15, I read you loud and clear."

"We have just returned to the village..."

Manuela was not able to stand the tension any longer. With trembling fingers, she reached for a cigarette.

"We have found some parts of an aircraft," said the helicopter pilot.

Staring out into the night, Manuela went ice-cold.

"The largest part we found was an aircraft engine. It showed clear signs of damage by rocket fire. Apart from that, we found a few pieces of aluminium, probably parts of an aircraft wing..." The pilot's voice faltered for a short moment. "That was all," he finally concluded. "There was no sign of life..."

Manuela's heart began to thump wildly against her ribs. Her face twitched and a sudden flood of tears ran down her cheeks.

"...and there were no bodies!"

For a few more seconds, the static disturbances on the radio waves continued to crackle through the silence of the room. Colonel Guario switched the transceiver off, his action the symbolic confirmation that the search for the Skyvan was over and that any hope of finding Stanfort and Oviero alive had gone.

Fearful of the President's reaction when informed about the loss of the diamonds, Roberto Cabral withdrew to his office and lifted the phone off the hook.

Later that evening, Manuela hurried down the narrow Rua do Esquadrao, her eyes swollen from crying. Since the Skyvan had gone missing, now more than ten days ago, Stanfort's picture had been constantly in her mind. In one of her nightmares, she had seen him lying wounded in the wreck of his aeroplane, with claw-like hands reaching out for her.

The relationship she had shared with Stanfort had been a very profound one. Days of powerful passion separated sometimes by weeks of loneliness, when Stanfort had to spend time in the mines and she was stuck in the office in Luanda. Now Anthony was gone and she felt utterly devastated.

"I wish they had found his body," she thought. It wouldn't make the pain go away, but it would put her mind at rest.

Lopes, only caring about the diamonds, didn't give a damn about her feelings. Barely able to conceal his impatience, he sat on the edge of his chair and made her repeat the events of that day.

"Well," he said softly. "That's it then, Manuela. Your fly-boy has lost the diamonds."

Manuela nervously wrung her hands together. Gathering all her courage, she looked Lopes straight in the eyes. "I've done what you asked me to do," she said. "Now, I cannot help you any more. Therefore, Comrade Lopes, I beg you. Let my father go free."

"I promised to help you," replied Lopes very quietly. He came out from behind his desk and took her arm. "I said I would give you my full support, *when* the diamonds were safe, here in Luanda."

Suddenly, he shouted, in an outburst of rage. "Where are those damned diamonds now, Manuela?" He yelled again, drops of spittle sprayed from between his lips. "Tell me, where are they?"

Violently, he pushed her towards the door. "Get out of here," he said hoarsely. "Don't ever dare to ask me for help until you can give me the answer to *that* question."

Without any further words, he slammed the door closed behind her back and left her alone in her despair.

PART THREE

1995

Heathrow Airport, 13 March 1995

"I've seen the most terrible things in Angola," said Rob to Ian and Jock. "Destroyed and looted villages, wounded and mutilated people. Children crippled by bullets or disfigured by stepping on land mines, and everywhere signs of famine and vitamin deficiency." He paused to take a sip of his coffee. "The main towns and airfields are well protected by Government troops. Therefore, getting caught up in the guerrilla war is not very likely. Clashes between MPLA forces and UNITA guerrillas mostly occur in the south, or in the deserted open spaces of the eastern provinces. Guerrilla activities in the northern provinces are restricted to brief and skilfully executed hit-and-run raids." Rob spread his hands to convey a veiled sense of cynicism. "Sobreiro also told me that UNITA is getting stronger and that the guerrilla war in the south is getting more and more intensive".

"Do you think our lives could be at risk?" asked Ian cautiously.

"Not exactly," replied Rob. "Of course, I don't have the gift of foreseeing the future, and I don't know how long the situation will remain stable, but I believe that for the next couple of years, the operation will be relatively safe."

Jock gave a low whistle. "We'll just have to be prepared to make a run for it as soon as the condition gets out of hand," he said nonchalantly.

"Any precautions we can take?" queried Ian.

"Yes, there are," replied Rob. "Sobreiro has been flying in Angola almost daily since the beginning of the guerrilla war, and he's never had a problem. He gave me some very valuable advice. For instance, to avoid being shot at by a SAM-7 or a Stinger, we should fly high over the countryside, but low and fast in the vicinity of airfields. We should also stay away from the coastlines."

Ian nodded slowly. "The skills we learned in the Air Force will come in very useful. However, the chance of being shot at with Stinger rockets does not appeal to me at all."

"That's why I have decided to make the deal financially more attractive," Rob remarked. "The contract is a good one. It pays very well, and it saves me from bankruptcy. Therefore, I can afford to pay you an extra hundred dollars per day, as danger money, agreed?"

"That sounds fine by me," countered Ian reflectively. "But don't misunderstand me, Rob, it's not the money that is my main concern. I just want to make sure that all operational and safety angles are covered."

"So do I, Ian," confirmed Rob. "I don't want to get killed for the sake of a few thousand dollars."

"Stop behaving like old women," interrupted Jock rudely. "Having extra money to spend is fine. What interests me more is the technical assistance we can get."

"Hold on, Jock. A few more items before I come to that. I was told that having a contract with the Government will give us a lot of privileges, but it won't put us above the law. The minister made it quite clear that we are foreigners, highly respected for what we'll be doing, but still foreigners. So, whatever you see, don't volunteer any comments, and if occasionally we have to operate a flight out of the country, don't give any information to journalists. If my own experience is anything to go by, we'll have to watch our step." Rob leaned back in his chair and revealed what had happened that fateful night, when he came back from Portugalia and discovered that Veleiro had been arrested by SECPOL. "Apparently," he explained, "I was also on the list of 'wanted criminals', but thanks to Sobreiro, I had the opportunity to clear my name and I got the contract." Rob pushed his frightful experience to the back of his mind and carried on with the briefing. "I also noticed a feeling of fear and insecurity amongst the population."

Ian looked mystified. "What do you mean by that?"

"I don't know how to explain it," replied Rob. "It must be something like in Germany during the second World War, where everybody was watching everybody and where anyone could be an informer for the Gestapo."

"It's a communist state, Rob, based on old Soviet doctrines and KGB disciplines," erupted Jock, raising his hands in supplication. "What else would you expect?" He drew a deep breath to calm down. "Now that you have given us all the frightful stuff, tell me something about the technical aspect of the operation."

"All right," said Rob, smiling at Jock's outburst. "The airfields are generally in good condition. Loading equipment, stairs, and conveyer belts are non-existent. On the positive side, there are hundreds of labourers to do the job."

"So it's as we expected," remarked Ian, "lots of missing factors, requiring a lot of improvisation."

"That's right." Rob turned his attention back to Jock. "As far as maintenance is concerned, we'll be completely on our own. Every piece of equipment we need, we'll have to take with us."

A worried expression wrinkled Jock's forehead. "Are you trying to say that we'll have to take care of the daily inspections and the repairs, Rob? In that case, we'll need a workshop, and..."

Rob raised his hands to thwart the argument. "There is a perfectly suitable workshop in Luanda, Jock. As for the spare parts, I've made a list, listen."

Referring to a handwritten list that lay on the desk in front of him, he began to read: "We'll need two spare engines, two propellers, several sets of brakes, twenty wheels, six radio transceivers, two weather radars ..." Remembering the rough and damaged condition of the landing strips, he added: "And tyres, especially tyres. Lots and lots of tyres. The runways in Luso and in Saurimo are like sandpaper. They will wear away our tyres as if they were made out of butter. Finally, we need fire extinguishers, a first-aid kit and a portable Honda engine to drive an emergency generator."

Ian raised his voice. "You mentioned the lack of motorized transport, Rob. To make us completely self-reliant, wouldn't it be wise to take your Land Rover with us, and two light motorcycles."

Rob nodded his head in assent and added the vehicles to his list.

Always practical where his personal comfort was concerned, Jock insisted on adding a large quantity of canned food. "To add some variety to that blasted diet of dried fish and rice."

It took them two months to finish the preparations for the exodus. On the 15th May, they were ready. The large cargo hold of the Britannia was loaded to capacity. The last item to be stowed was Rob's Land Rover. The vehicle had been transformed into a repair shop on wheels, the dark blue colour sprayed khaki, the inside furnished with drawers for tools, and the rear bumper strengthened to hold racks for jerrycans. Outside it was getting dark, with low hanging clouds drifting in from the north-east. The sinking sun illuminated the passenger terminals at the other side of the airfield in a strange reddish light. Everything beyond was already shrouded in dark shadows. A wretched drizzle began to fall.

Rob turned on his heels and walked out of the hangar. "I'll leave you to finish the job," he said. "I've got something to do in the office."

Jock manoeuvred the Land Rover inside the hold and secured the wheels to a set of metal rings in the floor. "Mission completed," he reported jokingly to Ian.

"Cargo loaded and all equipment on board."

They closed the big hangar doors, the electric motors whining through the gloomy vastness of the hangar. The drizzle had turned into rain, blanketing the far side of the field with sheets of spray. A strong smell of wet tarmac and grass perfumed the air. Jock ran ahead through the miserable downpour, his trouser-legs flapping about his knees. Just behind him he heard the heavy footfall of Ian sloshing through the puddles. Almost together, they reached the other side of the apron. Jock pushed the door of the office open.

A gust of wind slammed the door against the wall. Rob looked up with a start. "Jesus Christ!" he shouted. "Can't you be more careful?" Shaking his head with displeasure, he focused his attention again on a chart of Angola.

Jock slipped out of his sodden coat. "Will you never stop studying, Rob? You must have memorized that chart by now."

"Memorized," laughed Ian ironically. "That's too weak an expression. By now, he can draw it better than the best cartographer."

"All right," muttered Rob. "Cut it out you two. I was just toying with an idea. I admit it's a crazy idea. I don't even know how to begin to explain it."

"I knew there was more to this," interrupted Ian.

Rob nodded. "You remember what I told you, about this Skyvan and the lost diamonds."

For a moment, his memory jumped back to Angola, the immensity of the country and the dense tropical forests. "It's just possible that my father was on board that plane," he said, and he told Jock and Ian about the strange coincidence of his father's disappearance at about the same time the Skyvan had gone missing.

"That is rather strange," confirmed Ian, "... but what can you do about it. Is there any way to find out?"

"Once settled in our new operation, Ian," Rob replied, "I'll ask to have a look in the archives of DIANGOL." He studied for a moment the rain which ran in droplets down the window. "Not that I remember much about my father," he carried on, "... but if I could find the wreck of the Skyvan, it would solve the mystery about his death." As an afterthought, he added: "And we could get rich at the same time!"

"You can't be serious, skipper," sneered Jock. "I can't believe what I'm hearing."

"That you want to find your father's grave," said Ian gravely, "I can understand, but that you believe in lost treasures..."

"You must still believe in Father Christmas," Jock cut in.

"Or in pretty virgins and compassionate debt collectors," added Ian.

Rob's face twisted in an annoyed scowl. He tightly rolled the chart together and slipped it in a long cardboard container. "We'll see once we're there," he decided. "In the mean time let's go and have a couple of beers in the bar of the Aero Club, but..." He raised a warning finger to Jock. "No drunken feast tonight." A smile in his eyes defused the sting in his voice. "Tomorrow morning at first light, we must be on our way."

Early the next morning, Rob pointed the nose of the Britannia down the runway. "Roger Heathrow, cleared for take off," Ian confirmed. At the same time, Rob advanced the throttles and Jock leaned forward to tune the power of the four engines. "All temperatures and pressures in the green, Skipper."

Slowly the heavy aircraft began to move forward and the thin needle on the airspeed indicator sluggishly came to life. Twenty knots, forty knots... "80 knots," Ian called out.

"Roger, I have control." Rob pulled his left hand away from the nose-wheel steering and draped his fingers around the control column.

The huge wheels ran faster and faster over the runway, the nose-wheel rumbling in a rhythmic vibration over the lights on the centre of the runway. The cold, moist air condensed in graceful rivulets of water over the windshield.

Seconds later, Ian called out: "V1... Vr."

Vr was the speed at which the lift developed by the wings was great enough to pull the heavy weight of aircraft, fuel and cargo off the ground. Rob gently drew the stick backwards, the column feeling warm and smooth in his hand. His fingertips started to search for the subtle reaction of the plane, an almost imperceptible vibration like the sudden tension of a thoroughbred ready to jump an obstacle.

"There it is", Rob thought. "This is the moment."

With an elegant movement, the nose started to come up. For a few more seconds, the wheels of the main landing gear remained in contact with the earth and the nose-wheel moved higher and higher. Suddenly, a thin whisper of spiral vortex appeared at the wingtips. As if the main gear had been waiting for this moment, the huge wheels left the ground and the giant plane started to climb. "Positive rate of climb, gear up," Rob called out.

At one thousand feet, he ordered Ian to raise the flaps. Free of the drag of flaps and landing gear, the speed increased quickly to 200 knots. Jock pulled the throttles to climb power and started to read the after take-off check-list.

At five thousand feet, Rob reached forward and engaged the autopilot, then stretched his arms and pointed to the sun which was surrounded by a golden halo. "Look at that," he said suddenly, his voice loud in the interphone. "It's so good to be alive."

In a more prosaic manner, Ian and Jock also enjoyed the beauty of the early morning, the pure and clear crispness of the air and the milky-blue of the sky smeared with a thin veil of cirrus clouds.

The noble spire of Westminster cathedral slipped slowly by under the right wing. Beyond the U-turn in the river lay the London docks and far behind that the fog-shrouded fields of Kent.

The aircraft rocked gently when it passed through a thin layer of clouds. Rob set the heading selector of the autopilot on a south-easterly course to intercept the outbound radial from Biggin Hill VOR, a Very high frequency Omni Range navigation system, and turned around in his seat. "So boys, that's it," he said. "Goodbye London, and welcome adventure."

"From now on it's farewell to the mundane regularity and the security of a life in Europe," said Ian seriously.

"Well, I for one am glad to be away from it," added Jock. "I'm thoroughly fed up with the rat-race mentality here. At least in Africa we'll be our own masters."

"As long as you keep your nose clean," remarked Ian. "Remember Rob's experience with SECPOL."

Through a gap in the clouds appeared the wide double belt of the M 25, as usual at that time in the morning clogged with traffic. They watched for a moment, lost in silence. As they climbed higher, the land disappeared under a thick layer of clouds. The only sounds to be heard were the muffled growl of the engines and the surge of air over the windshield.

Five hours later they landed in Tamanrasset, an airfield in the middle of the Algerian Sahara. Looking void of life, the desert had a fascinating and lonely beauty. Around them lay a sandy wilderness, the colour a strange yellowish-brown striped with black, the air smelling hot and dry. Close by stood an almost derelict collection of airfield buildings, in their midst the control tower, daubed with decades of desert dust. From behind came the puff-puffing noise of an ancient fuel bowser. The driver was an old Arab, his head garbed in blue.

"Salaam Aleikum," he shouted.

"Aleikum es Salaam," replied Ian in Arabic, the few words a leftover of a mission they had flown in Aden.

"Jock, take care of the refuelling," instructed Rob. "Ian and I will handle the flight plan."

While Ian filled out the necessary documents, Rob quickly jotted down a couple of words on a telex form to advise DIANGOL in Luanda of their ETA, their Estimated Time of Arrival. Through the grimy windows of the control tower, he saw the fuel bowser pull away from the Britannia. In a sudden hurry to be on their way, he counted out the money for the landing fees.

"Shukran, wa massalamah," he said to the Arab air traffic controller ATC, whose English, apart from a couple of standard expressions, was non-existent. "Thank you and goodbye."

Ten minutes later, this time with Ian at the controls, they took off again. Each mile they flew brought a change of scenery, the colours altering from bright yellow to ochre brown. At times, for miles on end, they soared over patches of pure white sand, shining like silver and gold in the hazy heat of the sun. At other times, the desert resembled the bottom of a vast ocean, the earth criss-crossed by the rocky beds of broad rivers which had run dry, centuries ago.

Slowly, Algeria changed into Mali, then they crossed the border with Niger. The emptiness below became dotted with desert bush and small trees, and circular clusters of huts and mud walls began to mark the beginning of human habitation. As they passed the border with Gabon, the desert disappeared. Instead came the lush blanket of the equatorial forest.

"Another hour and a half," said Jock, stretching his legs to restore circulation. "Then we'll be there." Looking forward to getting out of the plane, he started to whistle softly.

When sunset came, it came fast, like a curtain being drawn. A short streak of bright blue, splashed with red, flashed for a second over the horizon, then it was dark. Rob tore his eyes away from the map. "It's about time we got there," he sighed. "I'm dying for a beer."

On the tarmac in Luanda, Sobreiro suddenly stretched his arm in a northerly direction. "Look, there they are," he yelled.

"I don't see a thing," said Mena. She was a slim girl, Angolan from Portuguese origin, with blonde wavy hair and vividly green eyes. She made a kind of funnel with her hands and concentrated on a point in the far distance. "No, I can't see them."

"Yes, there they are," Sobreiro yelled again. "You must be able to see the navigation lights." Excitedly he grabbed Mena by her arm. "There," he pointed. "There, a little to the left of the control tower."

Now she could see the red and green lights on the wingtips and the bright white flashes of the strobe lights which drew a tight arc as the plane circled the field and lined up with the runway. Upon touch down, the tyres made a loud screeching noise, each wheel sending a cloud of burnt rubber in the air.

"Gosh, that's a big plane. I never thought it would be so enormous," Mena shouted.

Rob turned the plane on to the tarmac and told Jock to shut the engines down. The loud whistling noise came to an abrupt halt and the large props slowly jerked to a stop. Rob rushed out of the cockpit and swung the cargo door open. The rich smells of Africa saturated the hold. Still slightly deafened from the droning of the engines during the last twelve hours, he climbed down the ladder.

"Hello, Sobreiro," he said, and introduced Ian and Jock.

"Rob, this is Mena," announced Sobreiro. "She is working in Flight Ops. She will be your coordinator with DIANGOL and..."

The rest of his words were lost on Rob. "It's a pleasure, Mena," he mumbled at last. With old-fashioned elegance, he bent down and brushed her fingers with a delicate handkiss.

A slow smile appeared on his face when he noticed a deep-red blush appear on Mena's cheeks.

She felt a sudden spark of attraction. With it came the memory of her husband, a geologist with DIANGOL, and the fatal accident when the mine shaft he was working in had suddenly collapsed. They had been married for only three years, and the pain she had felt at that time surged back to the surface. In an impulse of self-protection, she freed her hand and turned away.

Rob felt hurt and rejected, wondering why she acted so strangely. Beyond any doubt, she was the most beautiful woman he had ever met. A woman he could easily fall in love with!

Later that same evening, the telephone rang in Lopes' office, the same person who in 1975 had been a mere inspector, but who now, after twenty years of faithful service, had become SECPOL's Superintendent.

"It's Olunga," the voice said. "Just to let you know that Captain Stanfort and his crew have arrived. They'll start operations in a couple of days."

Olunga was one of Lopes' informers inside DIANGOL, not a member of the Council, but sufficiently high up to have access to all plans and decisions made by the management.

"Good," replied Lopes. "How does it look?"

"They seem to know their business," Olunga said. "The Britannia was loaded to the gills with equipment and spare parts. As expected, Sobreiro and Mena have been appointed as coordinators."

"Will you be able to keep me informed of all their movements," he asked Olunga.

"That's no problem at all, Comrade."

"All right," Lopes replied. "Keep me informed. Even the most insignificant facts, I want to know. You never know what might turn up."

"I understand," confirmed Olunga. "You can count on me!"

The first few operations in Angola were an example of how an airline should not be run. To repeat Rob's words, it was a disaster. Everything had to be improvised, from ground equipment to trucks, communications and labour.

With a lot of patience, help from the Base Commander in Benguela and the mining staff in Portugalia, they slowly managed to eliminate the problems.

Benguela, a harbour on the south-west coast, was an important centre of the fishing industry. It was also the base of a Squadron of MiG17 fighter Jets, Angola's most southern defence against infiltrating units of UNITA, who had several of their training camps just over the border with Namibia.

To supply the squadron with kerosene, Rob had developed a daily routine that brought them early in the morning to Benguela with a load of fuel for the Migs. After unloading the fuel in underground storage tanks, the Britannia was then loaded with eighteen tons of fish bound for Portugalia.

During the long flight at low level from Benguela in the far south-west, to Portugalia in the extreme north-east, they learned to love the country, its gently undulating savannahs alternating with formidable mountain ranges and impregnable tropical forests cut through by an abundance of wide flowing rivers, the far horizons lined by rows of pink and white Cumulus clouds.

Late at night, sometimes winding their way between heavy thunderstorms and blinding lightning, or floating peacefully below the shining belt of the Milky Way, they pointed the nose of the Britannia in a westerly direction and flew back to Luanda, where they enjoyed a glass of Casal Garcia before retiring to bed.

During the same period, based on the need for working together, Mena's attitude towards Rob changed from a businesslike manner to a fragile friendship. When being totally honest with herself, she had to admit that her feelings for Rob went much deeper. Sometimes at night, in the seclusion of her room, she imagined that they were together, caressing and kissing. It always resulted in sensations of longing and sexual arousal, but each time she felt guilty, as if she was betraying her dead husband. For conscience's sake, for as long as she was not free of the past, she decided that being friends with Rob was all she could afford to be.

At the end of August, Rob was informed by Sobreiro that the Ministry of Transport wanted to start regular flights to Henrique de Carvalho, or more precisely to the nearby airfield of Saurimo.

"Why there, Sobreiro?" Rob queried. "We already operate to Portugalia. As the crow flies, Portugalia is only a hundred or so miles to the north of Saurimo? Wouldn't it make more sense to operate to Serpa Pinto, in the south-east? Then the four corners of the country would be covered."

"Logically spoken, yes," replied Sobreiro, "... but for one thing. From intelligence reports, it has become clear that UNITA is infiltrating the province from across the border with Zaire. The Minister of Defence says that "The north-east province has become the jugular of Angola, with the guerrillas hacking at it with a rusty knife." To prevent that knife from getting sharper, the military want to strengthen the Government forces with Artillery and Infantry units. They also want to use the old American bomber station as a base for the 2nd Fighter Squadron, equipped with MiG21 jets." Sobreiro made a flapping movement with his hands. "However," he added. "It is 30 years since the Americans left. During that time, the place has been completely neglected. To provide lodgings for the squadron's personnel and adequate shelter for the planes, a lot of work needs to be done."

Rob was quick to grasp the meaning. "I see," he replied. "We'll have to transport the building equipment."

"As well as food supplies for the workers, who will be doing the repairs, and for the soldiers of a Unit of MPLA Airfield Defence Forces, who are already based there," completed Sobreiro.

General Pia took it upon himself to inform the Military Commander in Luanda of the new flight schedule, and coordinate the unloading of the plane with the authorities in Saurimo.

On the eight of September, he reported that no stone had been left unturned to ensure a smooth start of the new operation and that consequently, the flights could commence. "You will be met there by a committee of local dignitaries," Pia proclaimed.

Just before the crack of dawn the following morning, Rob and his crew left the hotel. The air felt fresh and cool, the sky was clear with only a thin layer of clouds on the eastern horizon.

By 6 o'clock, the sun rose quickly above the rim of the earth. They were airborne at seven and after an uneventful flight, they reached Saurimo. Ten thousand feet below the plane lay the long runways of the old American bomber base. Rob looked down at the airfield. Of the welcoming committee that General Pia had promised, he could see no sign. In fact there was nothing that indicated that they were expected at all. Jock stretched his neck to take a good look through the windshield. "I can't see a thing on the ground. Can you, Ian?"

"No, nothing."

"Are you sure this is Saurimo, Rob," Ian queried cautiously.

"Well, if it isn't Saurimo, my name is Julius Caesar," responded Rob peevishly. "During my inspection trip, when Sobreiro was showing me the sights, we passed over this airfield. As it was late in the evening we didn't land, but it is undoubtedly the same place."

Ian twisted around in his chair. "Jock, tell me I wasn't dreaming when Pia said that he personally notified the Commander in Saurimo of our arrival."

"Yeah, one day pigs will fly," Jock replied. He pulled a handkerchief out of his pocket and dabbed at the sweat on his forehead, then slipped a headset over his ears. "I'll try to raise our Ops Office in Luanda on the HF to let them know."

Remembering Sobreiro's advice to stay well above ten thousand feet, Rob stood the Britannia on its left wing and swung a tight circle over the airfield. "Look, Ian," he suddenly said in the interphone. "There are car tracks between the hangar and the runway. And there, between those trees, that looks like an aircraft." He pulled the throttles slightly back and rolled the wings level. "I think we should go down and have a look, don't you?"

Ian meditated whether that was really such a good idea. "I don't know, Rob. I've got a weird feeling about this place. Don't you think we should make certain that it's safe? Jock is on the radio with Luanda. They might know more."

"You're right, Ian," Rob admitted reluctantly. "It's useless to take unwarranted risks. After all, we're here to bring food and building materials to the people. Not to fight the war for them."

"I've got a reply from Luanda," called Jock from the rear. "They'll try to raise the Army Headquarters in Saurimo."

"God damn," shouted Rob, his patience running on a very short fuse. "That's a good start for the operation isn't it." He swung around in his seat. "Tell Luanda that we don't have enough fuel to turn around in the holding for hours, Jock. If we don't get a landing clearance within the next five minutes, we'll return to Luanda. All costs for the wasted flight at the Government's expense, of course!"

A shaft of sunlight fell through the side window. It reflected on the glass cover of the flight instruments. Squinting, Jock turned back to his HF radio. "Luanda Ops, Luanda Ops, from Skylift One, come in."

"Having to pay for a wasted flight, that will get them moving," stated Ian ruefully.

The cloud cover became more solid, dotting the earth with small drifting shadows. Ian adjusted his sunglasses on the tip of his nose and threw another look at the airfield. Craning his neck, he suddenly shouted: "Hey look, Rob, there is a car moving over the runway. The place is not deserted at all."

Rob reacted immediately. "That must be the promised reception committee," he said. "I'm fed up with waiting, Ian. Let's get this thing on the ground. Tell them we are going in, Jock," he shouted over his shoulder. "Tell them we'll call again after the landing." He pulled the throttles to idle and threw the Britannia in a steep turn. "Let's show the bastards what this plane is capable of doing. "Gear down, Ian, flaps at 20."

The aircraft sank in a narrow spiral towards the ground. At 500 feet, Rob kicked the wings level. "Full flap, Ian." With a jolt, much harder than intended, the Britannia touched down on the first few meters of the runway. "Full reverse!" Rob made his voice sound very matter-of-fact, as if he had intended to make such a positive landing. Out of the corner of his eye he saw Ian make a very rude gesture with two raised fingers of his left hand.

"Beautiful, skipper," said Jock sarcastically. "You really showed them what this plane can do."

Not willing to admit that he had made a bad landing, Rob reminded them of what they used to say in the Air Force: "A good landing is a landing you can walk away from, and..."

Before he could finish the sentence, he caught sight of a vehicle that suddenly appeared from behind, a sort of Russian made Jeep, with a MI.30 machine gun pointing in the direction of the cockpit.

To avoid a collision, Rob jumped on the brakes. Recklessly, the Jeep dashed underneath the left wingtip, it's wheels slipping on the loose pebbles of the tarmac.

"Look at that! These guys must be nuts," shouted Ian. He turned to Rob. "I told you we should have gone back to Luanda!" Anxiously, he pointed to another Jeep that shot out from behind a hangar. "Damn it, skipper, we should never have landed here."

"Yes, but we have, Ian, so stop shitting yourself."

Forcing himself to remain calm, Rob wiped his sweaty hands on the legs of his trousers. "If they had intentions to shoot us, they would have done so already," he claimed.

"You know, skipper," ventured Jock, "I think you're right. They must be just as confused as we are. We are most probably the first civil aircraft that's landed here in years."

"Keep trying to contact Luanda, Jock," ordered Rob. "Tell them what has happened. Meanwhile, I'll go down and talk to one of their officers."

Hurriedly, Rob threw the passenger door behind the cockpit open and put a foot on the ladder.

"PPPrrrrrrrtttttttt."

The full salvo of an AK47 assault rifle whipped over his head, narrowly missing the fuselage of the aircraft. Rob threw himself back in the safety of the hold. The air was heavy with the smell of cordite. "We are friends. NOS SOMOS AMIGOS!" he shouted wildly to the soldier who had fired the gun. "Get me one of your officers. We came from Luanda."

Rob turned around to face Ian. "Wait until I get my hands on that pompous imbecile Pia," he vented his anger.

As they sat waiting with the engines shut down, the temperature in the hold became rapidly unbearable, the stench of a load of dried fish overpowering. With his shirt sticking to his back, Rob looked at Jock. "Any reply from Luanda?"

"Nothing, and I have to switch off the batteries, Rob. Unless you want to run them empty."

"Then, we won't be able to start up again," replied Rob. "Go ahead, Jock, switch off all power and secure the cockpit."

"They'll be worried sick in Luanda," warned Ian.

"Can't help it," countered Jock. "It's either that or getting stuck in this Godforsaken hole forever!"

"This is getting too stupid," announced Rob desperately when consulting his wrist watch. "We have been here for more than an hour." Again, his anger rose to the surface. "God damn bastard," he yelled, thinking of Pia. "He is sitting there on his fat arse, reaping all the credit, while we have to pull the chestnuts out of the fire."

Racking his brains, he constructed a sentence with words left over from a year of Spanish lessons in his student days and a few words of Portuguese he had picked up from Sobreiro and Mena. He pulled himself upright and stuck his head out of the door. "Ai acqui algun que falu Engles?" he shouted. "Does anyone here speak English?"

One of the soldiers, squinting against the harsh light of the sun, wrinkled his lips in a smirk.

Another Jeep appeared from behind the hangar. An officer, a Major from his shoulder boards, stepped out. His nose was sharp like the beak of an eagle, his eyes dark and hostile.

"Ai acqui algun que falu Engles?" Rob repeated.

"I speak English," the Major said, putting his foot on the first step of the ladder. "I'm coming up."

Rob reached down to give him a hand. With a proud shake of his head, the officer refused help. "Who are you?" he asked. "Why have you come here."

"Who are you that you dare to threaten us with your guns?" retaliated Rob. "We came from Luanda with food, not to fight."

As he mentioned the word Luanda, the cold hostility disappeared out of the Major's eyes. He looked around in the hold to make sure that the plane was not carrying weapons or ammunition.

"I was not informed, Captain," he said. "You must understand, I have to make certain. This is a war zone, you know." Before Rob could formulate an answer, he pointed through the open door to a camouflaged battery of Anti Aircraft Rockets that stood by the edge of the tarmac. "They have been tracking you since you came overhead. It would have been easy for them to shoot you down." The bold tone of his voice almost made it sound as if he would have preferred it. "It's only because you fly a large aeroplane that you are still alive. The rebels don't have any planes. Therefore, we wondered whether, perhaps, you were one of our own."

In spite of the hot sun, an ice cold shiver ran down Rob's spine. His fear exploded in a blind fury as he remembered the smug and self-complacent voice of Pia "You may rest assured Captain, I have not left one stone unturned."

"I'll kill that bastard in Luanda," he whispered hoarsely to Ian. "That incompetent imbecile almost got us killed."

Eager to make his point, the officer pulled Rob's sleeve and pointed to a spot between the trees. It was the plane they had seen from the air. From this close distance, Rob saw that it was nothing but the burnt out fuselage of a DC3. "That pilot was not as lucky," he growled. "He was heading for the border with Zaire. We thought he had aggressive intentions, so we shot him down. Afterwards we discovered that he was transporting refugees." He raised his shoulders in a shrugging motion. "How was I to know?"

Rob did not reply. Shooting down a plane full of refugees was horrible, but somehow, it didn't feel as bad as being the target himself. After all, it was a war zone!

Motioning Rob to come with him, the Major started down the ladder. "I must verify your credentials, Captain," he explained. "Let's go to my office."

"What about my crew," asked Rob. "Can't they come with us. It's getting very hot and uncomfortable in here."

The Major nodded curtly and turned his attention to Ian and Jock. "You can leave the plane," he said, "... and stay in the shadow under the wings. It will be cooler there." Shrugging his shoulders dismissively, he repeated that they had to stay there until further notice. "Otherwise, you risk a bullet."

Rob followed the officer across the tarmac. They entered one of the rooms beneath the derelict control tower. The inside reminded Rob of an old picture in a history book, of a dugout in the trenches during the First World War. The place smelt musty and damp, the odour of eternal darkness and moist clothes. The windows were boarded up. A field mattress, covered with a roll of smudgy blankets lay in the dark recess in the far corner. Next to the bed stood a small kerosene burner and a plate with the remains of a frugal breakfast. As they came in, a number of mice, who had been feeding on the scraps, scurried away along the wall.

"Sit down, Captain," said the Major, an undercurrent of distrust in his voice leaving no doubt that Rob was still under guard.

Rob sat down on a wobbly canvas chair. The Major seated himself behind his desk, an old door placed horizontally across a couple of orange crates. Its surface was covered with a couple of old-fashioned telephones and a stack of documents. The Major vigorously swung the handle of one of the field telephones.

Rob listened to the conversation. At first, the officer spoke in a strong voice, pleased with himself. Gradually the belligerent tone calmed down. Then, in a slightly disbelieving tone:

"Autorisado?" All distrust disappeared, and his voice became very submissive.

"Si, Camarad," he muttered finally. "Immediamente. Muito obrigado. Thank you."

Grinning apologetically, he turned to Rob. "I didn't know, Captain. Some breakdown in communications. It will not happen again."

"Forget it," Rob said. "Let's get on with the job. We still have to make another flight today."

He pulled himself out of his chair and walked to the door. A squall drifted over the field, the rain came down in a torrent and splattered the tarmac with frothy bubbles. Rob declined a ride in the Jeep.

"I prefer to walk back through the rain," he shouted, revelling in his freedom.

In no time he was soaked to the skin, the rain washing the sweat out of his shirt. Rob deeply inhaled the damp and misty smells. We're not in smooth water yet, he pondered, but I'm sure that from now on, it will get easier. And safer.

In Luanda, they were received like members of a long lost tribe. Mena showed real concern and her voice trembled with emotion. "Sobreiro and I, we were so worried about you, Rob. First a radio message to tell us that, from the air, it looked as if Saurimo was deserted. Then another message saying that you were landing, followed ten minutes later by a report that you were held at gunpoint by a bunch of trigger happy soldiers. Then nothing, for hours, until finally, the news that the problems were solved and that you were airborne again."

Admiring the line of her eyebrows and the delicate curve of her mouth, Rob admitted that it had been chaos. "I'm sorry for the trouble," he said, smiling crookedly. "It was the result of Pia's lack of professional integrity."

"It was terrible," she confessed, her eyes glowing. "I was afraid that you had been shot."

"No such luck," joked Rob. Playfully, he laid his arm around her shoulder and walked with her to the Ops Office.

A slight shudder of desire ran through Mena's body. Briefly, she allowed herself to lean against Rob, until it came back to her that falling in love would be like setting one foot over the edge of a cliff, never being able to turn back.

She reached up and pushed Rob's hand away, but deep in her heart, she knew she was deceiving herself!

Luanda, 29 September 1995

As fast as the potholed road permitted, Rob was driving along the sunlit and mostly deserted Praya Copacabana. The sky was deep-blue, the temperature in the mid-twenties and the refreshing tang of sea water hung heavily in the air.

Two miles down the road, he turned left towards the airport. The road became narrow, the air hot and stuffy, and Rob's nose crinkled in disgust as he smelt the stink of garbage that choked the gutters.

The Britannia stood parked in front of the hangar. Rob threw an admiring glance at his aircraft, not unlike the glance of a young man in love with an older but very attractive woman, then he aimed the Land Rover in the direction of the Flight Operations Office. Before he had time to cut the engine, the door of the office crashed open.

"Don't bother to get out," shouted Mena. She waved a pink slip of paper above her head. More running than walking she hurried across the parking area, her breasts gently swaying under the thin cotton of her blouse. "I've tried to call you at the hotel," she panted, trying to catch her breath, "... but you'd already left. You're wanted urgently downtown..."

"Thank you, Mena," Rob interrupted jokingly. "I'm fine thanks, and how are you?"

A sudden red glow flashed over Mena's cheeks, making her look even more attractive. She pushed the slip of telex-paper into Rob's hand. "Read it for yourself," she muttered.

Anxious to know, Rob let his eyes run over the written text.

```
"To Skylift. Urgent.
     Flooded area in the East Province.
     Supplies urgently required!
     Signed: Amboni."
```

"Phew, that's strange," he mumbled when he was finished. A little slower, he read the document a second time. "What flooded area? Where? What kind of supplies? And who is Amboni?" He touched Mena's hand and looked in her eyes. "It's a little bit vague isn't it. Do you know anything more?"

Bashfully, she pulled her hand away, but couldn't stop a sudden flash of affection from flooding her mind. "Senhor Amboni is an official, working for the Minister of Transport," she said gently. "That's all I know." Avoiding his eyes, she told him to hurry. "He'll tell you all you need to know, Rob. He is waiting for you in DIANGOL's downtown office."

"You'll have to come with me," stated Rob. "I need a translator."

"No need for that. Amboni is quite fluent in English, and Sobreiro is already there."

"Just one favour then. Call the Tropico to inform Ian and Jock that I'll pick them up in fifteen minutes. For something like this, I want them to be present too."

He blew her a kiss and shifted the Land Rover into reverse gear.

Allowing his driving to be guided by habit, he let his mind dwell on the strange relationship that existed between himself and Mena. In brief and unguarded moments, her body-language told him that she was attracted to him, but each time he tried to get closer, she turned him away, as if something much stronger than love was ruling her emotions.

One day, in a confidential mood over a glass of wine, he had told Sobreiro about his growing affection for Mena and the worry that his feelings might never be reciprocated. Breaking his reluctance to talk about the past, Sobreiro had spoken about Mena's husband and his mortal accident in the mines in Dundo. "They were married for only three years, Rob. Three weeks after the funeral, she managed to get a job in Luanda, working as flight coordinator, but the past is still very much alive for her, so you'll have to be patient. She's a brave girl and I'm sure there is no one else, but don't do anything rash. It would only destroy your chances."

Destroying his chances was the last thing Rob wanted to do!

Ian and Jock were waiting in front of the hotel. Ten minutes later, they entered the meeting room of DIANGOL. Next to Sobreiro sat a perfectly dressed gentleman. He stood up and walked across the room. "Hello, Captain Stanfort," he said. His deep and warm voice betrayed him as a very accomplished speaker. "I'm Rico Amboni, deputy Minister of Transport."

Amboni's face was pleasant and round, his skin smooth and only slightly black. His neatly brushed hair was almost without curls, and a small David Niven moustache adorned his upper lip.

All the signs of a proud but very vain man, Rob thought, wondering what the next few minutes were going to bring. To get a hint, Rob looked at Sobreiro and lifted his eyebrows. Sobreiro replied by raising his shoulders.

"I've been looking forward to meeting you," Amboni said. "As you already know, we are faced with an emergency. I'll come straight to the point."

He walked over to a large geographical map which completely filled one of the walls. "Lukapa is a little village of some five hundred inhabitants," he began. "It lies in the Province of Dondo, in the north-east of the country, almost exactly in the middle of the diamond belt between Saurimo and Portugalia." He pointed to a place on the map. "Here is the village. As you can see, it is surrounded by low flatlands. Most of the male inhabitants work in the mines for DIANGOL. The women and children cultivate the fields and herd the cattle." Amboni's finger moved slightly to the south. "This is the Luena range, a high plateau," he said, aiming his finger as if it was a stabbing spear, "... and this is the Chiumbe river."

Rob got the impression that whatever Amboni wanted, was not going to be easy. Sobreiro pulled the wrappings off a fresh pack of cigarettes. He lit up and sucked the smoke deep into his lungs.

"Because of the heavy rains during the last few weeks," Amboni continued, "The Chiumbe has flooded its banks, isolating the village of Lukapa. They are running out of food, water and medicines. However..." His finger came to a halt on a certain position on the map. "There is a runway, four thousand feet long." He looked at Rob, his lips curling in a slightly twisted smile. "I believe that is long enough for a plane like yours, Captain."

The quiet intensity of his words sounded like a test, challenging Rob to raise objections. All at once, it dawned on him; a village in the north-east of the country, flooded land, a dire lack of food, and a runway.

"They want us to make a relief flight without even knowing the layout of the field and the condition of the runway," he thought. "They must be bloody mad!"

He looked at Ian and Jock. Ian spread his hands in exasperation. Jock made a funny gesture and raised his eyebrows to the ceiling.

Rob jerked his attention back to Amboni. "The roads have been swept away," Amboni stated, resolutely turning his back to the map and facing Rob. "The crops are destroyed and most of the cattle have been killed." To stress the point, he raised his voice. "Even the rescue teams of DIANGOL have not been able to get through to the village."

For a short while, the only noise in the room was the monotonous whirring of the ceiling fans and the muted sound of the horn of a seagoing cargo vessel.

Amboni slipped his left hand in his pocket. "I know, Captain," he said, his voice barely louder than a sigh. "It's quite different from the work you have been doing recently. It is also quite different from the work you came here to do."

To satisfy his curiosity, Rob raised his voice. "Due to the guerrilla war, there must be a number of villages lacking food supplies and medicines," he remarked. "So why this village, and not any one of the others?"

"Good question," replied Amboni. "As you know, the revenue generated by the diamond mines is of vital importance to this country. As DIANGOL is paying most of your bills, they have a say in the destination of your flights. Hence Lukapa, one of their 'own' villages!" He hesitated a moment, his shoulders sagging slightly under his fine suit. "I'm sorry to get you involved in this, but I beg you. Can you help? Please ..."

Rob saw the effort it cost Amboni to say the word 'please'. At the same time he noticed the expression in Amboni's eyes, the acute intensity of a man who really cares. In turn, he stood up. Studying the map, he traced the track from Luanda to Lukapa. "Finding the place will be easy," he declared. "It will take us about two hours to get there. It's the landing that's going to be tricky!"

"Tricky?" Ian interrupted. "I think it's outright dangerous."

"So what," declared Jock. "It's not any more dangerous than landing at night in Portugalia with only goosenecks to guide us in, or flying low beneath a storm over hills and forests."

"This is different," argued Ian. He started to count on his fingers. "First, we've never seen that strip, therefore we don't know whether it is long enough or solid enough. Second, it's possible, even probable, that the heavy rains have soaked the earth and washed some of the soil under the surface away. If we hit one of those holes we might destroy the aircraft. Or, at best, we could get stuck there for the rest of the rainy season. Third..."

Impatiently, Amboni waved his words away, his whole attitude showing real emotion and agitation. "Gentlemen," he shouted, "... there are children and old people. If they don't get help soon, they'll be the first ones to die."

"See," said Jock. "It's not a matter of safety any more. For those people, it's a matter of life and death. Under these circumstances, we should at least try."

"What do you think, Rob," asked Ian. "I'll go along with the majority. If you decide to go, I'll go with you!"

To make up his mind, Rob turned and looked out of the window. In his concentration, he didn't notice the deep, green colour of the lagoon and the blue of the Atlantic Ocean. From the way Amboni had explained the problem, Rob knew that there was no chance to wriggle out of this flight, but just in case something went wrong, he had to defend his own interests and the interest of his company. "As you said, Mr. Amboni," he said assertively, "... there are lives at stake. Therefore I'm willing to give it a try. However, you know as well as I that it's an enormous risk. I could lose my plane and my only means of existence." He paused before launching his challenge. "Are you willing to accept that same kind of risk, and guarantee full compensation if the Britannia is damaged, or destroyed?"

Amboni's face looked as if it was cut out of a block of wood. "We accept full responsibility, Captain, and will pay for any damages that might occur." With a solemn expression on his face, he pulled a document out of his pocket. "I anticipated your concern. This morning, I asked the President to sign this letter of guarantee." He smoothed the wrinkles in the document and handed it over to Rob. "Will that be good enough to put your mind at rest?"

Rob read the text and recognized the scratch underneath as Nevo's signature. "Yes, that's good enough for me," he confirmed.

Ian and Jock scanned the letter and nodded their approval.

Finally, Rob passed the letter to Sobreiro. "Hold on to that," he said flippantly. "If we break our necks, send it to my solicitor."

Seen from the air, the extent of the catastrophe looked even more dramatic. To the south of the village, the foothills of the Luena range formed a steep incline, their slopes covered in a coat of thorny bushes. Behind the incline, a sheer vertical cliff reared up for another 200 feet. From a wide cleft in the rock face, the swollen waters of the Chiumbe River dropped down into the flat fields of the Savannah, transforming the whole area around the village into a gigantic sea of water and mud. The huts and circular cattle walls of the village stood on a shallow copse, twenty feet above the level of the water.

Jock pointed to the south of the village, where a narrow red coloured strip marked the position of the runway. Built on a slight incline, the eastern end of the laterite strip looked safe and dry, the western end disappeared beneath a thin film of muddy water.

"If that is 4,000 feet, we can call ourselves lucky," Ian said.

"Well, no use in circling around," Rob exclaimed.

He pushed the nose of the plane down for a low pass over the runway, a careful check to see whether the strip showed signs of flooding or sagging. From a height of two hundred feet, it looked good.

"It's what is hidden under the surface that I'm worried about," Rob shouted. "Dangers such as holes and mud or hidden rocks."

He knew the enormity of the risk he was taking, they all knew it, and they all knew that they had only one chance to get it right. Too high and too fast, or too low and too slow, either way it would end up in disaster.

"Let's go in," he said assertively. "Flaps 20, Ian."

As they came closer to the ground, the red-brown waters at the end of the runway beckoned very threateningly, making the landing strip look much too short. To make matters worse, a gusty wind came rolling down the slopes of the Luena range and buffeted the plane. The flight controls felt like lead in Rob's hands. "Gear down, flaps 30, Ian," he ordered, and using all his skills to keep the aircraft lined up with the strip, he fought the plane down to the threshold.

"200 feet!" called Jock.

Rob knew that they were almost committed for the landing. Only a few more seconds to decide. One part of him cried out for adding power and pulling the nose up to fly back to the safety of the airfield in Luanda. Another part of him, his pride and all his professional instincts told him that it could be done.

Ian pointed to plumes of dust, which were blowing in streaks of red across the treshhold of the runway. "Crosswind from the left, skipper."

Aiming the nose for a landing at the very beginning of the strip, Rob rolled in a touch of left aileron to compensate for the drift. Just before touchdown, he kicked the right rudder to swing the nose parallel to the centreline of the strip. "Idle power, Jock."

The landing was hard and very positive. Nobody had any complaints this time. They knew there was no other choice. Every foot, every inch of the length of the strip counted.

"Flaps up, Ian, and full reverse, Jock!"

The engines howling under the strain of full reverse power, the plane started to slow down, the wheels lurching wildly through potholes and dents in the runway. Earth and mud flew up on both sides of the nose and small stones were banging like rifle bullets against the fuselage. A musty smell of laterite invaded the cockpit. Standing on the brake pedals, Rob's feet and hands fought the mass of the aircraft, forcing it to continue rolling in a straight line.

The end of the runway came rushing nearer. Rob felt a cold hand gripping his heart. The harsh reflection of the sun in the muddy water made it difficult to see where the runway ended and the mud began. Again, Rob threw a glance at the airspeed indicator. Barely perceptible, the speed started slowly to come down ... much too slowly. Half the length of the runway had already disappeared behind them and the speed was still well above 90 knots.

"Come on, you bugger," Rob grumbled between his teeth. "Stop, will you." As if the plane understood the urgency, the wheels grabbed a new hold on the surface.

They nearly made it.

Just before the end of the runway, at the place where the surface sloped gently down to the level of the water, the pelting rains of the previous days had dug a deep hole in the laterite. At the very last moment, Ian saw the danger. "Watch out, Rob, on the right. A hole in the runway!"

His shout came too late.

Rob turned the nose wheel to the left in an attempt to swing the plane around in a tight turn. Before he could manage to override the inertia of the aircraft, the right landing gear rolled over the edge of the hole and sunk away in the slippery ooze. The sudden resistance jerked the plane to an abrupt stop. As the landing gear disappeared below the mud, the right wing started to drop, the horizon slowly tilting over. It felt as if they were sitting in an elevator which was moving down and sideways.

"Shut down the engines, Jock," yelled Rob. "The props will break if they touch the ground."

Jock snatched the fuel cocks through their stops, cutting the kerosene to the engines. Slowly, the rpm counters milled to a halt. The whining cry of the engines changed their whistling tone to a low humming vibration which resonated through the fuselage.

"Bloody hell!" yelled Rob. "How the hell are we ever going to get out of here. How the hell are they going to get lifting equipment out to this bloody, flooded place?"

His face twisting in despair and on legs which felt like liquid rubber after the effort of working the rudders and the brakes, Rob rushed back and pushed the door open. Jock and Ian came close behind him.

Far away to the south lay the outlines of the Luena range, its contours now softened by a thin layer of haze which hung low over the flooded fields. Its blurred beauty was lost on Rob as he rushed down the ladder and hurried over to the landing gear, still hoping for a miracle.

It was worse than he had expected. The whole righthand bogie was sunk in a foul pool of mud, which smelled of decay and long dead leaves.

"It could have been much worse," Jock said.

Rob looked at him as if he were demented. "What do you mean, Jock? What could be much worse? Are you out of your mind?"

"The wheels must have found solid ground," Jock patiently explained, pointing to the strut of the landing gear which had stopped sinking down in the mud. "There must be hard rock below the surface. That's why the fuselage and the props didn't sink all the way down to the ground."

"There might even be a way of getting out of here," added Ian. "We could dig a trench and reverse out of the hole."

"Dig a trench!" Rob shouted bitterly. "With what, with our bare hands?" As he said that, he suddenly remembered Amboni mentioning something about the villagers working in the mines for DIANGOL, and he felt a ray of hope in the depths of his misery.

"I guess you're right, Ian," he replied with something like admiration in his voice. "There must be some sort of ground working or digging equipment here. That should do the trick."

Ian pointed over his shoulder to the narrow road that connected the strip with the village. "Judging by the cacophony of voices I hear, there will be no lack of helpers either. Listen."

From behind a fringe of trees appeared a long row of oxcarts, filled with people. They were pointing to the aircraft, cheering and shouting, slapping each other on the back.

"It's looks like a scene from the Bible," remarked Jock.

Still anxiously grinding his hand in his palm, Rob turned away from the commotion. Bubbling with fresh hope, he motioned Jock back with him to the plane. "First of all, let's start number one engine to keep the batteries charged, then call Luanda on the HF radio. They must be anxious to know how we are doing. When that's done, shut the engine and all equipment down. Afterwards, you and Ian can show the villagers how to unload the plane. I'll try to find the headman of the village to organize some help."

The sun began to drop down to the horizon, its glare mellowed by a curtain of red clouds. In their search for insects, a flock of birds wheeled low over the water. A shallow layer of fog rose like steam out of the earth, dressing the Britannia in a skirt of white.

Armed with shovels and trenching tools, the villagers dug a long and narrow ditch which ran from the sunken bogie of the landing gear to the surface of the runway. As soon as the trench was ready, they layered the bottom with a mantle of branches. It was now up to Rob and his crew to start the engines and attempt to reverse the plane out of its muddy tomb.

Outside the cockpit, it was almost dark, only a thin edge of daylight lingered above the horizon.

"Come on, let's do it, Jock," Rob said. High on a cocktail of caution, worry and anticipation, he gripped the control wheel.

Jock pulled the propellers into reverse, throwing clouds of red laterite curling and twisting in the beam of the landing lights. At first nothing happened.

"Give it more power, Jock," Rob yelled. "Give it all you've got!"

What they were doing was exceptionally dangerous. Not enough power, and they would remain stuck in the mud. Too much power, and the plane could drop down on to its tail and twist the landing gear. Then they would be stuck forever.

"Come on, move..."

As if talking to his favourite pet, Jock gently moved the throttles backwards, ready to chop the power at the slightest sign of danger. The needles on the counters reached 1,700 rpm. Almost imperceptibly, the aircraft gave a short lurch and produced a rumbling noise which sounded like faraway thunder.

Afraid that the rumbling sound was the indication of damage, Jock began to cut the power. Immediately Rob slammed his hands on top of the throttles, forcing Jock to give more reverse thrust. Suddenly, the plane rocked a foot backwards.

"Keep the momentum going," Rob shouted above the roar of the engines. "No time to fuss around now."

At eighty percent of full reverse and shaking violently, the plane started to move, one foot at the time. Slowly the huge wheels rose out of the mud.

Inside the cockpit, they felt the wings gradually come level. As the clinging drag of the mud lost its grip on the bogie, the plane gradually picked up speed until suddenly and effortlessly, it rolled out of the trench on to the level surface of the runway.

"We've done it..." Rob shouted. Very excited at their success, he gave Jock a thumping whack on his shoulder.

Once they were safe on the dry part of the runway, Jock chopped the fuel supply and set the parking brakes. For a moment the atmosphere in the cockpit was heavy with silence and disbelief. Then, in an explosion of nervous release, they all started to speak simultaneously.

"We needed a miracle, and now we have one," Ian slapped his thighs in pure delight.

"I would never believe it if I hadn't been here," said Jock smugly.

Rob turned around and tapped Jock on his arm. He pointed to the small box which was fixed above the entrance door to the cargo compartment. That box, during the military career of the aircraft, had contained an emergency flashlight. Now it was empty. One day, in a impulsive mood, Rob had written on it that, in the unlikely event that the Flight-Engineer did something right, the box would dispense a banana.

"I think you have deserved your banana today, Jock."

"If it's all right with you, Skipper, a dram of scotch would suit me better."

Outside, the world disappeared under a cloak of darkness. Above the layer of fog, a pale moon hung between the stars and the lights of the Milky Way. Looking out through the window, it dawned upon Rob that, although they had won a victory by getting the plane out of the mud, they had lost the race against time. Taking off in the dark on a fog-covered and partly flooded runway was an experiment they could not even consider.

"We'll have to spend the night here," he said, pointing out of the window. "Better call Luanda, Jock. Tell them we'll leave at first light, tomorrow morning. After that, we'll have something to eat. You can have your dram of scotch, then."

It turned out that they didn't have to drink their own scotch after all. Just as they finished their meal, a boy came down from the village with a message from the headman. As Rob read the text - a mixture of Portuguese and French - his eyes started to shine with anticipation. "I think I understand what it means," he said to his two friends. "To show his gratitude for bringing food and emergency supplies, the headman is offering us a drink. No scotch, I'm afraid, Jock, but home-made beer, or wine."

The glow of the moon showed them the way to the village. Their feet drew funny circles in the swirling coat of fog that covered the ground. Once in the dark of the forest, the dense canopy of leaves prevented the heat from dissipating in the clear air and the fog disappeared. From the water's edge came a concert of bullfrogs, and the grass by the forest path resounded with the high pitched buzz of crickets.

Above the village, the sky shone red with the light of a campfire. The smell of burning wood hung heavily in the air. They were met by the headman and a delegation of the elders who guided them along the pathways between the huts and led them to a row of low benches which had been placed in a circle in front of the fire.

Neither Rob, Jock nor Ian had ever been in a native village before. The darkness of the night, the huts and the campfire, combined with the striking postures of the people gave the experience a strangely mystical and bewildering aura. The setting was so far removed from the modern world that they had the uncanny sensation of having travelled through time and discovered a hidden village in one of the most primitive areas of Africa.

At first, the contact between them and the villagers was difficult, the conversation mostly limited to hand signals. After a few beakers of the local beer, a brew which tasted strangely sour but was extremely potent, communication stopped being a problem. One of the villagers threw a bunch of thick branches on to the fire. The flames soared high, sending a stream of sparks into the air. Suddenly, the slow and haunting sounds of a drum pierced the silence. As if by magic, a group of girls in their late teens appeared, sparsely dressed in short skirts of woven grass. Their young breasts stood proudly erect, their spines were lined by long supple muscles which ran down their backs and ended in tight rounded buttocks.

Fascinated by the sight of their lovely bodies, Jock forgot that he was talking to Rob and groaned like a bull in heat. On the beat of the drum, the girls started a slow twirling dance around the fire. The rhythm of the drum picked up, driving the girls into a trance. Their bodies became shiny with sweat, their breasts swayed wildly, and the beat of their naked feet on the hard-baked earth rose in harmony with the sounds of the drum.

A sense of desire bolted like fire through Jock's body. Finally, the beat of the drum slowed down, the rhythm of the dancers became slower and slower. One by one, the girls faded away in the shadows between the huts. The eternal sounds of the tropical night replaced the noise of the drum.

Much later, as the fire died down to a mere flicker of light, they took their leave from the headman and the elders. Ian and Rob declined the offer to spend the night with one of the dancing girls. Jock eagerly accepted.

"You're crazy, man," Ian mumbled drunkenly. "They might be full of V.D..."

"No fear, Ian," replied Jock, showing him a packet of prophylactics. "With a French Letter, or as the French say, avec une Capote Anglaise, I'm perfectly safe!"

Disturbed by the early light of the morning that fell in through the cockpit windows, Jock was the first one to stir. Amazed to find himself at that ungodly hour in the plane, he shook his head. With the movement came the sharp pain of a headache, as if a tribe of midgets were pounding his skull with hammers. Slowly, his memory came back - the relief flight, the disaster when the gear had got stuck in the mud and the feast in the village.

Shrinking back when the pulsating throb of his hangover shot again through his head, he carefully made his way to the galley and swallowed a couple of aspirins. Armed with the box of pills, he returned to the cockpit and shook Rob by his shoulder. With a snort of surprise, Rob opened his eyes. They felt swollen and his mouth tasted like mud. Jock handed him two aspirins and a glass of water.

"I feel rotten," Rob said. "Why the hell did I drink that much?"

"If you feel as bad as you look, your headache must be worse than mine," Jock replied.

"You're more used to drinking," Rob stated jokingly. "On top of that, you're a bloody sex-maniac."

Recalling his experience with the dancing girl, a new wave of desire crept up in Jock's loins. "I'll have to find myself a regular girlfriend in Portugalia or in Luanda," he replied enthusiastically. "Life is too short to be wasted in forced abstinence. I guess those vile carnal feelings are below your moral standards, Rob. You prefer to keep yourself pure and clean for your beautiful lass, don't you?"

"She isn't my girl ... yet," replied Rob. "But yes, I want to keep myself clean. You do whatever you like Jock, but be careful, will you!"

Twisting sideways, he pulled the sliding window of the cockpit open and sucked the fresh morning air into his lungs. The yellow circle of a watery sun was shining through a thin layer of mist. From the trees by the road to the village came the song of early birds. Rob threw a look at the right seat in the cockpit. "Where is Ian?"

"In the cargo hold..." Jock's voice sounded cruel. "When I came back from the village, I found him on the cargo nets, drunk as a skunk. I bet he'll be feeling like shit today."

Quiet and dependable Ian, Rob contemplated, who rarely drank more than one or two glasses of wine or beer. "The poor guy," he said. "He's not used to heavy drinking, you know. That local brew was too much for him. Wake him up gently, Jock. I'll make the coffee. Afterwards, I'll go down and have a good look at the runway. I don't want to run into another hole during take-off."

Ten minutes later, sipping his first coffee of the day, he carefully stepped down the ladder and began his inspection. The plane was in a shameful condition, the belly streaked in red and the struts of the right hand gear hidden under a coat of stinking slime.

Rob rubbed some of the mud away to inspect the hydraulic actuators and the thin metal supply lines. They were undamaged and a load of worry disappeared from his mind.

Sipping the rest of his coffee, he set out on a walk down the runway, briskly moving his legs to get his blood flowing again.

Ever attentive to details, he inspected the edges of the strip, looking for signs of damage such as cavities or wet, muddy spots.

Almost in the dead centre of the strip, he found one small patch of damp earth. He scratched the mud with the heel of his shoe. Barely one inch under the surface, he discovered solid soil. Upon reaching the end of the runway, Rob noticed that the mist was almost gone. Instead, the sky was covered with a layer of high Strato-Cumulus clouds which came streaking in from the west, a cloud base that promised more rain and gusty winds.

It was time to get out!

Eager to get back into the air, Rob hurried back to the plane. By the time he approached the aircraft, the gusty winds of the storm depression were already whipping the flood waters into a frenzy. As fast as he could, Rob climbed up to the hold, pulled the ladder up and slammed the door shut.

"I think we should sit out this weather on the ground," suggested Ian, his baggy eyes hidden behind a set of pilot's sunglasses.

"You must be joking. Getting away as soon as possible is important. We've already lost too much time with this blasted incident."

"That wind must measure between 20 to 30 knots! Can you cope with such a crosswind on this short runway?" asked Ian doubtfully.

Rather touchy because of his hangover, Rob was barely able to repress a stab of anger. "Can I cope with this weather?" he echoed. "Easily. What I'm worried about is not the wind on the runway. It's the weather between here and Luanda."

"I agree," interrupted Jock. "That will be the biggest problem of all." He stretched out his arm, sweeping his hand over the western horizon. "Look at those storm depressions, rolling in one after the other. What's more, it will be impossible to get the weather by radio," he added. "There's no way to get through on the HF with this static electricity."

"We'll just have to rely on the weather radar," Rob announced ruefully.

Suddenly, the rain slapped hard against the windshield, blotting out the view on the landscape. "That's the main reason why I want to get out of here," Rob explained, pointing to the big fat drops of water that washed the reddish dust from the windshield. "If we stay one more hour on the ground, the whole runway will become a quagmire."

They took off in heavy rain, the wipers dancing like mad. With the hold empty and only ten tons of fuel remaining in the tanks, Rob managed to pull the plane up with almost one thousand feet of runway to spare. At 6,000 feet, they found themselves between two layers of clouds.

Rob flipped the range knob on the radar to 160 miles. The sweeping beam painted the screen black with a mass of towering Cumulonimbus clouds which stretched for more than thirty miles to each side of their track.

"We'll have to dodge them," he said, switching the radar in the contour position to highlight the cells of the storms. Tracing the course he intended to follow with his index finger, he nodded his head. "If the storms remain isolated like that, we should be able to weave our way through the worst of it." As he said that, the first waves of turbulence hit the plane. The gusts shook the plane like a dead leaf.

Ian felt the first stirring of air sickness gripping his stomach.

Twenty-five minutes later, they ran into real trouble when the isolated clouds closed ranks and blocked their way. Shaken by bad turbulence, they had to tighten their safety harnesses to prevent themselves from getting hurt. Behind, loose equipment rattled down the hold and a door of the galley broke open, spewing cups and packs of powdered sugar over the floor.

Deciding that it was better to fly the plane by hand, Rob pushed the disconnect switch of the autopilot.

"As far as I can see, there are only two possibilities," shouted Jock. "Either we deviate to the north where the radar shows clearer skies, or we try to climb above this rubbish. Going down is something we can't risk. We don't know exactly where we are, and the country here is full of mountains."

Rob mulled this over for a few seconds in his mind. He turned to Ian to ask his opinion, but Ian, fighting hard to keep his bile down, was not paying any attention to what was going on. Shaking his head, Rob turned back to Jock. "If at all possible, I prefer to stay on this track and try to climb above the cells. God only knows how far we would have to swerve to the north, and our fuel reserves are not that good."

Jock turned the tilt knob of the radar antenna two degrees up. For a short while he studied the screen, then he scanned the antenna between four degrees up and two degrees down. "I think you're right," he acknowledged finally." I guess we can get on top of it. Look, with the antenna in a horizontal position, you can see what lies just ahead of us. One unbroken mass of storm clouds! But when I put the antenna two or three degrees up, it becomes a whole different picture." He turned the antenna two degrees up and pointed to the radar screen. "There, look!"

A few thousand feet above them, the radar showed a picture of isolated storms with wide open passages of clear sky between them.

"That was to be expected," confirmed Rob. His caution gave way to eagerness. "The size of this type of cloud is at its greatest in the middle heights but much narrower at the tops. Give me climb power, Jock."

Jock moved the throttles forward and Rob pulled the stick back. At 25,000 they were still in the clouds. To make matters worse, the outside air temperature was down to minus ten and the wings became covered with ice. A volley of hail hit the windshield. It sounded like gunfire.

"It's suicide to continue like this," shouted Ian, his stomach heaving with the gusts and his hangover pounding sharply between his eyes. "Let me out of here," he shouted suddenly. Disregarding all safety, he unbuckled his seat belt and lurched out of his seat. Seconds later they heard, above the noise of the hailstorm, a retching noise that came from the crew toilet and the acrid smell of vomit penetrated the cockpit. Jock wrinkled his nose in disgust.

They had been in the air for one hour now. Forty minutes of it had been spent fighting the storms. Rob began to feel tired. A dull ache of fatigue spread slowly between his shoulder blades and down his back, making his muscles feel like rubber. On the other hand, the intense concentration on flight controls and instruments had made his hangover disappear.

Ian slipped back in his seat. Rob was glad to see that the deadly pale colour of his skin was gone, and that his eyes were bright with a renewed interest in what was happening.

"My stomach is empty now," Ian said, smiling rather sheepishly. "I feel much better."

"If you are ready to do your share of the job," Rob grumbled, "... then you could take over the controls and..."

Before he could finish, the left inboard engine backfired. The loss of power made the plane swerve violently to the left. Almost immediately the Britannia shuddered at the brink of a loss of airspeed. Without hesitation, Rob shoved the stick forward and pushed the right rudder down, turning away from the dead engine to avoid the trap of getting stuck in a spiral dive.

"What's happening, Jock," he yelled, fighting with the rudder controls. "Is that backfire the result of ice on the air intake?"

"No, much worse than that. The fuel pressure is low but the engine exhaust temperature is running up. Something wrong with the fuel control unit, I think. We must shut that engine down."

Immediately, Ian pulled the throttle back and shut the fuel cock. He ran his eyes over the check-list, checking the vital actions. "Throttle closed, fuel shut off, prop feathered..." He pushed the knob of the feathering pump and the four huge blades of the propeller swung flush with the slipstream. "Checklist completed," he reported.

"Because of this engine problem, we can't hold our course," declared Rob. "On three engines, we haven't got a hope in the world of climbing above this rubbish, and the terrain below us is very high. We'll have to deviate to the north." He turned the yoke to the right and swung the plane on a heading of 360 degrees. Rolling in some trim to compensate for the drag of the failed engine, he let the plane gently sink down into the turbulent mass of clouds. Less than twenty minutes later, they broke out of the Cumulonimbus and found themselves in a narrow canyon of clouds, several thousand feet deep and one mile wide. Immediately the worst of the turbulence disappeared and the needles stopped their crazy dance over the dials of the instruments.

As they progressed further north, the gap between the clouds broadened rapidly until it opened up in a wide valley of cloudless sky. Beneath them, a broad river ran almost due north. For as far as they could see, the acacia forest of the tropical belt stretched out on both sides of the aircraft.

Very worried about the engine, Jock unstrapped his seat belt and shook Rob by his shoulder. "Now that it is safe to walk, I'll go back and have a look through the window. I want to make sure that the bang we heard did not cause any serious damage."

"All right, but make it short, and whilst you are in the back, Jock, have a look in the catering box and see if we have some food left. I'm starving."

Floating along in the calm air for another ten minutes, they followed the river which wound its way like a giant snake through the forest. A skirt of rain blocked the view to the east. Far away to the west, they saw another frontal depression building up. Straight ahead, the sky was clear.

Rob engaged the autopilot and pulled a topographical map out of his flight case. “You watch the controls, Ian,” he said. “I’ll try to find some reference points on the map to locate our position.”

Finding their position was very important. If they continued on the actual track, they would either wind up in Zaire or run out of fuel. Neither of the two options was acceptable!

The moment Jock came back, they were down to 5,000 feet and the placid waters of the river below had disappeared. Instead, a torrent of waters cascaded through a narrow gorge in the rocks, forcing its way between half-submerged boulders in a frothing mass of waves and foam.

“I can’t see any external damage,” Jock reported. “I don’t know what the real problem is, but I guess that the rough landing in Lukapa must have shaken an electrical connection in the fuel control loose.” Putting a sandwich in Rob’s hand, he shrugged his shoulders. “Anyway, there is nothing I can do about it now. It will have to wait until we are on the ground.”

Ian wrinkled his nose when Jock offered him a sandwich. “Thanks,” he said. “But no, thanks. My stomach already heaves when I think about food.”

He leaned forward and studied the contour of the land and the path of the river. “Look there skipper, to the left of the nose. Is that what I think it is?”

Rob looked out.

A couple of miles to the left of the river, he saw a cluster of tiny huts. It looked like a small native village. Closer by, where the banks of the river widened at the beginning of a long and curved lake, lay the straight and narrow line of a laterite landing strip. To get a better view of the land, he turned the heading selector of the autopilot to the left and selected a lower altitude. “Yes, you’re right, Ian, that is indeed an airfield. What do you guess? 5,000 feet long?” A surprised expression appeared on his face. “I wonder which one it is? It could be any one out of a hundred I suppose.”

At 1,500 feet above the ground, they were able to make out the dark shapes of a herd of cattle or sheep on the runway. Frightened by the noise of the engines they panicked and, closely followed by their shepherd, disappeared in the high grass that bordered the strip.

Munching on his sandwich, Rob scrutinized the layout of the terrain and the state of the runway. “I have an idea,” he said suddenly, pointing successively from the packed layers of clouds which came drifting in from the west, to the fuel flow indicators on the centre instrument panel. “We can’t go on like this. Dodging threatening thunderclouds, and flying on three engines at low level, we’re burning fuel like a blowtorch. At this rate, we’ll never get back to base.” He shook his head. “On top of that, our position is a mystery, we have no exact course to steer and don’t know the distance to go.” He took another bite of his sandwich and shrugged his shoulders. “On the other hand, down there is a place where we can land and sit out the storm.”

“The villagers must be able to tell us exactly where we are,” Jock pointed out.

“What about guerrillas,” risked Ian. “Are you sure this place is safe?”

“As far as I know, there is no danger of rebel activity in this part of Angola. I remember Sobreiro saying that in 1976, the combined forces of Nevo’s Army and the Cubans drove UNITA out of here.”

“Yes, that’s right,” confirmed Jock. “I was there when Sobreiro said that. I like the idea of landing here, Rob. It will give me the chance to have a look at that engine. Maybe even fix it.”

With a speed of 200 knots on the clock, Rob flew low over the strip. Ian and Jock kept their eyes wide open, looking for obstacles or other pitfalls.

In the mean time it had started to rain again, a dismal drizzle which clouded the forest in a shroud of mist and hid the other side of the lake from view. The rivulets of water on the windshield deformed the view and made the runway look like the surface of an ocean. The swaying motion of the treetops indicated a slight wind from the east. Rob brought them gently in, making the approach on three engines appear as if it was easy.

As soon as the props came to a full stop, a group of people emerged from the forest. Rob counted five or six men, and maybe a dozen children.

"They must have come from the village," Rob said.

"Good," declared Jack. "That will save us the effort of going there to find out where we are."

"If they speak English, Jock," remarked Ian. "That, I think, is highly doubtful."

"I'll go and try to talk with them," Rob volunteered. He slipped his navigation map in his pocket and, followed by Jock, hurried down the ladder.

Jock unlocked the cowling of number 2 engine. Armed with a torch, he plunged his arm into the innards of the engine.

Rob found his way through the high grass to the edge of the forest. As he came nearer, he noticed the shabby state of the clothes of the villagers and the unhealthy appearance of some of the children. He estimated the age of the adults between twenty and thirty, the children between five and ten. He soon discovered that they didn't speak English, but a weird-sounding Bantu dialect that he couldn't understand. Even pointing to the map and making inquiring signs did not help. Raising his hands in an apologetic gesture, Rob went back to the plane.

"No luck, Jock," he said. "No common language at all. Sobreiro should have been here. He would know that kind of lingo."

"So Ian was right."

"These people are in bad shape, Jock. Their clothes are worn to shreds and the younger children have very thin legs and swollen tummies."

Instead of giving a reply, Jock suddenly shouted with joy. "I was right skipper, look there." Proudly, he pointed the beam of his torch somewhere to the back of the engine.

Rob noticed the black box of the fuel control unit and a set of loose hanging wires.

"The wires have merely been chafed through," Jock added. "Most probably the result of the hard landing yesterday and the beating we got in the severe turbulence this morning. With a pair of pliers and a screwdriver, I can fix that in less than ten minutes."

"Take all the time in the world," Rob said. His arms made a sweeping motion. "We won't take off until all those clouds are gone and I can see clear blue sky from here to the west coast. In the mean time I'll go down to the lake to stretch my legs."

He turned on his heels and walked away. The rain fell in heavy drops on his head and shoulders. It felt like an open-air shower, cool and invigorating. Reaching the lake, he sat down on a flat rock by the shore. The rain made bubbles on the surface of the water. Suddenly aware that this was crocodile country, he backed away from the shore. Then the shepherd, seen from the sky previously, an old man with a weathered skin, stepped out from between the bushes by the side of the runway. Smiling a toothless grin, he said in Portuguese: "Boa tarde, Senhor. Como esta?" - Good morning, senhor, how are you?

One hour later, Rob came back to the plane, his hair and clothes soaking wet from the rain. He noticed that the cowling of engine number two was closed.

Ian and Jock were in the cockpit, both asleep and snoring. Rob quickly stripped and toweled himself dry. He changed into a set of spare clothes he carried in his overnight kit and prepared some coffee. A tray of steaming mugs in his hand, he woke up his crew.

"This runway is in very good condition," he said. "I also found the shepherd. Or maybe I should say he found me." He told Jock and Ian what had happened. "We had an interesting conversation in a combination of Portuguese, Spanish and sign language, but it's amazing what I discovered."

Over lunch, a simple piece of bread and corned beef, he told them that their Britannia was the first plane to land here in years and that a very long time ago, a plane had crashed into the lake. "There were no survivors!"

"Poor bastards," Jock mumbled.

"The old guy showed me a piece of wreckage," Rob went on. "It was the broken strut of a landing gear, with the wheel and tyre still attached. As far as I could make out, the tyre was an aviation Pirelli, but I haven't got the foggiest idea about what kind of a plane it was."

"Could it be the Skyvan?" Ian suggested.

"It's not very likely, Ian. This place is nowhere near the normal route from Portugalia to Luanda."

"Ask Sobreiro," advised Jock. "He might know."

"I doubt it," rebutted Rob. "I asked him when I was here, in March, before the start of our operation. He was a young teenager when it happened. He doesn't remember much of it. However, he promised to ask around, and try to find some reports about the incident in the files of DIANGOL. I might have a look in the archives myself."

"With Mena's help, I presume?" said Jock.

"That would be the day," replied Rob wistfully.

At that moment, the clouds broke open. The sun burned down on the earth, raising clouds of steam. The surface of the lake shone like a mirror, the water reflecting the rock wall at the eastern shore and the blue of the sky above.

"Incidentally," Rob concluded, "The name of this place is Massau. It's barely 200 miles to the north-east of Luanda."

Ten minutes later, they climbed through 5,000 feet, leaving the watery grave of the unknown aviators and the mystery that surrounded them behind.

Luanda, 30 September 1995

His eyes half closed and the smoke of his cigarette drifting in a cloud above his head, Lopes concentrated on what Olunga was saying.

"They spent the night in Lukapa," Olunga reported. "Then early this morning they came back to Luanda, but guess what? Instead of flying straight back, they made a detour to the north and landed in Massau. They pretended they were forced to do so by heavy weather and the extra complication of an engine failure. However, when they arrived here, the mechanics could find no traces of a technical problem. As a matter of fact, the plane has already been loaded for another flight, so there can't have been much wrong with it."

"Was the weather really that bad?" Lopes inquired. "Or was it just a pretext they used to deviate to the north?"

"This time of year, it is true that the whole country is saturated with storm depressions," Olunga confirmed. "I don't know whether Stanfort had an ulterior motive for a landing in Massau, but I thought it best to let you know. Maybe he is trying to make extra money by running guns or equipment for UNITA. A remote airfield like Massau would be perfect for that, and the border with Zaire is not that far away."

With the daily increase in guerrilla activity, Lopes admitted that Olunga's suspicion of Stanfort's motives was a very astute one, and true, UNITA had training camps across the border with Zaire.

His own sceptical mind suddenly found a possible connection with an event from the past when he was a young inspector, and a whole swarm of ideas flashed through his head.

Wasn't it in the vicinity of the Guillaume Falls that the Skyvan of DIANGOL had been shot down? Massau was not that far away from the Falls. Had Stanfort discovered something about the location of that lost aircraft?

The recollection of the enormous fortune in diamonds that was still lying somewhere in the jungle was sufficient to set Lopes' blood racing.

"Keep me advised about Stanfort's further movements, Olunga," he said, carefully hiding his emotions. "If ever they go back to Massau, I want to know it immediately, understood!"

Without waiting for a reply, he put the phone down.

"Imagine," he thought. "Just by following Stanfort, I might be able to recover the diamonds. It would earn me the eternal gratitude of the President and propel me to astonishing heights in my career..."

There was of course a second possibility! The disaster with the Skyvan was twenty years ago. Hardly anybody alive in Angola could still remember it. Hence, keeping the diamonds for himself would be easy.

It would be like being able to print his own money and becoming rich beyond all imagination!

Luanda, Wednesday, 8 November 1995

It was an exceptionally beautiful day. The late afternoon sky, entirely free of clouds, looked like a cupola of gold and blue which spanned the whole width of the horizon. A soft breeze came in from over the ocean, gently swaying the crowns of a grove of palm trees and flattening the long grasses which covered the slopes of the coastal hills.

Jock, assisted by Ian and two mechanics of DIANGOL, was doing a 50 hours check on the Britannia. Rob had spent the morning doing his paperwork and was now enjoying the rest of the day comfortably stretched out on a deck chair by the swimming pool of the Tropico. He let his eyes glide over the vast expanse of the Atlantic Ocean and the wide curve of the moon-shaped beach which turned silver and green when a long, rolling wave hit the shore and curled over in a mass of bubbling foam.

His sense of being alive was so intense that, in his mind, he could hear the swishing noise of the water on the coarse sand. This was in fact the best time of the day, he considered, a few short hours of coolness before darkness fell and the soil began to release the warmth it had accumulated during the day, wrapping the city in its nightly blanket of sweltering heat and moisture, with the added curse of buzzing and stinging insects.

With the sun still warm on his skin, he bent forward and lifted a bottle out of the ice-bucket. After sipping a few mouthfuls of beer, he leaned back in his chair and closed his eyes against the sharp light of the sun. Involuntarily, his mind drifted to the obstacles and adversities they had conquered during the past few months.

"We must have a party," he decided. "Something to commemorate the first few months of our operations in Angola." Busy thinking about the organization of the event, he took another sip of beer. "We'll need booze and music, and a large room. And a list of people to invite, and invitations..."

As far as booze was concerned, Rob knew he could rely on Sobreiro. With his contacts on the black market, getting all the drinks they needed would be easy, but finding a room large enough to receive fifty or sixty guests was an entirely different matter. Racking his brains, Rob suddenly remembered the function hall in the Tropico. He made a mental note to talk to the manager of the hotel. As for music and invitations, he would have to ask Mena! His mind now vivid with plans, he began to see how it would be, with a lot of guests, drinks, music and dancing. And of course, Mena.

Almost imperceptibly his thoughts became hazier and he fell asleep. Half an hour later, he awoke brusquely when a splash of cold water fell on his head and shoulders.

"What the hell," he shouted, jumping up.

Sobreiro laughed when he saw the furious expression in Rob's eyes. "Oh, Robby," he said, in his joy almost choking on his words. "Don't look so mad, it's nothing but the water from your ice bucket." To remove the sting out of the joke, Sobreiro folded his lips in a conspiratory grin. "In fact, I didn't come here to annoy you," he said. "I came to tell you that somebody in high places trusts you very much."

Suspicious of being tricked into another relief flight, Rob walked over to the edge of the terrace. The metal railing of the balcony felt hot to his touch. In a reflex action, he jerked his hands back and looked out over the harbour. On the north side, at a safe distance from the commercial docks, stood the installations and storage tanks of the Angolan Petroleum Company. A large oil tanker was moored by the pier, the warm yellows and reds of its hull gleaming richly in the clear green water. Anchored in the middle of the lagoon, surrounded by a fleet of small coastal vessels, lay an old Russian freighter, its rusty hull in stark contrast with the bright colours of the tanker. To get a clue of what to expect, Rob turned around and faced Sobreiro. "Explain what you mean, you treacherous friend."

"What would you say if I told you that, perhaps in two weeks from now, you could be having dinner in the Ritz in Lisbon?"

Rob raised his eyebrows. "The Ritz in Lisbon!" he exclaimed. "What do you mean?"

Sobreiro walked over to where Rob was standing.

Rob suddenly saw his chance to get even. Sly as a fox, he stayed motionless until Sobreiro was barely a couple of steps away. He then took a giant jump forward and pushed Sobreiro into the swimming pool. "That will remind you in the future not to wake me up with a bucket of ice water," he roared gleefully.

Coughing and sneezing, Sobreiro dragged himself out of the pool. He quickly stripped, draped his wet clothes over the back of a chair to let them dry in the sun and, totally at ease in spite of his nakedness, grabbed a towel to rub himself dry. As he hissed Rob to shut up and listen, his voice was a mixture of annoyance and irritation. "You know that the country is suffering from the effects of a black market in hard currencies," he began. "The official rate for the dollar is 25 Escudos, but in the city, dealers are offering 250 and sometimes even 260 Escudos for one dollar."

Culpable of changing dollars on the black market himself to pay for all his expenses in Angola, Rob guiltily dropped his eyes.

Unaware of Rob's embarrassment, Sobreiro finished drying himself. He wrapped the towel around his waist and let himself sink down into a chair. "I heard a rumour that some dealers in Lobito are paying up to 300 escudos," he added.

His lungs aching for a smoke, Sobreiro fished around in the pocket of his shirt. The cigarettes were sodden with water. As he pulled one of the sticks out of the packet, it came apart in a messy pulp of paper and tobacco. Immediately, another flash of annoyance lit up his eyes. Rob quickly turned his head to hide the grin that curled his lips. Sobreiro flicked his fingers to attract the attention of the pool waiter. He slipped him a bill of 200 escudos and ordered him to go down to the bar and fetch him a fresh pack of cigarettes.

"We could do with two more beers as well," added Rob.

When the waiter came back with the cigarettes and beer, Sobreiro told him to keep the rest of the money. The boy's eyes grew big with surprise at the largeness of the tip. As soon as they were alone again, Sobreiro carried on. "In order to get rid of that money problem," he said, pulling the wrapper off the pack of cigarettes, "the Minister of Finance and his assistants have invented something like the Marshall Plan." He lit his cigarette and blew a plume of smoke into the air. "Do you know anything about that?"

"Not at all, Sobreiro, it must have happened quite a while before my time."

"It was before my time as well, Rob, but I looked it up in a history book."

Sobreiro took another puff of his cigarette. "At the end of the Second World War, General Marshall, an American, came up with a plan to revive the economies of the war torn countries in Europe. His plan consisted mainly of shipping aid, such as tractors, machinery and equipment, worth billions and billions of dollars. Our Government in Angola came up with a slightly different version of the plan. They think that the secret of restoring the productive power of the country lies in getting rid of the money problem."

For a moment, Sobreiro let his eyes wander in the direction of two sparrows, who were having a fight in the shallow end of the pool. Absently, he sipped his beer. Then, as if afraid of being distracted again, he turned back to Rob. "The first step in their plan is cleaning up the black market in hard currencies. From the first of December, the old Escudo will cease to be a legal tender. Each citizen will be given two thousand new Kwanzas. By doing this, the Government hopes to kill two birds with one stone. All Angolans will be equally rich..." He suddenly sniggered, "... or equally poor if you prefer ... and the profiteering will stop due to lack of money on the black market."

Rob could not prevent himself from making the snide remark that it would only last until somebody high-up found a way of beating the system to make a huge profit for himself.

"True, Rob. Knowing the ways of Africa, it's something to be expected." Drinking deeply, Sobreiro drained his beer. "However, that's besides the point." He called the waiter and ordered two more beers. "The new Kwanzas are currently being printed on the presses of the National Bank in Lisbon," Sobreiro whispered confidentially. "Fourteen tons of them, and you have been chosen to pick them up."

Although very reluctant to leave Angola and Mena, even only for a couple of days, Rob immediately saw the positive side of it. "This flight comes exactly at the right moment, Sobreiro. The Britannia is coming up for a C check. That's a very important inspection and, due to the need for special equipment, can only be done in our home base. According to my contract with the DCA, the ferry flight to Europe and back has to be paid by them. Why not take the opportunity of this flight to Lisbon to get the maintenance out of the way. The checks can be done in less than three days. Afterwards, we fly back to Lisbon, pick up your newly printed money, and come back to Luanda."

"Very smart," acknowledged Sobreiro. "It would save the DCA a lot of money, and it would save you from having to make an extra flight to Europe."

"There is something else I want to ask you." In a few brief words, Rob told Sobreiro about his plan for a party and his need for a supply of booze. "I'm sorry to ask you for this favour," he said apologetically. "But, as I have to fly almost every day, I don't have the time to organize it all."

"Don't worry," replied Sobreiro. "That's what friends are for. It's a great idea and I'll be happy to arrange the booze. There's enough of that available if you're willing to pay the price. As for food, that's ..."

"I don't want any food," Rob broke in. "There's nothing decent available on the market, and I don't want to serve them a portion of 'Dried fish and rice à la Tropico'. Booze, music and dancing, that will be the theme of the evening!"

"Count on me," answered Sobreiro. "Tomorrow, I'm scheduled to fly a trip with the F27 to Sao Salvador. The following day, I'm operating a round trip to Mocamedes, but the day after that, I'll go shopping."

Early the next morning, shortly before the thin line of dawn commenced to pierce the dark of the night, they were ready for another day of flying. The glowing tail of a shooting star briefly scarred the sky.

"Make a wish," Rob said, thinking about Mena, and followed by Jock, he started across the tarmac.

The bowser pulled away from the aeroplane, its bulky mass partly hidden by a plume of exhaust vapours. There was a smell of dry dust and high-octane petrol. Behind the bowser, the dark shapes of the Britannia looked dreamlike and spooky.

Under the right wing, the security guard on duty stirred, the collar of his jacket pulled up to ward off the early morning chills. As he recognized Rob, he saluted.

The first rays of the sun abruptly appeared above the horizon. The narrow band of light became a halo of brightness, the rim of the earth a mixture of pinks and reds. A bright flash of light sparked against the base of the clouds which drifted like giant birds across the land. As if touched by magic, the thin veil of fog that covered the earth, lifted.

Silently admiring nature's glory, Jock draped his arm over Rob's shoulder. "I've seen this spectacle at least a thousand times," he murmured. "And it never stops to thrill me."

The milky-white clarity of the sky became painful to Rob's eyes. Small drops of perspiration appeared on his forehead and stuck the back of his shirt to his skin. He wrapped a pair of Ray-Bans around his eyes.

"Enough of this sentimental nonsense, Jock," he said jokingly. "Let's get on with the job. We have a long day in front of us," Rob let a secret grin creep over his lips. "... And I promise you, it will be a very rewarding day. We have to pickup a very special cargo in Benguela."

"What?" shouted Jock. "You mean that you have..."

Rob eagerly broke in: "Yes, after months of talking and begging and trying, I finally managed to make a deal with the Base Commander. The Motor Falcons are mine."

Jock's face became a picture of surprise. "How did you manage that?"

"Once it occurred to me how to tempt the Commander, it was easy," replied Rob smugly. "Just make sure that one of the motorcycles is on board."

"So that's the price you have to pay."

"That, and two pairs of my blue jeans," Rob chuckled. "They seem to be worth a fortune on the black market."

In Benguela, they unloaded 15 tons of kerosene into the fuel tanks of the Air Force. Ian supervized the loading of the cargo for Portugalia and Jock took care of the refuelling. Rob completed the deal with the Base Commander and they stowed the two Motor Falcons on board.

In Portugalia, they unloaded and stored the Falcons in the old hangar. Jock made a quick inspection of the two planes.

"I'm surprised," he remarked. "The years of neglect haven't caused any obvious damage. I'll have to tune the carburettors, replace the cables of the flight controls and clean the pitot heads. After that, your Falcons will be perfectly airworthy!"

Saurimo, Thursday, 16 November 1995

During the night, the Civil War, which had mostly been raging in the south, hit Saurimo. It was the result of a series of secret meetings held in Paris and Geneva during the early summer months between CEA, acronym for the Committee of Cuban Exiles in Africa, and the leadership of UNITA.

CEA consisted mainly of landowners and industrialists who had fled Cuba when Fidel Castro ousted General Fulgencio Batista and changed the country from an extreme right-wing dictatorship to an authoritarian Communist Republic.

On the 5th of October, at the conclusion of the final meeting in Geneva, CEA made a substantial offer in aid to UNITA. New weapons and equipment, and a group of 2,500 well-trained volunteers to fight alongside their African allies. In exchange, once the war against the communists was over, CEA wanted the right for the Cuban exiles to live in Angola, in a part of the country where they could live free and create new futures for themselves and their families.

UNITA accepted the conditions.

From the 10th of October onwards, large quantities of weapons and equipment started to arrive from secret supply points in Namibia and Zaire. Eight new battle groups were fitted out and trained. By the middle of November, UNITA was ready to launch a new offensive. In preparation for that, deep infiltrations into the eastern provinces began.

Shortly after midnight on the 16th of November, they crept out of the bush and attacked simultaneously in four different locations. The first to fall were Tumbi and Yema, two small towns to the north of Luso. At 3 o'clock, Maquila and Gumala, two villages in the vicinity of Saurimo, were overrun by UNITA units.

It was not until the sun came up that an infantry battalion, supported by two artillery platoons and a squadron of fighter jets, launched a counter attack. At the price of much damage and bloodshed, they managed to stop the advance of the guerrillas.

Unaware of the fighting, Rob and his crew left Luanda on time for their scheduled flight to Saurimo. They landed shortly after ten in the morning. As soon as the cargo door was opened, the sounds of distant gunfire flooded the cockpit. Rob instructed Ian and Jock to stay on board. "Call Mena," he instructed. "She is on duty in the Ops Office. Tell her what's happening. I'll go down and find out what the situation is. If there's any danger, we'll fly straight back to Luanda!"

"It's a new offensive of UNITA," explained the cargo supervisor. "But don't worry. Our own forces are in close contact with the enemy. They'll soon drive them back into the bush, where they belong."

A loud salvo of artillery fire drew Rob's attention to the east, where a red flare drew a glowing trail through the pale blue of the sky. Like a flight of hawks, two MiG21s dived down and plastered the marked position with a cluster of napalm bombs. Huge billowing clouds of smoke rose up and partially obscured the light of the sun. Rob estimated the columns of smoke to be approximately ten miles away from the airfield.

"For the time being, we're safe enough," he judged. "Let's get on with the job, but hurry!"

"I'm afraid it will take a little longer than usual," the cargo supervizor answered. "Half my work force hasn't turned up, and those who are here are worried shitless."

It took the better part of two hours to empty the plane. When Jock was ready to close the cargo door, a Jeep came shooting around the corner. It stopped by the plane, its tyres spewing gravel. A young Lieutenant jumped out.

"Wait," he shouted. "You have to take a load of wounded soldiers with you to Luanda."

Rob stepped out of the cockpit. "I'm not equipped to transport passengers," he shouted back. "There are no seats on board, and no toilets, and we don't carry oxygen in case of loss of cabin pressure at high altitude."

"Doesn't matter, Captain," replied the Lieutenant. "Our field-hospital is swamped with wounded. We're running out of bandages and painkillers." A distracted look appeared in his eyes as he recalled the intensity and savagery of the fighting. "You have to take them," he repeated. "You're their only chance!"

Four ambulances pulled up by the aircraft. The drivers, assisted by stretcher bearers, loaded row after row of stretchers in the cargo hold of the Britannia.

A tremor of worry and apprehension coursed through Rob's body. As the casualties were brought on board, he could hardly bear the look of the miserable shapes which were lying on the stretchers. Finally, compassion forced him to move in closer.

One of the wounded was moaning softly, his eyes big white globes filled with panic and despair. Rob noticed the bloody bandage around the lower part of his arms where his hands should have been. The soldier on the next stretcher was lying on his back, moving his body restlessly. The bandages around his belly came loose and Rob saw a succession of bullet holes which ran like a row of small red-mouthed volcanoes over his dark skin. Another soldier was breathing laboriously, a frothy foam on his lips. The head of the next one was completely bandaged, the bandage strangely deformed at the place where his chin had been shot away...

Confronted with those terrible injuries, Rob's eyes misted over and horror and compassion fought for priority in his mind. Drained by the intensity of his emotions, he wondered what he could do to help but, apart from rushing them to Luanda, there was nothing!

In total, they loaded forty stretchers, each one of them carrying a severely injured soldier. "There are many more of them," the Lieutenant stressed. "Please, come back as soon as possible."

During the flight, five of the wounded soldiers died...

That day, they flew three more stretcher flights and late at night, when the Britannia was being serviced, they fell exhausted on camp beds Mena had made in one of the rooms in the Flight Ops building and snatched a few short hours of almost comatose sleep. On Thursday, they operated four Medevac flights. Finally, on Friday, the front stabilized and the intensity of the fighting decreased. Rob and his crew had to operate only one more stretcher flight.

In the afternoon, they loaded a cargo of dried fish and rice, and operated a 'regular' flight from Luanda back to their home-base in Portugalia.

That evening, after dinner, they drank glass after glass of Casal Garcia. As the alcohol got hold of their tired and stressed bodies their muscles relaxed but their minds remained strangely lucid and refused to erase the awful sights their eyes had witnessed.

Outside, the weather was terrible, matching their moods. In the garden, swaying wildly in the strong winds, hibiscus and frangipani bushes were shredding their petals like confetti, covering the soil with a velvet carpet of white, pink and yellow.

Ian was standing on the balcony, leaning his shoulder against the door post and looking morosely at the spectacle of rain and wind. He took a deep breath of the musty air and returned to his place by the hearth. "I feel rotten," he stated. "Here we are, living in comfort and luxury while those poor soldiers die by the dozen, and innocent families are killed in their villages."

"I feel it, too," replied Rob. "What I feel most of all is anger. Anger against the leaders of the warring armies, who are using their soldiers as pawns in a game of political chess."

"May all unscrupulous politicians rot in hell," Jock roared. "They deserve it!"

"I'll drink to that," Rob replied.

They emptied their drinks in one go and threw the empty glasses into the flickering flames of the fire.

To get them out of their ominous moods, Rob went back to the bar and took a new set of glasses out of the cabinet. Pushing all thoughts about fighting and wounded soldiers to the back of his mind, he opened another bottle and poured the wine.

"We've done our best to help," he said. "But life must go on, and remember, tomorrow, we have a celebration to attend to."

Ian and Jock looked up at him, their eyes full of wonder.

"Have you forgotten what day it is, tomorrow?" Rob asked.

As he noticed their vacant stares, he laughed drunkenly. "Tomorrow, Saturday, we're flying to Luanda. For our party. Or had you forgotten about that, too?"

Saturday, 18 November 1995

Early the next morning, their sombre moods of the previous evening had been dissipated by a good night's sleep. Suffering only a slight hangover in spite of the amount of wine they had consumed, and looking forward to the coming party, they showered, shaved and had a light breakfast. Jock threw their overnight bags in the boot of the car and they hurried to the airfield.

In places, the road was still covered with puddles of standing water and mud. Clear of clouds, the sky slowly changed from grey to blue and the air which came wafting in through the open windows smelled clean and fresh.

Whilst Jock made the external inspection, Rob climbed into the cockpit and adjusted his seat to the correct position for the take-off, then he wrapped a headset around his head, checked the oxygen mask and flicked a few dozen switches and knobs to their pre-start positions.

In the co-pilot's seat, Ian went through the routine of reading the check-list to make sure that nothing had escaped Rob's attention.

As soon as Jock finished his pre-flight, he climbed up the retractable ladder and closed the door, thereby sealing them off from the outside world. Rob started the engines and they took off.

Barely free from the ground, slender wisps of dew wrapped themselves around the windshields. At 18,000 feet, the air felt as smooth as silk. The movements of the aeroplane were almost dreamlike, the stick and rudders so easy to handle that Rob had the eerie feeling that it was not him but somebody else, somebody much more capable, who was handling the controls.

Fifty miles before the coast, the pink and gold reflection of the sun on the walls and towers of Luanda became visible through the cockpit windows. After a routine approach and an extremely smooth landing, Rob taxied the Britannia to its normal place by the DCA hangar. His Land Rover was parked in front of the office. Next to it stood Mena and Sobreiro, their hands raised protectively against their ears to shut out the noise.

Jock cut the fuel supply to the engines. As soon as the props started to spin down, Rob slipped his side window open.

"What do you want first, Rob," shouted Sobreiro. "The bad news or the good?"

"Just give me a second," replied Rob. "I'll be right there!" Leaving the shutdown checks to Ian and Jock, he rushed down the ladder. Carefully hiding the apprehension in his voice, he told Sobreiro to give him the bad news first.

"Well," said Sobreiro gruffly. "With the money you gave me to buy drinks for the party, I've only managed to get five barrels of beer. For some reason or other, the black market in booze seems to have dried up."

"Oh, shit," shouted Rob. In his frustration he swung around and kicked the rear tyre of the Land Rover. "How the hell can I entertain fifty or sixty people with five barrels of beer?"

To stress the importance of what he was saying, he punched his fist against the car's body. "Damn it, as from tomorrow, I'll be the biggest joke in Luanda."

Trying to find a way out of the crisis, he mentally reviewed his own contacts and people who owed him a favour. Maybe, just maybe, there was enough time to go and comb the city to get some real booze, such as scotch or vodka. He turned back to Sobreiro. "Jee, man, you let me down," he snapped disappointedly, "but the day is still early and maybe I can find..."

In spite of his anger, his eyes caught the smile that puckered Sobreiro's lips. Suddenly, he knew that he had been duped and his depressed expression made place for a look of relief.

"You bastard," he sighed. "I should tie you to a blade of the propeller and give the engine a few swings."

"Just repaying you for throwing me in the swimming pool, Rob." Without waiting for Rob's answer, Sobreiro added: "The good news is that I also have lots of white and red wine, five bottles of vodka, five bottles of gin and ten bottles of scotch."

In a surge of companionship, Rob gave Sobreiro a playful whack on his chest.

Sobreiro aimed his hand in the direction of the car. "Come on, let's not waste the rest of the day at the airport."

They seated themselves in the Land Rover, Sobreiro, Ian and Jock in the front and Mena and Rob on the narrower bench in the rear. Sobreiro gave a full report of what he, with Mena's help, had been able to accomplish. Chuckling with delight, he uttered: "Your party will be the success of the year, Rob. The whole of Luanda is talking about it. It's a very rare event, you know!"

"Who is coming, Sobreiro?" asked Ian.

"Most of the guests are people who have been very helpful, others may be useful in the future. There are also managers of DIANGOL and the DCA, senior staff members, a delegation of Army officers..." Sobreiro suddenly laughed. "Some of them will be there to be seen. Others, will be there to drink as much and as fast as possible. They'll make real fools of themselves, but that's normal in a war torn country like this."

"Have a short life, and a good one," remarked Jock.

"Some of the guests will come with their girlfriends instead of their wives," interrupted Mena, a certain disdain in her voice making it clear what she thought about that kind of 'girlfriends'.

"I hope there will be one or two unattached ladies to take care of people like me," said Jock expectantly.

"I'm sure you'll find a suitable companion," replied Sobreiro, adding that there would also be delegations from foreign embassies and some members of the Angolan Government.

"For music," he concluded, "Mena has borrowed a jukebox with all the great favourites of the fifties and sixties. So it's all arranged. Nothing to worry about!"

"That's fantastic," said Rob. He playfully caressed Mena's cheek with his lips. Strangely enough, she didn't pull away, a reaction that strengthened his belief that her attitude towards him was changing.

He didn't have the slightest inkling about how much Mena's attitude had really changed.

The confrontation at the airport in Luanda with the wounded and dying soldiers had shocked her out of an emotional limbo, making her accept that her husband was dead and belonged to the past, and crystallizing her feelings for Rob, who was alive and belonged to the present! It had also come to her that it was useless to worry about the future, about things that might or might not happen. What counted was today as there might never be a tomorrow, especially now that Rob was getting involved with Medevac and the military. If he got killed, she would never know what it meant to lay in his arms and be loved by him. To enjoy whatever time they had left, she had decided to give love a chance!

Sobreiro swung the Land Rover in a skidding turn to the right. In front of them lay the wide and sunlit Largo de Serpa Pinto, the long road that ran from the airport to the centre of town. In the turn, the vehicle listed over steeply, throwing Mena sideways against Rob.

"Hey, Sobreiro, take it easy, man," shouted Jock cheerfully.

In a protective gesture, Rob slung his arm around Mena's shoulders.

Sitting so close together, she could feel the heat of his body through the thin fabric of her summer dress. She could even smell the faint scent of his aftershave. Shock waves of longing shot through her body.

Sobreiro took another turn, more gentle this time.

The rays of the sun fell strongly on Mena's face. In a reflex, she closed her eyes and let her head rest against Rob's shoulder. Her thoughts went to the party. She imagined herself dancing with Rob, with his body close to hers. That would be the right time to show him her true feelings. Afterwards they could go somewhere together, where she could spoil him rotten and give him all the love she had to give. Moving sideways, she slipped closer to Rob and put her hand in a silent pledge over his hand.

At the end of the airport road, instead of turning right in the direction of the Tropico, Sobreiro turned left and headed away from the city.

"Hey Sobreiro, you missed the turn," shouted Jock, pointing to the right. "The Tropico is that way."

"Not at all, Jock," Mena answered. "Tonight, we'll go to the Tropico for your party. This afternoon, we're going deep-sea fishing." Leaning forward in her seat, she tapped Jock on the shoulder. "Have you ever done that before?"

Jock swung his head around. "Have we ever done that before?" he roared. "Did you hear that guys? Did she really have the cheek to ask *us* if we have done any deep-sea fishing?"

With his face folded in an artificially piqued scowl, Ian remarked that it was like asking whether there were craters on the moon.

Sobreiro butted in.

"These boys pretend not only to be flyers, but also experienced divers and fishermen, Mena!" He ignored the furious howls of protest his remark provoked. In a slow and teasing way he continued: "To go by their stories, because we don't have any actual evidence, it seems that the North Sea is a rather more difficult place to go fishing than the South Atlantic."

Shifting down the gears, he swung the Land Rover from the main road onto a narrow track which, like most of the roads in Luanda, was potholed and smelt of mud and dumped rubbish.

"I think they are bluffing," Mena said mockingly.

"We'll see about that later," countered Jock. "I'll bet you one hundred dollars against ten of yours, Sobreiro, that I will catch more fish than you. And sooner."

To avoid cracking the springs of the Land Rover in one of the deeper holes in the road, Sobreiro concentrated on winding his way between the obstacles and stopped short of two rusty, but still majestic old gates. A middle aged man, dressed in the faded brown uniform of a DIANGOL security guard, stepped out of the watch house. As he recognized Sobreiro and Mena, a huge smile split his face.

"Bom dia," he chanted and threw the gate open.

Sobreiro slipped a packet of cigarettes in his hand, released the clutch and drove the car into the shade under the wide canopy of a dozen long stemmed palm trees.

"Welcome to Mussulo," Mena said exuberantly. "Welcome to the Luanda Yacht Club."

"It's not quite the luxurious tropical paradise it used to be," stressed Sobreiro more soberly, setting the parking brake. "To tell you the truth, compared with what it was, the place is rather run-down now..."

"It's still the best kept secret in Luanda," added Mena. "Mainly because of DIANGOL's influence!"

"And half a dozen security guards," completed Sobreiro.

A slightly teasing smile on her lips, Mena explained that nobody but prominent employees of the Government, DIANGOL, or visiting VIPs were allowed to use the club, but that none of them seemed to be interested. "Believe it or not, Rob," she disclosed, giggling. "As pilots on contract to the Government, you and your friends are rated VIPs. So from now on, whenever you are free, you can come here and use the boat."

"What boat," asked Rob.

"A 150 hp Chris-Craft," she replied. "And there's more. I'll show you later."

She jumped out of the car and ran barefoot over the hot white sand to the edge of the water. Rob was quick to follow. Standing next to her, he shaded his eyes with his hands. Ahead, the surface of the lagoon glittered like gold in the light of the sun. Just inside the reef lay a small island, its green vegetation contrasting vibrantly with the colour of the sky. On the island stood two small villas. Slightly further to the north, at the place where a break in the reef gave access to the ocean, the colour of the water turned from green to dark blue.

Eager to discover what he could find on this side of the lagoon, he slipped his arm gently around Mena's slim waist and turned their backs to the water. Slightly to their left stood the buildings of the Yacht Club. Or what was left of them, for the boat house was in a pitiful condition, the windows broken and some of the roof tiles missing. The beach was cluttered with boats. Amongst them, Rob noticed a couple of large sailing yachts and several big cabin cruisers. His interest aroused, Rob walked over to take a better look. As he came closer, he became aware of the neglected condition of the yachts. What he had believed to be a row of beautiful boats was in fact nothing but a collection of derelict hulks.

Mena explained that those yachts had been left there by their previous owners. "It all happened a few weeks before Independence," she said, making a sweeping motion with her hand. "At that time, the airport was closed and the last passenger ships had left a long time before that."

Listening to Mena's voice, Rob could almost sense the frantic desire of the families to get away.

"Getting out of the country on board their own boat was the only way of escape," Mena continued. "When they applied for a permit, it was refused by the military. Some took the risk and got away in the dark of the night." She shrugged her shoulders helplessly. "Others were not so brave."

"I see," replied Rob. "And rather than leave their boats as toys of luxury for the new communist rulers, they ran them on to the beach, destroyed the engines and left the hulls to rot." Slowly, he moved his head up and down. "What a shame, but yes, I can understand it."

Very conscious of each other, they turned around and walked to a long wooden pier which pointed far into the lagoon. Above their heads, long leaved palm trees were rustling softly in the wind. A flock of pink flamingos came in from over the trees and splashed down in the lagoon. At the very beginning of the pier, attached to its mooring by a set of brand new painters, lay a twenty foot Chris-Craft, its colours a delicate shade of green and blue.

"That's the boat I was talking about," pointed Mena.

After poking around for a while in its cockpit, Rob discovered that the craft was equipped with a 150 hp Evinrude Z-drive motor and a modern fish finder with depth sounder.

"This is a first rate vessel, Mena. Outfitted like that, it must be pure bliss to go fishing."

"You'll find out soon enough," replied Mena. "and ..."

Happy at the idea, she threw her head back and laughed, her voice ringing clear and bright. She ran ahead to the end of the pier. When Rob caught up with her, she stretched her arm and pointed in the direction of two small white painted villas on the island. "They belong to DIANGOL as well, and you may use them whenever you want. Since nobody else bothers to come to the club, they'll be as good as your own private holiday resort!"

Somewhere deep in her mind, she felt a twinge of excitement as it occurred to her that if all went well, she would be able to share some of that free time there with him. A flash of sunlight made her blonde hair look like a crown of gold. Instead of looking at the villas, Rob stood close behind her, studying the line of her neck and the shape of her body which was barely concealed by her thin cotton dress. It was the first time ever that he had seen her so spontaneously happy. It was almost as if, now that she was far away from the city, she had become a different person. Whatever the cause of the change, it made her beauty even more evident, her appeal even more irresistible. A spark of desire rose from somewhere deep in the pit of his stomach. Afraid of destroying the delicate happiness they now shared, he stopped himself from pressing his lips in the nape of her neck.

They were quite alone now, the others busy stowing a box of wine and food supplies in the cockpit of the Chris-Craft. Mena felt Rob's closeness. As if she was physically holding on to him, she could perceive his yearning. Slowly, she turned around, looked deep in his eyes, and wetted her lips with the tip of her tongue. The sight of her tongue drove Rob crazy with desire. "Mena, I..." he said, reaching out for her. She took a step forward and he wrapped his arms around her waist, pulling her close.

At that moment Jock shouted something behind them, breaking the spell. She drew back, the magic of the moment irretrievably gone. Although disappointed, having seen the light in Mena's eyes, Rob felt certain that becoming lovers was only a matter of time! Savouring the tangy smell of the beach, he took a deep breath of air.

"Hey, you two," shouted Sobreiro over the noise of the Evinrude engine. "Are you coming with us?"

Hand in hand and rather self-consciously, they walked down the pier and rejoined the boat. Jock untied the painter. Less than a second later, Sobreiro threw the throttle open and raced the Chris-Craft across the lagoon in the direction of the island with the two villas.

As the speed increased, long moustaches of spray came sprouting from underneath both sides of the bow. Close to the island, where the depth decreased rapidly, Sobreiro pulled the throttle back and Ian threw the anchor in the shallows by the beach.

After unloading the boat, they pulled their swimsuits out of their overnight bags and changed. Following a sweet-scented path that wound its way through a growth of giant palm trees, they set out to explore the island.

Rob kept thinking that there was something amiss, but he could not put his finger on it. He tried to hide it away in the back of his mind. The thought kept coming back until he suddenly realized that it was the feeling of peace and untouched beauty of the island that made it so different from the war torn country he had learnt to know. A country where the population was permanently engaged in a struggle for survival, where the days and nights were a combination of poverty, shortages, dangers and the risks of sudden death by an incurable illness or the bullet of a guerrilla's rifle. Here, it was as if history had stood still, leaving the island untouched by the events which had ripped the country apart.

Soon they reached the west side of the island. Behind a thick screen of hibiscus plants and palm trees, they found the beach, its sandy surface littered with ripe coconuts.

Beyond the beach lay nothing but the vastness of the South Atlantic. Pushed by a strong breeze, rows and rows of waves came rolling in. Where submerged heads of coral obstructed the course of the water, the waves exploded in a rainbow of spray. At other places, giant rollers broke frothing and foaming on the broad band of white sand.

All too soon, Sobreiro's voice jerked them back to reality. "It's almost noon," he said. "If we want to have lunch, we have to go fishing." Out of habit, he pointed to the far horizon where a thin layer of clouds was building up. "That will become a storm later this afternoon. Nothing to worry us now, though."

Small sea shells cracked softly under the soles of their sandals as they found their way back to the villas. Ian volunteered to stay behind and get organized for the barbecue.

Sobreiro occupied himself with the preparation of the fishing gear. Mena sat down behind the wheel and started the engine. Carefully navigating through narrow passages which ran between low, coralline formations, she pointed the bow to the open sea. At certain places the colour of the water changed rapidly from deep blue to emerald green, indicating very shallow depths.

Rob sat happily watching Mena. At one moment he heard the scraping noise of the propeller-guard against the sediment on the seabed, then they were in the channel that connected the lagoon with the ocean. Mena rammed the throttle forward, the deep throaty roar of the open exhaust filling the quiet air with thunder. Once in the unprotected waters of the Atlantic, the narrow hull of the boat became a playball for the high rolling waves. Meeting each wave head on, the Chris-Craft struggled up the steep slopes before plunging with a sickening lurch in the trough beyond, throwing showers of water into the open cockpit.

Two miles out from the coast, the waves became longer and the slopes more gentle. Rocked by the motion of the boat and his skin caressed by the warm rays of the sun, Rob felt his eyelids grow heavy. Completely relaxed he let his hand trail through the water.

"I wouldn't do that, Rob," shouted Mena, indicating a series of lines which shot rapidly towards the boat. "Barracuda!"

Quickly, he jerked his hand away. It made her laugh, again that happy, carefree laugh that raised butterflies in his stomach.

"Remember, Jock, these waters have not been fished for many years," Sobreiro pointed out. "The Benguela current, which runs along the west coast of Africa, is very rich in fish. It should not take us long to catch our lunch."

Mena swung the wheel around and steered the boat towards a spot where the swirling motion of the water indicated the presence of a large shoal of fish.

At the prospect of the chase, Sobreiro yelled excitedly: "That's most probably a shoal of tarpon, or maybe king fish."

Jock and Sobreiro let their lines down into the water. Mena adjusted the power of the engine to maintain a steady 5 knots, a speed just fast enough to keep the slack from the fishing lines.

A moment later they were in the heart of the shoal, a mass of white and green flashes which darted at breakneck speed underneath the keel of the boat. Rob threw handfuls of small bait overboard. Immediately, the shoal became a throng of wildly milling fish.

"Not too much, Rob," warned Sobreiro. "We don't want to attract the sharks."

His thumb ready on the brake lever of the reel, Jock kept his eyes locked on the place where the fishing line disappeared under the surface. Slowly, he turned the handle on the reel, the clicking noise of the gears sounding clear above the hiss of the water.

"Come on, you buggers," he mumbled impatiently. "I can see you. Don't keep me waiting too long."

At low speed, with the sun reflecting off the mirror-like water, it became very hot. Mena held on to the rudder with one hand and bent far out over the side of the boat, splashing handfuls of water over her head and face. Rob admired the slim line of her waist and the fullness of her breasts.

Suddenly Jock's fishing rod jerked forward. Simultaneously, his right index finger pushed the brake on the spool. As soon as the rattling sound of the reel stopped, Jock raised the rod high above his head. "I've got him now," he yelled. "He won't get away any more." As he wound in the line, the muscles on his forearms were clearly marked under his tanned skin. For a moment, Jock's attention was distracted when a loud clattering noise indicated that Sobreiro had also hooked a fish.

After a fight of twenty minutes, a catch of six large fish lay on the bottom of the boat. One small barracuda, which looked very much like a perch, three king fish, and two tarpons.

"Enough for a king's meal," pronounced Sobreiro.

In their pursuit of the shoal of fish, the Chris-Craft had slowly drifted away from the coast. The boat started rolling heavily in the swell. With a very competent movement of her hand, Mena turned the Chris-Craft to the south where the low profile of the lagoon, as if outlined in dark oil colours, lay barely visible on the far horizon.

The sky, which until then had been perfectly clear, started to cover up with high clouds and the sun sometimes disappeared for minutes behind their ragged edges.

Closer to the beach, another motorboat, a Whaler by the look of it, came up fast as an arrow from behind, and swung in a tight skidding turn through the shallows into the lagoon.

"I think we are getting a visitor for lunch," declared Mena.

Turning around to look at Rob, Sobreiro nudged his head in the direction of the motorboat which in the mean time had disappeared from view. "There's only one man I know who is capable of handling a Whaler like that," he said. "Tommy Morgan!" He added that Tommy was working for the Government as Captain of the Petrolua. "That ship is a PROBO," he defined.

The blank stare in Rob's eyes told him that Rob didn't have a clue about what a PROBO was, and Sobreiro explained that the letters stood for *Product, Oil, Bulk and Ore* carrier.

Rob suddenly remembered the big ship he had seen in the commercial docks a few days previously.

"The ship is owned by the Angolan Petroleum Company, Rob," Sobreiro explained. "It's as large as an aircraft carrier, capable of carrying one hundred and ten thousand tons of oil or bulk."

"The cargo to be sold for much desired hard currency," ventured Rob. "Always useful for some, I suppose. I wonder who puts..."

"As such," interrupted Mena, who obviously did not want to listen to an exchange of ideas about who was putting the hard currency into his pocket. "Tommy is considered a VIP, just like you. That's the reason why he's allowed to go out in his Whaler. I'm sure you'll like him."

To preclude any further discussion, she gunned the engine and steered the Chris-Craft through the narrow channel into the lagoon.

Tommy was a tall, well-built man, his face almost completely hidden behind a full black beard. With him was a small and very tanned woman. Her lovely, oval face was framed by long hair, its colour so black that it had a blue shine on it. Her eyes were of a most fascinating light-blue colour.

"Glad to make your acquaintance," Tommy said, vigorously pumping Rob's hand up and down.

Rob felt as if his hand was being squeezed in a vice.

After meeting Jock, Tommy countered by introducing Joanna.

"She is my best friend, my wife, my lover and my destiny," he said in his deep and melodious Welsh accent. Frowning, he added jokingly: "Who sometimes, when I do something to annoy her, behaves like a wild dragon." To take the sting out of his words, he quickly bent down and pecked a kiss on Joanna's lips.

"We got some cleaning to do," remarked Sobreiro, pointing to the Chris-Craft. Accompanied by Jock, he went back to the boat. The rest of them made their way towards the two small villas. Halfway up the beach, behind a large brazier of charcoal, stood Ian, his forehead awash with sweat and his chest and arms marked with black stripes from the smoke. By his side, on a small table, lay an assortment of large knives and forks he had found in the kitchen of one of the villas.

"That's my Co-Captain," announced Rob. "You wouldn't say that from the look of him, but he's got an excuse for looking so filthy. He is on cooking duty today."

As soon as Ian saw them coming, he waved and said hello to Joanna and Tommy. He then took a dangerous looking skinning knife in his hand. "Sorry," he said. "Must get on with it. My charcoal is ready and I haven't even started to gut the fish yet."

"Please, let me do that, Ian," said Joanna immediately. "You just take care of your fire." Without waiting for his reply, she took the skinning knife out of his hand. In one deft move she slit the belly of one of the tarpons open and scraped the intestines in a ditch in the sand where the remains could serve as food for ants and crabs. Next, she cut a series of slits in the white flesh of the flanks and filled them with a clove of garlic, some sweet smelling herbs and a few drops of olive oil.

"I see you know how to prepare fish," said Ian admiringly.

Without being asked, Mena made a start with the preparations of the salads.

Tommy, obviously very much in love with his little woman, followed each of Joanna's movements with his eyes. "She's the best thing that ever happened to me, Rob," he said offhandedly.

Leaving Ian and the two girls to do the cooking, they walked to one of the villas where they sat down in the shadows of the veranda under a canopy of woven palm leaves.

Rob gestured with a bottle of Casal Garcia in the direction of the Chris-Craft. Then he pointed to the sun. "Sobreiro and Jock haven't finished cleaning the boat and stowing the fishing gear," he said. "As far as I can see, 'O sol' is well over the yardarm. I don't think that they will hold it against us if we start without them."

Tommy nodded his agreement.

The cork, when Rob pulled it out of the bottle, made a loud plopping noise. Rob poured a small quantity of wine into his glass, tasted it, and smiled. "First class, Tommy," he said. Smacking his lips in an appreciative gesture, he filled two glasses with the slightly fizzy green coloured wine. "First class indeed."

After a long sip from his glass, Tommy coughed to clear his throat. Lifting his shoulders in a helpless gesture, he started to speak. "A couple of years ago I went through a lousy period, Rob. At that time I was still married, but my wife was a real bitch who permanently nagged me and made my life a living hell."

Rob, never having been good at listening to other people's problems, felt slightly embarrassed. "You don't need to..." he started.

"I want to, Rob. I guess I *have* to talk about it." For a moment, Tommy let his eyes scrutinize Rob's face. After another sip of his wine, he carried on. "One day, I found out that during my absences at sea, my wife was never lonely. It seemed that she had a couple of friends who regularly visited her, or took her out." His eyes drifted away to the horizon. "Finally, one day, she ran off with one of her lovers, leaving me a letter to say that she was setting me free to go ahead with my life and career." A narrow smile slipped over Tommy's lips, but Rob could see that the pain was still there, deep down but masterly disguised.

"At first I was heartbroken," Tommy went on. "I went into hiding for weeks at the time, living out of a bottle. Slowly, I began to realize that that kind of woman was not worth killing myself for, and that I had to get a grip on myself. Gradually, I fought back to the surface."

Looking down, Tommy began to fill his pipe with an aromatic mixture of Clan and Cavendish tobacco.

In the few minutes it took Tommy to light his pipe, Rob discovered to his greatest surprise that it was not embarrassing at all to listen to Tommy's confessions. It was as if he had known him for years, and that they were just catching up with events long gone.

"Shortly afterwards I got the offer of this job with the Angolan Petroleum Company," uttered Tommy, breaking the silence. "I grasped the opportunity with both hands. For me it was a way out of my blind alley. I poured my liquor down the drain, sold the house and put the few possessions I had left in storage."

Rob refilled the glasses. Tommy noisily sucked on his pipe and blew a large cloud of scented smoke into the sky. A swarm of tiny mosquitoes drifted away when they smelt the fragrance of the smoke.

"I have never regretted my move, Rob. It brought me freedom and inner peace."

The voice of Joanna, who shouted something to Ian, carried clearly to where they were sitting. Mena, busy laying the table under the sun-awning, shouted something back. It made Joanna laugh. As if her voice had a magical power to it, Tommy swung his head in her direction. "Joanna is Angolan," he said, pointing with the stem of his pipe. "After I met her, my lonely existence became a life again. She's a woman with a strong character. A real woman, Rob. What's more, she loves me for what I am, not for what I give her." Saying that, as if touched by a sudden spark, Tommy's eyes lit up. "To make things really perfect, the company allows Joanna to live with me in my suite on board the Petrolua. She travels with me wherever I go. That makes us virtually inseparable."

"You must be very happy now," Rob said, a touch of envy touching his heart. "I'm very glad it turned out so well for the two of you."

Lifting his glass in a tacit salute, he drank deeply. "I went through a broken marriage as well," he divulged in turn. "As a young officer in the Air Force, flying became the most important thing in my life. My wife and I grew apart and it ended in a divorce. Luckily, there were no children." Rob looked up into the sky to find the right words to express his feelings. "I was a young fool then, Tommy. I didn't know the difference between real love and a short-lived crush based on sex." He stole a glance in Mena's direction. "Now I know better," he added meaningfully.

"What made you come here?" asked Tommy.

Rob told Tommy about Skylift and the financial problems which had prompted him to accept the contract.

Next, they discovered that they were both Capricorns, Rob late in December and Tommy early in January, that they both loved the sea, adventure and nature.

Later, when the barbecue was over and the sun started to go down, it was only natural for Rob to invite Tommy and Joanna to join them that evening at the Tropico.

"On one condition only," boomed Tommy, slapping Rob on his back. "You have to come and visit us one day on board the Petrolua, for drinks and food. Soon!"

He lifted Joanna in his arms as if she weighed no more than a feather and put her gently down in the cockpit of his Whaler. "We'll see you tonight then, in the Tropico. At eight!"

Never during the twenty years since the Declaration of Independence, had the Gala Room in the Tropico Hotel seen so many guests. It was now half past nine in the evening, and the party was in full swing. Thanks to Sobreiro's inventiveness, the bar was stocked with an impressive collection of vodka, gin and whisky, a choice of red and white wines and barrels full of ice-cold beer. What light there was came from a discreet mixture of coloured spots and strobes, which transformed the movements of the dancers into a succession of spasmodic jerks. The music, produced by an old fashioned jukebox, was very loud, and everybody was having a good time. That is, everyone except Rob. He stood by himself by one of the pillars in the corner of the room, briefly following the movements of a liveried waiter who, carrying a tray with canapes and other delicious titbits high above his head, made his way through the crowd.

Earlier on, having Mena all to himself, he had been ecstatically happy. Until an Army officer, a Major, already drunk but still behaving like a gentleman, had monopolized her. Rob had tried to stop him, but with a delicate sign of her head, Mena had made him understand that it was better to stay out of the way than to risk trouble.

Rob felt nothing but dislike for the officer. If he was really honest with himself, he had to admit that he was behaving like a love-sick teenager. Knowing that people were watching him, he forced his lips into a smile that looked like a grimace, as if his mouth was full of broken glass. Never leaving Mena for long out of his sight, he accepted a vodka & orange from a passing waiter.

A shout of enthusiasm rose up from the direction of the bar where Tommy, holding a whisky the size of a mug in his hand, was making a successful imitation of a Zulu-dancer. Jock, accompanied by a pretty young mulatto girl, slipped quietly out of the door.

The booming sounds of Elvis Presley's 'Jailhouse Rock' fell silent. Instead came the haunting tones of Paul Anka's 'Crazy Love'. Hoping he could get this dance with Mena, Rob quickly swung around but the Major was already there, looking very possessive now. To give himself something to do and to calm his nerves which were taut as springs, Rob emptied his glass and walked over to the bar. He was just about to order a refill when above the soft sound of Paul Anka's voice, he heard a shriek of pain and a slapping noise. At exactly the same moment he heard a roar of anger. Rob swung around, fearing that this meant trouble, and trouble it was.

Mena stood frozen in the middle of the dance-floor, her hands raised in a frightened gesture. In front of her stood the Major, stooping down threateningly, one hand rubbing his cheek, his mouth wide open and a furious snarl on his lips.

In a flash, Rob was across the floor, eager to find release for his frustrations. Through the mist of his rage, he heard the soft and pleading voice of Mena. "Don't do it, Rob, for my sake, please, don't do it." She placed her hand on his arm and managed to stop the swing of his fist. Rob turned halfway to look at her, an unspoken question in his eyes.

"It's all right," she whispered softly. "Let him be. He's had too much to drink.

He couldn't help it."

Rob turned back to the officer. "Come on, Major," he said, smiling but his blood still boiling. "Let's forget what happened and enjoy the rest of the evening." He held out his hand: "In peace!"

The Cuban drew back, spittle dripping out of a corner of his mouth. "La Puta," he shouted, pointing his finger threateningly to Mena. "She hit me!"

"Yes, she was right to do that," chipped in a girl who had come to the party as the guest of the Russian Consul. "You had your hands all over her. I saw it." A compassionate look in her eyes, the girl turned to Mena. "If he had done that to me, I would have scratched his eyes out or..." She raised her knee in a very well understood gesture. "Or I would have crushed his cojones."

Most of the guests started to laugh. The face of the Major changed from red to purple. Knowing that he had the laugh on his side, Rob tried to defuse the situation by gently pushing the man in the direction of the bar.

The Major, who by now was very drunk, tripped over his own feet and hit the ground with a bang.

Rob decided not to waste any more time on him. Turning deftly on his heels, he draped his arm around Mena. "I'm sorry that it got a bit out of hand," he whispered, brushing her hair with his lips. "Why don't we call it a night and go somewhere, just you and me?"

Rob held her close. He could feel every curve in her body. His lips went lower and he caressed the silken skin by her throat.

"Yes!" she sighed, her eyes big and shiny and full of love. "Let's go out on the terrace, I feel the need for fresh..."

Abruptly she fell silent, the sudden fear on her face unmasked. Screaming at the top of her voice, she pushed Rob away from her. "Watch out Rob, he's behind you, and he's got a knife!"

Rob had barely the time to swing round before the Major was on to him. He lifted his right hand to block the thrust of the knife. At the same time he launched his left fist against the Major's chin. It felt like punching warm, moist clay. Then, quick as lightning, he dropped his right hand in the hollow of the man's stomach.

The Major's mouth flew open in a soundless scream, expelling a cloud of booze-smelling breath. He slowly began to topple over but, crazed by alcohol and in an ultimate desire to inflict pain, he threw his knife-hand forward.

Rob felt the sting of the blade as it ripped through his shirt and cut into the soft flesh beneath his ribs.

The Major fell to the ground, unconscious.

Rob's side began to burn like hell, a trickle of blood colouring his white trousers and shoes with stains of red. He pulled a handkerchief out of his pocket and pushed hard down on the wound to stop the bleeding. Someone switched the jukebox off and turned the lights up. Two Army officers rushed forwards and forcefully dragged the Major to the door.

His face very pale now, Rob was afraid he was going to faint. His breathing sounded very loud and laboured, as if he had been climbing a steep mountain. As soon as Mena noticed the blood, her eyes widened into pools of despair.

"Get a doctor, someone," she shouted loudly. "Please, hurry. He's badly wounded!"

"Don't worry!" Trying hard to sound reassuring, Rob added: "I'll be all right." He risked a feeble smile. "Just a couple of stitches and I'll be like new again."

He saw Mena's lips twist in a desperate plea for help.

"Don't worry, Mena," he repeated. "I'll be all right."

Suddenly a bolt of pain shot through his side and everything went dark.

Much later, Rob opened his eyelids a tiny fraction. The only thing he saw was a blurred, dull grey mass which seemed to be moving backwards. I must be flying in the clouds, he thought, drifting again into a state of unconsciousness. A short while later, the sound of fast walking footsteps penetrated his mind. That woke him up. The grey mass above his head was still there. This time, he noticed that the grey surface, at regular intervals, was illuminated by rows of small spotlights. It reminded him of the centreline lights of a runway. It can't be a runway, he mused. A runway would not be hanging above my head. Besides, I can't hear the noise of engines, but the sound of footsteps. After briefly analyzing what all that meant, he decided that the grey mass had to be some kind of a ceiling. The next thing he discovered was that he was lying flat on his back on a stretcher and that he was being wheeled rapidly through a long and narrow corridor.

In a flash it all came back to him, the party, the drunk Major, and Mena. *Mena*!

He opened his mouth to cry out for her but all he managed was a barely audible croak. Rolling his head from left to right, he tried to see where she was. She was right there, by his side, holding on to his hand. "Hold on darling," she said. "We're almost there. The doctor is waiting for you."

"So that's where I am," Rob concluded. "In a hospital."

With the return of consciousness came the pain. Wincing, he lifted his head and looked at his body. His shirt and trousers were sodden with a mixture of blood and sweat.

As they progressed through the long corridors, Rob noticed the presence of other people, either sick or wounded. All the hospital wards seemed to be full. From one of the wards came the sound of crying children.

To provide berths for the abundance of patients, long lines of stretchers had been placed along the walls of the corridors; the stretchers standing bumper to bumper like trains in a shunting yard. The smell that pervaded the whole place was disgusting, a mixture of disinfectants, vomit, urine and putrefaction.

Entering the emergency room was a relief.

The doctor cut Rob's shirt and carefully studied the wound. "Well, what have we got here?" he said, peering myopically through a set of thick-lensed glasses. "Been playing rough?" Gently removing the rest of Rob's shirt, he clicked his tongue when he probed the ragged edges of the wound.

Feeling as if the whole right side of his body was immersed in scalding liquid, Rob forced his mind to concentrate on something else. "How," he asked Mena. "How did I get here?"

"Courtesy of the Base Commander in Luanda, Rob. You were out cold, covered in blood. He seemed to be very worried." Mena brushed some hair away from her face, then she smiled contemptuously. "Come to think of it. I guess he reacted more out of embarrassment because of the outrageous conduct of one of his officers than out of concern for your health." She glanced over to the right and noticed that the wound in Rob's side had stopped bleeding. Also the deadly paleness of his skin was slowly disappearing. The intense anxiety in her eyes began to make place for a more hopeful look. "Whatever his reason, Rob, he insisted that we use his Mercedes and his driver."

Chuckling mockingly, she revealed that in any case, it had been the only way to get him to the hospital. "Because Tommy, Sobreiro and Ian were too drunk to drive and Jock had disappeared with one of the girls." She smiled. "I'm afraid you've left spots of blood on the seat cushions of the car, Rob."

"Bugger his cushions, Mena, I don't give a damn." To illustrate his indifference Rob shrugged his shoulders. That was a mistake and he cringed with pain when a new flash of fire shot up through his groin.

"You are a lucky man, Captain," said the doctor when he finished examining the wound. "I haven't got an X-ray machine, but I'm pretty sure that the knife went clean in and out, without touching any of your organs. You'll live," he said as an afterthought. His accent was heavy.

"If the pain is anything to go by, I must be very much alive," hissed Rob.

Reaching behind him in a cupboard marked with a red skull and crossbones, the doctor removed a small glass phial which contained a transparent liquid. "I'm going to give you a shot of anaesthetic," he explained, holding up the needle of the syringe and squirting a little jet of liquid into the air. "It's supposed to be a local one, but still, it will make you feel rather dopey." He added apologetically that he preferred to use Lidocaine, but that Morfione was the only anaesthetic he had. Rob hardly felt the prick when the tip of the needle pierced his skin.

Immediately, the effect of the drug ran through his body and he felt his muscles go limp. Drifting away in a condition of semi-consciousness, he closed his eyes.

"It won't be a pretty scar," the doctor remarked to Mena as he started to stitch up the wound.

"I don't mind the scar, as long as he is all right," she replied. Her mind more at rest now, she remembered something the doctor had said previously. "How come you don't have an X-ray machine, doctor? That's one of the most basic tools in a hospital, isn't it?"

The doctor shook his head. "The general situation for health care is terrible here," he explained. "Since Independence, we are in need of everything. We don't have enough doctors, we don't have enough beds, and above all, we don't have enough medicines." He took a surgical swab and dabbed a remnant of blood away from Rob's wound, then he resumed the stitching. "The Captain here, with his status of Government Pilot, is very lucky. I *have* to give him priority." He nudged his head in the direction of the corridor. "Those poor people out there have to wait until we finally find the time to treat them. For many of them, it will be too late."

"That's horrible," Mena mumbled. "I had no idea the situation was that bad."

"If you think that's bad," replied the doctor, "... then you should see the children's ward!" His voice suddenly became hoarse with sadness and anger. "Some of them are dying because of malnutrition, others because they caught a stray bullet or stepped on a mine. I've got children in there who have been blinded by flying shrapnel. Others are missing an arm or a leg, or both!"

He turned to look at Mena. "Can you imagine a five year old, blind and both arms amputated?"

Mena's eyes clouded with tears. "But surely, doctor," she said falteringly. "The Government must be able to do something about those inhumane conditions."

The doctor shook his head, an attestation of despair and hopelessness. "Your ideas are an illusion, my dear. Not one of the leaders of this country has ever set foot in this hospital. They don't want to know about it. Why should they anyway?" His voice sounded desperate now. "They don't need it," he answered his own question. "Whenever they need medical help, they fly to Moscow, where they are treated in the best clinics, enjoying all the advantages of modern medical science." Although they were all alone in the room, afraid of being overheard, he looked over his shoulder. "I'm afraid that for the leaders, the citizens of this country don't rate very high on their list of priorities."

He finished stitching Rob's scar. To prevent infection, he gave Rob an anti-tetanus injection, then took off his glasses and rubbed them clean with a piece of bandage. Talking in a low voice, he started to dress the scar. "In the beginning," he said, "I rebelled against these atrocious conditions. I tried to force the Government to do something about it. It was to no avail. I was even threatened with a jail sentence if I continued to make a nuisance of myself. Now I have accepted that it will never get better, but it makes me feel very bad."

At that moment, Rob came out of his comatose condition. His brain still fuzzy from the anaesthetic, he heard Mena ask the doctor why he stayed on if he felt so unhappy with the conditions in Angola?

"And leave them all behind in their misery?" the doctor almost shouted. "No, I couldn't."

He paused briefly, then, his eyes absently focused on a dirty speck on the wall, he added: "Besides, even if I would like to leave here, there is nowhere else for me to go."

A question arose in Rob's mind. He tried to raise his voice, but his tongue felt thick and swollen like a sausage and the noise he made sounded like a dry cough.

The doctor looked at him with his myopic eyes. "I know what you were going to ask me, Captain," he said. "Why is there nowhere else for me to go? Let me explain. I'm Belgian, actually born in Zaire, formerly known as the Belgian Congo. I studied in Brussels, but returned to Zaire as a volunteer with 'Docteurs sans Frontieres'." For a moment he searched his memory for the correct words. "That means 'doctors without Borders', I believe. I'm sure you have heard of that organization."

Rob nodded, and the doctor went on.

"It was the usual story of idealism, believing that I was doing something good. One day, a very young girl who had been butchered by a local quack, claimed that I was the doctor who had performed the abortion. I swear to you I had nothing to do with it, but nowadays in Africa, white men are always wrong until proven innocent. My word was worth nothing, Captain, so I had to flee. Europe didn't appeal to me and finally, thinking I could help the people here, I came to Angola. I think that answers your question."

As if the discussion had never taken place, he took two small bottles of pills out of the medical cabinet. "The blue pills are antibiotics," he explained. "To prevent infection of the wound, you'll have to take two of them three times a day. The other bottle, the red one, contains painkillers." He filled a glass with water and told Rob to swallow two of the red pills. "That will keep the pain away for the next few hours. They will make you very drowsy, but it's the best I can do."

He handed the pills to Mena. "Give him two of these tomorrow morning. Or at any time during the night if the pain becomes too unbearable."

The doctor helped Rob into a wheelchair and walked them back to the car park. Rob felt very sleepy now, his muscles weak and shaky. Before he closed the door of the car, the doctor put his hand on Rob's shoulder. "Remember what I said, Captain," he whispered. "Nowadays in Africa, white men are always wrong!"

The driver of the old Mercedes slowly found his way through the labyrinth of puddles which scarred the surface of the darkened streets. Occasionally, the headlights of the car swept over piles of rubbish and litter swarming with vermin. Now and then the light fell on the skeleton of a car which had been stripped of everything but its most useless accessories.

Rob lay on the back seat, his head safe in the hollow of Mena's lap. The old seat had the rich smell of leather and old polish, very much like the smell he remembered from his riding days, when he had spent hours cleaning his leather saddle and bridle.

Looking out of the window, half-drugged from the combined effect of the Morfione and the two pills the doctor had given him, he got the impression that he was watching an old, black and white movie, the images faded and smeared by the speed of the car. Even the faint screeching noise of the worn out suspension sounded like the rickety whirring of an antique cinema projector. After a while the screeching noise became very soporific. Rob's eyes fell partially closed. Drifting away in the strange twilight zone between consciousness and drugged sleep, he knew that he was beginning to hallucinate, but he didn't care. In fact, he enjoyed the apparent state of weightlessness, his muscles still partially able to execute the commands of his brain, but his mind floating higher and higher as if he was drifting a few inches above the seat. In the chimerical depths of his brain, like the beatings of a jungle drum, he heard the words the Belgian doctor.

"A white man is always wrong... wrong...wrong!"

Then the rhythm of the drums became faster and the face of the doctor exploded into a thousand fragments, which became a ring of dancing girls who jumped naked around the campfire in the flooded village.

Rob began to giggle happily. Mena gently wiped the sweat away from his brow.

It worried her deeply to see him in such a drugged and weakened state. For a moment she pondered whether it had not been a mistake to take him away from the hospital, where he could be monitored by the doctor, or by one of the nurses. About to order the driver to turn the car back, she recalled the permeating stink of the hospital and the squalor of the wards, and she decided that she could take care of Rob much better than any one of those overburdened nurses.

By the time they reached the Yacht Club, Rob felt very lethargic, his legs barely capable of supporting the weight of his body. In his drugged condition, it looked as if the beach had tilted, the lagoon and the island a strange mixture of colours ranging from dark green to midnight blue. Even the pier looked like a long, steep incline.

Supported by Mena, he fought his way to the place where the Chris-Craft was moored. Having forgotten all about the island, he wondered where he was, and why Mena wanted him to get into a boat. "Leave me here, Mena, in the soft sand," he grumbled. "Or better still, in the water." It would be like a return to the womb, where he would be safe from knives, pain, and danger. Where nobody would be able to hurt him.

As they reached the island, Rob was so far gone that, supported by Mena with his feet moving more from habit than from reason, he staggered like a drunk out of the boat.

Under the wide expanse of the night sky and guided by the brightness of Orion, they hesitantly made their way up the beach, slipping between the shadows of sweetly smelling rhododendron and frangipani bushes.

Inside the villa, not bothering to undress and oblivious to any pain or hurt, Rob let himself down on his bed. Before his head touched the pillow, his body surrendered to a deep and drugged sleep. Mena put the pills and a glass of water by his side on a small bedside table.

Five hours later, shafts of pain cut like fire through his side. Rob's eyes shot open. He felt like crying out, but he couldn't. His tongue was as sticky as treacle, his throat parched and sore. Desperate to find the painkillers the doctor had given him, he raised himself on his elbow. In the twilight that fell through the thin curtains of his room, he found the pills. Not bothering to read the instructions on the bottle, he swallowed three of the pills and washed them down with a mouthful of water. According to his watch, it was 6.30 in the morning.

Rob looked around the room. Still partially sedated, he could only vaguely remember the events of the previous evening, the party, the fight and the hospital. After that, his memory was blank. To find out where he was, he dragged himself out of his bed and found his way through the kitchen to the balcony. The reluctant glow of a new dawn was beginning to mark the horizon. The sky was covered with heavy clouds. Rob could just make out the tops of the trees at the other side of the lagoon. The glow of the early daylight threw shimmering patterns in the moisture on the sand. Attracted by the peacefulness, Rob walked slowly over to the waterline, where the smell of ozone was strong and heady. The soft sand of the beach felt cool under his feet. Carefully, he let himself down and peered out over the calm surface of the lagoon. A soft drizzle came down from the sky. He lifted his face and let the cool and damp air refresh his feverish skin. By now, the pills started to numb the pain in his side until only a faint, throbbing soreness remained. Feeling very tired, Rob wanted to stretch out on the beach, to be one with nature and at peace with the world. Before he could lay down, a pair of soft arms wrapped themselves around his neck. "So this is where you've got to," Mena whispered softly in his ear. The warmth of her skin felt good against his naked back, her long hair pleasantly tickling his shoulders. She squatted down next to him on the soft sand and, almost motionless, they sat together for a long time, silently watching the birth of a new day. When the drizzle turned into a real downpour, they slowly made their way back to the villa.

The rooms inside were still full of shadows, the high canopy of the palm trees a screen that effectively concealed the house from daylight, as if it was a secret sanctuary.

Mena helped Rob to bed. Before he closed his eyes and allowed himself to drift away in sleep, he was aware that Mena, at the other side of the bed, threw the covers back and lay down by his side. He rolled over and clung to her like a child to its mother.

When, much later, Rob woke up, he felt very refreshed and extremely well rested. The cobwebs of the drug-induced lethargy had disappeared and his brain seemed to be able to function again. His wound felt only slightly painful, a dull pounding sensation that was more noticeable in his brain than in his body. Outside, it was still raining. He could hear the gurgling noise of water that ran down the corrugated metal slope of the roof and fell bubbling and splattering down on the sand. In the semi-darkness behind the curtains, against the background noises of incessant rain, the small bedroom felt very cosy. Judging by the small amount of light that remained, Rob decided that it was already getting dark again.

Suddenly, with a comfortable feeling in the hollow of his stomach, he knew that it was not the sound of rain nor the passing of the day that had pulled him out of his sleep. It was the unfamiliar but gentle touch of Mena's hand.

Slowly, Rob turned his head to the right. Sighing happily, he inhaled the delicate aroma of Mena's presence.

As soon as she saw that he was awake, Mena pressed a soft kiss on his lips. Next, as if her mouth had developed a life of its own, her lips began to move, gently pulling the hairs on his chest. Her hands, first caressing his shoulders, slipped down and began to explore his body.

Forcing himself to breathe slowly, Rob was not able to thwart a tremor of passion that contracted the muscles of his stomach. He wanted to reach out for her, kiss her, make her also feel good.

"Not now, my darling," she whispered, lowering herself on to him. "Remember your wound! This first time, let it be my time to spoil you."

Rob's eyes swept down her body and he caressed the flatness of her stomach. Mena began to moan softly. Rob exploded in a hot rush of desire. Not able to control his emotions any longer, he reached out and pulled her down.

"I love you so much," he cried. His mouth sought her mouth and his tongue met hers.

Their movements became gradually faster and deeper. Rob felt the shivers of an orgasm run down Mena's spine.

"Yes, darling!" she sobbed, digging her nails in the flesh of his shoulders. "Now, please, yes!"

Rob let himself go in an explosion of intense pleasure.

Afterwards, they lay close together, listening to the rain and the beat of their hearts. From far away in the distance came the monotonous cry of a bird. Closer by a big lizard slipped noisily through the undergrowth. Wrapped in each other's arms, they fell asleep.

The next morning, Rob opened his eyes to a bright day. The grey hue of the previous evening was replaced by glorious sunshine. Outside he heard the voice of Ian, who yelled something unintelligible. Somebody must have understood what he said, because Rob heard a shouted reply. He thought he recognized Sobreiro's voice and a little later he heard the deeper voice of Jock.

"So," he thought. "Our tipsy friends have finally returned. They must have come with Tommy, in the Whaler."

Looking down on Mena, who lay curled up against him, a warm feeling of belonging flooded his stomach. Stretching the minutes, he remained still for a long time, enjoying the smell of her hair and the warmth of her skin. "This is what I want," he decided. "This woman with me for the rest of my life."

After a while, Rob quietly got out of bed. Compared to how he had been the night before, he felt very steady on his feet. A towel wrapped around his waist, he made his way to the kitchen where he quickly washed and shaved.

Remembering the provisions they had brought with them, he opened the cupboard above the sink and retrieved a jar of Nescafe. On the sink lay two coconuts and a pineapple. Carrying two cups of coffee and a plate full of sliced fruit, he returned to the bedroom and drew the curtains partly open.

"Rise and shine, darling," he called out. "Room service."

As if the bright light of the day had changed everything, Mena felt strangely shy after the intimacy of previous night. She greeted Rob with a timid "Good morning." Finally, she found the courage to ask the question that was foremost on her mind: "Do you really love me, Rob?" Then even more shyly, "Don't you think I behaved rather wantonly last evening?"

Sensing that it was important to her, Rob put his cup down on the night table. "I love you more than anything else in this world," he said very sincerely. "And, Mena, if you were wanton, then so was I. It was exactly the way I like it."

Craving for the confirmation of his love, Mena stretched out her hand. Carefully, Rob lay down next to her, kissing her eyes, her lips, her breasts. Soon, they both lost all perception of time and surroundings in a spiral of passion. As their breath finally came back to normal, Rob kissed her gently on the forehead and said impulsively: "I'll give my life for you if I must." He spoiled the solemnity of the moment by adding that, if he had any choice in the matter, he preferred to grow old with her.

It made her laugh, the happy and carefree laugh of a woman in love, a laugh which made it clear to Rob that she was all right and that all questions and doubts had been swept from her mind.

Careful not to strain his wound, he lifted himself out of the bed and slipped into a pair of shorts from his overnight bag. "It's beautiful out there," he whispered. "Let's go for a walk and have a picnic. There's still some food left, and a bottle of wine."

Mena quickly washed and dressed.

To avoid having to face the others, they sneaked out of the villa and headed for a narrow path that ran between thick clusters of frangipani and rhododendron bushes. The ground, as a result of the storm, was covered with a thick carpet of pink and white petals.

On the far south side of the island, they found a wide moon-shaped beach, protected on all sides by a growth of old and twisted mangrove trees. The wind was light, the air had a faint salty smell to it and the sun was hot. The sea, after the storm, was still rough, the waves high as towers, their green crests breaking in a milky froth.

They settled down on the sand, the rays of the sun warm on their skin. Rob rested his head on the soft skin of Mena's stomach, his right hand gently caressing her leg. "Why did you bring me here," he asked. "That night, after the party?"

"I considered taking you to the Tropico, Rob, but I thought it was not such a good idea. I guess I was afraid of running into that Major again."

Rob chuckled. "I don't believe you, Mena. I think that you, with your wicked mind, just decided to bring me here to take advantage of me in my weakened condition."

"Stop that, Rob," she replied reproachfully. "You'll never know how worried I was. All that blood, and you looked so deadly pale."

Rob took her hand and gently kissed her fingers. "Sorry, darling. Just joking."

"I wish I'd known you a long time ago, Rob," Mena said with the unspoiled spontaneity of new lovers. "The last couple of years, I was so lonely. I had forgotten how wonderful it is to be with somebody you love."

Carefully, Rob propped himself up on his elbow and tenderly kissed her lips which tasted like the sea from the salt that was suspended in the air. "I know about what happened to your husband," he said, reaching down and letting a trickle of sand run through his fingers. "I also have been quite alone," and in almost the same words as he had used with Tommy, he told her about his broken marriage. "Your husband's death, my divorce, that's a long time ago," he concluded. "Now, we have each other, forever and ever."

"You're right," she replied. "I feel alive again, but..."

They were disturbed by the loud voice of Sobreiro. "So, this is where you two love birds are hiding," he said jokingly, then, with concern in his voice, asked how Rob felt.

"Very well, Sobreiro. With this woman by my side, it's pure bliss. It's so good that, to force her to stay, I'm thinking about having another fight."

"Don't count on it," said Mena, giving him a playful slap on his arm. "I've had enough of hospitals and blood and gore for a while."

Sobreiro, suddenly serious, lit a cigarette and looked at Rob. "Last week, you told me about that crashed aeroplane in Massau," he began and Rob felt a sudden rush of excitement in his stomach. "Since then, I've been asking some discrete questions, but nobody in Portugalia remembers anything about the Skyvan. However, I was given two names. Manuela Rodrigues and Roberto Cabral. Manuela was a secretary, working for DIANGOL. And more..." Sobreiro blew a cloud of smoke in the air and looked significantly at Rob. "What exactly do you know about your father's life here in Angola, Rob?"

"I don't know much about it at all," replied Rob, absently scratching his chin. "He died such a long time ago. I can hardly remember him."

"Then it won't hurt your feelings," Sobreiro said mysteriously. "... Manuela was your father's girlfriend..."

"Good for him," said Rob spontaneously. "My mother died when I was still a baby. I never knew about Manuela, so they must have met after I left in 1975." He made a rapid calculation in his head. "By that time, he had been widowed for ten years!" His voice turned suddenly pensive. "The significant part is, of course, that Manuela must be able to tell us all about his disappearance."

Sobreiro shook his head. "Unfortunately, her father died in 1985. After the funeral, she emigrated to Portugal. Address unknown!"

“Shit,” said Rob vehemently. “Why...”

“However, I managed to get hold of Roberto Cabral,” Sobreiro cut in. “He was Chairman of DIANGOL in 1975, and fell in disgrace when the Skyvan was lost. He could have been executed for losing the diamonds. Instead, he spent six years in jail, then was pardoned and got a job as a waiter in a restaurant on the Praya. He’s an old man now, living in a tiny flat in the old part of the city, but his mind is still as sharp as a razor and he remembers a lot about the disappearance of the Skyvan. I went to see him yesterday. He told me that...”

Sobreiro reported his conversation with Roberto Cabral in a few short sentences; the treasure of diamonds in the mines in Portugalia, the accident of the Chipmunk with Oviero’s broken leg and the unfortunate episode with the armoured convoy. “Now listen to this,” continued Sobreiro, looking meaningfully to Rob. “After the disaster with the military, a member of the council came up with the idea that Oviero could train your father to fly the Skyvan.”

“Then my hunch was correct,” exclaimed Rob, impulsively squeezing Mena’s hand.

“Yes, it was!” confirmed Sobreiro. “He and Oviero spent one day doing bumps and circuits. The next day, they loaded the diamonds and took off, to disappear somewhere between Portugalia and Luanda. DIANGOL organized a rescue attempt with two Search and Rescue helicopters.” Sobreiro made a pause to pour himself a glass of wine and took a sip. “They all thought it was only a matter of days before the wreck would be found, but in spite of all the sophisticated SAR equipment, they only managed to find an engine and a blue and white painted cowling in the forest by the Guillaume Falls.”

As if touched by lightning, Rob sat up. “What did you say, Sobreiro,” he queried. “A blue and white painted cowling?”

“Yes, that’s what Cabral told me, blue and white!”

“That’s it, then,” Rob shouted. “I’ve got it!” He picked up a stick and sketched a crude map of Angola in the sand. “Look,” he said. “Here is Portugalia, and here is Luanda.” He drew a line across the map between the two cities. “This is the course a plane would follow if it came in a straight line from Portugalia to Luanda. Here is the Rio Cuango and the Guillaume Falls, and here,” he pushed the point of his stick deep in the sand. “Here is Massau!” His voice very agitated now, he turned to Mena. “You see, Mena, the village is on the shore of the Rio Cuango, barely 30 miles to the north of the track.”

“What is the meaning of all that, Rob?”

For effect, Rob waited a few seconds, then said dramatically: “It means that I feel quite certain that my father’s remains are lying somewhere on the bottom of that lake!” Again, he turned his attention to the crude map in the sand. “Look, Mena. It ties in perfectly with everything we know. The missing plane, the engine cowling they recovered in the forest beneath the waterfall, and the old strut and wheel of the landing gear I found in Massau. That strut was painted bright blue. It must have been a part of the Skyvan.”

Fearing that Rob would not let go until he had found the wreck of the Skyvan, a stab of dark premonition pierced Mena’s heart and she cursed Sobreiro for having raised the subject.

Abruptly, Rob’s attention shifted to the cargo that had been stowed on board the Skyvan.

“Is it true what they told me, Sobreiro,” he blurted out. “Is it true that the value of the diamonds is estimated at more than 12,000,000 dollars?”

Feeling trapped, Mena shuddered. “I don’t give a damn about the diamonds, Rob,” she shouted. The hand she laid on his arm trembled with fear and worry.

"Forget about them. Those stones are cursed. They've cost the lives of your father and Oviero, and so many other people."

Although moved by her simple honesty, Rob knew he couldn't stay out of it. He pressed his lips together. "I can't let it go," he confessed. "I don't like to run away from things. I *have* to find out." Quite unexpectedly, he chuckled and added. "Think about it, Mena. If we find the diamonds, what a fantastic story to tell our children!"

To give his wound time to heal, Rob returned to the Tropico and took four days leave. Ian and Jock, assisted by Sobreiro, operated the flights to Benguela and Portugalia.

Sobreiro, with his long experience as Captain on the Fokker and his thorough knowledge of Angola, proved to be a perfect First-Officer.

Mena spent the days working in the Ops Office and the evenings with Rob, walking on the beach and making plans for the future. It was only when Rob began to talk about diamonds that dark clouds of disagreement threw a shadow over their otherwise idyllic existence. At the end of the four days, Rob felt much stronger. They went back to the hospital where the doctor removed the stitches and declared Rob fit for duty.

The Government, in urgent need of the new Kwanzas, pushed for an early departure to Lisbon. To oblige, and to give his scar the time to heal completely, Rob scheduled the flight for the 2nd of December.

Early that day, a storm depression moved in from over the Ocean. As they went out to the airport, the rain came down in rods and a strong gusty wind made the preparation of the Britannia for the long flight even more strenuous. It was not until 6 p.m. that the plane was ready, the fuel tanks containing forty tons of kerosene, sufficient for twelve hours of flying time. The cargo hold was loaded to the ceiling with crates and boxes of used spare parts. To add extra punch to the performance of the engines, Jock had polished the leading edges of the wings and the propellers. Sobreiro pointed at his watch.

"Time to go, Rob!"

His hair dripping wet from the rain, Rob draped his arms around Mena. "Are you sure you won't come with us?" he asked.

She looked up, a nervous tic twitching the corner of her mouth. "You know I want to, Rob, but my passport is expired and it would take weeks to get a renewal. Besides," she added, throwing her arms around Rob's neck: "You'll only be gone for a week." Gently caressing his shoulders, she whispered a tearful: "Vai com Deus, my darling...!" Then she abruptly turned away. Rob climbed up the ladder and slipped into his seat in the cockpit. At that moment, the layer of clouds that covered the sky broke open and a shaft of golden sunlight touched the ground. The damp surface of the tarmac began to steam and clouds of vapour drifted in a thin layer of fog over the field. Immediately, the temperature inside the aeroplane rose by ten degrees. Rob opened the top two buttons of his shirt, a futile gesture in a cockpit which felt as hot and sticky as a Turkish Bath.

When lined up on the runway, Rob wriggled his back against the padding of his seat and lifted his head to study the position of the sun. The glowing disc was sinking visibly fast below the horizon, the sky overhead gradually changing from blue to dark-red and black. Also the wind seemed to have gone, leaving the windsock by the tower hanging as limp as a wet rag. By the DCA hangar, the big tarmac lights came on. Rob threw a last glance at Mena, who was standing by the Ops Office, then turned his attention resolutely to the job at hand.

"Let's go," he said. "Full power, Jock..."

Back on the tarmac, Mena followed the profile of the Britannia until it disappeared in the hazy distance. As the noise of the engines slowly faded away, she felt strangely lost, as if part of herself had gone with the plane.

Shortly after the departure of the Britannia, Olunga dialled Lopes' number. "They've left," he said. "Only Stanfort with the First-Officer and his Flight-Engineer are on board. Mena is in the Flight Ops room with Sobreiro, listening to music."

"Good," responded Lopes. "If Mena's there we can be sure that Stanfort plans to come back. He wouldn't dream of leaving her behind." He didn't tell Olunga that, to prevent Mena from leaving the country, his agents had been standing by at the airport. After all, if Rob Stanfort discovered the location of the lost diamonds, Mena was his best weapon of blackmail!

"All right, Olunga," he said finally, "Keep an eye on Mena and call me as soon as you know the time and date of the return flight." He put the phone down, poured himself a brandy and let his ideas wander to the fortune the diamonds represented.

London, Monday, 4 December 1995

London was wet and miserable! It was raining continuously, the lowest layers of the clouds almost touching the ground with the visibility down to half a mile. In the pelting rain, Brompton Road looked like a dark grey river, the raindrops spotting the surface with bubbles. Straight ahead, Rob could just distinguish the trees of Hyde Park, the naked branches wrapped in veils of mist. The pedestrians crowding the pavement, moving all more or less in the same direction, reminded him of a crowd of ants. Rob's thoughts flashed back to the rich colours of Angola, where far away on the horizon the blue of the sky merged with the green of the forest; where most people, although poor and oppressed, still knew how to smile.

Spinning the wheel, the taxi driver turned his car into Knightsbridge. Almost immediately, he jammed on his brakes. "What the hell!" he yelled. "Look at that!"

In front of them, long queues of vehicles were solidly blocking the road, the air filled with a cacophony of honking horns. Through the windshield of the taxi, Rob noticed the blue and white strobe-lights of a police car.

"That does it," cursed the driver. "Another bloody accident." He set the parking brake and relaxed in his seat.

Rob stole a glance at his watch. Already twenty past ten, and still so much to be done. Since he had discovered that the lost Skyvan could very well be found at the bottom of the lake in Massau, he had taken the idea of recovering the diamonds very seriously. Although it sounded simple to go diving for lost treasure, a lot of problems had to be solved and a lot of questions asked.

The first item on Rob's program was a visit to the Zoo, to talk to Rick Martin, one of his old school friends. After obtaining his doctorate in Biology, Rick had spent a couple of years in the jungles of South America and Africa, and was now head of the Reptile Department. He would be able to tell Rob all he wanted to know about crocodiles and what had to be done to protect himself against these ferocious creatures. Then, at 3 p.m. he had an appointment in the Diamond Club with Patrick, another old friend who was a dealer with United Diamond Brokers, to get more detailed information about diamonds. Especially about the value of large gemstones.

Impatiently, he looked out of the window at the endless rows of cars blocking the road. Nothing seemed to be moving at all. Suddenly his eyes brightened. Barely twenty yards from where he sat, a blue, red and white shield marked the entrance to the Knightsbridge Underground. On sudden impulse, he pulled his wallet out of his pocket. "I'll get out here," he said, pushing a wad of bills into the hands of the cabbie. "I'll take the tube." His head covered with an old felt hat, he quickly sprinted across the road. A few cold drops of water dripping down from the trees found their way between the collar of his coat and the brim of his hat. A shiver ran down his back and he sneezed. Inside the Underground, the narrow corridors smelled wet and stale, but it was dry. Rob joined a throng of miserable looking commuters. Less than twenty minutes later he arrived at Regent Park Station. He ran upstairs and walked the short distance to the Zoo. Inside he turned immediately to the right and hurried by the cages of lions and tigers. Although in a rush, he could not resist a quick look in the Dolphinarium where two giant dolphins were lazily swimming the length of the pool. The clear blue colour of the water and its salty smell reminded him of the lagoon in Mussulo and Mena, and his heart missed a beat.

In the 'House of Reptiles' he knocked on a door which bore the title "DIRECTOR". He waited couple of seconds, then stuck his head around the door.

Doctor Rick Martin looked up from his desk, an absent look in his eyes. "Stanfort!" he exclaimed, catapulting himself from his chair. "Come in, man."

Pulling a chair from under the desk, he gestured Rob to sit down. "Well, look at that!" he uttered when taking in Rob's sun-tanned features. "You do look good, I must say." Very glad to see his old friend again, Rick spent a couple of minutes chewing the fat about their schooldays.

As soon as Rob got the chance, he came straight to the point. "Nowadays, I'm based with my company in Angola. Once in a while I have the opportunity to go hiking in the jungle."

Doc Martin leant back in his swivel chair. To hide his rising curiosity, he reached in his pocket for his favourite pipe. "Yes," he said. "Go on!"

"Next week, I may be visiting the swamps of the Rio Cuango, a very interesting area which seems to be swarming with crocodiles."

Martin's face lit up. As a frequent visitor to Africa, he could almost paint a picture of the river in his mind.

"The reason why I'm here," Rob concluded, "is that I'd like to learn all there is to know about these reptiles. I like to discover the country, but I don't want to become the next meal of a crocodile."

With a lover's expression on his face, Martin wriggled his back in a more comfortable position. "You're lucky," he said. "Crocodiles are my hobbyhorse."

At the airport, Ian spent the whole morning interviewing new co-pilots. Although still uncomfortable with the idea of Rob going to dive in the Rio Cuango - only accompanied by Sobreiro and Mena - he had to admit that Rob's suggestion of hiring a new co-pilot made a lot of sense.

Stopping the flights altogether would cause too much loss of revenue! Worse, it would make it obvious that something very strange was going on.

With an extra pilot, the flights could continue normally, and if anybody in Portugalia asked about Rob's whereabouts, they could pretend that he was taking care of business in Luanda. In Luanda, they could spread the rumour that Rob was in Portugalia, studying the possibility of opening a new line to Cabinda, in the Angolan oil fields.

It sounded very easy but, after this morning, Ian despaired at the feasibility of it all. He had interviewed half a dozen of pilots. Instead of being driven by the holy fire for flying and adventure, they had been asking questions about salaries and pension and living conditions. The chance to fly in an exciting new environment appeared to be totally unimportant!

In his mind, Ian classified them all in the category of boring bureaucrats who were just playing at being pilots. He was sick and tired of them. Sighing deeply, he opened the door and called: "Next one."

Contrary to the previous applicants, this one was not dressed in a nice suit and tie. He was wearing a well-worn leather flying jacket and a pair of jeans. His head was covered in a wild bush of flaming red hair and when he looked at Ian, his eyes stood sharp and alert.

"My name is Donald Thomas," he said. "Just call me Don."

His handshake felt strong and honest.

"Listen, Don," Ian began. In carefully chosen words he described the country and the extreme beauty of the land. He told Don about the rainy season when, in the early morning under the effect of the tropical sun small Cumulus clouds seemed to develop a life of their own, swelling and bulging with inner currents until they became towering thunderstorms forcing them to fly at low level over the tops of the trees. He painted a picture of the far horizons, only visible when the clouds dissolved in a clear blue sky. He also warned Don that in Angola, a civil war was raging and that life could be very dangerous. Once finished, Don didn't waste any time asking questions about salaries and pensions and guarantees. Instead, he inquired: "When do we leave?"

Later that night, Ian, Jock and Rob were sitting together in the lounge of Rob's house in Maidenhead. Large French windows offered an unrestricted view on the garden where evergreen pines added a little colour to the drabness of winter.

The lounge felt cosy and comfortable. An open fire was lit in the fireplace, filling the room with a pleasant aroma of burning wood. Pieces of antique furniture were arranged against two of the other walls. The fourth wall disappeared almost completely beneath an impressive collection of firearms and swords.

"The diving equipment you ordered from the British Sub Aqua Club has arrived," began Jock. "There is a large semi-rigid Zodiac inflatable, an Evinrude outboard engine, two scuba tanks with regulators and buoyancy compensators, an air compressor and a metal detector."

Rob looked up from the large glass of cognac he was warming up in the palm of his hand. "That's the most important item of all," he replied. His voice sounded smothered with the onset of a cold. "With a metal detector, it will be possible to search the bottom of the lake for the remains of the Skyvan without wasting too much of our precious time. We'll stow all that equipment in the lower front belly hold, Jock, safe from prying eyes, and the money can be loaded on the main deck."

"I hired a new First-Officer," reported Ian. "He's experienced and very willing. He'll do fine."

Happy that all the pieces of the plan were falling into place, Rob walked over to the fire and turned his back to the flames, the heat pleasantly warm against his buttocks.

"I've spoken with Doc Martin in the Zoo," he said. "He went on and on about crocodiles. I guess I know enough to write a book about these wretched animals." Deciding to keep his explanation short and sweet, he took a sip of his cognac and started. "In a nutshell, crocodiles are untrustworthy creatures, voracious and vicious. They kill their victims by dragging them under the water and hiding them under the roots of a tree or a cave in the rocks. Then, after a couple of days, when the meat is rotten and soft, they eat it."

Just about to sip his drink, Ian spluttered. As soon as he caught his breath, he shouted: "If crocs are that dangerous, you can't be serious about diving in the Rio Cuango."

"Oh yes, Ian, I'm very serious about it," Rob retorted. With four quick steps, he crossed the room and pulled a Mauser K 98 rifle out of a rack; one of the many rifles and guns Rob, in his passion for military equipment and weaponry, had collected over the years. He worked the bolt to make sure the chamber was empty, then walked back to Ian and placed the weapon in his lap. "Take a good look at that," he said. "That's a Mauser K 98, the standard issue of Hitler's Wehrmacht. It's old, but in pristine condition. The bullets are soft-nosed 08/57 IS, capable of killing an elephant."

Studying the rifle, Ian asked Rob what that rifle had to do with diving.

"That rifle comes with us to Angola, Ian. And, of course, lots of ammunition." As if looking at the steamy depths of the forest and the foaming waters of the river, Rob's eyes became dreamy. "Did you know that Sobreiro has quite a reputation as a big-game hunter?"

Slowly realizing what Rob was leading up to, Ian nodded.

"Well," Rob said, slapping Ian on his back. "When I go diving, Sobreiro will be my bodyguard. So you don't have anything to worry about."

With a sad and troubled frown on his face, Ian's logical mind focused on other problems, the invisible but mortal ones such as running into a group of guerrillas who might be passing through the forest. He started to formulate his objections, but Rob cut him short.

"Stop it, Ian," he snapped curtly. His tone sounded very agitated now. "Grow up, will you! Or did you imagine that we could lay our hands on a fortune of diamonds without taking any risk at all?" His words gave the impression of great mental strength, but deep inside his head, a small voice cried out that he was acting like a fool, belittling the risk of the crocs and the dangers of the forest.

He turned around to look out of the windows.

A fresh gust of wind whistled through the gap below the doors and made the flames in the fire flicker with the sudden draught of cold air. "I have to confess, Ian," he said. "It's not only the loot. It's also the attraction of the unknown and the chance of finding my father's grave that's making it so fascinating for me. And there's more. This afternoon, I discovered some hard evidence about the lucrative aspect of discovering the wreck."

Rob returned to his seat and pulled a thin folder out of his briefcase. "This is the inventory of the lost diamonds that Mena got out of a dusty file for me." He ran his finger down a row of figures. "Initially, when Mena spoke about 30,000 carats, I thought they were small industrial stones. When examining the inventory, I discovered that one quarter of the stones are big uncut diamonds, weighing more than one carat each." Rob's eyes briefly scanned the paper. "Even better, eight of the stones are big whoppers of more than two carat." He waited a moment for effect, then pulled another piece of paper out of the folder. "To know the approximate value of this treasure, I went to see a friend who is a merchant in the Diamond Club." He tapped his finger on the printed price-list. "This tells me that the larger stones have a value of nine to ten thousand dollars per carat. If we are able to recover the whole lot, the total value would be..."

Immediately, Ian's lips started to move like a calculator. "That must be close to twenty million dollars," he mumbled.

Rob leaned back in his chair, smirking with satisfaction. "Between twenty and thirty million to be exact, Ian. Do you agree now that the search is worth the risks I'm taking?"

"Oh sweet Jesus," muttered Jock. "Thirty million dollars."

Sipping his cognac, Jock sank back in his chair. Ian tried to imagine what a pile of thirty million in one-hundred dollar bills looked like.

Rob emptied his glass and put it back on the wooden surface of the table. Stretching his arms, he yawned. "I don't know about you," he remarked. "But it's getting late and I'm going to bed. I must take some medicine to get rid of my cold."

As soon as Rob was gone, Ian started talking in a whispered voice. "You know, Jock, Rob is right when he says that there is no gain without risk." He suddenly smiled. "I admire his guts, so I'll help him wherever I can!"

"Me, too," Jock replied, lifting himself out of his chair. "If necessary, I'll follow him through hell and high water!"

The maintenance checks of the Britannia were done at 6 a.m. At 9 o'clock, they landed in Lisbon and loaded forty crates of banknotes. In less than an hour, the job was done and they continued their journey.

It was now four in the afternoon. Cruising at an altitude of 24,000 feet, the needle of the outside temperature gauge stood at 28 degrees below zero and the True Air Speed was a steady 340 knots. Far above, the sun hung like a red ball in the sky, its light a dazzling mixture of white, red and gold that transformed the whirling disks of the propellers into circles of fire.

Don was flying the Britannia. Ian, having flown the first half of the trip, was having a nap, and Jock was busy completing his engineer's log. Enjoying the peaceful rocking of the wings and the synchronized vibrations of the four engines, Rob sat lazily in the left hand seat. At the beginning of the trip, probing for Don's technical knowledge about the plane, he had fired a load of questions. Having thoroughly studied his flight handbook, Don had been able to answer them all. Not once fooled by Rob's apparent show of complacency and knowing that nothing less than perfection would do, Don was concentrating very much on keeping track and altitude. Two hours later, he pushed the interphone button on his control-wheel. "Another twenty minutes to Luanda, Skipper. Time to start our descent."

Rob nodded.

Don pulled the throttles slightly back. The nose of the aircraft dipped down, the altitude started to decrease. With his left index, Rob pointed to the aeronautical map which lay folded in his lap. "I'll tune the radio beacons," he proposed, selecting the frequency of 'Lima Delta', the initial approach aid of Luanda, and listening for the identification Morse code in his headset. The needle swung to a bearing of 160 degrees.

Far below, the waves of the South Atlantic drew parallel lines of foam on the green surface of the ocean. Helped by a favourable tailwind, the ground speed of the plane reached 385 knots. Minutes later a dark line, a little more solid than the thin line of the horizon began to rise slowly out of a shimmering layer of haze. To find out exactly where they where, Rob bent forward and strained his eyes to recognize a particular point on the coastline. Out of the corner of his eye he noticed that Don had the same instinctive reflex. With his right hand, Rob made a distinct motion to the right and advised Don to take a more southerly heading. "We shouldn't cross the coastline too far to the North of Luanda," he explained. "According to the Notice to Airmen, NOTAMs, the military have designated that part of the airspace as a restricted area, only to be used by military traffic."

As if to emphasize his words, two MiG21 fighters appeared out of nowhere and shot straight up in the sky, the exhausts of their engines spewing two widening jets of white-hot vapour. Seconds later they disappeared in the hazy overcast.

At 9,000 feet, Rob suddenly pointed to the left. "There," he said, studying the outline of the coast. "At least I think..."

As they came closer, the city and the airport jumped into view. Rob's heartbeat rose wildly in anticipation of seeing Mena again. "Yes, that's it." Rob's voice sounded very certain now. "Look, Don, there is the Bay of Luanda and just to the east of it, the airport."

Gazing in the direction of Rob's hand, Don saw it too, the Bay of Luanda, the water dotted with ships. At the same time he realized that the haze had played a dirty trick on him. Everything was much closer than expected. Instead of still having a lot of distance to play with, the city and the airport lay barely fifteen miles in front of the plane.

In a perfectly synchronized movement, he eased the throttles back and wound the trim a couple of degrees nose up to prevent the nose of the aircraft from dropping with the reduced power setting "We are much too close and much too high," he exclaimed. "I'll have to make a very steep descent!"

Rob agreed.

At 6,000 feet, they hit a strong thermal which made the wings roll violently Don corrected the motion smoothly with an easy pressure on his control yoke.

"He's good," Rob thought. "A natural pilot."

The voice of the ATC controller burst through the headset and cleared them to land on Runway 19.

"Your game, Don-boy," Rob remarked loudly, exhilarated by the steep angle of the flight deck and the howling sound of the slipstream around the cockpit. "A straight-in. They make it easy for you."

Sharply concentrating on making a fine job of the approach, Don shifted his eyes from the long, grey ribbon of the runway to the DME, the distance measuring equipment. "Ten miles out," he announced. As the altimeter passed through 4,000 feet, the speed was a steady 190 knots. Don mentally calculated the ratio of height on distance. Realizing he was still too high and forty knots too fast, he wriggled nervously in his seat.

"Maybe we should fly an orbit before committing us for the final approach," he called out, quickly sneaking a look at Rob's face in the hope of finding a hint about what to do.

Rob's face stood frozen. "It's up to you, Don," he said. "It's your check-flight. Do whatever you think is right."

Don snapped himself out of indecision. "I can make it," he declared. "I must make it!" All his instincts now locked into the plane's behaviour and knowing that he had only one chance to do it right he instructed: "Gear down, flaps twenty and landing check-list." Nothing else but flight procedures, speeds and height existed in his brain. It felt as if the plane was merely an extension of himself. He faintly heard the increased noise of the engines when Jock pushed the prop-controllers to full fine pitch. As the height decreased and the runway came close, he called out for full flaps and rolled the trim slightly back to stabilize the rate of descent. The airspeed stood at 125 knots, the altitude was just right.

At ten feet from the ground, Don gently pulled the stick back. Seconds later the giant plane touched down, soft as silk. A knot of tension fell away from Don's stomach when he analyzed his performance and concluded that his judgement had been correct.

"That was exciting, skipper!" he shouted, his flow of words so fast that it sounded as if he was caught in a rapid.

"Well done, Don," Rob replied. "Very well done indeed."

As they came closer to the hangar, the first thing Rob noticed were four enormous trucks and a cordon of armed soldiers. "They are obviously very eager to get the money," he remarked.

"Can't blame them," added Jock. "I wouldn't leave fourteen tons of newly printed banknotes overnight in a plane. Certainly not in a place like this."

On its normal parking spot by the office building stood the Land Rover with two small figures next to it. Rob recognized Mena and Sobreiro. As soon as the engines started to run down, he couldn't control his patience any longer. With an abrupt gesture he unlocked his safety belt and struggled out of his seat. As he opened the cargo door and hurried down the crew ladder, the heat of the afternoon hit him. He shook hands with Sobreiro, then he took Mena in his arms, his lips brushing her hair.

"I'm so glad you're back, Rob," she whispered. "I've missed you so much!" Although she had promised herself to be strong, she couldn't prevent a tear from running down her cheek. Rob took his handkerchief and gently wiped her tears away. "In about an hour, we'll be on our own, in the Tropico," he hinted. "Then we can catch up with everything we've missed this week."

She caught the insinuation in his voice and started to laugh. He kissed her at the nape of her neck. She smelled sweet and clean like freshly cut flowers. Through the thin cotton of her dress, he felt a shiver run down her back.

With regret in her voice, Mena announced that 'catching up' would have to wait till later. "We're all invited for a meal on board of the Petrolua, Rob. Tommy was quite adamant and I couldn't refuse."

"I'll have to control my libido a little longer," replied Rob jokingly. Turning his mind to more serious matters, he lifted her chin and stared into her eyes. "We've got all the equipment we need, Mena. So the search for the Skyvan can begin."

Having prayed for a miracle that would make Rob forget all about the possible existence of sunken treasure, Mena shook her head. "I hoped you had given up on that, Rob."

"You know I can't, darling. I've taken all possible precautions to keep us safe. I'll tell you later about the plan. Now, bear with me for a while, until the plane is ready. Then we'll be off." He turned around and climbed back on board the Britannia.

As soon as the crates with the banknotes were unloaded, Ian instructed the cargo handlers to stow the load for Portugalia on board. "I presume ..." he said to Rob, "... that you haven't changed your mind about tomorrow."

"No, I haven't, Ian. I still want to get out in the morning. First stop Massau. Afterwards, you continue on your own." More softly, Rob added: "And load a couple of extra tons of dried fish for the villagers in Massau. They could do with some decent food." About to run down the ladder, Rob suddenly remembered: "Make sure to lock the belly compartment, Ian. Otherwise everybody in Angola will know that we are planning a diving expedition."

Rob rushed over to the control tower. As the success of their search in Massau largely depended on weather conditions, he spent ten minutes studying the movement of storm depressions which were building up over the Ocean. By the time he returned to the aeroplane, the cargo door was closed and the refuelling completed.

"We're ready to go," reported Jock.

They struggled into the Land Rover. Sobreiro swung the four-wheel drive through the afternoon traffic, mostly vans and trucks from the military and a few old and dilapidated cars which had been rebuilt with usable parts from scrapped wrecks. Closer by the harbour, the traffic became thinner. Ten minutes later, Sobreiro turned on to an asphalt road which, quite uncommon for Luanda, was in a very good state of repair. At the end of that road, Sobreiro shifted the gears down and brought the Land Rover to a stop in front of a ten foot wide gate. The gate posts were marked with large placards which said:

Luanda Harbour
No entrance
Authorized personnel only

Behind the gate stood three heavily armed guards. Menacingly, they pointed the black snouts of their assault rifles at the car. Rob's eye fell on the fully loaded Kalashnikovs and the curved magazines, each holding 35 high velocity armour piercing AP bullets.

By the quay, a large Russian roll-on roll-off freighter was discharging its cargo, an endless stream of military vehicles and equipment. Rob immediately understood the reason for the guard's nervousness.

"Boa tarde, Camarades," shouted Sobreiro, waving his DCA pass. The red colour of the document flashed like a bright beacon in the light of the sinking sun. One of the guards, back erect and finger ready on the trigger of his rifle, made a show of inspecting their passes. Satisfied with what he saw he stepped back, slung his rifle over his shoulder and swung the gate open. Sobreiro saluted him and drove off. He followed the road that led to the north, circled the harbour, and stopped by the enclosure of the Angolan Petroleum Company. There, clearly standing out against a background of billowing clouds and huge oil storage tanks, Rob noticed the high bridge and the stark functional lines of a very large tanker. "The Petrolua?" he asked.

"How did you guess," replied Sobreiro.

Rob was surprised at the sheer size of the ship. He had expected to see a medium-sized tanker. What lay there before him was the largest ship he had ever seen. He remembered that Tommy had told him that the Petrolua was one of the very first PROBOs. "One of the biggest and most modern actually afloat!" Now, from up close, he saw that Tommy had not been exaggerating. The deck of the Petrolua lay more than ten meters above the level of the dock and was at least 200 meters long.

Following Sobreiro and Mena, Rob climbed the gangway and reached the deck where Tommy stood waiting to welcome them. They followed him through a maze of corridors, up several sets of stairs and across the bridge which lay three levels above the deck and spanned the full width of the ship. As he saw the rows of dials and switches, Rob immediately realized that this was the heart of the ship. To his surprise he also recognized a LORAN and a DECCA navigator system, an HF radio and two VHF transceivers. They looked almost identical twins to the ones he had on board his Britannia. On the poop of the Petrolua, he noticed a helicopter landing-pad and an idea flashed through his mind. Those VHF transceivers could be the answer to one of his problems: a way of communication with the Petrolua, offering a secondary escape route in case they had to make a run for it! "Tommy," he started. "Are you working those VHFs on the same air band as we do?"

"Sure," replied Tommy. "Anything between 118.00 and 135.50 Megahertz."

"I didn't know that ships carried VHF radios," remarked Rob.

"Normally, we don't," explained Tommy. "It is a requirement of the military, because of the war. It enables us to talk directly to Air Force jets and helicopters for identification purposes." He frowned and asked, "What's on your mind, Rob?"

"Just a thought, Tommy. We'll talk about it later."

In the corner of the command cabin, Tommy opened a door and descended a spiral staircase. They found themselves back in a short corridor with doors leading off to four cabins, two on either side of it.

"This is my cabin," explained Tommy, pointing to one of the doors. "Two of the other cabins are for VIPs. They are luxury suites, normally reserved for the use of managers of the shipping company." A smile lit up his face when he revealed that he didn't often have the opportunity to welcome one of the managers on board. "None of them have sea legs," he clarified, and pointing to the door at the far end, added: "This is the lounge."

The first thing that occurred to Rob when he stepped over the door-sill was that he had entered the Royal Suite of a luxury hotel. Under his feet lay an inch thick carpet and the colours of the room were a tasteful combination of green and gold which contrasted delicately with the dark wooden furniture and the leather of the chairs.

Outside, the sky turned slowly grey with rain, a slight drizzle that hesitated to turn into a tropical downpour. They sat down in deep comfortable armchairs. Tommy opened a bottle of Dom Perignon and proposed a toast.

"To happiness," he said.

"Yes," added Joanna, raising her glass. "To happiness! Or as you English say, 'Up your bottom'."

They all burst out laughing. Tommy almost choked on his drink. "No, my darling," he said when he found his voice again. "The correct expression is 'Bottoms up'."

"That reminds me of a girl I once knew," Jock butted in. "She was French and one day after a pretty nasty experience, she told me that life was not always like a row of beds. It was only after a minute or two that I realized that she meant a bed of roses."

In buoyant mood, Jock stood up and refilled their glasses.

"Now tell me," voiced Tommy, "how was Europe, Rob?"

"Europe was fine," Rob replied. He took a sip of his wine. "But I don't want to talk about Europe, Tommy. I want to talk about diamonds and a lost aeroplane."

"Diamonds?" said Tommy, a tone of wonder in his voice. "An aeroplane?" Realizing that he was going to hear something out of the ordinary, he closed his mouth with a snap. The noise in the room dwindled away like the sound of big waves dying on a sandy beach.

"What I'm going to say will come as a surprise to most of you," Rob began. "In fact, only Jock and Ian know all about it. Mena and Sobreiro have the general idea but don't know the details of the plan. Therefore, I'll start at the beginning."

Rob told the story of the missing diamonds. He spoke about the disappearance of the plane that had carried the treasure from Portugalia to Luanda and the futile search in the forest by the Rio Cuango. He also revealed how he, on the way back from Lukapa, having lost an engine and threatened by a storm, had made an emergency landing in Massau. Still talking, he pulled a map from his flight case and spread it out on the table. With a pencil, he drew a line from Portugalia to Luanda and traced the course of the Rio Cuango. Finally, he drew a circle around the place where Massau was.

As he progressed with his story, a sensation of growing excitement invaded the room. "In Massau," Rob told them, "I learned from an old shepherd that many years ago, an aeroplane had crashed into the lake."

Tommy raised his voice. "One cannot always believe the story told by some..."

Rob impatiently raised his hands. "Just bear with me, Tommy. I'm sure that this tale wasn't born in the imagination of the old chap. He showed me a piece of wreckage, an old blue and white strut of a landing gear with the tyre still attached to the rim."

Again, Tommy raised his voice. "A blue and white strut, Rob? What does that mean?"

Rob tossed his hair back from his forehead. "It's the link between the wreckage in Massau and the missing Skyvan, Tommy," Rob said. "Two days after my encounter with the knife of the drunk Major at our party, I had a long conversation with Mena and Sobreiro in Mussulo. It was Sobreiro who gave me the final clue when he told me that the colours of the Skyvan were white and blue, exactly the colours of the wreckage I saw in Massau!"

Tommy sucked his breath in between his teeth. "From that, you deduce that the wreck of the Skyvan should be somewhere on the bottom of the lake in Massau?"

"It's probable, Tommy. I can't be one hundred percent sure, but all the evidence I have points to it! Take a look at the map. Massau is not far to the north of a direct track from Portugalia to Luanda. When talking with Roberto Cabral, the former Chairman of DIANGOL, Sobreiro found out that the mechanics in Portugalia did *not* install extra fuel tanks in the Skyvan. Without extra fuel tanks, Oviero could never have made it non-stop, therefore he must have flown the direct track." Rob paused to let his words sink in. "Now there are two things we can do," he said, looking them one by one in the face. "Either, in the hope of getting a fair share of the loot, we can go to the Government and tell them about our discovery. Or we do it very secretly on our own."

Sobreiro shouted loudly, a sharp edge to his voice: "You must be crazy to talk about going to the Government, Rob. Most of them are hard-core communists, utterly devoted to the cause. Others are selfish maniacs who are only interested in bettering themselves. Even if that means putting a bullet through your head."

"I agree," replied Rob scornfully, "Especially if you consider that the total value of the stones is in the region of thirty million dollars."

As if he had suddenly sprouted horns and a tail, they stared at him in utter stupefaction, then they all started to talk at once.

"You realize that such an amount of money is enough to drive everybody in Angola crazy with greed," bellowed Tommy.

"Yes, you must be crazy to consider talking to the Government," repeated Sobreiro.

"Thirty million dollars? That much?" Mena gasped, a look of utter concern on her face. "What about the legality, Rob. That money legally belongs to the people of Angola."

"The people of Angola," shouted Sobreiro. "You're bloody naive, Mena. If your dear President ever gets the money, he'll use it to buy weapons and ammunition, to kill the people of Angola. Is that what you want?"

"No, Sobreiro, I want the fighting and the killing to end, and I would like to see this money used to help those who have been wounded or maimed, but there is something else..." Her voice spiralling a few octaves, she turned to Rob. "When we were talking about this in Mussulo, I never thought you were crazy enough to push things this far. What you plan to do is extremely dangerous. This country is at war, Rob, and the diamond industry is one of the main sources of income for the Government. They are very anxious to keep it like that. Lately, two workers in Portugalia were shot, because they tried to smuggle a few stones out of the mines to sell on the black market." She fell silent for a moment and looked at the others to find support. "The value of those stones was nothing compared to the 30,000,000 dollars you're talking about, Rob! Do you realize what SECPOL would do with you if they ever find out?" In her anxiety, she jumped up and her voice became high and desperate. "They are ruthless, Rob," she cried. "They'll stop at nothing to get their hands on those diamonds! For that reason, I want you to forget about it!"

Rob took her hand and guided her back to the couch. "There will be dangers," he agreed, "but I've taken all precautions I could to eliminate them."

"What is the plan?" asked Sobreiro.

"A model of simplicity," began Rob before Mena could start another contest in words. "Tomorrow, Ian will drop us off in Massau. Only Mena, Sobreiro and I will stay there. Ian, Don and Jock will continue to Portugalia."

"How are you going to prevent SECPOL from coming after us," Mena cried. "How are you going to explain our absence from Luanda?"

Rob put his hand on her arm. "Calm down, will you. SECPOL will not even know that we are hunting for the stones." Turning around on his heels, he pointed to Don. "That's why we hired Don. As far as everyone is concerned, the flights will go on as normal. As for our absence from Luanda, we'll explain that by spreading the rumour that we are studying the feasibility of opening a new line between Luanda and Cabinda, and that's a very plausible destination."

It was beginning to dawn upon Mena that Rob seemed to have planned the search to the finest detail and that nothing she could say or do would make him change his mind. She might as well hope for the moon to rise in the west, or for the waters of the Victoria Falls to flow back up the waterfall! Forcefully, she pushed her worries to the back of her mind and comforted herself with the idea that she would be there, with him...

"The beauty of it all is that," Rob continued, "if we don't find any diamonds, officially nothing has happened and we can go on with our flights as before." He turned his lopsided smile to the rest of the group. "However, if we find the stones..." His voice rose vibrant with enthusiasm: "Then we have enough money to get out of here and start a new life, anywhere we fancy to go, Kenya, South Africa, the Far East maybe, and..." He switched his attention to Mena, "... to put your conscience at rest, my darling, we'll give a generous donation to the Belgian doctor who treated my knife wound. I trust his integrity, I admire his devotion to his patients, and he'll be able to use that money to improve conditions in that miserable hospital."

Tommy had a question. "Why involve me in all this, Rob. You obviously have it all set up with your own team."

Smiling secretively, Rob gathered the papers from the table and slipped them back in his flight case. "You are my safety net, Tommy. Even the best made plans can sometimes go wrong. Tomorrow, before we leave, we'll have a talk about a contingency plan, and I want Ian to be present. It's got something to do with your VHFs and an alternate escape route in case we have to get out of here in a hurry."

Massau, 14 December 1995

The sun rose like a ball of fire above the steep rock wall at the eastern boundary of the lake. Instantly, the thin layer of mist which covered the water became a veil of gold. Minutes later, the sunlight reached the sandy beach on the western shore and crept further inland until it fell on the canvas roof of two small tents which were shielded from the runway by a growth of thorny bushes and waist-deep grasses. Disturbed by the sudden increase of brightness in the tent, Rob opened his eyes. The unfamiliar sight of canvas walls and the drumming noise of falling dew drops on the roof made him frown in wonder. "Of course," he suddenly remembered. "Massau ... the lake ... the diving expedition."

Mena lay curled up in a ball next to him. He noiselessly unzipped his sleeping bag and crawled on all fours out of the tent. The air was scented with the smell of wild flowers, wet grass and dusty soil. Yawning, he stretched his arms above his head, his yawn becoming a groan when the sharp pain of stiffness shot through his muscles, a leftover from the hard work the previous day when, with the help of the villagers of Massau, they had set up camp.

With thin branches and dry leaves, Rob built a fire and brewed the coffee. Tempted by the tantalizing aroma, he sat down and poured himself a cup. The caffeine flooded his body with new energy. Armed with another cup, Rob crawled back into the tent and woke Mena. Sipping her coffee, she asked him where Sobreiro was.

"I haven't seen him, Mena, but I remember him saying yesterday that he intended to go to the village to hire two trackers."

"What for, Rob?"

"Well, if we find the Skyvan, I'll have to dive. To make it safer, Sobreiro came up with the idea of killing a water buck or a gazelle and putting the carcass on the opposite shore to draw the crocodiles away. That's why he needs two trackers to help him with the hunt."

Mena forced the idea of the dangers Rob would be facing out of her mind. She quickly dressed in a pair of shorts and a light coloured blouse. As she came out of the tent, the sun highlighted the gold in her curls. Rob pulled her close and kissed her.

"Your chin feels like sandpaper," she complained, rubbing her hand over his stubble.

Rob shaved in the remains of lukewarm water that was left from making the coffee. Afterwards they walked to the edge of the lake. As the sun rose higher in the sky, the heat burned the fog away. The Zodiac lay bobbing up and down on small waves which glittered like silver. On the other side of the lake, in the shadow of the rock wall, the water lay flat and dark.

Mena jumped when a frog croaked and vaulted from a large boulder into the lake. Rob made sure that there were no crocodiles in sight, then they stripped and splashed around in the shallow water. Forgetting the world around them, they frolicked for a while like two young seals. Feeling very much alive and ravenously hungry, they rubbed each other dry with a towel and walked back to the camp. They caught the delicious smell of broiling meat. "Good old Sobreiro," Rob laughed. "He must have caught some game. Imagine, fresh meat for breakfast. All the comforts of home." Hand in hand, they started to run.

Whilst savouring his food, Sobreiro told Rob that he had hired two experienced trackers. "I also found out that there are no guerrillas in the area. Massau is like a little sanctuary, far away from the roads the guerrillas use to travel between their training camps in Zaire and Angola."

"Good," replied Rob. "That's one thing we don't have to worry about." He took a stick in his hand and sketched the outline of the lake in the dust. Next, he partitioned the surface into separate sectors, each sector subdivided by a set of parallel lines. Pointing his stick to the extreme eastern part of the lake, he started to explain his plan. "Each line represents a search track. They all run straight from north to south." His voice full of zeal, he looked at Mena. "In Luanda, I've seen how well you handled the Chris-Craft. Therefore, it will be your task to steer the Zodiac. Start out by following exactly along the first line, then, at the end of the first run, you turn around and..." Again Rob gestured with the stick to his drawing. "Follow a line parallel to the first one, a little more to the west, but exactly in the opposite direction, and so on, until..."

Sobreiro smiled widely. "Until the metal detector finds a chunk of metal on the bottom."

"How far should the lines be apart?" asked Mena.

"About thirty yards, I guess," replied Rob, judging the depth of the lake and the sensitivity of the detecting equipment.

"What speed?"

"Not more than 5 knots."

Mena looked over her shoulder to the lake which now glittered like molten lead in the hot glare of the sun. Quickly she calculated the total surface of the lake, divided it by the number of lines and the average speed of the Zodiac. Her eyes widened in an exasperated frown. "At that speed it will take us a whole day to search the lake," she sighed.

"That's right," agreed Rob. "However, we don't need to bother about the whole lake, my darling. This shore is much too close to the end of the runway. Remember what the shepherd told me. The plane made a rough landing, jumped up in the sky and plunged into the lake. Therefore, considering the speed of the Skyvan, it must be lying far away from the shore." He stared out over the water. "Somewhere between the middle of the lake and the rock wall at the other side, I figure." As he said that, it suddenly hit him that only a short distance away, the remains of his father might be lying on the bottom and a cold sensation crept over his skin.

Sobreiro doused the fire and slung the Mauser over his shoulder. Rob and Sobreiro carried the metal detector between them.

The deep blue of the morning was gone. Instead, the sky was beginning to cover with the typical cloud formations of the rainy season, the east still clear and sunny, the west already dotted with small Cumulus clouds. By the shore they were met by a group of villagers from Massau, men, women, and half a dozen children.

"What are they doing here?" asked Mena.

"Hoping that we'll give them a job," ventured Rob.

"No, they're just satisfying their natural curiosity," explained Sobreiro. "You'll see, for as long as we are on the lake, they will stay. As soon as we stop, they'll return to their village."

"Take a look at the children, Rob," Mena whispered.

Rob observed the unhealthy condition of the children, their arms and legs thin like reeds, their bellies swollen like balloons.

"Total malnutrition," he stated. "I wish there was something we could do to help."

Sadly, Mena climbed on board the raft and opened the fuel cock. Sobreiro took a seat in the prow. Rob installed himself on the starboard float, put the streamlined body of the metal detector over the side and adjusted the acoustic level until the tiny loudspeaker emitted a faint squeaking tone. Sobreiro shielded his eyes with one hand and studied the surface of the lake. At the place where the Rio Cuango forced its way between huge shoulders of rock, the water was swirling rapidly.

"Look there, Rob," he said. "That current must be 8 to 10 knots. We'll have to..."

His words were drowned by a blast of noise when Mena started the engine. Rob tried to visualize the bottom of the lake, the huge water-washed boulders, the mud flats between, and the forest of algae that slowly swayed to and fro in the lively current.

Hour after hour, they crossed the lake in neat parallel lines. Once, a crocodile, attracted by the hope of easy prey, emerged close by the Zodiac, its monstrous head breaking the surface of the water without making a sound. Mena screamed, a loud and piercing noise that scattered the peace of the afternoon. A flock of birds, scrounging for food in the shallows by the shore took off in a mass of wildly fluttering wings. Sobreiro drew the Mauser to his shoulder and fired, corrupting the fresh air with the sharp smell of cordite. The first bullet went through the mouth of the reptile, the second transformed its left eye into a pool of blood. Thrashing its tail in deadly convulsions, the monster slipped away to the bottom.

As the sun slowly continued its travel to the west, the protecting shadow of the rock wall grew shorter. It became unbearably hot. Sobreiro grabbed the bailing bucket and made himself useful by throwing pails of water over the rubber seats of the Zodiac. After what seemed like an eternity, they finished searching the first half of the lake. Rob looked down at the dial of his watch. His eyebrows shot up when he saw that it was already 2 p.m. The first half of the lake had been the most likely place to find the wreck and not once had the detector given the slightest indication of metal on the bottom.

Discouraged and exhausted by the heat which seemed to affect him more than Mena and Sobreiro, Rob winced at getting it all wrong. "We should have found something by now," he muttered. Feeling that something was trying to emerge from the back of his mind, his voice trailed away. It was something important he knew, but what? He forced himself to focus his thoughts. Each time he felt he was coming close, the idea slipped away like a mirage. Doggedly they continued the search. Shortly after three, the Evinrude ran low on petrol.

"Time to refuel," announced Mena, adding that she could do with a bite to eat as well.

"So could I," affirmed Sobreiro.

After a late lunch of tinned sardines, hard bread and fresh coffee, Rob felt refreshed. As an added bonus, the idea that had been so evasive had germinated but he decided to eliminate all doubt by sticking to his original plan and finish the search in the eastern part of the lake. Stretching out his hand, he touched Mena's arm. "Four hours to sunset," he said gently. "Shall we give it another try?"

The next hour they searched another six lanes but the metal detector remained mute. The absence of sound did not disturb Rob any more. On the contrary, with the passing of time, he seemed to become more sure of himself as if the silence of the detector was the final proof he was looking for. "It's becoming very obvious now," he said suddenly, a mysterious edge to his voice. "Let's go back. It's enough for today!"

They dragged the Zodiac on to the shore and secured its painter to a huge boulder. Darkness, as usual in the tropics, came fast. The sun disappeared like a giant red ball behind the green wall of the forest. Whilst they were walking back to the camp, the mosquitoes came out of their hiding places and started to whine around their ears. Later they sat by the tents under the great canopy of the African sky. To keep the mosquitoes at bay, Sobreiro built a roaring fire. In silent companionship they sipped their drinks and listened to the noises of nature, the rustling from branches in the soft evening breeze and the cry of a bird or the roar of a lonely predator, hunting for food. Just about to explain what he had in mind, Rob suddenly pricked up his ears when another tone added itself to the sounds of the night, the high pitch of aircraft engines that steadily increasing in volume, came heading their way. He looked at his watch. "That's the Britannia," he shouted. "Ian is exactly on time." He pulled the microphone of the small portable VHF from its holder. "Skylift One, this is Rob. Do you read?"

Immediately Ian's voice came through, loud and clear.

"Hello down there, this is Skylift One. Yes, I read you five by five."

In brief words Rob explained the result of the day's work. "We need another day to finish the search," he concluded.

As he spoke, the blinking navigation lights of the plane passed overhead, a set of tiny coloured stars that slowly moved from east to west amongst the stationary but much brighter lights of the Milky Way. Rob could almost visualize the faces of Ian, Don and Jock, sitting in their seats in the cockpit.

"Understood," replied Ian.

"By the way, Rob," interrupted Jock, "I believe that your ruse is working. Nobody has missed you, yet."

"I don't know whether we should be so complacent about it," stated Ian. "Remember what Mena told us two days ago on board the Petrolua about the dangers involved with the possession of diamonds. Therefore, I wouldn't be surprised if somebody is closely watching what we are doing. So, for God's sake, don't be too long, Rob. The whole thing could blow up in our faces before we know what's happening."

"I'll make it as fast as I can," replied Rob. "I'll talk to you tomorrow."

"Just a moment, Rob," added Jock. "There's something else."

For a moment it remained quiet on the frequency, with only the muted echo of a static discharge piercing the silence of the night. "Yesterday evening," Jock finally said. "Don and I finished overhauling the Falcons. They are both now in perfect flying condition, refueled and ready to go."

"Well done," said Rob. "Thanks, and enjoy your night in Luanda." He switched his portable receiver off.

The lights of the Britannia slowly disappeared to the west. When the noise of the engines was completely gone, Sobreiro stood up and threw two logs of wood on the fire. His face, illuminated by the flames, looked as if it was carved out of a block of amber. Rob quietly sipped his scotch.

"Ian is right," Sobreiro said. "Knowing the system, I'm sure SECPOL has spies in Luanda and in Portugalia. Lopes is an old experienced fox. Given the slightest hint, it won't take him long before he discovers that we're missing."

"We'll give it one more day," responded Rob. "Now, I guess that both of you are anxious to know what went wrong today. " Smiling regretfully, he turned his attention to Sobreiro. "It was my fault. I recall from your conversation with Roberto Cabral that, in 1975, during the search for the missing Skyvan, the only thing they found was the right hand engine which showed signs of damage by rocket fire."

Sobreiro nodded slowly.

"Well, that substantiates my theory," Rob said.

"I don't understand," started Mena.

"Let me explain," declared Rob. "From Roberto Cabral, we learnt that my father was flying the Skyvan and that Oviero was sitting in the right hand seat. We also know that the right engine was shot out of the wing. Therefore, I believe that Oviero was badly wounded by shrapnel from the rocket that hit the engine."

"How can you be sure, Rob?" asked Sobreiro.

"I can't be sure, but think, man. A crack pilot like Oviero! With him alive, even with one leg in a cast, they would never have crashed into the lake. He would have been able to guide my father safely to the ground."

Slowly Sobreiro began to realize what Rob was driving at.

"Oviero must have been dead when the Skyvan came here," Rob repeated. "My father had barely five hours experience on twin engines, and shocked out of his mind by being shot at, with his best friend mortally wounded in the seat next to him, he was forced to cope on his own with a plane that was very badly damaged."

"I see your point, Rob," Sobreiro admitted. "With the engine shot out of the wing, your father must have had a hell of an asymmetrical problem."

He held a match to the tip of his cigarette. "I agree with you that if Oviero had been alive, they probably would have made a safe landing, but how does that help us find the wreck?"

"That's easy," Rob replied. He slapped at a mosquito that was trying to suck his blood. "Only a matter of imagining the flight path of the Skyvan."

"Would anyone please explain what you're talking about," Mena broke in. "I don't know anything about flying, and what you're saying sounds like Chinese to me."

"You see, Mena," explained Rob. "When flying a twin, the power of the engines is distributed evenly on each side of the plane. The resulting force pulls the plane straight ahead. However, if only one of the engines is working, the plane has a tendency to turn towards the dead engine. Unless the pilot corrects it by pushing on the opposite rudder. That requires a lot of experience, the kind of experience that my father didn't possess."

With his hands, Rob demonstrated what he meant, the movement of the plane and the pivoting moment around its own vertical axis.

"So far, I understand," Mena said. "Go on."

"In the case of the Skyvan, only the left engine was working. To keep the Skyvan going in a straight line during the overshoot, it would have needed a lot of rudder to the left. I guess, when he made that bounced landing, my father must instinctively have thrown the throttle forward and I fear that, in the rush of the moment, he forgot all about correcting the swing of the nose with the left rudder." Rob's hands painted a picture of how it had been, the high nose-up attitude, the turn to the right and the resulting roll with loss of airspeed followed by the stall.

Sobreiro jumped up. "With the result that the plane plunged in the water, not in the lake but far more to the right, in the river by the rapids," he shouted excitedly. With admiration in his voice, he acknowledged that Rob was right. "We really have been looking in the wrong part of the lake, Rob." He stood up and flipped the stub of his cigarette in the fire. "Since it looks very promising now that we are going to find the wreck tomorrow, I'm going to bed. I have to get up early, because I have some hunting to do." He revealed that one of the trackers in the village had discovered the footprints of an old water buck in the northern part of the forest. "The ideal bait to lure the crocodiles away from where you'll be diving, Rob."

It suddenly struck Rob that his rendezvous with the wreck was coming close, and a cold shiver of apprehension ran down his spine.

At the same time, in Luanda, Lopes sat brooding in his office. Earlier that evening, Olunga had told him that Rob, Mena, and Sobreiro, were missing. Although loosing trace of Rob did not say much about Olunga's efficiency, Lopes was not unhappy about it. It could be that this sudden disappearance was the sign that Stanfort had found the location of the lost treasure, or at least a trace leading to it. Stretching out his hand, Lopes reached for the phone. Halfway there, he changed his mind and his hand froze in mid-air.

"No", he mumbled. "I'm not going to order a general alert." Unwilling to share the loot with anybody else, a cunning smile slipped over his lips. "Let Rob and his comrades get the chestnuts out of the fire. Only then shall I make my move." Savouring already the satisfaction of snatching the diamonds away from Rob, he dialled Olunga's number.

Massau, 15 December 1995

Sobreiro stood just inside the edge of the trees by the extreme northern shore of the lake, at the spot where a narrow river came snaking out of the forest. Ndjungu and Kabila, the two black trackers he had hired the previous day, were studying a set of hoof prints which were leading from the nearby shore and disappearing into the forest.

It was 7 a.m. Dawn had broken an hour ago when the sun came surging like lava above the far rim of the earth.

With the eye of an experienced hunter, Sobreiro carefully surveyed his surroundings. At that early hour, the shore was already teeming with wildlife, the air reverberating with the loud screams of kingfishers and the more delicate clucking of a flock of white and pink flamingos. Away from the shore, on the mud flats in the estuary of the river, a couple of large crocodiles were warming their lizard-like bodies in the heat of the sun. Behind him lay the forest, deep and dark and virginal, as if untouched since the early days of creation.

Captivated by the pure beauty of it all, Sobreiro stood still in admiration. After a short moment and somewhat reluctantly, he went down on one knee to examine the trail. Immediately, he noticed that it was a series of tracks, all made by the same animal. A new set of prints partly overlaid the old ones, the new indentations so fresh that it looked as if they had been cut out of the soil with a knife.

"The track of a Punja Buck," whispered Ndjungu.

"An old animal," Kabila added. He made a movement with his hand in the direction of the forest, then crept slowly forward along the narrow track that twisted its way through a dense screen of leaves and foliage. Full of purpose, Sobreiro followed. Ndjungu came last, protecting Sobreiro's back.

The forest floor, covered by centuries of dead leaves and mouldy twigs, felt springy and moist. At first, Sobreiro thought it was a blessing as it absorbed all the noises they made. Soon however he discovered that instead of a blessing the very resilience of the soil was a curse, making the spoor very faint and hard to follow. Deeper in the forest, the track became even more arduous. At times, the trees stood so close together that they blotted out most of the sunlight. To avoid loosing the track completely, they sometimes had to go down on all fours.

Entirely captivated by the thrill of outwitting his prey, the noises by the shore became nothing but a vague impression of sound on Sobreiro's mind. Sweat running in rivulets down his forehead and his shirt clinging like a soaked rag to his shoulders, he lost all sense of time. As he followed the track around the trunk of a fallen tree, something moved in the undergrowth and his skin suddenly started to crawl with the perception that he was coming close to another living being.

Kabila went down on one knee and put a finger across his lips.

Sobreiro understood that he had to remain immobile, and very silent. "Was it the Punja or was it a predator of the forest that was sneaking up on them?" His weapon at the ready, he searched the shadows between the trees. Apart from the eternal twitching and fluttering of leaves and creepers and branches, nothing stirred.

Kabila made a motion with his hand, signalling him to come close.

Without making a sound, Sobreiro crawled further down the track. As he reached the position where his tracker was hiding, Kabila pointed his finger to a small clearing which had been formed years ago when a storm had uprooted a couple of trees and left the forest with a small but almost perfectly carved circular scar. At first, Sobreiro did not realize what Kabila was pointing at. Suddenly, he became aware of a discrepancy in the pattern of green; a dark and mottled brown that had nothing to do with the colours of the forest. Immediately he recognized the form for what it was.

The Punja!

Sobreiro's pulse jumped. Slowly but firmly he placed the Mauser against his shoulder and took up the slack in the trigger. A light breath of air caressed the left side of his face, the signal that he was still on the downwind side of the animal. For as long as he stayed in this quarter, the Punja wouldn't be able to catch his human scent, a scent which in the savannah or the forest only meant one thing: *Danger!* At one time, the buck looked directly in his direction. Fearing he had been detected, Sobreiro mustered all his willpower to remain immobile. Seconds later - seconds which seemed like hours - the water buck turned his head away and started to scrape the soft soil of the forest with his hoofs, looking for fungus or roots to fill its stomach.

Sobreiro let go his breath. With animals it was as with humans. Feeding came secondary to the primal instinct for safety and survival. The fact that the water buck was starting to look for food *was* the irrefutable proof that the animal was unaware of his presence. In a gut reaction, Sobreiro lowered his rifle and decided to crawl closer to make sure of the kill. As he moved nearer, he could see that the Punja affered a sore sight, its coat hanging in folds down its skinny chest. Sobreiro moved his eyes down the old animal's body. He took in the split hooves which sagged from age like a pair of old shoes. The large head and shoulders, as evidence of a long and hard life full of fierce battles, were covered with dozens of scars. Sobreiro pondered that once, the buck must have been the leader of a herd. Now weak and frail, it had been chased away by a younger and stronger male. Left on its own, sooner or later the old animal would find a lonely and miserable death. Visualizing the agonizing fate it would suffer when falling prey to one of the predators in the forest, Sobreiro reflected that killing the buck now was not an act of cruelty but a gesture of mercy. Without further hesitation, he raised the rifle and supported the barrel against the trunk of a tree.

The shot tore the peace of the early day apart. Above Sobreiro's head, a group of monkeys began to scream. Wild with panic, they swung away through the tops of the trees. A shower of broken twigs and leaves whirled down to the earth. As if the spring that held it upright was suddenly broken, the Punja plumped heavily down to the ground. Its nostrils opened wide, then the animal stretched its legs and exhaled its breath in a last spasm of life.

Sobreiro chambered a new round. Continuously scanning the forest to make sure that no danger was lurking behind his back, he walked over to where the buck had fallen. His shot had gone straight through the heart, but experience had taught him that a wounded or dying animal could be very cunning and very dangerous. To be sure that the Punja was dead, Ndjungu touched one of the eyes with the tip of his hunting spear. The eyes didn't twitch.

"Punja dead, Bwana," he said. "Nice shot..."

Sobreiro left the unappealing task of cutting the animal apart into manageable chunks to the two hunters. They both went down on their knees and sliced the belly of the old buck open. The sickly warm smell of blood pervaded the air. Whilst Ndjungu cut the legs from the rest of the carcass, Kabila began to lay the intestine in a trail to the shore of the lake, a trail that would lead the crocodiles to an easy prey and keep them far away from the spot where that afternoon - if all went well - Rob would be diving.

It took them the best part of an hour to finish the job. By then, according to

Sobreiro's watch, it was already approaching 9 o'clock. Startled, he made a short-cut through the forest until he came out on the narrow strip of sand that lined the western shore. The soft white sand made a faint crackling noise under the rubber soles of his shoes. To get rid of the stink of killing that stuck to him like a second skin, he washed his hands and face in the fresh water of the lake.

A group of villagers, eager to watch the spectacle, stood waiting by the shore where the Zodiac lay tugging at its mooring line. It reminded Sobreiro that they would have to find a way to bring the diamonds ashore without arousing the curiosity of the villagers. Otherwise they might know in Luanda about the discovery before the stones could be loaded on board of the Britannia.

Rob and Mena had already checked the dinghy and installed the metal detector. "Hello, Sobreiro," Rob called out when he saw him coming near. "Come on, hurry up, man. We've been waiting for you."

Sobreiro flicked the safety catch of the Mauser to safe, untied the mooring line and settled himself on the narrow wooden bench in the front of the Zodiac. Pushed by the current, the Zodiac drifted away from the shore. Mena pulled the starter cord and pointed the nose of the Zodiac to the south, in the direction of the rapids and the river.

As an aside, Rob asked: "We heard a shot, Sobreiro. Did you get your prey?"

A thoughtful look slipped in Sobreiro's eyes. "Yes, I got it," he replied. "The bait for the crocs is ready. Whether it will work, that's another question." To emphasize his words, Sobreiro made a sweeping movement with his hand, a movement that took in the whole surface of the lake. "Yesterday, I saw only a few crocodiles, but today, the northern shore of the lake is literally swarming with them."

Immediately, Rob felt his fear surge to the surface. Since his talk with Rick Martin at the Zoo, he had been plagued by terrible dreams, images of rotting bodies and fearsome crocodiles who were lurking in the wreck of the Skyvan. Maybe more afraid of showing fear than of fear itself, he had not told anybody about his nightmares. Now that his rendezvous with the wreck was becoming a distinct probability, a reminder of all the risks he was taking was as useful to him as a set of roller blades to an elephant, and his blood started to boil with anger.

On the verge of giving a spiteful reply, he suddenly understood the deeper meaning behind Sobreiro's words. It was not an attempt to tease or goad. It was merely a plea for extreme carefulness. An expression of a deep and loyal brotherly love. Trying to hide how touched he was, Rob tapped the barrel of the Mauser. "I feel very confident that my life is in good hands, Sobreiro," he said gently. "After all, you *are* the expert with the rifle, aren't you? Why else do you think I asked you to come along?"

Because of the abundant rains during the previous few days, the river had risen to a very high level. Huge rocks, which normally stood high above the waterline, were now barely visible. The water in the narrow channel between the rocks was swirling with eddies, each one of them betraying the location of submerged rocks. One touch against one of these razor sharp stones could tear the rubber floats of the Zodiac to shreds.

If that happened, we would not stand a chance of survival, pondered Mena. "Why not wait another day, Rob?" she said loudly. "Diving in smooth and calm waters will be much safer, won't it?"

Tempted to follow her advice, Rob looked up into the sky. By the look of the clouds which were already beginning to form, he felt sure that it was going to rain again soon. "Look up there," he said, pointing. "Before the day is over, we are going to get another pelting. That means even more water to swell the river."

"The rains won't stop until the beginning of the dry season, Rob. That's in four months from now."

"We don't have the time to wait for the dry season, Mena," he answered mockingly. "Remember, there is that little matter of our absence from Luanda. The longer we stay away, the more likely it becomes that somebody is going to get very curious about what we are doing."

Mena knew that trying to make Rob change his mind was just a waste of breath. She had tried it before. It had not worked then, it would not work now.

"If anything else," she heard Rob add. "Fast currents and swirling waters are just what I need to keep the crocodiles away. So let's get this show on the road, shall we?"

Mena steered a direct course to the centre of the narrow channel that connected the lake with the river. Once there, the speed of the current increased rapidly. The water became a roaring flood full of rapids and the Zodiac started to buck like a wild horse. After what seemed like hours, they reached the deeper waters behind the rapids. The river, instead of a progression of unpredictable spins and twirls, became a flood of long and steady, fast-flowing waves. Now that the danger of submerged rocks was behind them, Rob turned his attention to the metal detector and adjusted the volume until the squeaking sound was clearly audible above the roar of the river.

"Careful, Mena," shouted Sobreiro suddenly. He made a frantic sign to the port side of the prow. "A floating tree!"

Mena looked in the direction of Sobreiro's hand. A mass of broken twigs and splintered branches came charging through the current with the speed of an express train. In a split second, she turned the rudder to port and snatched the throttle in reverse pitch. The Zodiac spun around on the spot and started to drift backwards, missing the threatening branches of the tree by inches.

"Watch it," yelled Rob. "Keep her nose in the current or she will turn over."

His warning came too late. With a hard, slapping noise, the Zodiac slipped sideways in a trough between two giant waves. Another wave washed under the semi-rigid bottom. To prevent the Zodiac from flipping upside down, Rob flung his weight on to the starboard float.

At that moment, when everything seemed to be lost, something snapped in Mena's mind. "What am I doing," she thought. "I can't let *this* happen!" She swung the rudder hard to port and gunned the engine. The dinghy reared up like a charging horse. Mena pushed the throttle to its full forward stop. "Come on, move!" she yelled.

Pushed by the full power of the Evinrude, the Zodiac fell on an even keel and shot forward through the waves. Behind two huge shoulders of rock, Mena noticed a passage where the rocks were folding back on themselves like two overlapping curtains. Between them lay the access to an almost perfectly oval cove. In a reflex action, she swung the Zodiac between the two rocks. Inside the cove, the water lay flat and docile. Almost immediately, the strong current disappeared and the rocking and rolling motion of the dinghy calmed down.

"Well done, Mena," shouted Sobreiro. "I couldn't have..."

He was interrupted by the loud shriek of the metal detector.

"Jesus," Rob yelled. "That must be it. Switch the engine in reverse, quick."

As soon as the Zodiac lay still, Rob let the anchor down and attached a red marker buoy to the anchor chain. "This is it," he said, turning back to them. "The moment of truth."

Anticipation of what they were going to find galvanized Rob and Sobreiro into an outburst of activity. Sobreiro started to check his rifle, making sure that the magazine was full. Rob, energy radiating from every pore, carefully made his way to the poop of the dinghy. To protect himself against the cold of the water, he donned a thin neoprene diving jacket. Next, he put his arms through the straps of an air tank and tossed the heavy tank in a swinging movement over his head and down on to his back, a movement that betrayed great expertise as a diver.

Mena gave him a hand in fastening all the straps of his equipment and turned the valve of the air tank open. Rob sucked on the mouthpiece to check the air supply. To complete his preparation for the dive, he strapped a weightbelt with attached diving knife around his waist, slipped the loop of an underwater torch over his wrist, and put on a pair of flippers.

Mena's mouth suddenly twitched.

Rob understood the turmoil of emotions that went on in her. He gently pulled her against his chest. "Don't worry about me," he said, pointing to the surface of the water. "The water is clear, and there's only a very slight current. It will be all right." Reluctantly, she let him go.

Rob moved over to the side of the dinghy and sat down on the float, his back towards the water.

As an occupational therapy for Mena, he instructed her to keep a listening watch on the VHF. "Right now, Ian should be on his way back from Luanda. I told him yesterday to give us a call when flying over the lake. Tell him that we'll dismantle the tents at first light tomorrow morning, and ask him to land in Massau as early as possible. He will understand."

Ready to dive, he placed the mouthpiece of his regulator between his teeth and pulled the face mask over his nose and eyes. He made a small circular gesture with his thumb and forefinger to indicate that all was well and let himself roll backwards into the water. The first contact with the water was surprisingly cold. It made him gasp for breath. Also the visibility was bad, the water at the surface saturated with thousands of air bubbles and micro-organisms which shrunk the world around him to a circle of less than three feet. Rob let himself glide down along the anchor chain. Beneath a depth of ten feet, the air bubbles and organisms suddenly disappeared. As if a curtain had been pulled open, the visibility increased rapidly. The sunlight drew slanted lines of light through the water. Enthralled by the magic that revealed itself in front of his eyes, Rob felt as if he was floating on air. Slowly descending, he admired the moss-covered algae which gently swayed in the mild current. A couple of nosy tilapia fish fluttered by and fearlessly studied him through his face mask. Carefully checking his depth gauge, Rob discovered that he had reached a depth of forty feet. The density of the growth of algae increased, strengthening his impression that the bottom was coming near. Slowly, a more solid form began to rise up from between the waving plants.

As he came closer, Rob realized that he was looking at the wing of an aircraft. His stomach abruptly cramped in a spasm of excitement. Slower now, he worked his way down and studied the position of the plane. It lay roughly level on its right side, partly concealed behind a large boulder. The right wing had broken off and lay buried under the fuselage. The left wing, with the engine still attached, rose like a symbol of distress straight up from the bottom. To prevent himself from being swept away by the light undertow, he grabbed hold of one of the struts of the landing gear. Hand over hand, he pulled himself forwards along the belly of the plane. With his glove, he rubbed the thin layer of moss and slime away. Due to the filtering effect of the water in the depths, he couldn't make up his mind whether the colour of the wreck was green or blue.

It was only when he came round the nose of the plane and discovered the shrapnel holes in the side of the cockpit that he became sure that this was the Skyvan. Carefully avoiding the sharp edges of metal, he worked his way forward towards the large hole where the right windshield had been. Preparing himself for the gruesome sight of finding the bleached skeletons of the pilots still strapped in their seats, he looked inside the cockpit. It was empty! There were no dead bodies, and there was no obvious sign of any bag, box or container that could hold the diamonds.

"If they are on board," Rob thought. "They must be somewhere else."

From the pressure in his chest, Rob realized that he had been holding his breath. He let a long flow of bubbles escape from his mouthpiece. More relaxed now, he studied the cockpit.

The canvas covers of the seats had rotted away, the needles on the instruments stood frozen in their last position. The water that flowed in through the broken windshield moved the stick slowly forwards and backwards, as if a ghostly hand was still flying the plane. The right side of the cockpit lay hidden under a layer of mud and silt.

"A possible hiding place for a container of diamonds?" Rob asked himself.

Considering the emptiness of the cockpit, he decided it was not very likely, but he filed the information away in the back of his mind, with a reminder to subject the cockpit later to a more meticulous examination.

Eager to enter the plane via the cargo hold, he allowed the current of the water to push him gently back to the rear of the plane. As he reached the far end, he gave a few quick kicks with his flippers and went down under the double rudders to the sandy bottom of the river. From there he pulled himself forward to the wide open mouth of the cargo door. Inside the hold, the light was very dim. To make it worse, the moss that covered the tiny windows painted everything in a dark green hue.

As Rob swam into the fuselage, a strange kind of vertigo seemed to grab hold of him. It felt as if he had lost all feelings of balance. After a while it dawned on him that it was because the plane was lying on its side. The metal floor underneath him was not the floor of the plane but the right side, and the ceiling above him was the left side of the fuselage! Once he had sorted that out, it was easy to orientate himself and he let the beam of his torch sweep through the cavernous space. Almost at the end, by the cockpit door, he could distinguish a dark object that lay hidden under the rotting remains of a cargo net. From this distance, he couldn't quite make out what it was. Suddenly he was startled by a movement in the water. A dark mass seemed to make itself free from the forward end of the hold, a mass that was moving in his direction!

Afraid that he had disturbed a crocodile in its lair, Rob recoiled, his hand grabbing for the hilt of his diving knife. To his profound relief, when the *thing* came nearer, he saw that it was only a shoal of small fish that had made the fuselage their home.

Slowly, he started to move deeper into the hold. Small bubbles of air escaped from the mouthpiece of his mask and drifted like silver pearls to the ceiling. Careful not to touch the bottom and to disturb the sediment, he slowly flipped forward through the hull, the beam of his torch probing the corners and the sides for any sign of the diamonds. As he came closer to the bulkhead between the hold and the cockpit, he recognized through the maze of the cargo net the square forms of a crate. Rob's heart jumped, then a sudden stab of doubt flashed through his mind. "Would it be that easy?"

After analyzing his options - an apparently empty cockpit, and only one possible hiding place for the diamonds in the hold - he decided that working the crate out of the plane and hoisting it up to the surface was the only way to make sure whether or not he had found the diamonds.

He pulled his diving knife out of its sheath and began to slash the rotten strings of the net away. To get a better hold on the remaining strands of rope, he swam around to the other side of the crate. As he turned around the corner, he wasn't prepared for the horrible sight that met his eyes - the skeleton of a man, a few strands of hair still attached to the bleached bones of his skull, the empty eye sockets staring him straight in his face.

Rob's breath froze in his lungs. In a sudden reflex of self-protection he wanted to get out. He pushed himself vertically up. Seconds later, his head contacted hard with the left side of the fuselage. Rob lost all sense of direction. He started to gasp for air. The noise of the air bubbles sounded like the roar of thunder, his heart felt crushed against the cage of his ribs. In his frenzied movements, he loosened the mud and silt that lay on the bottom. It spread out in the water and blotted out the light. Rob's confusion became an uncontrollable panic. Completely disorientated and blinded by the drifting silt, he searched for the exit, but in his panic he couldn't remember where the exit was. Death by hyperventilation and exhaustion was only a matter of time.

Somewhere deep in Rob's subconsciousness, a tiny voice began to shout for attention. It said that giving in to panic would lead him nowhere. Forcing himself to listen to that voice, Rob focused his eyes on a tiny sliver of light that fell in through one of the cabin windows. As if that minuscule light was the only thing that mattered in the whole universe, Rob stuck the glass of his dive mask against the partly moss-covered window and concentrated on what he could see outside. With his eyes, he followed the gentle movements of the swaying algae, forcing the picture of horror he had seen to the back of his mind. Slowly, his hysteria began to give way to reason, and he mentally started to count: "One... two... three, breathe in! One... two... three, breathe out!" Again and again until gradually his breathing became normal and his heartbeat started to slow down.

Five minutes later, or was it ten or fifteen, the clouds that were flooding his brain lifted and he was able to think clearly again. He remembered that the metal wall above him was the left side of the plane and that the exit was at the end of the fuselage and not somewhere above him.

"Air," he suddenly thought. "Do I still have enough air?" Raising the pressure gauge of his scuba tank in front of his eyes, he noticed that he had still 2,100 psi left. Enough at this depth for another thirty minutes of dive time. Satisfied that he was not going to become trapped in the wreck without any air to breathe, Rob let his thoughts wander back to the skeleton he had found. "Who is it," he wondered. "Father, or Oviero?"

Now fully at ease with the idea of coming face to face with the skeleton, he swam back to the crate, cut the remaining strands of the cargo net loose and slowly pushed the crate towards the rear of the fuselage where he let it drop to the sandy bottom of the lake. A quick glance on his pressure gauge told him he still had 1,000 psi of air left in his tank.

Remembering the layer of mud in the cockpit, he swam forward and swept the beam of his torch through the dark recesses under the dashboard. Next, he plunged his hand in the silt that covered the bottom. Working blind, he felt his way around the rusted struts of the cockpit seat. About to give up, his fingers brushed against something that felt smooth and soft. As he pulled the package clear from the mud, his first impression was that he had found the container of a life jacket, the kind of jacket pilots wear when they make extended flights over water.

Rob rubbed the mud away and knew instinctively that it was a bag full of diamonds, but a stab of scepticism flashed through his mind. "What's that single bag doing in the cockpit," he asked himself. "And what about that crate?"

By now, the needle of his pressure gauge was fast approaching the red low-pressure mark. Time was up. Rob threw a last look on the frozen flight instruments.

As in a caress, he let his hand rest for a moment on the stick. He wondered whether he should raise the skeleton to the surface and give it a decent burial, but then decided that after twenty years, the best grave for the unknown pilot was the wreck of his own aeroplane.

As soon as Rob emerged into the green water outside the fuselage, he allowed some air into his buoyancy compensator and let himself slowly drift back to the surface, wondering whether all his work to push the crate out of the hold had been in vain. The first thing he saw when he came up was the indescribable expression of relief that brightened Mena's eyes. He spat his mouthpiece out and, holding on to her hand, shouted: "It's the Skyvan! Catch!" He threw the bag with diamonds over the side.

Aided by Mena, Rob pulled himself on board and sat down astride the rubber float. After swallowing a couple of mouthfuls of water to wash the metallic taste of compressed air away, he began to explain what he had found in the wreck, omitting all mention of the skeleton.

"I've looked everywhere," he announced. "Apart from that single bag of diamonds, the only other object I discovered is a wooden crate."

"It's weird that the leather of that bag has survived twenty years on the bottom without rotting away," Mena remarked.

"It's because the bag was buried deeply under the mud," said Rob. "The mud actually sealed the leather from contact with water and oxygen. It simply could not disintegrate." Rob turned away from Mena and threw a quizzical glance at Sobreiro. "Do you know whether the diamonds could have been shipped in a crate?"

"I've never heard anything about that, Rob. Nowadays, diamonds are transported in small metal boxes, but it is possible that in 1975 they used wooden crates or leather bags, like the one you found...." He hesitated briefly before finishing his sentence. "It was war then," he said. "Therefore, yes, I guess it's possible."

"How heavy is that crate, Rob?" asked Mena.

"I guess somewhere in the region of 200 to 300 pounds."

"That's sounds quite heavy for 30,000 carats of diamonds," Sobreiro commented. "However, if the diamonds were on board of the Skyvan..."

"We know they were," interjected Rob, "but I can't figure it out. If the diamonds are in that crate, what was this single bag doing in the cockpit?"

"That crate could contain anything," remarked Mena. "Let's presume that the diamonds were in the cockpit. The fact that you found only one bag would indicate that all the others have been sucked out by the bottom current."

"In which case we've got nothing to lose by hoisting the crate to the surface and check the contents," countered Rob.

"True," replied Sobreiro. "Only, I don't see how we are going to hoist a 300 pound crate on board the Zodiac."

"We don't have to haul it on board at all, Sobreiro. Remember, water has a much higher density than air. As long as the crate remains suspended in the water, we won't even notice its weight, and hoisting it up from the bottom will be no problem at all. The two of you can handle that. We'll secure it under the keel of the Zodiac." Rob suddenly smiled. "A supplementary bonus of having that crate suspended under the boat is that it will add to the stability. This time, crossing the rapids will be easy." He took the spare air tank out of its rack and lifted it on to his back. "Tonight," he added, "after dark, when the villagers are gone, we'll beach the crate on the sandy strip by the shore and open it up."

"Very clever," said Sobreiro. "And if I may ask, what will you be doing whilst Mena and I work as slaves to hoist that crate to the surface?"

"I'll be down under the water to make sure that our precious cargo doesn't slip out of the slings. Finding a crate in the fuselage of a plane is one thing. Trying to find it again if it drops down and disappears in a forest of algae and weeds on the bottom of the river is a rather more difficult task."

Later that evening they sat together by a roaring campfire.

"What a disaster!" Sobreiro mumbled.

Rob nodded.

His thoughts went back to the moment that, in a mild mood of hope, he had opened the crate. Again, he felt the bitter disappointment he had experienced in the pit of his stomach when he had discovered nothing but an old, rusted engine. To swallow the sour taste of failure and defeat, he downed his scotch as if it was a glass of water. "It's not entirely a disaster," he argued, his eyes red from the water and fatigue. "That single bag of diamonds is worth a hundred thousand dollars."

"Just enough to throw a fantastic party," Sobreiro replied in a self-mocking manner. "It's a far cry from the millions we had hoped to find."

Instead of being happy that the search was over and that they were all safe and well, Mena felt strangely subdued and afraid. "I wish we had found nothing at all," she said timidly.

"Why?" asked Rob. "What's the problem?"

"I'm afraid that somebody will find out about this," Mena blurted out. "I couldn't stand it if something would happen to you, or to anyone of us because of those diamonds!"

To soothe her fears, Rob pressed his lips on her cheek. Putting a lot of conviction in his words, he said: "Nothing will happen, Mena. Nobody knows anything about the diamonds. Tomorrow, the operation will be back to normal! As soon as we are in Luanda, we'll go to your apartment and pack your belongings. You'll move in with me, and we'll ask DIANGOL to give you two weeks leave. Then, when I fly, you fly. Where I go, you go. That way, you'll be safe!" His gentle voice worked like a caress to Mena's frightened mind.

After Sobreiro had gone to bed, they sat for a long time alone by the fire, until the skies covered over and showered them with sheets of drizzle. They withdrew to their tent and very much in love, they huddled close together in their sleeping bags.

Rob's last thoughts, before he drifted away into a deep sleep went to the diamonds, wondering where he would find the rest of the thirty million...

Luanda, 19 December 1995

Mena read the large sun-bleached letters above the shuttered windows of an old house in the Rua Cabras. "SELANO'S JOALHARIA Y OURIVESARIA," she said. "That's it, Rob. Selano is the jeweller Sobreiro mentioned."

"It doesn't look as if there's anybody home," remarked Rob, studying the dilapidated condition of the house and the peeling paint on the wooden window sills. "From the look of it, this shop has stopped dealing in jewellery a long time ago. Maybe Senhor Selano has moved out."

"I don't think so," voiced Mena. "I understood that he stopped trading when the communists came to power, but Sobreiro didn't say anything about him moving out!"

"I hope you're right," answered Rob. "He is the only trustworthy source we have to get an evaluation of our diamonds."

He rapped his knuckles on the door. After what seemed like an eternity, a small spyhole in the door swung open.

"Are you Senhor Selano?" asked Rob.

"I am," replied the jeweller. "What do you want?"

"You've been recommended to me by a friend," began Rob. "His name is Sobreiro."

"Ah, him ..." chuckled Selano. He closed the spyhole and unlocked the door to let them in. "Where the hell do you know Sobreiro from?"

"We are both pilots for DIANGOL," replied Rob. "Sobreiro told us that you are an old friend of his family, and that you could tell us confidentially something about the value of uncut diamonds." He opened a small purse and deposited half a dozen diamonds on the counter.

"Only because you're a friend of Sobreiro," Selano said, reaching behind him to switch on a strong spotlight that painted a bright circle of light and made the stones erupt in a myriad colours. He carefully took a small sliver of stone between the prongs of his tweezers and examined it with a strong magnifying glass. "This is undoubtedly a diamond," he confirmed, "but the quality is bad, barely sufficient for industrial use or for very small jewels."

He let the magnifying glass dangle by its string around his neck and put the stones on a pair of scales. "Well," he finally grumbled, raising his shoulders in an apologetic gesture. "As I said, the clarity of the stones is at best SI 2, maybe even P1 or P2. As for the weight, the largest stones are about half a carat. And that's the weight as they are now." He explained that another ten percent would probably be lost in the process of cutting and polishing. Drifting away in a mental calculation, his lips began to move rapidly.

"In Europe, you might get 200 US dollars per carat, if you're lucky. Here, not more than 100."

"I was already afraid of that," replied Rob, satisfied that the jeweller's appraisal was correct as the figure of 200 dollars closely matched the value on the price-list he had brought from London, bringing the total value of the whole bag to a mere one hundred thousand dollars.

Looking over the upper half of his glasses, the jeweller studied Rob. "Don't go around showing them to everybody," he stressed. "They are a very dangerous commodity!"

Rob slipped Selano a bill of ten US dollars. "To cover your fee," he said.

"No way," replied Selano, pushing the money back into Rob's hand. "Sobreiro's friends are my friends, and I don't take money from a friend. If we don't help each other, nobody else will, you know. Maybe one day, you can do me a favour."

He stepped out from behind his counter and walked to the exit. As he pulled the door open, a smell of ocean air mixed with the oily odours of the harbour drifted in.

Compared with the stale and stuffy atmosphere in the shop, it almost smelt like a breeze of fresh air.

Driving down the Rua Cabras, Rob put his hand on Mena's knee.

"First to your apartment, Mena," he said assertively. "To pack your belongings. Next stop, the Tropico, and at 2 p.m. we'll fly to Saurimo."

Mena reached over and caressed Rob's cheek. "That's great," she said, and added timidly: "I know you're not happy with the result of the search for the diamonds, Rob, but I'm very glad that this madness is finally over."

Headquarters SECPOL, 19 December 1995

Frowning with concentration, Lopes listened to what Olunga was saying. Only once in a while did he ask a short but very concise question. "Well done," he said finally. "Be assured, Olunga, I won't forget." He banged the phone back on the hook and, as if propelled by the force of a spring, he jumped up, ran to the door and called for his two aides. "Toni, Carlos, come here!"

Toni was an albino, with a blotchy pink-white skin, a hairless face and thickset lips. He had joined SECPOL when Luis Cordi had died from the wasting sickness, the more common name for AIDS. Carlos, a newcomer in the department, was a tall, strongly built, very dark-skinned man in his late twenties.

As soon as they were seated, Lopes began to talk quickly.

"Yesterday night, Stanfort and the girl arrived back in Luanda. This morning, they went to the airport and spent some time in the office. When they left, Olunga managed to follow them, and guess where they went?"

Carlos raised his shoulders. Toni muttered that he had no idea.

"They went to see a jeweller!" shouted Lopes. "Do you know what that means?"

"That your hunch about Stanfort and the diamonds was right, boss," replied Toni respectfully.

"Right," said Lopes. "I want Stanfort and Mena arrested. You, Carlos, cover the Tropico, and you, Toni, watch the Yacht Club in Mussulo. Arrest them on sight and bring them here."

"What about Sobreiro?" asked Carlos. "What about the other members of Stanfort's team?"

"Forget Sobreiro," responded Lopes. "I don't need that treacherous creep, and I don't need the rest of the crew." His voice sounded glacial. "It's Stanfort I want. He knows where the diamonds are, and his girlfriend is the key to that knowledge!"

In the Tropico, it didn't take Carlos long to find out that Stanfort and Mena had arrived in the hotel. Two by two and closely followed by an armed guard, he ran up the stairs.

In his room, Rob was sitting on the bed, toying with the bag of diamonds. "One hundred thousand dollars," he said. "Two months ago, that would have been a great deal of money, Mena. Now, compared with thirty millions, it is..."

At that moment somebody kicked the door open and a strongly built man came in. Behind him, an armed soldier entered the room. In an effort to defend himself, Rob jumped from the bed and threw the bag with diamonds at Carlos' head. Carlos stepped aside and hit Rob over the head with the barrel of his gun, splitting the skin of his scalp. Rob collapsed unconscious.

Mena's knees suddenly felt very wobbly and she screamed. Carlos looked at her and smiled. Not a gentle smile, but the sneer of a sadist who suddenly found himself alone with a defenceless victim. Mena's fear turned into panic. Carlos stepped nearer. As if she weighed no more than a sparrow, he lifted her up with one hand. With the palm of his other hand he smacked her hard across the cheek. Tears sprang from her eyes. Without uttering one word, Carlos slapped her again. The guard grabbed her by her hair and pushed a dirty rag which smelled of chloroform over her nose and mouth. Struggling wildly to get rid of it, she kicked back. Her heel connected with something soft. The bitter fumes of the liquid on the rag caught the back of her throat. For a moment she gasped for breath and her head started to spin, then it became dark and her body went limp.

As he came to, Rob found himself in a stinking cell, his chest and legs tied to a chair and his hands cuffed behind his back. His head felt as if he had been hit by a truck, and dried blood clotted his hair.

"Where are the stones, Stanfort?" Carlos shouted.

Rob shook his head to get some clarity in his mind. "I suppose you have them," he whispered. "I threw them at you."

Carlos smashed a cudgel against Rob's head.

"Not these stones," another man said. "The other ones. The valuable ones."

Rob turned his head in the direction of the new voice. This man, he had never seen before.

The man nodded. "My name is Lopes, and I want the other diamonds."

"There are no other stones," Rob replied. "Believe me. If I had them, I would give them to you." He briefly explained what had happened in Massau.

"So that's all there was?" echoed Lopes. "Just one bag."

"Right, only one bag," Rob repeated, "and a crate that contained nothing but an old rusty engine."

Lopes smiled. "Why is it that I don't believe you, Stanfort?"

He looked over to Carlos and made a nodding gesture. Carlos stepped forward, raising the rubber cudgel.

"Remember, Stanfort," Lopes said. "You can still stop him by telling the truth."

"I told you the truth. There are no..."

The pain when Carlos whacked his shoulders was agonizing, but it was nothing compared to the suffering Rob felt when Carlos methodically started to beat his body.

"I'll ask you once more, Stanfort," said Lopes menacingly, "and I warn you. If you remain stubborn, I'll be forced to use other methods."

Rob had the sudden premonition that something terrible was about to happen, not to him but to Mena. He shouted desperately, "Believe me, Lopes, please, there are no other diamonds. If I had them I would tell you."

"Your choice, Stanfort," replied Lopes, his voice cold like ice. "You'll regret it."

He told Carlos to put a gag in Rob's mouth. "Then bring him to the other cell. He has to realize that I mean business."

Mena's tongue felt as dry as sandpaper and her mouth tasted of bile. Still suffering from the after-effects of the chloroform, she was only vaguely aware of her surroundings. Slowly the recollection that something horrible had taken place started to fight its way to the surface of her mind. Forcing her eyelids open, she saw four bare stone walls, dripping with moisture, and the medieval type of cuffs that secured her hands and legs to the four corners of a heavy table. The room stank of vomit, faeces and some other undefined substance that reminded her of the smell of death, a smell she remembered well from the time when her father took her hunting, when she was present whilst the shot animals were skinned. A powerful light bulb hung above her head. The corners of the room were hidden in darkness. She tensed up and arched her spine in an effort to pull herself free. The rough iron handcuffs cut deep into her skin.

From far away came the sound of Lopes' voice.

"My dear Mena," he remarked tauntingly. "What have they done to you?" He touched her shoulder. She twitched with terror, rolling her head from left to right. "Look who's here," Lopes added.

Carlos and Toni stepped out of the dark, dragging a chair. On the chair sat Rob, his eyes wide with dread and his mouth covered with a piece of surgical tape.

Mena started to cry hysterically.

“Relax,” said Lopes in a calm and impersonal way. “Just tell me where the diamonds are, then both of you can go free.”

“We only found one bag of diamonds,” cried Mena. “Believe me, please...”

“Another liar,” sniggered Toni. “Disgusting.”

“I know a way to loosen her tongue,” volunteered Carlos. “For each lie, we cut one of Stanford’s fingers off, then his arms, and so on...”

“Yes, and when he kicks the bucket, we feed him to the sharks,” added Toni.

“That would be crazy,” admonished Lopes. “Stanfort knows where the diamonds are. We don’t want that secret to die with him!”

“We’ll have to punish Mena, then,” suggested Carlos. “Maybe that will revive his memory.”

Lopes nodded. “I like that idea.”

Rob violently shook his head. Tugging impotently at his handcuffs he tried to speak but only managed to make a weak muffled noise.

Lopes stroked Mena’s head as if she was a pet. “Carlos and Toni can’t wait to get their hands on you,” he said obscurely. “And your dear Captain is the one to be blamed for it. If only he would stop being stubborn, all this nastiness wouldn’t be necessary.”

Lopes stepped back and disappeared into the dark. The door of the cell closed with a resounding boom.

The knowledge that they were both at the mercy of two potential murderers threw Mena into an hysterical fit. From somewhere came a whimpering voice. After a while, she discovered that it was her own...

Toni stepped forward. With the tip of his knife, he ripped the buttons of her blouse and started to fondle her breasts. Carlos walked around the table and placed himself at the far end. With one hand he caressed the inside of her legs.

Rob went crazy with helplessness.

Carlos reached down and unzipped his pants.

Mena’s voice spiralled in an outcry of horror. “Oh, God ... no ... not that!”

Her terrified reaction seemed to excite Carlos even more. He laughed cruelly and forced her knees apart. Toni licked his lips in perverse anticipation.

Rob’s head started spinning. To draw Toni’s attention, he kicked his heels against the legs of the chair.

Toni turned around and hit him hard on the head. For the second time that day, Rob passed out.

“Oh God, let me die,” prayed Mena.

Trying to knock herself out, she battered the back of her head against the table. Slowly, she felt herself sink away in a trough of darkness. Before she lost consciousness, she heard the voice of Lopes who shouted: “That’s enough, Carlos, stop. You too, Toni. I’m sure they have learned their lesson.”

One hour later, Rob slowly started to stretch his legs. All the time, he had been lying like a discarded rag in the corner of his cell, his right leg folded under the dead weight of his body. As his blood started to flow again, his leg came alive with pins and needles. That brought some clarity to the hazy depths of his mind. Rob’s first thoughts went to Mena.

“Where is she?” he asked himself in near panic. “What did they do to her?”

He was startled when his ears picked up the rattling sound of a key in the keyhole. The door swung open and Carlos stepped over the sill. He coarsely ripped the surgical tape from Rob’s mouth. “Let’s go,” he said, and escorted Rob up the staircase to Lopes’ office.

The only other person there present was ... Mena.

Carlos closed the door and left them alone. Mena wrapped her arms around his neck and wept. Noticing her blouse with the ripped buttons, he couldn't prevent himself from asking: "Are you all right? Did Carlos ...?"

In a subconscious gesture of self-protection, Mena hugged her body. "No," she said, "Lopes stopped him just in time." A tone of puzzlement slipped in her voice. "It's as if he is playing a very cruel game with us."

Suddenly the door swung open and Lopes entered the room. Carlos positioned himself behind Rob. Toni remained standing by the door. A cold hand of fear clutched Mena's stomach.

"So," said Lopes conversationally. "Are you now ready to tell me where the stones are."

"I told you the truth," shouted Rob defiantly. "There are no other diamonds. What do you want me to do? Pluck them out of thin air?"

Carlos pulled the cudgel out of his pocket and gave him a hard whack on his left shoulder. The pain hit him like a flash of lighting and he almost fainted. Mena cried out with terror.

Indulgently waving his hand in the direction of the clock, Lopes shook his head. "No, Carlos. We don't need that any more. It's late in the afternoon, and we don't want to start another interrogation at this time of day." He lit up a cigarette and blew a plume of smoke to the ceiling, then looked at Rob. "I have decided to use a completely different strategy, Captain. You'll have the whole night to think about it. In a short while, we'll move you both to a cell in the Old Fort." Lopes smiled contemptuously. "The cells are not very comfortable. Some of them are so deep that they get partly flooded when the tide comes in. However, I'm sure that you'll be too busy discussing my proposition to notice that small interference with your comfort. Tomorrow morning, we'll bring you back here and let you decide about your own future."

"I don't have anything to think about," Rob shouted. "I'm not hiding anything."

"Somehow, I don't believe you, Captain. Therefore, I'll give you two options. The first one is that tomorrow morning, you tell me straight away where you have hidden the diamonds. In that case, we'll go and retrieve them together. Afterwards, you'll be free to continue your freight operation as if nothing has happened." Lopes' voice became suddenly very threatening. "The second option is that if you persist with your stupid denials, then...." He purposefully turned his head towards Mena.

Rob's mind suddenly began to fathom what Lopes was driving at and he went cold with horror.

"I'll have you strapped down on a chair," said Lopes, "and I'll force you to watch when Toni and Carlos beat Mena up. If after that you still refuse to talk, I'll tell Carlos to rape her, and this time, I won't interfere. After that, they will beat her up again and so on and so on, until you decide to answer my questions."

Rob's eyes turned lifeless and somber with desperation.

Lopes chuckled. "Love is such a handicap," he said scornfully. "Look at you, Captain. For the sake of a woman, you'll tell me everything I want to know."

"You murderous bastard!" Rob shouted. Blinded by hatred, he jumped forward and reached for Lopes' throat.

Carlos had been waiting for that. Rob felt the hard thump when the cudgel hit the back of his head. Again, everything went dark.

The next time Rob regained consciousness, he found himself back on his own in his cell. His head felt sore, and all his muscles and joints were aching. Feeling utterly miserable and desperate, he crawled to the wall and rolled himself into a tight ball, wondering what he could do to prevent Mena from being raped. The irony of the whole affair was that, even if he wanted to, he couldn't tell Lopes where the diamonds were.

Pushed by hopelessness, Rob racked his mind to come up with a solution. Hopeless minds sometimes turn into geniuses, and it came to him that there was a way to buy them a little more time. It all depended on Lopes' greed and the fact that most people believe what they want to hear. He decided to discuss it first with Mena, later that night, when they were together in a cell in the Old Fort. If she agreed, he would tell Lopes that he had hidden the more valuable diamonds in a cave under the water of the Rio Cuango.

Knowing Lopes as exceedingly perceptive and suspicious of everything and everybody, Rob knew he would insist on coming along with them to Massau. That, Rob didn't mind, as long as Mena would be spared the horrible fate of being beaten and raped. Once in Massau, he would be in a much stronger position. Almost certain that only he and Mena had any diving experience, he might find a way to lure Lopes and the others to come with him in the boat to help him with the diving equipment. Once he had the scuba tank strapped on to his back, he would capsize the Zodiac and drag Mena with him under the water, buddy-breathing from his own mouthpiece, whilst the three others fought for their lives in the wild currents of the crocodile infested river...

Now that he had the embryo of a plan, Rob's mood rose from bottomless despair to reasonable optimism. Suddenly feeling very tired, he drifted away in a fitful sleep, a short and troubled sleep in which he dreamt that Mena had been killed. With a start he woke up. To chase away the horrible dream, he forced himself to concentrate on happier times, when his mind had only been on doing his job, flirting with Mena, and finding the right way to persuade the Commander in Benguela to sell him the Motor Falcons.

Before Rob's eyes appeared the picture of the two Falcons in the old hangar in Portugalia. He remembered the broken parts of the Chipmunk lying discarded in a corner, the floor covered with junk and rubbish, such as rusted tools, cracked cylinders and old corroded pistons. "Corroded pistons..." Rob jolted when, in a flash of inspiration, he saw where his father could have hidden the diamonds. Looking at it from all angles, he let the idea ripen in his mind. "Of course," he finally decided. "That's the way it must have been. Why else would he bother to take that crate with him to Luanda? Oh, father, you really were a fox."

Rob's mood lifted as he fully understood the significance of his discovery. He would not have to rely on a risky plot any more. To gain their freedom, it would be sufficient to tell Lopes where the diamonds were really hidden.

"Are you sure that Lopes will let you go?" asked a suspicious voice in his brain.

A fortune in diamonds was indeed a very dangerous commodity for Lopes. Leaving anybody alive who knew about it would leave him wide open to blackmail, for a man like Lopes a totally unacceptable risk.

"That's right," Rob said out loud. "Once Lopes has the diamonds, we will have to die, and so will Toni and Carlos." He made up his mind to keep the knowledge of the possible hiding place of the stones to himself and continue with his original plan.

Several hours later, what time it was he didn't know because they had taken his watch away, Rob jumped with fright when the door of his cell was suddenly thrown open. His mind was dopey and his body felt stiff like the broken branch of a tree that had been lying for days under the scorching sun.

Carlos dragged him upstairs. According to the clock in the corridor, it was almost midnight. Outside, by the light of a pale moon, Rob saw a black Ford Escort standing by the curb, Mena already seated in the back and an armed soldier in the front. Carlos pushed Rob on the seat next to Mena, slammed the door closed and slipped behind the steering-wheel. As if he was afraid that they were going to try something foolish, the soldier pointed the barrel of his AK 47 between Rob's eyes.

The rear tyres spewed a spray of dust as Carlos pulled away. Upon reaching the corner of the Rua Do Esquadro, he took a turn to the right and steered the Escort in the direction of the Old Fort. With the noise of the high-revving engine reverberating from the walls, the needle of the speedometer touched 70 miles per hour. Out of the corner of his eye, Rob suddenly saw an enormous truck shooting out from one of the side-streets. Instead of slowing down to give them priority, the driver of the truck swung his vehicle directly in front of the Escort. "Watch out, Mena," he cried.

Carlos, pumping the brakes, threw the wheel to the left in an effort to slip between the bumper of the truck and the line of trees that bordered the road.

Rob pulled Mena down with him on to the floor. Less than a second later, the bumper of the truck hit the bonnet of the Escort. With a resounding thud, Carlos' head flew forward against the steering-wheel. It knocked him out cold. The soldier was not so lucky. He was lifted from his seat and launched through the windshield. The shock broke his neck.

Safely protected from the impact by the front seats, Rob slowly started to pick himself up from the floor. Mena was dazed but unhurt. Somebody pulled the door open and dragged them out of the car. The first thing Rob noticed was the dead soldier on the bonnet, his neck unnaturally crooked and his eyes staring wide open. Next, he saw the same hands that had pulled him out of the car, wrenching the AK 47 out of the soldier's hand.

"Get in the front of the truck, you two, quick."

Rob recognized the voice.

"Sobreiro, is that you? What... How...?"

"No time for explanations, Rob. We must be quick! Go ahead, Mena, climb in," he urged.

Holding the AK 47 in his left hand, Sobreiro climbed into the cabin and slammed the door close. Tommy shifted the gears in reverse. With the screeching noise of tearing metal, the bumper pulled free from the wreck of the Escort.

"How did you manage to get us out of this mess?" Rob asked. "How did you know we were in that car?"

"You have to thank Sobreiro for that," replied Tommy. He turned the heavy truck into a narrow side-street and pushed the throttle down to the floor. "As soon as he found out that the two of you had been arrested, he came to see me. At first, he wanted to call one of the Ministers and ask for help."

"Yes, but we decided that it wasn't a very good idea," added Sobreiro. "We didn't want them to know that Lopes was questioning you about a treasure in lost diamonds."

"How right you were," replied Rob. "Some of them would sell their own sister for that kind of money." He flinched as the wheels of the truck bumped through a pothole.

"I knew that SECPOL never kept their prisoners overnight in their HQ," Sobreiro disclosed. "So Tommy 'organized' the truck, and we decided to take matters in our own hands. We parked the truck in a narrow street by the HQ. I kept watching the door, until I saw Mena come out and take a seat in that Ford Escort. I then ran back to Tommy, and you know the rest." Emotion suddenly choked his voice. "I was afraid that either of you would be hurt in the crash, but it was a risk we had to take."

At that moment, they passed a long and high fence of rusty wire-meshing. Tommy slowed down and steered the truck into a narrow lane. At the far end, above the shrubs and rubbish that covered the sides of the road, rose the gates of the yard where the trucks of the Angolan Petroleum Company were kept overnight.

"That's where you got your transport!" Rob exclaimed.

Halfway down the road, Tommy brought the truck to a stop. Chuckling, he pulled the handbrake up. "Bribes in cash and a lot in kind, my friend. It works all the time." He lit a match and sucked fire into the bowl of his pipe. As soon as the tobacco was burning to his satisfaction, he took the pipe from between his teeth and pointed to the left. "I stopped here because that's where we hid your Land Rover."

Beneath a thick growth of thorny bushes, Rob saw the faint glint of moonlight reflecting from the bonnet of his vehicle.

Tommy spoke again, this time with a very serious tone to his voice. "Decision time, Rob."

"What do you mean?"

"Well, look at it this way. Whatever happens in Angola, you've cooked your goose." Tommy successively pointed the stem of his pipe to Rob, Mena and Sobreiro. "You can bet your sweet fanny that Lopes knows about the little escapade the three of you made to Massau. From now on, the three of you are blacklisted. Three outlaws, to be arrested on sight."

"The three of us? What about you, Tommy?" asked Rob sarcastically. "You're in it as much as we are."

Tommy quietly puffed a cloud of smoke in the air. "No, not me," he said, raising a hand. "Nobody suspects that I had anything to do with it. Carlos hasn't seen me. I stayed in the cabin of the truck, remember, and he was out cold. The soldier? He's dead. He'll never talk again. No Rob, the only thing that can be held against me is that I organized the truck by bribing the guard of this yard, but you can be sure that he will never say a word. By doing that, he would compromize himself."

"Tommy is right, Rob," interjected Mena. "We're burned."

Somewhere in the bushes, a cricket started to chirp. A large cloud slipped in front of the moon and hid the path in gloomy darkness.

"There is only one way out for you," continued Tommy. "Tonight, join me on board my ship. There are sufficient places where I can hide you. In two days from now, I'm scheduled to leave Luanda in ballast for Sao-Tome. So in two days from now, you'll be free. End of the story."

Gently rubbing his forehead and massaging the skin around his eyes, Rob remained quiet for a while. "It sounds very good," he finally admitted. A slow smile curled his lips. "There is only one problem."

Mena felt as if suddenly a huge weight was falling on her shoulders. "I'm not sure that I want to hear what you have to say," she whispered.

Rob felt as if he was a magician who had invented a new trick, eager to show it to his fans but also dreading their reaction. Finally, unable to control his growing impatience, he blurted it out. "When I was lying in that stinking cell, a very funny thing happened to me. I discovered something I want to verify before I leave Angola."

Mena drew in a sharp breath. Sobreiro lit up a cigarette.

"You see," Rob said, studying them one by one, "I think I know where the diamonds *really* are, and therefore I have to go back to Massau."

Tommy and Sobreiro looked as if Rob had just uttered the most vile blasphemy. Mena's mouth dropped open in astonishment.

"You want to do what?" she shouted, a shocked expression on her face. "You must be utterly and dangerously insane. They ought to lock you up."

"That's what Lopes did, but Sobreiro and Tommy got me out of there," countered Rob. Despite the seriousness of the moment, he smiled at the absurdity of what he had just said.

Mena forcefully grabbed his hand. "Tell me that you are not serious, Rob. Promise me..."

Rob looked at her. The expression in his eyes told her all she wanted to know and her heart froze. "I know it sounds stupid, Mena, but I can't give up now."

"It's not worth the danger," she cried in utter frustration. "Tonight, a soldier has been killed and Carlos has been badly wounded. For Lopes, it's not only a matter of getting the diamonds. It's a personal vendetta now!"

Remembering what Lopes had threatened to do, Rob suddenly felt his anger soar.

Still sobbing, Mena blew her nose. "I want us to get out of here," she yelled. "I want to get out, now that we still have the chance! I want you to..." She fell silent as Rob grabbed her rudely by her shoulders and shook her.

"I can't leave," he shouted, rage clouding his mind. "I want revenge." In his anger, Rob began to thump his fists on the dashboard of the truck. "Remember what Lopes had in store for you, Mena. That bloody bastard was going to have you raped and beaten."

It was a rude explanation. Rob felt Mena shrink with horror. He took her in his arms. "I don't take graciously to that," he said, grinding his teeth in anger. "My only way of revenge is to make sure that he'll never lay his hands on the stones."

"What if Lopes launches a nationwide search for us?" asked Sobreiro.

"Lopes isn't a fool, Sobreiro. He won't launch a search. He is too greedy for that. To launch a search, he would need to explain his reasons. As a result, President Nevo would find out about the diamonds. That would blow his chances of keeping the stones for himself. No, Sobreiro," Rob concluded. "Believe me, Lopes will try to work it out on his own."

"I think that makes sense, Rob," Tommy threw in, "... but how in the name of Christ are you planning to do it, and for that matter, where are the diamonds?"

Having anticipated that question, Rob chuckled. "You remember we found a crate in the wreck, a crate which only contained an old engine?"

"Yes, I remember."

"Well, when I was lying on the floor in my cell I think I discovered how clever father was."

He leaned back in the seat and started to explain. "As a manager of DIANGOL, my father knew damn well that he was sitting on a fortune. In 1975, the area around Portugalia was thick with guerrillas. Father must have feared that sooner or later, they would raid his office and steel the loot. Suspecting that hiding the stones and leaving the vault empty wouldn't work, he filled some leather bags with cheap fragments and stowed them in his safe. It must have been one of these bags that I found in the cockpit of the Skyvan. The expensive diamonds, father hid in a much safer place."

Sobreiro felt a feeling of excitement rise in the pit of his stomach and began to wriggle in his seat. "Stop the suspense," he begged. "Where are they?"

Rob laughed.

At that moment, the moon appeared from behind the cloud and drowned the land in a silvery shine that made the long leaves of palm trees look like silver. Rob decided that he had kept them waiting long enough. "I believe that father stripped the pistons out of that old engine," he disclosed, "and hid the diamonds inside the empty cylinders."

Sobreiro sighed deeply. "So we have to return to Massau," he said. "How are we going to get there, Rob. The Britannia is not here, you know. Ian and the crew left yesterday afternoon. They won't be back until mid-morning tomorrow. By that time, Lopes and his wolves will be searching for us."

"I don't intend to fly," Rob replied. "I'm going to drive."

He jumped out of the truck and walked over to the Land Rover. "Look, the two spare jerrycans are full. That's enough to get me there."

"What do you mean 'ME'," cried Mena. "Don't tell me you intend to go on your own."

"Exactly."

"No way, Rob. Over my dead body. If you go, I go!"

Rob knew that it was useless to start an argument about that. For sure, that was something he couldn't win.

"And so am I," confirmed Sobreiro.

"I'm afraid that's not possible, Sobreiro. You see, we need a decoy, something to prevent Lopes from thinking that we've gone to Massau. Therefore, before leaving Luanda, I'll drive you and Tommy to the Yacht Club in Mussulo. Once there, you put the Chris-Craft into the water."

"Tommy can do that on his own," Sobreiro interrupted, but Rob cut him short. "No Sobreiro, Tommy can't, you of all people should know that. One man has to work the winch, the other has to guide the boat down the ramp. Tommy cannot possibly do all that on his own."

Sobreiro nodded resignedly.

"The best bit comes now," added Rob. "With the Chris-Craft, you and Tommy return to the Petrolua, navigating along the coast. As soon as you reach the ship, lock the rudder of the Chris-Craft on dead ahead, point it in the direction of the ocean and give it full power."

As he listened, the edge of incredulity slowly disappeared from Sobreiro's face.

"It will take a while before Lopes finds out that the Chris-Craft is missing," continued Rob. "His first idea will be that we are trying to get away along the coast to Zaire. By the time he realizes that he's been had, Mena and I will be in Massau."

It became very quiet as they considered Rob's words.

Tommy was the first to break the silence. "I like your way of thinking, Rob. That plan to get to Massau might work, but what then?"

"Then," stated Rob, "Mena and I will try to recover the diamonds. In the mean time, it will be up to you and Sobreiro to prepare an escape route for all of us."

"For all of us," queried Sobreiro. "What do you mean by that?"

Rob chuckled sarcastically. "Bloody hell, Sobreiro, do you honestly think that it would be safe for Ian, Jock and Don to stay here?"

"Shit no," cut in Tommy. "I didn't think about that, but you've hit the nail on the head, Rob. Now that you have escaped, once they arrive in Luanda, Lopes won't hesitate one second to throw them in jail!"

"That's exactly right," affirmed Rob. "You're the only one who is in the clear, Tommy. The rest of us are totally compromized and we all have to leave." Rob raised his hand and put it on Sobreiro's shoulder. "For you," he said, "the only way, is to hide on board of the Petrolua and leave with Tommy."

"I suppose you're right," admitted Sobreiro reluctantly.

"What else do you want me to do?"

"As soon as you arrive on board the Petrolua, call Dundo on the HF and speak to Ian. Tell him to change to frequency 8879 minus the date of the Battle of Hastings. That way, if Lopes' men are watching the frequencies, they will not readily know which one to use."

"I don't know the date of the Battle of Hastings," admitted Sobreiro.

"It's 1066," said Tommy helpfully. "The frequency to be used will be 8879 minus 1066 ... 7813 kilocycles. But don't tell Ian that. Let him make his own calculation!"

"Right," confirmed Rob. "Once contact is established on that frequency, explain to Ian what happened and tell him that, under no circumstances, should he fly to Luanda. Instead, by about four tomorrow afternoon, he should come to Massau with enough fuel in the tanks to reach Sao-Tome. Instruct him also to dismantle the Falcons and put them on board the Britannia, with all our personal possessions."

"Consider it done, Rob," replied Sobreiro." He pushed the AK 47 into Rob's hands. "To be prepared for all eventualities, take that with you."

"Good thinking," said Rob.

He put the Kalashnikov on the front seat of the Land Rover and switched his attention to Tommy. "If all goes well, in a couple of days, we'll meet in Sao-Tome, but remember the contingency plan we talked about on board the Petrolua. Explain it to Sobreiro. Then, when he talks to Ian over the HF, he can remind him what to do if something happens to me or to the Britannia.

"Trust me," replied Tommy, "As I'm leaving the day after tomorrow, that part of the plan will work out fine."

The first thing Lopes contemplated when he was told that Rob and Mena had escaped, was to order a general alert. Immediately realizing the implications of launching such an extensive operation, he decided to think it over

Shortly after 11 a.m. he was informed that also the Chris-Craft was missing. Initially, he figured that the fugitives had escaped along the coast.

A little later, his cunning mind came up with another idea. "If all the signs point so obviously in the direction of the ocean, it could be that they are *not* heading in that direction at all," he said.

"If it is a diversion and they are heading inland, where are they going?" asked Toni.

"To the place where the diamonds are really hidden!" replied Lopes. His eyes slowly drifted to the large wall map of Angola. "And if that is what they are doing," he mumbled, "I wouldn't be surprised if they are heading for Massau."

Massau was not far away from the border with Zaire. To prevent insurgents from entering the country, that border was regularly patrolled by helicopters of the Border Patrol.

Without further delay, Lopes called the Commander of the Squadron and instructed him to send one of his helicopters to Massau: "To have a look. If they see any sign of the fugitives, or of the Britannia, make sure that they don't get away," he said. "They are enemies of the state."

Massau, 20 December 1995

According to the phosphorous pointers on Mena's watch, it was exactly fifteen minutes past one when they left the last houses of Luanda behind. The country roads were empty and the first miles were easy. Later, a thin layer of mist began to cover the ground. As the night wore on, the temperature cooled down and the layer of mist became a blanket of fog. Rob was forced to slow down and kept his eyes locked on the faint trail of black and brown that marked the edge of the road.

Mena pointed with the muzzle of the AK 47 towards the fog. "Why is it that now, when time is of the utmost importance, even the elements have turned against us?"

"I don't know," Rob replied. "I hope it will get better once we are further inland."

At 4 o'clock in the morning, it started to rain, a light and miserable drizzle that muffled the sounds of the night and soaked them to the skin. As the raindrops hit the still warm surface of the road, they evaporated into clouds of steam. The fog became more dense than ever, with silhouettes of low trees and bushes looming out of the greyness like silent ghosts. Rob put his foot on the brakes and skidded to a halt. "Let's pull the canvas hood in place," he shouted over the sound of the engine.

Feeling wet and cold, her morale at its lowest from fatigue, Mena placed the AK 47 on her seat and helped Rob to raise the stiff canvas cover of the hood. In less than three minutes they were done. Rob took the opportunity to top up the fuel tank, then jumped back behind the wheel and let out the clutch. With the windshield wipers on high speed, they crept slowly forward through the darkness and the rain.

"One advantage is that we don't have to fear an encounter with a security patrol," Rob commented. "In this lousy weather they'll be inside by a cosy fire, most probably getting drunk on home-made beer."

He got no reply and looked over to the right. Mena was sitting upright in her seat, her eyes tightly closed. Her head occasionally lolled down to her chest. Despite his own tiredness and aches, he smiled faintly. Carefully, he took the AK 47 out of Mena's hands and pulled her sideways until her head was resting in his lap. Rob felt the heat of her skin and the frantic rhythm of her breath. Driving with one hand, he gently caressed the nape of her neck. Soon, her tensed muscles began to relax. She wriggled herself in a more comfortable position, mumbling something Rob could not understand and fell into a deep slumber.

Mile after mile, Rob doggedly drove on. Sometimes the Land Rover staggered through potholes or skidded on a patch of mud. Later in the night, the drizzle became a genuine downpour. The wind picked up and drove the fog away. It looked as if a shade had been abruptly opened. Now that he could see where he was going, Rob pushed the Land Rover to its maximum speed. If this visibility held, they might be able to reach Massau early in the afternoon. Sporadically, the moon showed herself through a ragged hole in the clouds. The rain then stopped, only to restart a little later with renewed vigour. Slowly, a shine of watery light started to break through the darkness. It was one of those wretched mornings, when everything looked drab and sombre, the rain hiding the rich and warm colours of Africa behind curtains of water and low hanging clouds. Even the air was heavy, with a musty smell to it; a combination of moist earth, decomposing leaves and dust.

Looking down at the clock in the dashboard, Rob was surprised to see that it was a quarter past six. "Another six hours to go," he muttered resignedly. To chase the aching stiffness from his muscles, he stretched his back and rolled his head on his shoulders. His bruises began to throb badly. To forget about the pain, he forced himself to think of Massau and a glow of expectation warmed his stomach as he thought about what he would find when removing the cylinder heads of that old engine.

"A fortune in glittering stones," he mumbled. "That's what I'll bloody well find." His mind wandered and his eyelids became heavy. Rob caught himself nodding off. He rubbed his eyes and forced himself to concentrate on driving the car, but the monotonous view of the rain-swept road worked soporifically, and again he drifted away in a dream.

With a bang, the left wheel of the Land Rover hit a deep rut by the side of the road. Rob snapped his eyes open. With a frightened cry on her lips, Mena pulled herself upright.

"What happened?" she asked, her voice thick with sleep.

"I must have dozed off," Rob admitted. Very determined not to let that happen again, he stuck his head out of the speeding vehicle. Squeezing his eyes half-closed against the flailing effect of the rain, he let the water poor down his face until his mind was clear and his skin tingling with cold. Dripping wet, Rob pulled his head back behind the protection of the windshield. Barely five minutes later, his eyelids started to flutter and once more he fell asleep. This time, he completely missed a turn in the road. The Land Rover jerked to a stop, its bumper only inches away from the trunk of a giant Baobab tree. Rob jolted awake, stopped and set the handbrake.

"It's no good," he said. "I need some rest, just ten minutes of sleep and I'll be all right again."

Mena studied the lines of exhaustion that marked his eyes.

"I'll take the wheel!" she said decisively. To make her point, she tapped her finger on the dial of her watch. "Look, Rob, I've been sleeping for three hours."

Rob had to admit that she was right. Fighting against extreme fatigue was useless. From previous experience he knew very well that, once his body was utterly tired, it would switch itself off, whether he wanted it or not.

"Come on, move over," Mena insisted. "I'm in a much better shape than you." Her voice left no room for discussion.

Rob stopped by the side of the road and pulled a Michelin road map out of the seat pocket. "Look," he said, tracing the red coloured ribbon that connected their position with Massau. "The route is easy to follow, Mena. It's the only more or less hard surfaced road in this neck of the woods."

"Don't worry," she replied. "I won't get lost."

With a tired grin on his face, Rob climbed over his seat and stretched out in the back of the car. Before Mena had the time to drive on, he was already asleep.

The next time he opened his eyes, the sun was shining and the sky was blue. The orchestra of drumming raindrops had disappeared. Instead, the air was filled with the lively noises of a new and bright day. With renewed interest in what was happening, Rob sat up and looked around him. The Land Rover was covered with mud and red soil, the result of the long and perilous drive. To the right, through the trees, the sun reflected dazzlingly from a wide stretch of water. Beyond stood the almost vertical slope of the rock wall.

"The Rio Cuango," he shouted elatedly. "Mena, you've made it."

Mena sped down the runway and stopped by the shore. The old crate still lay where they had left it. Rob worked himself out of the car. Feeling very stiff and hurting where Carlos had hit him on the shoulders, he clutched the AK 47 in one hand and the toolbox in the other, and stumbled and staggered over to the crate. Studying the engine inside, he discovered that it was an old Perkins diesel, the nuts and bolts, after having spent twenty years under the water, an almost solid block of rust, mud and corrosion.

"Let's hurry," he said. "I want to get this thing over with before we get any visitors from the village."

He pushed the AK 47 in Mena's hands. With a screwdriver, he scraped the mud away from the top of the engine. Next, he took a pipe-wrench from the toolbox and slipped its hollow head over the first nut that held the cylinder head cover. Gathering all the strength he could muster, he pulled the wrench to the left. The nut didn't budge. Rob pulled a little harder. From the effort, he turned red in his face. Mena saw his biceps swelling. He suddenly cried out when a sharp lance of pain shot through his bruised muscles.

"No bloody good," he whined. "I need a lever to give me more strength..."

He went back to the Land Rover and removed the vertical strut of the wheel-jack from its hiding place under the bonnet. It was a square steel pipe, about one and a half inches in diameter and three feet long, cogged on one side and smooth on the other. "That's exactly what I want," he said, fitting the hollow end of the strut over the grip of the wrench. "Give me a hand, Mena."

She put the AK47 down beside her on the ground. Together they threw their full weight against the resisting nut. Accompanied by a screeching sound, it suddenly came loose. The second and the third nut soon followed. After removing the last one, Rob drove the cutting edge of a chisel into the narrow slit between the gasket and the body of the engine. With a sucking noise, the top part came loose. Impatiently, Rob threw it on the ground. Something was hidden in the cavity of the cylinders! Something that looked like old leather.

"There," he shouted. Hastily, he removed one of the bags and pulled it open. It was filled to the brim with large diamonds, each one a gem of one or two carats.

"Look at that, Mena!" Wild with joy, Rob turned around and reached for her.

Wrinkling her nose, she pushed him away. "Get off," she said playfully and roaring with laughter. "You smell."

Rob smelled his own stink, a mixture of unwashed clothes, sweat and filth. His clothes looked rumpled and dirty, his arms were covered in oily smears. Wildly ecstatic at having found the treasure, he ran to the shore of the lake and threw himself head first in the beautifully blue water. As he came up, he turned around and shook the water out of his hair.

"We are rich, Mena," he shouted. "We are rich."

He saw Mena's lips move in a wild exclamation, not in a joyous way but in some kind of panic. Reading her lips, he finally understood what she was shouting. "Watch out, Rob, there behind you!"

In one quick movement, Mena picked up the AK 47, raised the gun to her shoulder and pulled the trigger. The booming sound of the shots hit Rob's ears, the bullets cutting a frothy wake through the water and missing him by inches. Rob swung his body around. His eyes looked straight into the open jaws of a crocodile, the monster so close that he could smell the stench of putrefaction and decay that came from its mouth.

Horrified by the view, Rob drew back. The AK bullets knocked giant bits of flesh out of the monstrous head. Mortally wounded, the beast disappeared under the surface of the lake. Feeling very shaky, Rob crawled out of the water. Having so narrowly missed death, his mind was a maelstrom of nausea and horror.

Mena dropped the rifle and threw herself in his arms. "My God, Rob," she blurted out. "You jumped almost straight on top of that crocodile. It must have been lying there all the time, and we were so preoccupied with that blasted engine that we didn't even notice it."

She leaned back in his arms and burst into tears, her face as white as chalk.

For a moment Rob was afraid she was going to faint. "It's all right now, darling," he said reassuringly, his voice stronger than he felt. "Don't think about it any more."

Sobbing loudly, Mena clutched him in her arms as if she wanted to make sure that he was real. Abruptly, she tilted her head and kissed him full on his lips. Rob tasted the salt of her tears and smelt the sweet aroma of her hair. Bending down, he gently nibbled the lobe of her ear. With it came the desire to make love to her. Perceptive to his rising passion, Mena responded immediately. She stiffened her back and pressed her hips against his. "I want you," she whispered. "Now!"

"We'll be bothered by the villagers," he grumbled. "They must have heard the shots."

"No fear," she replied, pulling him down to the ground. "They'll be too frightened to come here! We won't be disturbed!"

Instead of by the villagers, they were disturbed by the noise of aircraft engines that rapidly grew louder. In a reflex, Rob looked down at his wrist. As he noticed the pale mark on his sunburned skin, he remembered that Carlos had stolen his watch. Thoroughly annoyed, he jumped up and crossed over to the Land Rover. By the clock on the dashboard, it was a quarter past three in the afternoon. "That must be..." Rob said, raising his eyes to the sky. "Yes," he shouted. "Look."

The streamlined profile of the Britannia suddenly appeared above the eastern shore of the lake. The nose came down and the plane swung around in a tight left hand circuit. It touched the ground at the very beginning of the runway and slowly coasted to a stop.

At the end of the strip, Ian turned the Britannia into the parking bay, a position one thousand yards away from where Rob and Mena were standing. Rob rushed back to the Land Rover, took a rucksack out of the back and began to fill it with bags of diamonds from the old engine.

"Whilst I'm doing this, Mena, drive over to Ian," he suggested. "Tell him the good news. Also tell him to be ready for a quick departure. As soon as I've recovered the gems, I'll join you and we'll get out of here." He smiled and added: "Next destination Sao-Tome!"

Mena slipped behind the wheel of the Land Rover and disappeared down the strip in a cloud of dust.

As soon as the old engine had surrendered all of its treasures, Rob closed the zipper of the rucksack and rose to his feet. Just as he started to walk down the runway, another noise hit his eardrums. He turned his head so fast that he almost strained a muscle. Far to the west, a plume of dust appeared above the line of the trees. By the sound of the noise, Rob knew that the plume was made by the rotor wash of a helicopter. His stomach cringed in a dreadful premonition.

The waves of noise sounded sometimes nearer. At other times, when the shallow crest of a hill rose in between him and the helicopter, the noise of the rotor blades seemed to be retreating in the distance. For a moment, Rob hoped that the helicopter was just flying along the road on a routine inspection and that it would not come as far as the airfield. Soon however, he could recognize the individual blop-blop-blop of the rotor blades.

Suddenly, the wasp-like silhouette of the chopper sprang into view. Rob recognized the type. It was a Mi3 of the Border Patrol. The helicopter slowly curved around and moved along the runway until it hung in a hovering position in front of the Britannia. Suspecting that his ruse had failed and that Lopes had outguessed him, Rob's stomach turned into a coil of barbed wire.

"Bloody hell," he shouted angrily. "How are we going to get out of this mess?"

On board of the helicopter, the mood was victorious. Dreaming already of praise and promotion, the helicopter pilot was talking in his microphone, reporting the location of the Britannia to HQ. The gunner was pointing the barrel of his heavy machine-gun in the direction of the cockpit. Knowing that he had them outgunned, he relaxed in the easy way of an experienced soldier who was facing an unarmed target. Both he and the pilot failed to look down the landing strip, where Rob stood rooted to the ground like a pillar of salt.

Feeling cheated by fate, Rob let himself down by the side of the runway. As he wedged himself into a narrow gully, his eyes fell on the AK 47. Wondering whether there were still any bullets left, he crawled out of his hiding place and recovered the weapon. The magazine contained six more bullets. "Hardly enough to attack a helicopter," he mumbled, but he knew the only way to avoid capture was to shoot the helicopter down. The question he asked himself was: "How?"

Carefully, he studied the terrain. He discovered that the narrow gully was part of an old drainage system that ran along the edge of the runway. It had been dug a long time ago. Since then, it had been completely neglected. Now mostly covered with small bushes and grass, it was almost invisible from the air. If he could slide along that and get close to the helicopter, six bullets might be enough!

Rob looked up into the sky. The sun was already starting to go down. Rob estimated he had a good three hours left before it would be too dark to do anything. His boldness kicked into second gear. Behind him stood the strangely formed pyramid of a termite hill, its sides full of crannies and holes. To get the freedom of movement he desired, he stowed the rucksack with the diamonds deep into one of the cavities, then threw himself into the gully and began to crawl through the tight screen of thorny bushes and grass. Everything around him was covered in a thin layer of red dust. Soon his arms and shirt looked as red as the landscape, making him blend in perfectly with the surroundings. Once in a while the thorns of the bushes got tangled in his clothes and he lost some time pulling himself free, ignoring the pain when the sharp thorns cut into his flesh.

It took him half an hour to reach the other end of the runway. As he came closer to the helicopter, he could see the rows of rivets on its fuselage and the smears of crash helmeted heads in the cockpit. The distance was still too great to risk a shot. Trying to figure a way of getting underneath the Mi3 without being seen, Rob stretched out on to the ground.

The helicopter was hanging almost immobile above the dry surface of the runway, the rotor blades throwing huge clouds of red dust into the sky. In the light of the sinking sun, it looked as if the whole horizon was on fire. Rob wondered why the Mi3 didn't land. Was it because the blowing dust prevented the pilot from seeing the ground, or was it because he preferred to stay in a hovering position to keep his mobility, to be able to act faster in case the Britannia would make an attempt to get away?

Whichever the reason, Rob was grateful for it. The dust was exactly what he needed. If judged right, he would be able to run across the runway under cover of the billowing clouds and get close enough to the helicopter. Once more, he inspected the AK 47 to verify that the weapon was cocked and the safety off, then, at the right moment, he launched himself in a fast sprint.

By a fluke of bad luck, just as he reached the middle of the runway, the rotor wash blew the dust cloud apart. Rob felt as if he stood naked in the middle of a crowd. From the sudden change in the sound of the engine, he knew that he had been seen. Looking up to the cockpit of the Mi3, he noticed the gunner, his mouth open in a shout, his hands gesturing the pilot to swing the helicopter to the right to give him a clear field of fire.

Faced with the threat of being shot, Rob had no other choice but to run back to the gully. Still facing the helicopter, he withdrew rapidly, but stumbled over a stone and fell over backwards. As if in a slow motion, he saw the gunner swing the long barrel of the gun in his direction. In a reflex, Rob aimed his rifle at the most delicate part of the helicopter, the complicated set of pipes and cables and push rods in the heart of the engine.

The gunner began to shoot. Rob flinched when he heard the unbroken ripple of gunfire, the loud noise of heavy calibre bullets when they hit the ground and the whining sound when some of them ricocheted against rocks. He saw the impact of the bullets on the red surface of the runway, and the line of fire which ran towards him. Expecting any moment to feel the bullet that would split his body apart, he didn't care any longer whether he lived or died. As long as the others could get away. In a wild rage, he pulled the trigger. Compared with the loud thunder of the shots of the machine-gun, the AK 47 sounded like a toy. After what seemed only a second, Rob heard the metallic click of the percussion pin on an empty chamber. His bullets were spent. Above him, the gunner in the Mi3 was still firing.

Rob knew he had lost. Resigned to fate, he closed his eyes. Suddenly his ears picked up a different sound. The pitch of the rotor blades had changed! Rob's eyes flew upwards. Through the shiny plastic bulge of the cockpit he saw that, more by luck than by skill, his shots had gone home. The pilot had been hit! Instead of holding the flight controls, he had his hands in front of his face, blood dripping from between his fingers.

Without any steering inputs, the helicopter slowly rolled over on to its back. Abruptly, the machine-gun stopped firing. Rob saw the gunner grabbing hold of the controls, desperately trying to prevent the helicopter from stalling. The rotor of the helicopter suddenly lost grip on the air. The Mi3 fell out of the sky. Upon touching the ground, the rotor exploded into a thousand pieces. The fuel tanks burst open and flooded over the hot exhaust of the engine, throwing geysers of flames towards the sky. From inside the cockpit came the terrified screams of one of the aviators. Part of the grassland by the helicopter caught fire. The hideous screams brusquely stopped.

Strangely enough, Rob felt no regrets at having killed two people. "It was them or us," he said to himself.

The glow of the flames felt hot on his face and the stink of melting rubber and burning flesh rose sharp in his nostrils. He drew further back into the narrow confines of the gully.

The remaining ammunition of the machine-gun started to explode, some of the bullets clanging loudly against the fuselage and the wings of the Britannia. Rob prayed that none of his friends were hit. After what seemed to be hours, the explosions stopped. Only the faint crackling noise of the fire remained. It was safe to move around again.

Rob dragged himself to his feet and walked over to the Britannia. In the cockpit, the first one he saw was Mena, her face streaming with tears. She jumped up and threw her arms around his neck.

Ian breathed in deeply and said that the Britannia was badly damaged. "One of the main fuel tanks on the wing has been pierced, Rob!"

Don pointed to the fuel quantity indicators. "We are loosing fuel rapidly..."

"... And one of the hydraulic supply lines to the landing gear has been slashed," elaborated Jock.

Ian, with something like distress in his voice, added that, before they left Portugalia, he had talked with Sobreiro over the HF. "He gave me the full story of what happened with SECPOL, Rob. Because of that, I understand that we have to get out of Angola in a rush, and that you were planning to fly directly from here to Sao-Tome, but…" He hesitated briefly before delivering his final verdict. "...You can forget it. In this condition, the Britannia is going nowhere."

Rob studied the fuel gauges and let his eyes sweep the hydraulic panel. "We'll see about that, Ian," he stated finally. "Maybe there is something else we can do. For instance, to prevent the landing gear from collapsing because of lack of hydraulic pressure, Jock can insert the gear locking pins."

"And, to prevent fire, I can drain the remaining fuel from the leaking fuel tank," proposed Jock.

"With the gear down and one of the fuel tanks empty, we'll never reach Sao-Tome," declared Ian. "Even Brazzaville is too far away."

"I agree," replied Rob, "Let Jock get on with the emergency repairs. In the mean time, I'll go and recover the diamonds from their hiding place. Then we'll decide where to go."

Luanda, 20 December 1995

At a quarter past four in the afternoon, the C.O. of the Helicopter Squadron informed Lopes that the Britannia had been found on the ground in Massau and that two more helicopters had been dispatched to arrest Rob and his crew.

A powerful flush of anticipation instantly warmed Lopes' heart. Finally, after all those years, the diamonds would be his!

It was now 6 o'clock, and Lopes was still waiting for the confirmation that the prisoners were on their way to Luanda! As time went by, his thoughts became poisoned with the idea that something was badly wrong. He started to behave like a caged animal. Lighting his twentieth cigarette of the day, his eyes drifted to the clock. As he noticed the time, he cursed. "Shit, what's going on in Massau? What are they waiting for?"

Toni looked up from the file he was reading. "I don't..." he started to say.

To thwart Toni's attempt to make conversation, Lopes curtly shook his head. Driven by impatience and not able to sit still, he jumped up and walked over to the window. Outside, the sun was sinking fast behind a far bank of clouds, the dying light still casting a golden glow over the top floors of the highest buildings.

Rapidly drifting into a cantankerous mood, Lopes drew the curtains. The shrill ringing of the phone abruptly broke the silence. Lopes ran over to his desk and snatched the receiver from the hook.

Toni heard the squeaking voice that came out of the phone, the rapid flow of words sounding as if a hundred crabs were crawling over a surface of glass.

"What did you say?" Lopes suddenly screamed. "They are gone?" His mouth flew open in astonishment as he pressed the receiver closer to his ear. "What?" he shouted again, very agitated this time. In a gesture of utter frustration, he turned his eyes to the ceiling and smashed his right hand down on his desk. "You are bloody idiots!" he yelled, blinded by rage. "Nothing but a bunch of stupid lizard brains." Little specks of froth appeared in the corners of his mouth.

From where he sat, Toni could hear the indignation in the voice on the other side of the line. To stay out of harm's way, he gave the impression of concentrating on the file he was reading.

"I don't give a damn that you take offence at my words," Lopes yelled. The pitch of his voice rose to a level of near hysteria. "If your bloody crew had done their job properly, they wouldn't be dead now. So shut up and let me think."

Muttering unintelligible words, Lopes threw the phone down on the desk and burrowed his head in the palms of his hands. Gone were his dreams of sudden wealth, gone the vision of spending the rest of his life in luxury. Instead, his mind reeled from bitter disappointment at having lost the treasure and the prospect of having to explain to the President why he had sent a single helicopter to Massau instead of launching a general alert.

If he wanted to clear himself from the suspicion of having acted solely in his own interests, his explanation would have to be a very plausible one. Experience had made him a master at shaping the truth in such a way that it suited his needs and blinded his foes. If played cleverly, he still could get away with it.

Calmer now, Lopes lifted the telephone to his ear. "I haven't decided exactly what to do yet," he scowled. "In the mean time, put your whole force on alert. As soon as I make up my mind, I'll call you back."

With trembling fingers, he shook another cigarette out of a pack and lit up.

Sunk in thought, he stood up and studied the map as if it would give him a clue about what to do next.

Toni winced when Lopes started to speak.

"You know what's happened?" It was a rhetorical question. Without waiting for an answer Lopes continued: "To arrest Stanfort and his crew, the Commander sent two additional helicopters to Massau. But they arrived too late. The Britannia had gone."

Lopes explained that upon their arrival, the helicopter crews had discovered the burned out wreck of the first Mi3, and a huge puddle of oil and fuel at the spot where the Britannia had been parked.

Thinking about that, something suddenly clicked in Toni's mind. "To cause so much spillage, the Britannia must have suffered a lot of damage, Comrade Lopes. In that condition, they couldn't possibly get far."

"That's right," said Lopes. "I think you've got something there, Toni."

Lopes dropped his cigarette and crunched the stub under the heel of his shoe. He traced the course of the Rio Cuango and marked the runway in Massau with a large red circle. Next, he drew a line between Massau and Kananga, the nearest airfield in Zaire. The distance was a little over 200 miles. Lopes also drew the tracks between Massau, Brazzaville and Kinshasa, two other airfields that could be used as a safe haven. "That's the situation, Toni," he said. "The closest airfield abroad is Kananga. Farther away are Kinshasa and Brazzaville."

"They might not be abroad," stated Toni. As if drawn by a magnet, he stood up and let his finger follow the track that connected Massau with Kananga. Almost directly on that track, but much closer to Massau, was Portugalia.

"They could be there," he suggested. "The idea of going there is so ridiculous and against all logic that it might just be the thing that Stanfort would do."

Lopes's face became an expression of hope. The more he thought about it, the more he felt sure that Toni's arguments were valid. Deep in his guts, excitement of a new chase began to replace the gloom of defeat. "Well done, Toni," he admitted. "They must be there. It's the only place in the close vicinity of Massau where they can make repairs and stock up on oil and fuel."

Propelled by the urge to know, Lopes dialled Olunga's telephone number and instructed him to radio Dundo, to find out whether they had heard from the Britannia. Fifteen minutes later, Olunga called back and confirmed that the plane had landed in Portugalia. "Badly damaged, but safe!" Olunga specified.

Angrily, Lopes swept his hand in the direction of the window. "It's too late now to send in the helicopters. In this damned darkness, they'll never find the place."

"We have a squadron of all-weather MiG21s in Saurimo," offered Toni. "Whether it's dark or light, they can patrol the area."

"You're right again," praised Lopes. "Then at first light, if Stanfort tries to take off, they can intercept and force him to land."

"What if he refuses to follow orders? The border with Zaire is only a couple of miles away."

"I see your point," acknowledged Lopes. His voice turned slightly reflective, as if he was reluctant to consider that alternative. "If he refuses," he eventually decided. "They'll have to shoot him down. We can't afford to let him get away with it."

Toni refrained from saying that up to now, Stanfort had a very good record of getting away with everything he had set his mind to. Lopes reached for the telephone. "Connect me with the Commanding Officer of the Fighter Squadron in Saurimo," he instructed the operator. "Afterwards I want to talk to the C.O. of the Helicopter Squadron."

Saurimo, 20 December 1995

The order to put the Fighter Squadron on readiness arrived at 10 p.m.

The crews assembled in the briefing-room, a Spartan-looking place measuring forty by thirty feet, the white-painted walls covered with large scale aeronautical maps and instructions to air crew.

At the far end of the room, on a low stage, stood the C.O.

"Sit down, Comrades," he said curtly. Behind him, on an easel, hung a map with the weather systems currently affecting the area. A second easel held a very detailed chart of the north-east province of Angola, with a red line marking the track between Saurimo and Portugalia.

Looking very expectantly, the pilots found their seats and tried to get a hint of the mission by glancing at the red line which was prominently displayed on the chart.

When the scraping of chairs had finally calmed down, the C.O. took a long ruler in his left hand and pointed to the map.

"Your mission is to intercept a Britannia," he began. "That's a four engine freighter, now on the ground in Portugalia. Yesterday, they destroyed a helicopter that was flying a routine patrol over Massau, causing the death of two of our comrades. We cannot accept that. Those criminals must be brought to justice."

Driven by fear of repercussions from SECPOL in case of failure, the C.O. raised his voice to a high pitch. "Prevent them from taking off," he shouted. "If they are already in the air, which is doubtful because of the bad weather, intercept them and force them to land in Saurimo. If they refuse, shoot them down. Under no condition should they be allowed to escape."

The C.O. sat down and the Met Officer drew their attention to the low pressure zone which had its centre only 150 nautical miles to the south of Saurimo. He told the pilots that the bad weather was slowly moving to the east.

"Look at this, Comrades," he said, putting his finger on a maze of isobars which looked like cobwebs. "This is the position of our airfield. As you can see, the warm front has caught up with the cold front, resulting in an occlusion of the frontal systems. That means layers of low clouds hugging the ground, mixed with huge thunderstorms billowing up to 60,000 feet. And no weather improvement until early tomorrow evening."

After giving the pilots the time to study the maps, the C.O. ordered Red Flight to take off immediately and patrol over Portugalia until midnight. They would be relieved by Blue Flight, followed by Green and Black.

Flight Lieutenant Ruish, leader of Yellow Flight, was given the task of patrolling the area between 5 and 7 a.m.

Since checking out on the MiG21 in September 1994, Ruish had flown nothing but boring missions, such as strafing ground targets or dropping napalm on guerrillas.

"An interception, Mendez," he said to his wingman. "That's what being a fighter pilot is all about."

Portugalia, 21 December 1995

It was almost 5 o'clock in the morning, the sky obscured by low drifting clouds. It was still very dark and it was raining. The only point of light in the darkness came from a single ceiling lamp in the old hangar, its yellow glow falling on to the tarmac and reflecting wetly from the fuselage of the Britannia.

Rob stood under the left wing, pushing and pulling the handle of a wobble-pump. One end of the fuel pipe was connected to the bowser, the other end looped over the leading edge of the wing. Sweat and rain running down his face and his hands moving like automatons, he pondered how fickle luck could be. First, that spectacular escape from prison. Then the discovery of the diamonds, his fight to death with a helicopter of Border Patrol, and the resulting damage to the Britannia.

It was in fact nothing less than a miracle that they had reached Portugalia, with the Britannia behaving like a badly trained horse, bucking and swaying with the gear hanging down in the slipstream and the empty fuel tank causing an almost uncontrollable lateral imbalance.

Jock, Ian and Don had concentrated on the repairs. Rob and Mena, after devouring a hastily prepared meal of tilapia and bread-root at the villa, had snatched a couple of hours of badly needed rest before returning to the Britannia.

Repairing the hydraulic line had been relatively easy. A mere exchange of the damaged line with a new part from the stock of spare parts.

The hole in the fuel tank was a completely different kettle of fish. The bullets of the machine-gun had gone clean through the tank, leaving a row of ragged exit holes the size of a fist. Removing the wing panels, sealing the holes in the fuel tank and riveting it up again had cost Jock the better part of four hours. It was only now, on the verge of a new day, that they were ready to go.

On top of the wing, Jock was holding the nozzle of the bowser in the neck of the tank. Miserable from the constant rain and soaked to the skin, he looked around in disdain.

"Sunrise will be late today," he remarked.

Sorely needing a short rest from handling the wobble-pump, Rob stretched his back and looked up in the sky. A couple of raindrops dripped down the point of his nose.

"We should be grateful for that," he countered. "If the weather was gorgeous, we could have been swamped already by a fleet of helicopters." Anxious to get away, he carried on pumping kerosene. "Because of this rotten weather, we have a good chance of slipping away! How much more time do you need to get the plane ready, Jock?"

"Another thirty minutes and the tanks will be full."

"We'll finish refuelling," Rob decided. "Then I'll go and get the others."

Saurimo, 21 December 1995

At 3 o'clock, Ruish's batman woke him up with a cup of coffee. After breakfast, accompanied by his wingman, he went to the dispersal room and opened the door of the locker which held his flying suit, crash helmet and maps.

The old familiar room smelled of rain and dust, mouldy paper and stale cigarette smoke. An ancient looking record-player stood on a low cupboard in a far corner. In the centre of the room, a collection of comfortable armchairs surrounded a table which was sagging under a load of dog-eared books and magazines.

As he was closing the zipper of his anti-G suit, Ruish reviewed the tactics of the interception in his mind. Eager to fly a real air combat patrol, he allowed his mind to feed on the hope that the pilot of the Britannia would refuse to follow instructions. Mentally already savouring the moment of pulling the trigger on his stick and feeling the recoil of the guns, he couldn't stop himself from smiling.

Ruish and Mendez walked across the sodden tarmac towards the two MiGs which, in the steadily falling rain and glittering in the beam of strong overhead lights, looked like prehistoric predators. The ground mechanics had just finished refuelling and arming the planes. The internal tanks, augmented by 4,000 pounds of fuel in the tiptanks, contained enough kerosene to give Ruish three hours of operational range, providing he didn't use the afterburners too much.

On racks under the wings, the MiG21 carried four AA-20 air-to-air missiles. As additional armament, there were two 20 mm cannons, each one of them loaded with 300 shells. A formidable armament to face an unarmed Britannia.

With the rain beating his face, Ruish made a quick walk-around inspection of his plane. After all, it was his life that was at stake, and taking off in a plane that was not fully airworthy was very dangerous. Only an idiot would do that.

He shook the rockets and the tiptanks to verify that they were securely attached to the plane. Standing on tiptoe, he reached up and looked inside the air intake of the engine. Circling the plane, his eyes wandered over the control surfaces and checked the dynamic and static air inlets. Finally satisfied that the plane was ready, Ruish slapped his ground chief on the back. "Bom," he said, climbing up the short ladder to the cockpit. "Well done."

Whilst the ground crew armed his ejection seat, his fingers ran quickly over a dozen switches and handles to initialize the aeroplane's systems. Lastly, he slipped the dome shaped crash helmet over his head and pushed the pickle-switch on his stick down.

"Yellow One to Yellow Two, status report," he articulated in his microphone.

"Yellow Two to Yellow One," replied Mendez. "Ready to start."

With a nonchalant gesture of his left hand, Ruish signalled his ground crew and pushed the starter of his engine. At twenty per cent rpm, he opened the fuel cock and carefully monitored the rapidly rising exhaust gas temperature (EGT), and as soon as it stabilized at 290 degrees Centigrade, he closed the cockpit and released the brakes. As he taxied out, he punched the timer of his clock on the flight instrument panel. It was 4.40 a.m. and it was still raining.

Ruish looked up at the tormented clouds. The ceiling was less than 200 feet, the wind gusting from the north-west.

At 4.45 a.m. the two jets took off, the sound of their afterburners blasting the silence of the day apart. Barely free from the ground, Ruish flipped his undercarriage switch to up. The green lights extinguished and Ruish swung the nose of his MiG on a heading of 340 degrees.

The two fighters adopted a tight wingtip to wingtip formation, climbing at a rate of 4,000 feet per minute. Studying the radar, Ruish found his way between severe concentrations of thunderstorms. At 5 a.m. the two jets reached their assigned patrol area. The ground lay hidden under layers of clouds.

Ruish knew it was useless to try to pierce the base of the clouds as they were most probably hugging the ground. Trying to get a glimpse of the airfield in Portugalia could only result in a crash. He decided to stay in the clear above the weather and locate the target on his attack radar. To conserve fuel, he reduced his speed to 210 knots.

One hour later, the light of pre-dawn became strong enough to distinguish grey nebulous valleys between formations of billowing clouds. Ruish switched his gun selector to 'fire'. Immediately, the yellow ring of his attack-control system lit up. He drew his eyes away from the radar and scanned the valleys between the clouds, 5,000 feet below the belly of his plane. He didn't have the slightest premonition that for his wingman, the encounter with the Britannia would become a date with disaster.

Twenty-five thousand feet lower, the Britannia was ready for take off. The slanting sheets of water indicated a very strong wind that blew at right angles across the runway.

Ian switched the weather radar on and pointed his finger to a line of black spots on the screen. "That's the most severe storm I've ever seen," he announced on the interphone.

Rob bent forward in his seat and looked out to study the weather. The precipitation was so massive that the rain on the windshield resembled a wild river. Barely perceptible through the layers of water, Rob noticed a blotch of light in the east, the first light of dawn that coloured the clouds and made them look like the brush strokes of a mad painter. "No more time to waste," he decided. "Thunderstorms, severe crosswind or heavy rain, we have to go."

Jock selected the wipers to high speed.

Rob threw a quick glance behind him.

Don sat far back in the cockpit, in the navigator's seat. Mena occupied the seat just behind Rob, her eyes wide and dark, betraying the depths of her apprehension.

Rob reached back and squeezed her hand, then, with a resolute gesture, unlocked the brakes and pushed the four throttles forward.

The whine of the engines rose above the howling noise of the wind. The disc of the propellers dissolved in a spiralling vortex of water vapour. As the heavy plane started to accelerate, the tyres of the landing gear threw geysers of liquid into the air. Strong gusts of wind kicked against the fuselage and caused very noticeable vibrations in the rudders and ailerons. The rain became a curtain of mist that reduced the forward visibility to less than 300 yards.

"80," announced Jock.

Unexpectedly, the left landing gear hit a pool of standing water that struck the plane like a hammer blow. Inside the cockpit, it felt as if they had run into a rock. Immediately, the plane slewed across the runway in the beginning of a ground loop. Rob pulled the throttles of the starboard engines to idle. At the same time he kicked the starboard brake to force the aircraft back to the middle of the runway. Shaking with vexation and fearing a crash, he started to curse.

Fighting against inertia, the Britannia slowly swung back towards the centreline and Rob gradually restored power on all four engines. Outside the cockpit, he saw nothing but a vague blur of grey, the rest of the runway lay hidden behind sheets of fog and rain. Whether there was still enough concrete left to complete the take-off, he would only know when reaching the end. Boldly, he pushed the throttles wide open. Like a tortured animal, the engines screamed under the abuse.

"The rpm limits!" Jock yelled. "We are over-revving the engines."

"Screw the limits!" Rob shouted back. "We have no other choice. It's a matter of do or die."

Ian threw a glance at the airspeed indicator. "90 knots," he called. "Rapidly becoming 95, now 100."

At that speed, the plane became more easy to handle. The stick lay lighter in Rob's hand.

"V1," called Ian. Barely ten seconds later: "Rotate."

Rob yanked the stick back.

Like a bird of mythology, badly buffeted by the gusting wind, the Britannia rose into the air. At a height of 100 feet, the plane entered the clouds and the ground disappeared from view. All external impressions of speed were lost. Only the severe buffeting remained. On the airspeed indicator, the thin needle jumped wildly between 130 and 150 knots.

"Positive climb, Ian. Gear up."

With a loud clonking noise, the wheels disappeared in their wells under the wings. Rob rolled the trim wheel forward and increased the speed to 170 knots. At 600 feet, the buffeting became worse, the safety belts cutting deep into their flesh. From the galley came the sound of falling gear and breaking glass. At 2,000 feet, Rob accelerated to 190 knots and ordered Ian to raise the flaps. The screen of the radar was dotted with thunderstorms. To avoid the cell of an exceptionally large Cumulonimbus, Rob threw the Britannia on its left side. Only seconds later, another storm appeared in front of the plane. To avoid being hacked to pieces by the terrible forces of nature, Rob reversed the manoeuvre.

They all jumped when at 7,000 feet, a crooked arrow of lightning flashed horizontally between two huge clouds, its light so bright that it hurt. Immediately after the flash came the noise of thunder. In an instinctive gesture of self-protection, Rob closed his eyes and swung one hand in front of his face. For a moment he saw nothing but yellow, red and blue sparks, as if somebody had lit fireworks in his head. When he reopened his eyes, it looked even darker in the cockpit, but the fireworks were gone. Jock turned the instrument lights to full brightness.

The fuselage groaned under the sudden impact of a thousand hailstones. It sounded as if they were under machine-gun fire.

"Jesu-Maria," screamed Mena. The heavy turbulence made her feel sick and her stomach turned over.

Rob's hands were hurting from fighting the stick. His arms felt as if they were being wrenched out of his body and his heart was beating wildly against his ribs.

A new burst of turbulence and hailstones hit the plane. The instruments on the dashboard were vibrating so badly that Rob could not tell whether they were climbing or descending, flying or falling. Suddenly, the noise and the vibrations stopped. The silence became so unearthly that it appeared as if they had gone deaf. A surprised expression on his face, Rob looked at the altimeter. The last altitude he remembered before entering the storm was 7,000 feet. Now the dial was showing 18,000 feet. Without even noticing it, the storm had sucked them 11,000 feet up!

With an external show of calm, Rob switched the automatic pilot on.

"Lucky the storm didn't push us 11,000 feet down," he said to Ian. "If that had been the case, we would now be a dirty smudge on the slope of a hill."

Gradually the light inside the clouds became brighter, their ragged edges growing radiant with pink and gold. A few strips of milky-blue began to appear through gaps in the clouds. Ian pointed to the right, where a wall of bulging clouds blocked the way to the north. To the left lay a long valley of immaculate blue air.

"That's the way to go," decided Rob.

About to turn into the clear blue sky, he suddenly felt a severe shock, followed by a ripple of vibrations that started somewhere in the rear of the plane and ran forward through the fuselage. For a moment Rob thought he heard the sound of hail again.

"Hail out of a clear blue sky?"

In a flash of comprehension it dawned on him that this time, they were under real fire. Scared out of his wits, he threw the plane on its side.

"Don't do that, Rob," said Ian. "Look there!" Rob quickly rolled the wings level. Ian, very agitated now, repeated: "Look..."

By the left wingtip, a mere thirty feet away, hung the eagle-like silhouette of a MiG21, it's aluminium skin bright in the light of the sun. Behind the canopy, Rob saw the yellow crash helmet of the pilot, a dark visor shading all view of his face.

The MiG pulled ahead and positioned itself slightly in front and to the left of the nose. As if on cue, a second MiG appeared from behind and took up position by their right wingtip. They were neatly boxed in.

Having forgotten the first lesson he ever learnt in the Air Force 'Look in the sun, that's where they'll come from', Rob blamed himself for what had happened. Like an imbecile, knowing that danger could be lurking, he had flown out of a cloud without even as much as a careful look-around.

"Rob, the outer starboard engine is losing oil," Jock called out. "It must have been damaged by machine-gun bullets."

At that moment, the engine ran out of oil and the shaft of the turbine seized up, causing the Britannia to yaw sharply to the right. The left wing shot up and the plane began to roll over. With an edge of hysteria to her voice, Mena shouted: "Rob, please, do something!"

Her scream launched Rob into action. He threw the stick into the high wing and kicked the left rudder to its stop. "Ian, feather number four," he yelled simultaneously.

Slowly the propeller began to wind down. Ian started to read the check-list. "Throttle number four ... closed. Fuel number four ... cut off ..."

He was interrupted by a loud voice in heavily accented English that came in through the overhead speaker. "Skylift One, this is Flight Lieutenant Ruish, do you read?"

"He is transmitting on 121.5," said Ian, pointing to the radio panel. "The international emergency frequency. We've got that on VHF 2."

Rob selected his transmitter to VHF 2. "Yes, Flight Lieutenant," he acknowledged. "I read you. Go ahead."

"I notice you have a slight problem with one of your engines."

Rob could hear the arrogance in Ruish's voice.

"I have orders to escort you to Saurimo," Ruish continued. "Follow me, and don't attempt anything foolish. The shots I fired are only an example of what could happen if you don't obey. Understood?"

With one engine out, the Britannia was badly crippled. Following orders was Rob's only choice. His voice sounded very defeated as he acknowledged Ruish's message.

"Steer a heading of 150 degrees and start a slow descent to 10,000 feet," instructed Ruish.

Rob slightly reduced the power and adjusted the trim. The altimeter started to wind down.

Jock slipped out of his seat. "I'll go and have a quick look in the back to check the damage," he said.

Ian pulled a plastic covered aeronautical map from his bag and studied it briefly. "Ruish is leading us slightly to the south of Saurimo," he announced. Pulling his eyes away from the map, he looked out to the horizon. "No doubt to avoid that squall line over there."

Rob bent over and looked in the direction where Ian was pointing. There, the northern horizon was hidden behind a line of thunderstorms. Slightly more to the right lay the Kiokos, the tree-topped hills that marked the boundary between the low fields of the Savannah and the high plateau of Saurimo. A low layer of Stratus clouds was partly covering the patchwork of forests, rocks and long twisting rivers, and fusing it in a hazy mixture of colours and shadows.

"I don't blame Ruish for trying to avoid that squall," Rob retorted. "Flying on your own in such a storm is traumatic enough. Escorting a plane through it is sheer madness."

At that moment, Jock returned. "There's a large hole in the cowling of number four engine, and a couple of bullet marks on the upper surface of the stabilizer," he reported.

"No signs of structural damage?" Rob asked.

Shrugging his shoulders, Jock strapped himself down in his seat. "I don't think the wings are about to fall off," he remarked. "But I can't vouch for the conditions of the control cables."

Rob focused his eyes on the line of thunderstorms. If Ruish persisted in maintaining a heading of 150 degrees, they would be passing very close by the clouds that covered the foothills of the Kiokos, two or three miles upwind of the main storm.

"If only we could distract Ruish for a couple of minutes," Rob said wistfully. "Then I could dive down and disappear into those low clouds."

As he said that, something clicked in Rob's mind. His mood changed from resignation to determination and he wriggled around in his seat. "Listen," he said, his voice loud enough for them all to hear. "We can't afford to land in Saurimo. It would be death for all of us. You know that, don't you?"

Ian sat up with a jerk. Mena's eyes became two big pools of anguish. Don's mouth fell open and Jock looked suddenly very alert.

"You're right, Rob," Mena said bravely. "Once Lopes has got the diamonds, he won't need us any more."

"I'm sure he'll organize a perfect accident to get rid of us," added Jock.

"Correct," replied Rob. "Therefore, we should try to get away while we still have the opportunity. After all, what have we got to lose? Once we're on the ground, our fate will be sealed."

"I agree," announced Jock. "Let's try something."

One by one, Rob reviewed mentally the manoeuvres he had learnt as a pilot in the Air Force. One manoeuvre in particular he remembered. They called it 'the spin', an aerobatic exercise whereby the speed of the plane was gradually reduced until the airflow over the wing was so critical that the slightest jerk on the controls was enough to send it down in a twirling movement like a dead leaf drifting down to earth.

Rob threw another glance on the squall line. The nearest clouds were barely five miles away. "Listen, Ian," he said finally. "That MiG by our wingtip is our best chance. If I can trick him into a spin, we can slip through the gap and get away."

"It's risky, Rob," he replied. "But it might just work. We might as well go down fighting, hey?"

Ian turned around in his seat and explained to the others what 'a spin' meant, and Rob flipped his transceiver button to transmit.

"Skylift One to Ruish," he said. "My airframe is vibrating badly. I must slow down or the plane will come apart." He paused a moment to let his words sink in. "Damage from your bullets, I suppose."

Ruish acknowledged the message without querying it. Rob reduced the power on the three good engines by a fraction of an inch. The airspeed crept slowly back until the needle stabilized at 190 knots. The noise level in the cockpit fell with the reduced speed. One minute later, Rob again pulled the throttles back. Gradually, the speed fell to 180 knots. At any moment, Rob expected to hear a shout of warning from Ruish, but the loudspeaker remained silent. A warm trickle of nervous sweat ran down his back. "Ruish is behaving like a fool, Ian," he remarked. "At this slow speed, his MiGs are almost useless."

Slowly descending, the Britannia approached 13,000 feet. Rob estimated there was barely 5,000 feet between the belly of the plane and the tops of the Stratus clouds. Slightly to the north stood the menacing wall of the thunderstorm.

Once more, he threw a quick look out of the window. The second MiG, not designed for flights at a low speed of 180 knots, was flying in an extremely vulnerable nose-high attitude. "It's now or never, Ian," Rob announced. "When I shout 'GO', give me 20 degrees of flap. That will save us from stalling. As soon as I feel the movement of the flaps, I'll turn to the right and cut in front of the MiG by our wingtip. If he doesn't turn away," he added reflectively. "We'll hit him and we'll both go down, but if he turns away, and I reckon he will because reflexes are faster than thoughts, he'll stall and we'll dive for the clouds."

Ian nodded his approval.

"For heaven's sake, Ian," reminded Rob. "Don't forget to retract the flaps once we are established in the dive. At the speed we'll be doing, the air pressures would tear them out of the wings."

Rob turned around in his seat and ordered Mena, Jock and Don to fasten their seat belts as tight as they could, then forced his mind to wipe out all thoughts about the risks he was taking and shouted: "Go, Ian!"

As soon as he felt the flaps coming down, Rob threw the ailerons in a violent move to the right, the centrifugal forces of the turn pushing him deep into his seat. Behind him, he heard Mena gasp with the suddenness of the manoeuvre. Steeling himself for the crushing impact if the MiG didn't turn away, Rob pulled the throttles to idle and pushed the stick fully forward. The Britannia went down like a ton of bricks. The airspeed ran wild.

Ian called out: "190 knots, flaps coming up, Rob. 210 knots now."

Rob risked a glance at the altimeter. The needle was spinning so fast that it looked like a disc. "Where is the MiG, Ian," he shouted. "Can you see him?"

Instead of telling him where the MiG was, Ian glued his face to his side-window. Jock reported: "Speed 230 knots."

Somewhere in the tail of the plane, a loose piece of metal started to shake. The controls felt like a live animal in Rob's hands, a clear sign that he was pushing the damaged plane well over its limits, but the clouds were still too far away and he resisted the temptation to pull the stick back.

"Speed 260 knots and rising," yelled Jock.

The protective layer of the clouds came rapidly nearer. Rob yelled again, with an urgent tone in his voice: "Ian, where is the MiG?"

Abruptly, Ian pulled his head back from the side-window. "Did you see that?" he shouted. "We turned right in front of the MiG, Rob. In his haste to get out of the way, the pilot overreacted and stalled. The last time I saw him, he was spinning down." Ian's voice suddenly became very cold. "I don't think he'll make it."

"Tough luck," remarked Rob sarcastically.

The first tendrils of clouds floated by the windshield. Thrilled that his gamble had paid off, Rob suddenly remembered the second MiG and a cold shiver of fear ran down his spine. In a reflex, he threw the stick over to the left and kicked the rudder, away from the path he had been following for the last two minutes.

"Where is that other MiG, Ian?" he shouted desperately. "Ian, where is Ruish?"

When Ruish heard the scream of alarm from Mendez in his headset, he pushed the throttle to full afterburner and shoved the stick down. As his airspeed built up, he swung the MiG around in a tight turn. The first thing he saw was the reflection of sunlight on the spinning wings of Mendez's MiG.

"Pull up, Yellow Two," he yelled in his microphone. "Stick forward and opposite rudder."

Instead of a reply, Ruish could hear nothing but indistinct noises on a background of static. In his panic, Mendez must have had his thumb stuck on the transmit button. Hoping to see his wingman recover from the spin, Ruish followed him down.

Mendez's MiG was two or three miles in front of him, still a good thousand feet above the top of the clouds. A puff of what looked like white smoke suddenly appeared above the jet. Ruish's first impression was that the MiG had exploded. Only when the whitish smoke developed into the long shrouds and bulging canopy of a parachute did it occur to him that Mendez had ejected.

Now that his initial worries for Mendez were over, Ruish's instincts took control of his actions. Being outwitted by a crippled cargo plane was too much for his pride. "I'll kill the bloody bastards," he growled, selecting his attack radar to a scale of ten miles.

Less than six miles away, on a bearing of 220 degrees and almost hidden between the clutter from ground echoes, he discovered a faint blip that was moving away from him. In one well coordinated move, he swung the nose of his MiG in that direction. Rapidly approaching the speed of sound, Ruish pulled his eyes away from the radar and scanned the sky in front of his cockpit. The Britannia was almost invisible, its fuselage slicing in and out of the clouds like a dolphin playing in the waves. Ruish's attack radar was one of the older types that had no look-down/shoot-down possibility; a radar that, once close to the ground, was completely useless. If he wanted to make a kill, he would have to hurry and risk a shot from this distance. One thing in his favour was the AA-20 missile. It had a powerful infrared seeker, capable of sensing a heat source from as far as 5 miles out. The hot exhausts of the Britannia's engines were a perfect target. Providing the cargo plane maintained the same heading, it would be like shooting a sitting duck.

Abruptly, the infrared seekers of the AA-20s locked on. Ruish heard a constant bleep in his headset. Instantly, he pulled the trigger. With a noticeable jolt, two rockets left their pods under the wings.

Exactly at the moment his missiles came close to their target, Ruish saw the plane turn sharply away to the left. Almost at the same time the blinding red flash of an explosion lit up the clouds.

As he checked his radar, Ruish noticed that the blip showing the position of the Britannia had disappeared. It could be indicative of the destruction of the plane. Or was it because his radar was saturated with echoes from the ground? For a moment, doubt clouded his mind, then again, he saw the red-hot flash of the explosion on his retina. "They are dead," he decided. "One of the AA-20 missiles must have gone home."

A quick glance on his fuel panel told him that he was rapidly reaching his minimum fuel reserves. It was time to return to base and organize a search party for his wingman, Mendez.

Rob's impulsive turn to the left saved them from the worst. One of the AA-20 missiles was not able to follow the sharp turn of the Britannia. It overshot its target and went ballistic. The proximity fuse of the second missile sensed the closeness of a heat source. It detonated with a blinding flash and ripped engine number 3 out of its bracket, rupturing fuel lines and setting the spills alight. Other pieces of shrapnel punctured the side of the cockpit. During the explosive decompression that followed, a maelstrom of maps, documents, rulers, drinking cups and dust were sucked out through the gaping hole. The nerve-racking chime of the fire alarm added its shrill sound to the confusion. Jock punched the button of the Halon fire extinguisher. After what seemed like an eternity, the fire agent extinguished the blazing fuel and the warning stopped. Only one noise remained, the high-pitched scream of somebody who was badly wounded.

"It's Ian," shouted Jock. "Ian has been hit."

Rob looked to the right. Ian was hanging in his straps, his head lolling on his chest and blood staining the back of his shirt. "Oh God, no!" he yelled. "Damn it, Damn it ... NO ..."

From the effort of keeping the plane straight and level, and fighting the two good engines on the port wing, Rob's left leg began to shake badly. To reduce the asymmetric pressure, he turned the rudder trim all the way to the left. The pressure was still too much to bear.

"Jock," he shouted. "Help Ian out of his seat and let Don take his place. With the two starboard engines gone, I can't handle it on my own."

Once Don put his foot on the rudder, controlling the heading of the aeroplane became much easier.

Leaving Mena to take care of Ian, Jock hurried back to his seat. Holding on to the armrest, he looked out of the window. His face turned grey when he saw the damage. The upper surface of the wing was a mass of holes, the ragged sheets of metal on the right aileron flapping like branches in a strong gale-force wind.

"Handle the plane like eggs," he shouted in Rob's ear. "Otherwise the wingtip will come off."

With the additional drag of the damaged wingtip, Rob was unable to maintain altitude on two engines. He had to make a decision fast. Turning back to Portugalia was a solution he rejected immediately. It wouldn't be long before Lopes found them there. Turning away to the west and putting as much distance as possible between themselves and their foes was the only possibility. He gently turned the plane on a westerly heading.

Now that the plane was flying with more stability, he switched his attention to Mena. "How is Ian?" he shouted. Waiting for the reply, he concentrated on his flight instruments. Inside the clouds the visibility was bad. Rob could hardly see the tips of the wings. Surprisingly, the turbulence was much lighter than expected. He tried to fly level at 7,000 feet. It was pointless, even with full thrust on the two remaining engines, they kept sinking at a rate of a little over 100 feet per minute.

"At this rate, we'll touch ground in about one hour from now," Don calculated.

"I don't think so," Rob disagreed. "As we use more fuel and the weight becomes less, we should be able to keep her flying for quite a bit longer."

Mena gently placed her hand on his shoulder. Rob swung his head around. As he saw Mena's face, her skin ashen and her eyes wide from the shock of seeing sudden violence, he feared the worst.

"How is Ian?" he repeated. "Will he be all right?"

She shook her head, and from the tears which suddenly filled her eyes, he knew that Ian was dead. A deep pain shot through his heart. He felt as if he had failed Ian. He wanted to scream with anger and frustration. Deep down he knew he had to concentrate on the living. The time to mourn would have to come later!

Forcefully he buried Ian's death somewhere far in the back of his mind where it caused no pain nor distraction, and tried to remember what the country looked like between here and the Zaire border. Was it a flat open space, or was it solid forest all the way to the coast?

It was now thirty minutes since the disastrous encounter with the missile. The needle of the altimeter passed through 4,500 feet. They seemed to be losing height slower than expected. Also the fuel quantity was no problem. With what remained in the wingtanks, they would reach the ground a long time before running out of fuel. "Where do you think we are now, Don?" Rob asked.

Don pulled a map out of his flight kit, folded it open and clamped it on to his knee-board. He located their last known position on the chart, then traced a line along the heading they were flying. "I make it about 180 Nautical Miles due south of Kinshasa. We should be able to get there."

Mentally, Rob analyzed the topography of the ground between his actual position and Kinshasa. He remembered the mountain chain that lay like a forbidding arc between Malanje in the south and Kinshasa in the north, a mountain range whose tops peaked more than 4,000 feet above sea level.

"Use your brains, Don," he remarked rather bluntly, pointing to the map. "Look at the terrain... We're already down to 4,000 feet, and going down steadily. There is no chance in the world that we can cross the mountains. We must take another route."

To remain over the lower fields of the Savannah, Rob selected a heading that took them slightly more to the south. Half an hour later, they were down to 3,000 feet, flying in and out of Stratocumulus. Through holes in the clouds, Rob got a glimpse of forest and trees, and a river which was winding a rust-coloured track through a steep and narrow valley. Beyond the valley, the land was a mixture of forests and grasslands, the terrain here and there interspersed with large boulders of rocks. From this low altitude, the impression of speed was tremendous, the colour of the land a blur of green and brown.

Rob sharply studied the horizon. Ahead, he could see some kind of an escarpment, with feather-like puffs of clouds rolling over the edge of the cliffs. Between the clouds and the top of the escarpment was a gap, the distance between rock and cloud just wide enough to squeeze the plane through without losing sight of the ground. On the other side of the escarpment lay a wide expanse of deep-blue water, with the sun reflecting brightly on long rolling waves.

"That's it," Rob suddenly yelled. "That's the coast." He slapped the central pedestal with his right hand. "We'll make a wheels-up landing on the beach. That's our only chance."

Don's face turned into a picture of horror. "But that's still in Angola!"

"I know that, Don, but I can't help it. It feels like the plane is coming apart. We must land as soon as possible. I can't keep it in the air much longer." To drive his point home, Rob began to shout. "I'm heading for the beach, and that's final."

"It's the right aileron," confirmed Jock. "If that breaks off, the wingtip will go as well, and..." He did not complete his sentence, they all knew what he meant.

Ten minutes later, the outline of the coast became visible on the radar screen. As if the plane sensed that the end of the trip was near, it started to vibrate badly, a strange rhythm that ran in long ripples through the fuselage and made the controls jerk wildly in Rob's hand. As a bonus, with the lower altitude, the air became more dense and the rate of descent decreased to less than 50 feet per minute.

The altitude was now down to 1,000 feet, the top of the escarpment so near that it looked as if they could touch it. Once over the escarpment, the land fell away to the level of the sea.

With only feet to spare, Rob managed to clear the top of the rocks. He made a shallow circle to the left and aimed the nose of the Britannia towards a long and narrow stretch of pure white sand. Closer to the ground, Rob saw that the sandy surface was a labyrinth of knee-high rocks, bushes and boulders.

"Flap 20," he called. "And brace yourselves for a crash landing."

At twenty feet above the ground, he ordered Jock to shut the two remaining engines down and at a height of ten feet, he pulled the stick towards his belly. As soon as the plane touched the ground, a spray of sand and pebbles whipped up into the air. Instead of the steady drone of the engines, the loud noise of tearing metal and breaking propellers filled the cockpit.

Gradually slowing down, the plane slithered over the sand. The left wingtip hit the top of a large boulder. The impact swung the plane around and it skidded sideways across the beach. With a thud, it came to rest against the base of the escarpment, almost completely hidden from the air by the overhanging top of the cliffs. Rob switched the main switches off. After the pandemonium of the last two hours, the cockpit fell eerily silent.

Rob released the clasp of his seat belt and walked over to where Ian was lying on the metal floor of the cockpit. He knelt down on one knee and gently caressed Ian's shoulder. The heady smells of kerosene, oil, and the sickly sweet smell of blood filled his nostrils.

"Forgive me, Ian," he said, tears filling his eyes. "Forgive me..."

Later, they climbed the rocky slopes of the escarpment, carefully carrying Ian's body between them. High above the beach, they buried him in a deep natural cavity, a discreet place that was shielded by overhanging blossoms of wild bougainvillaea. They covered Ian with a tarpaulin and filled the cavity with rocks and stones to prevent wild animals from desecrating the grave. The colours of the bougainvillaea looked bright and fresh, their red and pink flowers contrasting sharply with the dull brown colours of the rocks and the blue of the sky. The aroma in the air was a delicate mixture of fragrant flowers and the sharper tang of ozone that drifted up from the beach. Rob said a few words, not from a book but from the heart. Sudden tears blurred his vision as he remembered the man Ian had been and the years they had spent together.

"It's a beautiful place here," Mena said as she saw the depth of his pain. "When my time comes, I wouldn't mind being buried in a place like this."

Rob bit his lip to regain his composure. It was indeed beautiful here, he thought, and very peaceful, apart from the noise of an overflying jet. Rob looked up. High above, a thin contrail drew a pencil line through the azure blue of the sky. As he saw that, something in his mind cried for attention. It was something important, he knew, something that had to do with their safety. The more he tried to remember what it was, the more illusive it became. He shrugged his shoulders, knowing that it would come of its own if he let it rest.

"Yes," he whispered finally. "Indeed, it's very beautiful here, a nice place to be buried." Rob hesitated a moment. "Hardly the place to spend the rest of our lives though."

He pointed down to the beach. Down there, the wreck of the Britannia looked forlorn and small, its propellers bent, the wings a mass of crumpled and twisted metal. "As it stands, getting away in that plane is impossible. Unless we want to remain stranded on this deserted beach, miles and miles away from civilization, we'll have to use the Motor Falcons and revert to the contingency plan I discussed with Tommy and Ian."

He was met by a stunned silence.

"Contingency plan? What do you mean, Rob?" Jock said, his face wrinkled in puzzlement. "I don't know anything about a contingency plan. I remember Sobreiro talking about it with Ian over the radio, but Ian never had the time to tell us, and I don't see where the Falcons fit in."

A slow smile slipped over Rob's face. "Inside the hold of the Britannia, we have two aircraft, Jock. They are not big and certainly not fast, but they can get us out of here."

"If they have not been damaged by shrapnel," Jock said pensively. "It would be easy to make them flyable. Just a matter of attaching the wings and connecting the flight controls." He hesitated for a moment. "But how far can we get in those silly little planes?"

Rob raised his eyebrows. "Far enough to get us to Zaire," he answered. "I don't know exactly where we are, but I guess that the mouth of the Zaire river is not more than 150 Nautical Miles to the north. Do you agree, Don?"

Don slowly nodded his head up and down.

"The Falcons carry enough petrol to cover that distance," continued Rob.

"Then what?" remarked Don. He sounded agitated. "Refuel where?" He shook his head in a desperate manner. "Hop along the coast all the way to Sao-Tome?"

Rob smiled cunningly. "We don't need refuelling," he stated. "That's were the contingency plan comes in. Tommy didn't go straight to Sao-Tome. He has dropped his anchor seventy miles to the west of Moanda, well outside Zaire's territorial waters."

"How can we let Tommy know that we are not able to reach Sao-Tome?" asked Mena.

"Simple," said Rob. "The Petrolua is equipped with VHFs, capable of communicating with our aircraft radios. I've arranged a radio schedule with Tommy to let him know our final destination. Tommy's radio operators are keeping a 24 hour listening-watch on a prearranged frequency to make sure that they don't miss any of our transmissions."

Rob suddenly looked very thoughtful. "However, Tommy isn't going to wait forever. If he doesn't hear from us by tomorrow at sunset, he'll set course for Sao-Tome." Again, Rob pointed to the wreck on the beach. "Our main problem is that we can't use the powerful VHFs of the Britannia any more. From here, the range of our portable VHFs is insufficient to reach the Petrolua." Rob paused briefly, his eyes already studying the beach to find the best place that could be used as a runway. "Therefore," he emphasized, "we need to fly north in the Falcons, to get within range of Tommy's VHF."

He looked up to the sun and estimated its angle to the horizon. "By the time we reach Moanda, it will be very close to sunset, still bright enough for us to land on the beach. Before we land, we'll contact Tommy and give him our coordinates. After that, we'll just have to sit and wait until one of his motor launches, under cover of the dark, can come and pick us up."

"You cunning bastard," shouted Jock. "Let's get started!"

Luanda, 21 December 1995,

The news that the Britannia had been shot down reached Lopes at 10 a.m.

"They tried to get away by diving for the clouds," the Commanding Officer of the base in Saurimo reported. "Flight Lieutenant Ruish had to open fire. According to his battle report, the Britannia went down in the forest. I've sent out a squadron of SAR helicopters to search for the wreck, but bear in mind, Comrade Lopes, it's a very wild place over there. It may take hours." He added that the helicopters were not only searching for the Britannia, but also for the wingman of Captain Ruish, who had gone down in the same area.

At noon, Lopes was told that no traces of the Britannia had yet been found.

"However, one of our reconnaissance MiGs has detected the signals of an Emergency Transmitter, somewhere on the west coast, about 100 miles to the south of San Antonio do Zaire," the C.O. elaborated. "Those signals could be coming from the Britannia."

As he gave the order to dispatch a squadron of helicopters to that area, a tremor of hope, mixed with uneasiness, crept up Lopes' spine.

One hundred miles to the south of San Antonio, 21 December 1995

Guided by Jock, they pulled the disassembled pieces of the motorgliders out of the hold and dragged them over the beach. Under a wide canopy of palm trees, they found a protected spot where they could work in the shade. To Rob's profound relief, Jock reported that the planes had not suffered any damage from rocket fragments.

The heat came wafting down from the rocks of the escarpment. It became stiflingly hot and the job was tough. Soon they were all covered in sweat and dust. Mena gave them food and water from the Emergency Rations. It was barely enough to still their hunger and thirst. Without complaining, they continued to work. As the shadows on the beach became longer, the rock wall cooled down and the air currents turned from the sea to the land. Rapidly gaining in strength, the sea breeze pushed the layers of hot air away and replaced them with cool ocean air.

Mena let her eyes swoop over the wide expanse of the ocean and listened to the gentle slapping of the water on the beach. She admired the blue of the sky that, unbroken by clouds, stretched all the way from horizon to horizon. A thin but insistent noise pierced her thoughts, a whining noise that came from the sky. Startled, she looked up and saw a web of vapour trails above the exact position of the crashed Britannia. "Hey, Rob," she yelled, pointing in the air. "Look there."

Busy inserting the last locking pin in the aileron control of his Falcon, Rob threw his head up. Recalling the jet he had noticed earlier after Ian's funeral, he let his eyes follow the erratic circling movements of the high-flying plane. A tingling sensation suddenly ran down his back. With a sharpness of mind that was hurting, it dawned on him what it was and a muscle started twitching in his cheek. "The Emergency Locator," he shouted. "I forgot all about the Emergency Locator."

Jock heard him shout. Surprised at the intensity of Rob's reaction, he swung around.

Rob shouted again. "The ELT, Jock! I forgot about the bloody ELT." Very excited now, he pointed up into the sky. "That jet must have picked up the signal and is homing in on us."

"What is an ELT?" asked Mena sharply.

"It's an Emergency Locator Transmitter," explained Jock. "It's a homing beacon that is installed in the tail of the Britannia. It automatically starts transmitting in event of a crash. Ironic, isn't it," he added ruefully. "In the case of a real crash, when you want to be found, it most likely won't work, and now that we don't want to be found, the bloody thing is transmitting."

"Oh shut up, Jock," Rob exploded.

Realizing the immensity of the mistake he had made, Rob stiffened at the prospect of having ruined their chances. "We have to get out of here, immediately," he shouted. "We haven't got any time to waste." The thought hit him that Lopes could already have a squadron of helicopters in the air. At the top of his voice, he yelled: "We have to take off as soon as possible, Jock. The more distance between them and us, the more I like it. Are the planes fully ready?"

"All flight controls and cables are connected," Jock reported, "but..."

"... the fuel load is merely enough to cover 300 miles," completed Don.

"We have a couple of jerrycans with petrol in the hold of the Britannia," said Jock. "The fuel reserve for our emergency generator. We won't need that any more. I could use it to top up the tanks. It will take only..."

Rob made a quick calculation. Three hundred miles should be enough. In his imagination he could already hear the noise of rotor blades. The idea of being trapped on the beach became a phobia, the urge to fly away an obsession. "It will have to do," he decided, "... and don't bloody argue with me, Jock. It is far too late for that now."

Turning to Don, Rob shouted: "Let's go. Let's get out of here! Take off as soon as you can. Keep your portable radio tuned to 128.95 megacycles. Then we can communicate once we are in the air. Incidentally," Rob clarified, "that's also the frequency Tommy is monitoring."

"If that's what you want, then that's what you get," grumbled Jock.

He scrambled behind Don through the loose sand, to the spot where their Falcon stood parked beneath a palm tree. Whilst Jock settled himself in the right hand seat and tightened his seat belt, Don went through the starting procedure.

With beads of sweat rolling down the narrow of his back, Rob ran behind Mena across the coarse sand towards his own Falcon. He stumbled over the root of a tree and fell hard on his knees. The sudden pain urged him on. Panting from the effort of running, he jumped into the tiny cockpit. Mena was already there, strapped in and ready to go.

"I stowed the bag with the diamonds in the bucket seat under the cushion," she revealed. The bucket seat was the place where normally parachutes would be carried, a luxury they didn't possess.

As Rob closed the buckle of his own seat belt, he saw the tiny propeller of Don's plane swing around. A small puff of smoke came out of the exhaust and the 60 horsepower Limbach engine roared to life.

Rob scrambled through his own check-list, one of his hands searching for the choke, his other hand finding the starter. The engine coughed, turned over and stopped. He pulled the starter again. This time the engine backfired explosively. Below her tanned skin, Mena's face turned grey with worry.

Rob desperately tried the starter again. Quite abruptly, the engine caught on. With the roar of the engine echoing against the rocks of the escarpment, the propeller disappeared in a translucent disc. Rob pulled the throttle to idle and checked the oil pressure. As soon as he was certain that all the instruments indicated normal operating conditions, he closed the canopy, grasped the stick in his left hand and pushed the tiny throttle all the way forward.

Ahead of him, Don's Falcon was already lifting off, trailing a widening plume of dust in his slipstream. Rob's Falcon slowly accelerated over the uneven ground. Soon, the airspeed reached 30 knots, then the bumping sensation disappeared and the rumbling noise of the landinggear fell away. They were airborne.

At 4.30 p.m. Lopes received a radio call from Tenente Santini, the leader of the helicopter flight he had sent out to locate the position of the Emergency Transmitter.

"We've landed on the beach, Comrade Lopes. We've found the wreck of the Britannia but apart from a couple of suitcases and some tools, the plane is empty." After a brief pause, he added: "There are also traces in the sand which indicate that two light aircraft have taken off in a northerly direction."

Lopes' feelings turned into deep anxiety and a dark shadow of despair overhung the hope he had previously felt. "Hurry up," he ordered. "Go after them and find them before they cross the border with Zaire!"

South of San Antonio, 21 December 1995

Rob threw a careful glance over his shoulder. The sky was very blue and empty, with no signs of pursuing helicopters.

At one thousand feet, Rob caught up with Don. Side by side, they steered a northerly heading, the stick and windshield vibrating in harmony with the swiftly running engine. Underneath, the beach formed a curved line. At times, the escarpment came quite close to the shore and formed small half-moon shaped coves where the water was deep and blue compared to the faded green of the sandy shallows.

Although late in the afternoon, the sun was still very strong. It became increasingly hot under the plastic hood of the cockpit. Rob opened a tiny vent. The pitiful small amount of air that came in was hardly capable of cooling the heat. Sweat started to pearl in drops on his forehead. Mena, too, was suffering from the heat. With the thin cotton of her dress sticking wetly to her body, she was fanning herself with a handkerchief. Rob thought that she looked extremely desirable. He drew his eyes away from her breasts and concentrated on studying the run of the coast.

At first, the map made no sense, the sheet a puzzle of lines and colours. Later, he saw the white houses of a small city on the horizon. It had to be San Antonio do Zaire, a small city that sat astride the border between Angola and Zaire.

Elated with his discovery, Rob pushed the button of his transmitter down. "Hello, Don. Look slightly to your right. That's San Antonio do Zaire."

To acknowledge the message, Don clicked his transmitter twice.

Overflying the small town would be too risky, Rob judged. It would betray their presence. To slip by unnoticed, he made a slow turn to the left and flew out over the sea until the coastline was nothing but a thin line on the horizon. After ten minutes Rob estimated that they were far enough away from San Antonio and he turned the nose of his plane back towards the coast. Don followed him like a shadow.

Impatient to see the mouth of the Zaire river, Rob stretched his neck. Slowly, the waves of the ocean gave way to the rise of the land on both sides of the estuary. Soon Rob could see the place where the blue waters of the ocean were mingling with the muddy brown waters of the river. "That's the Zaire river," he shouted. Excitedly, he pointed to the left. "Only five more miles to the coast."

Overjoyed with the success of their escape, he groped for Mena's hand. "Angola is now behind us, my darling. We've made it." He took hold of his VHF. "We must be within range of Tommy's ship, Don," he said. "Let's give it a try."

He keyed his microphone. "Petrolua, Petrolua, this is Skylift One, do you read?"

Rob pricked his ears to hear the response. The receiver remained silent. Again, he pushed the transmit button down. "Petrolua, Petrolua, do you read on 128.95, over?"

At that very moment, the VHF came to life, the sound a mixture of garbled words and static that barely rose above the clatter of the engine. A short while later, Rob heard the noise again, a little stronger this time. His heart lifted when he recognized the voice.

"Skylift, this is Tommy, reading you weak but clear, over."

Rob's face broke into a wide grin. "Hello, Tommy," he yelled in his microphone. "Nice to hear you, listen..."

He hastily reported what had happened during the last two days. "We are going to land on the beach in Moanda," he concluded. "We'll wait there for your launch to pick us up."

His words were barely cold when he noticed a slight change in the visibility, a thin layer of haze that began to cover the surface of the sea. Driven by the westerly wind, the layer slowly drifted towards the land. Abruptly, Rob got very worried. "Sea mist," he cursed. "Bloody rotten sea mist!"

That phenomenon was quite common at this time of the year, a result of the confrontation between the cold waters of the Benguela current and the relatively warm waters of the Zaire river.

"We must reach land soon," Rob said to Mena. "Otherwise the whole coast will disappear under the mist."

Groping for his microphone, he shouted: "Full throttle, Don. We must stay ahead of the fog, otherwise we'll never be able to land!" With their tiny engines at full power, the two Falcons dropped down like hunting birds on their prey and went for the coast.

For a moment it looked as if they were winning the race but as the beach came closer, the rolling banks of clouds became thicker and more dense. When they were still two miles away from the land, the mouth of the Zaire river and the forest disappeared from view. Where the beach should have been lay nothing but a dense layer of fog. It was as if the two small aeroplanes were the only things that existed in the whole universe, as if they had come from nowhere with no place to go.

"What shall we do now, Rob?" Don asked, his voice a mirror of his anxiety.

"I don't know," Rob replied. He clenched his lips so tightly together that his mouth looked like a thin red line.

"Back to where we came from?" Don suggested.

"Useless, Don, we don't have enough petrol for that."

Rob stared blankly at the unbroken flatness of the cloud layer. Against better judgement, he searched for a hole in the clouds, but the white blanket of fog stretched as far as he could see in all directions. Looking down at the needle of his fuel tank, Rob estimated that he had a good 40 minutes of flying time left.

Of course, they could attempt a descent, flying blind through this swirling mass of fog in the hope of piercing the cloud base and miraculously finding a suitable landing place.

If the terrain below would have been flat and free of obstacles, Rob might have been tempted to do just that, but here, where the land was a jumble of rocks and hills and trees, it would be like committing suicide.

To conserve petrol, he throttled the engine back to a lower power setting and keyed his microphone. Sounding bitter with disappointment, he told Tommy that a landing in Moanda was now out of the question.

"The whole coast is fogged in," he stated. "At best, we can stay in the air for another forty to fifty minutes. After that we'll have to ditch."

On board of the Petrolua, Tommy stared out of the wide windows which encircled the bridge of his ship. His eyes studied the weather and the movement of the waves. Here, far away from the coast, the weather was not that bad. He estimated the visibility close to half a mile and the cloud base at three hundred feet.

Tommy's heart ached when he thought about his friends, how desperate they must be in their tiny planes. After all they had gone through, they deserved better. Worst of all was the feeling of helplessness he felt, knowing that there was nothing he could do to assist Rob.

Or was there?

It suddenly came to him that over the sea, there were no hills or mountains. "Why not," he mumbled, his hand already reaching for the microphone. "Skylift,

Skylift, this is Tommy, do you read?"

As if Rob had been waiting, the answer flashed back immediately. "Read you loud and clear, Tommy. Go ahead."

"The weather here is not too bad," he said. "Visibility half a mile, wind from the south-west, 17 knots. Pick up a heading of 270 degrees. My position is as we agreed, about 60 miles due west of the mouth of the Zaire river. With the petrol you have left, you should be able to get here. To help you locate my position, we'll fire a flare every two minutes and as soon as I pick you up on my radar, I can guide you to the ship."

"And then Tommy," asked Rob. "Where do we land?"

For a moment the radio remained silent. Rob started to fear that the battery of his receiver had gone dead, then he heard again Tommy's voice.

"There are two possibilities, Rob. I can put my lifeboats into the water, and you can ditch next to them, or..." Tommy hesitated a moment before expressing his idea. "Do you remember the Petrolua, Rob," he asked finally. "Do you remember the shape of the deck?"

In his mind's eye, Rob could see the deck of the PROBO, a deck that was as long and wide as the deck of an aircraft carrier. A deck with big open spaces, but also a deck whose sides were cluttered with a maze of pipes enabling the crew to fill the tanks with oil or inert gasses.

"You mean land on your ship," he shouted. "You must be joking."

"Not really, Rob. Think about it. I know that the deck is not a perfect runway, but in between the pipes are large hatch covers. They are free of all obstacles and should be long enough for your Falcons to land on."

Rob immediately realized what Tommy was trying to say. The maximum speed of the Petrolua was 16 knots, the wind 17 knots. That made a combined relative headwind for landing of 33 knots. The minimum flying speed of the Falcons 39 knots. That meant a difference of only six knots! With such a small difference in speed, it would almost be like landing a helicopter.

Trying to decide whether landing on the Petrolua was safer than ditching in the ocean, Rob evaluated the risk of the Falcon going down to the bottom of the sea before they would be able to get out of the cockpit - and if they managed to get out, there might be no time left to retrieve the diamonds from underneath Mena's seat. But landing on a PROBO?

"Is it safe to land on the deck, Tommy," he queried. "I mean, if we hit one of the pipes on the side of the hatches, it could cause..."

"Don't worry, Rob," interrupted Tommy. "Remember what I told you a couple of days ago. The Petrolua is in ballast. We don't carry any crude, and all the tanks are sealed and filled with inert gas containing less than four per cent of oxygen. In addition, the hatch covers are electrically earthed. No risk of an explosion."

"That's good to know," replied Rob.

"Also, my crew are well trained to assist you in case of a hard landing..."

"It's getting better all the time," said Rob sarcastically, but the more he thought about the plan, the more he liked it. It was very dangerous and risky, but left with the choice between certain death when running out of petrol over land and crashing in Zaire, or having a chance of surviving by flying out over the sea in an attempt to find the Petrolua, his choice was easy.

Locating the position of the ship would be the difficult part, but with the help of flares and the Petrolua's radar, it should be feasible.

"We'll give it a try," Rob shouted in his microphone, his voice strong with new hope. He turned his Falcon to the west and set the hairline of his compass on 270 degrees. The needle of his airspeed indicator stood just over 80 knots. At that speed and taking the headwind into account, it would take them about forty minutes to reach the ship.

To increase their chances of finding the Petrolua, he instructed Don to spread out and fly a parallel track four miles more to the north.

Luanda, headquarters SECPOL, 21 December 1995

Shortly before dark, Tenente Santini reported to Lopes that the whole coast was covered in thick fog.

"If the fugitives are somewhere in this area, they can't possibly survive, Comrade. There is no place left to land. To reach the safety of our own base, we have to turn back immediately."

It dawned on Lopes that, again, Stanfort had escaped. Whether he would find a place to land was totally irrelevant. Alive or dead, Stanfort had outwitted him.

Cursing loudly, he chased Toni out of his office. Brooding about the unfairness of it all, he sat down behind his desk and poured himself a glass of brandy.

At 10 p.m. he was still sitting in his chair, drinking brandy and smoking steadily.

As the level in the bottle went down, his muscles relaxed, but his judgement remained strangely lucid. He began to see what the result of Stanfort's escape signified for him. Intuitively, he knew that he would never be able to convince the President of the righteousness of his decisions. All his acts pointed too accusingly to the truth that he had been working with the intention of keeping the diamonds for himself.

His future as Chief of SECPOL was over. Despair and terror began to fight for priority in his mind. He could see himself already, strapped on the interrogation table, tortured by the likes of Toni, the life slowly ebbing out of him.

"Never!" he said, slurring his words. He drained his glass and immediately refilled it to the brim. "Never!"

Caught in his own web of intrigue and deceit, and not willing to become a victim of his own system, he knew that there was only one way out.

Resignedly, he pulled the gun from his shoulder holster. The click, when he cocked the gun, sounded unnaturally loud in the emptiness of his office.

"There has to be an end to everything," he muttered. "Even to life."

He drained his glass and raised the gun to his forehead.

"You Stanfort, I hope you crash in the fog and rot in hell," he said, then he shrugged and pulled the trigger.

Over the South Atlantic, sixty miles of the Zairean coast, 21 December 1995

In each Motor Falcon, two pairs of eyes were scanning the horizon. The sun was sinking towards the horizon. As always in the tropics, it started to get dark rapidly. The angled rays of the sun transformed the upper layer of fog into a giant mirror. A hundred times, Rob thought he saw the red flash of a flare. Each time he realized that it was the dying light of the sun that was playing tricks with him.

Another ten minutes went by.

Rob checked his fuel quantity indicator. The needle was barely moving. Soon, his engine would be running on fumes. A spurt of adrenaline shot through his blood and set his heart racing.

"How much fuel have you got left, Don?" he inquired.

"Fuel, I don't know," Don replied, his voice artificially calm. "Another fifteen minutes, maybe more. Anyway, I guess we'll run out of daylight before my tank runs dry."

Rob had to admit that Don was right. The sun was sinking visibly fast in the fog. At best, they had another ten minutes, then they would have to ditch and it would be over.

Outwardly putting up a brave face for Mena's sake, he felt more like screaming with frustration and fear. Perversely, he wondered how cold the water would be and how long his Falcon would remain afloat before it dipped its nose towards the bottom. He threw a covert glance at Mena. Her jaw set in a tight line, she was absorbed in searching the far horizon, slowly moving her head from left to right. Suddenly, she got hold of Rob's arm.

"What is that?" she gasped, her voice hoarse with tension.

Slightly to the left, Rob saw the red flash of a flare cut across the darkening sky.

"That's a bloody flare!" he shouted. "That's Tommy's ship!"

They were barely five miles away from the flare. Rob whooped with joy. As soon as he got his voice back, he keyed his microphone.

"Petrolua, this is Rob. I've got your flares Tommy, almost dead ahead."

"Yes," replied Tommy. "I'm getting weak returns on my radar. Steer a heading of 260 degrees."

Rob made the slight course correction to the left and told Don to rejoin formation. As soon as the other Falcon was flying in position on his right wingtip, Rob started to descend.

At a height of six hundred feet, the sky disappeared and the swirling layers of clouds closed above them. Inside the fog layer, the light became very diffused.

"Look down, Mena," Rob said. "As soon as you see the sea, give me a shout. I don't want to make a splash."

Around them, the world was blind, the swirling mist layers creating false impressions of motion. Sometimes, Rob thought that his aircraft was spinning to the left. It was only with an extreme effort of willpower that he could force himself to believe his airspeed indicator, his compass and the tiny artificial horizon.

As the altitude decreased, the tension in the cockpit rose. With minuscule pressures on the rudder, Rob kept the needle of the compass steady at 260 degrees and the speed at 80 knots.

"Altitude four hundred feet," he shouted out loud. "Keep looking, Mena, we should be getting close."

Mena concentrated so hard on looking down through the fog that her eyes started to blur with tears. Suddenly, she could see the phosphorous reflections on top of the waves.

"We're breaking through," she yelled.

A sudden gust of wind rocked the wings of the Falcon. Tiny holes appeared in the glue-like substance of the fog. Instinctively knowing that the surface of the water was very near, Rob felt the hairs rising on the back of his neck.

At three hundred feet, flashes of dark green water speckled with white became visible, then vanished again.

"Altitude, 250 feet."

Mena put her hand on his arm. "There," she said. She hesitated for a moment, then, "Yes, there! That's the sea, Rob."

As Rob looked up from his instruments, he noticed that the visibility was less than half a mile, the cloud base blurred and grey. The water looked extremely close and very green.

"Well done, Mena," he shouted, levelling off at two hundred feet.

Afraid that he would see the Petrolua too late and ram the side of the ship, he reduced the speed to 40 knots. Suddenly a set of green navigation lights grew out of the haze. Rob recognized the solid metal sides of a huge ship that lay comfortably rolling on the long swells.

Immediately his worries disappeared. Instead came the exhilaration of having once more pushed his luck to the limit and won.

"I've found you, Tommy!" he shouted in his microphone, turning to the left towards the poop of the Petrolua. "Time to tell your Chief-Engineer to push his engines to full power, and tell him to hurry. Our fuel is running out. Whether you like it or not, we are coming in."

As he was still talking, Rob noticed the widening wake behind the ship, with the Petrolua accelerating rapidly, its bow pointing fifteen degrees to the left of the prevailing wind direction.

"Approach from the port side and aim for the front hatch," instructed Tommy over the radio. "To have a longer landing distance, land across the hatch."

Rob acknowledged the message by clicking his transmit button.

To help him with the landing, Tommy switched the deck lights on, brightening the deck as if was high noon. To catch up with the ship, Rob had to push the throttle to full power.

In the powerful beam of the deck lights, the small open gaps between the hatches were clearly visible.

Out of the corner of his eye, Rob saw the other Falcon, following him like a hunting dog at the heel of its master.

EPILOGUE

On board the Petrolua, 21 December 1995

Rob's landing on the deck of the Petrolua was almost perfect. It was only when coasting to a stop that the wingtip of his Falcon hit one of the vents on top of the hatch. Don, not as adept as Rob in flying light aircraft, made a much harder touchdown. When forcing his plane down, his undercarriage collapsed.

One hour later, after a shower and a meal, they were all comfortably seated in the lounge of the Petrolua. The ship was making thirteen knots, the bow easily cleaving the low-crested waves which came rolling in from the west. The fog had dissipated and the light of the waning moon threw a yellow glow over the water.

After their spectacular escape, they should have been in high spirits, but Ian's death lay heavily on their minds. Not even the view of the diamonds, which were laid out on the table, was able to pull them out of their sombre moods.

Rob suddenly put his scotch down and stood up. "What I'm going to say is something that Mena and I have been considering for a long time," he said. "It started when we were discussing the legality of keeping the diamonds. The daily confrontation with suffering children and wounded soldiers further crystallized the idea, but it was Ian's death that finally convinced us of the righteousness of our plan. We talked it over after our take-off from the beach where we crashed the Britannia, and we decided that..." He gestured somewhere over his shoulder. "You all know what is happening in Angola, the fighting, the poverty and the misery."

Bitterness rose in his voice and he started to pace through the cabin. "Everybody in Angola is affected by the war, but the most touched are the innocents, the children. They suffer from malnutrition and lack of vitamins. Lots of them are wounded, hit by stray bullets or maimed for life by stepping on a land mine."

Rob pulled his handkerchief out of his pocket and blew his nose. Mena took over. "Due to the lack of medical care and adequate food, children die by the hundreds."

"And none of their corrupted politicians give a damn about it," added Rob. "I can't help thinking that somehow, by working for the MPLA Government, we've been making matters worse. Instead of flying weapons or ammunitions, we've been carrying humanitarian aid and wounded soldiers, but frankly, we've been some kind of mercenaries, and I feel that the diamonds don't really belong to us. Keeping the stones gives me a feeling of doing wrong."

"What do you mean?" cried Jock, his voice edged with incredulity, "They don't belong to us?"

"I know, Jock, we fought for them. We fought hard, and we got them, and we had our losses too. We lost Ian, I lost my plane, but compared to the daily misery of those children, we are very lucky. We still have a future and we still have each other."

Sunk in a moment of reverie, Rob went back to the table and took a sip from his glass. "We have a future," he repeated. "The children in Angola have nothing. If I kept the diamonds, I wouldn't be able to live in peace with myself. Each time, when buying myself another item of luxury, I would see their eyes." Rob's emotions burst to the surface and his voice started to tremble. "Those big beautiful sad eyes which, time after time, would ask me: Why does it have to happen to us? Why do we have to suffer?"

Again, Rob blew his nose. "Mena and I," he finally blurted out. "We have decided that with our part of the money, we are going to do something about that.

First of all, we'll send money to Ian's mother. It won't compensate for the loss of a son, but it will give her a steady income. We'll also find a way to send 1,000,000 dollars to the Belgian doctor in Luanda, and I'll use some of the money to buy another plane. A Boeing 707 freighter perhaps, and I'll continue flying as before. Somewhere in South America or in Asia, and you're all very welcome to join me."

Mena cut in. "The rest of our share will go to charitable institutions, which will use the money to help children. Not only in Angola, but all over the world. UNICEF, Children of the World and Save the Children."

The first to react was Jock. "I had already made some terrific plans," he admitted. "An expensive sports car and a sailing yacht, but I also know that the attraction of being rich would soon wear off and my life would become extremely boring. I don't have any family, you know." He made a broad movement with his arms, as if encircling them all. "You are my family. I need you more than I need money." He turned around and put his hands on Rob's shoulders. "Take my part, Rob. Give it to the children. I'll be happy to continue working with you on your new plane."

It was the longest speech Rob had ever heard from Jock.

"Me too," came Don's voice. "I think you're right, Rob. It's a good plan."

"And you Sobreiro," asked Rob. The tone in his voice was a mingling of hope and faith. "What do you think about it?"

Standing by the bar to refill the glasses, Sobreiro looked back over his shoulder. "I was born in Angola," he replied. "I am more Angolan than Portuguese. Therefore, Rob, if you and Don and Jock, who are strangers to my country, are so concerned with the fate of the children, I am very glad to join in."

Tommy's voice rose above the applause that followed Sobreiro's words. "I'm getting fed up with tramping the seven seas. I want to settle down with Joanna. Instead of my part of the loot, give me a job in your company, Rob, as commercial manager for instance. That would suit me fine."

Rob tried to say how grateful he was. He opened his mouth to speak, but before he could utter one word, his eyes glazed over. Abruptly he turned around and walked out on to the deck. Mena found him there, standing alone in the darkness. After the warmth in the lounge, the air felt damp and cool. Mena shivered. Quietly wrapping her arms around Rob's waist, she pulled him close to her chest.

Silently they stood together, staring out over the empty sea.

Rob's mind went back to the cavity in the rocks above that lonely stretch of beach where Ian was buried, the image so real that he could almost smell the aroma of bougainvillaea and hear the wash of the waves on the beach.

Like a voice from the past, he heard Sobreiro's words: "This is a whole new world, Rob, with a whole new set of rules. If you want to survive, you'll have to learn fast."

"Obviously I didn't learn the rules fast enough," he whispered in Mena's ear. His mouth quivered with sorrow. "That's why Ian is dead."

"I know it hurts," she replied, "... but you can't go on living with a ghost, Rob. Ian is at peace now. You have to let him go."

She squeezed her arms a little tighter around his waist.

Rob knew she was right. To continue living with this feeling of guilt was wrong. It would end up by destroying him.

"If it were not for you, Rob," Mena asserted vehemently. "We would all be dead by now. You're the one who pulled us through."

She stood up on tiptoe and kissed him, her lips warm and soft. "It's getting very late, and you must be exhausted," she said. "Don't you think it's time for bed?"

Rob smiled faintly. "That's the best proposition I've had all day," he replied.

Mena turned her head once more in the direction of the coast.

"Vai com Deus, Angola," she whispered, then, arm in arm they walked back to the lounge.

Their ordeal was over.

Their future could begin.